'The undisputed queen
of crime writing'

Erwin James

MARTINA COLE

Author of 23 novels – and counting…

15 No. 1 bestsellers

4 screen adaptations

3 stage shows

Over 15 million copies sold across the world

Celebrating 25 years of record-breaking bestsellers

Stay in touch for film and TV news,
book releases and more…

🐦 @MartinaCole
f /OfficialMartinaCole
www.martinacole.co.uk

Martina Cole's 23 bestsellers (so far) –
in order of publication.
All available from Headline.

Dangerous Lady (1992)
The Ladykiller: DI Kate Burrows 1 (1993)
Goodnight Lady (1994)
The Jump (1995)
The Runaway (1997)
Two Women (1999)
Broken: DI Kate Burrows 2 (2000)
Faceless (2001)*
Maura's Game: Dangerous Lady 2 (2002)*
The Know (2003)*
The Graft (2004)*
The Take (2005)*
Close (2006)*
Faces (2007)*
The Business (2008)*
Hard Girls: DI Kate Burrows 3 (2009)*
The Family (2010)*
The Faithless (2011)*
The Life (2012)*
Revenge (2013)*
The Good Life (2014)*
Get Even (2015)
Betrayal (2016)*

On Screen:
Dangerous Lady (ITV 1995)
The Jump (ITV 1998)
Martina Cole's Lady Killers (ITV3 documentary 2003)
The Take (Sky 1 2009)
Martina Cole's Girl Gangs (Sky Factual documentary 2009)
The Runaway (Sky 1 2011)

*Martina Cole's No. 1 bestsellers – at time of press she has
spent more weeks at No. 1 than any other author

MARTINA COLE
TWO WOMEN

HEADLINE

First published in Great Britain in 1999 by
HEADLINE BOOK PUBLISHING

First published in paperback in 2000 by
HEADLINE BOOK PUBLISHING

This edition published in paperback in 2016 by
HEADLINE PUBLISHING GROUP

23

Cataloguing in Publication Data is available from the British Library

ISBN 978 0 7553 5057 5

Typeset in Galliard by Avon DataSet Ltd, Bidford-on-Avon, Warwickshire

Printed and bound in Great Britain by Clays Ltd, Elcograf S.p.A.

Headline's policy is to use papers that are natural, renewable and recyclable
products and made from wood grown in well-managed forests and other
controlled sources. The logging and manufacturing processes are expected
to conform to the environmental regulations of the country of origin.

HEADLINE PUBLISHING GROUP
An Hachette UK Company
Carmelite House
50 Victoria Embankment
London, EC4Y 0DZ

www.headline.co.uk
www.hachette.co.uk

For Christopher, Freddie and Lewis.
Son, daughter and grandson, keepers of my heart.

Also for Sally Wilden
In your lovely suits and posh shoes!
To me you will always be Sally Wally.
Childhood playmate and late night bottle of wine artist!
A friend for life, a mate for ever.
(Remember the tech wall?)

Prologue

The sweatbox was humid inside. The heat of the summer day seemed to be amplified by the metal casing. Susan Dalston felt a trickle of sweat drip between her breasts and raised her hands to her face in a tired gesture.

'Any chance of a cold drink?'

The prison officer shook her head.

'We're nearly there, you'll have to wait.'

Susan watched as the woman took a long swallow from a can of Pepsi and then smacked her lips deliberately. Forcing herself to stare at the floor she fought against an urge to slap the supercilious bitch's face. It was what the woman wanted, Susan Dalston on a charge, her appeal fucked by one rash move. Instead she looked the PO in the eye and grinned.

'What's so amusing?'

She shook her head sadly.

'I was just thinking, poor old you, stuck in here on a day like this. Unfair really, ain't it? Now you've got all that journey back to Durham again. Long old day, eh?'

The PO nodded.

'Aye, but tonight I'll be lying in my nice bed, watching telly and playing with my old man's cock. What will you be doing? At least I've got something to look forward to.'

The sweatbox lurched to a halt. Susan's handcuffed wrists were aching. She knew the PO could have removed them, but also knew that she wouldn't. Danby was a hard screw, everyone said so, and Susan wouldn't give her the opportunity to refuse. As a lifer, a murderer, she had long ago resigned herself to just how difficult people like Danby could be.

It was as if they enjoyed lording it over the prisoners. In a way Susan understood this. She knew from gossip that Danby's old man had a wandering eye, that her kids were always in trouble at school, that her house was always on the verge of being repossessed.

Screws gossiped like inmates.

And she understood the woman's need to belittle everyone around her. It was human nature after all. How Danby coped with her crap life and her crap job.

The sweatbox began moving again and Susan breathed a sigh of relief. The London traffic was horrendous, especially early-afternoon. She had been cooped up in the van since five-thirty that morning and only once had they stopped for her to go to the toilet and have a bite to eat. Danby had brought a picnic with her and had eaten and drunk to her heart's content, knowing that Susan, handcuffed and cramped, could do nothing about it.

The viewing grille opened and a male voice boomed, 'Nearly there, girls. About ten minutes and we'll all be able to stretch our legs.'

He left the grille open and Susan could hear the strains of David Bowie singing 'Life on Mars'. She closed her eyes again and sighed heavily.

Danby watched her, a closed expression on her face.

'Dalston!'

It was an urgent whisper.

Susan opened her eyes and just moved her face aside in time as the last of Danby's Pepsi was aimed straight at her. The dark liquid went all over her prison whites.

'They ain't letting you out, madam, not if I have anything to do with it.'

It was an empty threat and they both knew that.

She held her head down and stared once more at the floor. They travelled in silence until the van pulled into the main entrance of Holloway prison. The door was finally opened fifteen minutes after their arrival. Susan was half dragged out by Danby, and as she stood in the startling daylight, feeling a fresh breeze on her face, a sense of futility washed over her.

The grim façade of the prison was a stark reminder of what life held in store for her here; the closing of doors, the clanging of gates, the sound of keys in locks, all she could expect from now on.

Even though she had lived like this for two years it was the move for her appeal that had finally brought it all home to her; this brief glimpse of freedom had heightened her awareness of prison life.

Susan knew that unless she co-operated she would never get out and, equally, that she could never let on what had happened to her, could never tell anyone the truth. It was too frightening, too real still, to be talked about. Some things you kept inside.

She smiled at the irony.

She was registered and the handover went without a hitch. Danby kept up a constant stream of invective but the Holloway PO didn't bother to answer her. She had heard it all before.

Interrupting in mid-sentence she said quietly, 'Go back to main reception and you'll be taken to the canteen with the others. You can't go any further than here.'

Susan allowed herself a slight smile as the door was clanged firmly shut in Danby's face. Looking through the well-spaced bars, she winked at the other woman.

'Be seeing you, Dalston.'

'Not if I see you first, Mrs Danby.'

The screw unlocked her handcuffs and, rubbing her wrists, Susan followed her along a dusty corridor.

'Northern arsehole! It's Durham that does it to them – think they're better than all the other POs 'cos they run a hard nick there. Well, they want to try this shithole for a while. Twenty-three-hour lock up on remand . . . even the shoplifters get a bit shirty after a while, let alone the real cons.'

The PO unlocked yet another door.

'You eaten?'

Susan shook her head.

'Not since this morning. I had a drop of Pepsi, though.'

She laughed but the screw didn't return her smile. She didn't understand the joke.

'Make it easy for yourself here, Dalston, we know all about you and your sock trick. Now I heard through the grapevine that the other bird was asking for it, and that's fair enough, but don't try it on here. We all have enough to do without babysitting you, okay? You want to give anyone a kicking, you do it in the comfort and privacy of your own cell. Nothing seen. Understand me, eh?'

Susan nodded, serious now.

'Remember, there's lesbians coming out of the woodwork here, and they're not all inmates. You take care of yourself. You do anything, do it discreetly – that's the only advice I can offer you. Your rep has preceded you but you guessed that much. The way you slaughtered your old man goes against you from the off. Take my advice, love, keep your head down and your nose clean and we'll all feel the benefit.'

They were silent until they came towards the wing. The noise made by hundreds of women was deafening, growing louder and louder as they approached.

Once on the wing Susan was assailed by smells as well as sounds. The deep stench of overcooked cabbage from lunch was everywhere, in between sharper smells like sweat and cheap soap and deodorant. Wirelesses blared and people talked louder to compensate. Susan knew they were watching the new arrival and held herself straight, pressing her bundle into her chest. The women were the usual prison mixture: prostitutes with outrageous hair and make up; mousy kiters – credit card thieves; hard-faced prison junkies. Same faces, different prison.

It was all so depressing.

As she walked up the stairs to the first landing she heard a loud laugh and turned to stare into a pair of lovely green eyes that seemed to be open to their utmost. The owner of the eyes was tiny and doll-like. She smiled widely at Susan who nearly smiled back.

The PO pushed the girl away.

'One of the baby killers, Dalston. Watch out for her. Looks like an angel but she's madder than a rabid dog. She dropped her baby on to the gravel from her council flat – she was sixteen floors up.

Post-partum depression. She'll walk. But until then we're stuck with her.'

She followed the PO until they came to an open cell. The PO walked inside and Susan followed her, a feeling of apprehension washing over her. You never knew who you were to be celled up with, and until you'd found out, sussed them out and knew you could relax, it was a difficult business.

Lying on the top bunk, her hair immaculate, her make up perfect, was Matilda Enderby. Dark-eyed, with masses of chestnut hair, she sat up and gave Susan the once over. Then, turning to the PO, she said gently, 'You're putting this in with me?'

The voice was deep and husky with a middle-class accent.

Susan looked the woman in the eye and attempted a brief smile.

The PO ignored her, saying briskly, 'Listen, Enderby, you don't pick and choose in here, love. You gave up that right the night you murdered your old man. And as you're both in for the same thing I think you two might have more in common than you think.'

She left the cell and pulled the door to behind her.

Susan placed her bundle on the bottom bunk and pulled it open. The first thing she did was take out the photos and letters from her children. Then she quickly unrolled the few belongings she had and put them into the empty drawer of a small bureau.

Matilda Enderby watched her every move.

When Susan had finished she slid on to the bunk and, lying down, gazed at her children's faces. Especially the baby's.

Matilda left the cell and came back with two large mugs of tea. She opened a packet of Digestives and placed a few on the bunk beside Susan.

'Did you really hit your old man . . .'

Susan interrupted her acidly.

'One hundred and fifty-two times with a claw hammer? Yes, I did, I counted the blows, it gave me something to focus on.'

Matilda nodded. Even her face seemed still now. Gone was the perpetual eye movement betraying someone who was carefully observing what was going on around her. The two women were quiet for a while.

'What happened to you then?'

Matilda half smiled.

'Don't you recognise me? I'm the focus of a lot of media attention at the moment. I'll be out of here soon. Mine was one stab through the heart, and the bastard deserved it after what he put me through.'

Her voice was full of bitterness as she asked, 'Why did you do it?'

Susan shrugged.

'Who knows?'

'Well, you know, surely, even if you're not telling.'

Susan didn't answer her.

Instead she lay back on the bunk and tried to empty her mind. She had never told anyone what had led up to the murder and she didn't think she ever would. There were too many people involved, too many secrets to keep.

But then, that was how she had lived her whole life: one lie on top of another lie, one secret on top of another secret.

Later that day, as the prison noise calmed down and the cell door was finally clanged shut until the morning, Susan was left to her own thoughts. The same thoughts she had night after night. It was only in her own head, in the dark of night, that she could allow herself to think about what she had done and, more importantly, why she had done it.

She knew that to understand her own actions she had to go way back into her early life. That held the key to everything that had happened to her later. After the last two years of listening to psychiatrists repeatedly trying to find out the reason behind her crime, Susan finally understood why she had done what she had to Barry.

Book One

1960

Nothing begins, and nothing ends.
That is not paid with moan;
For we are born in other's pain,
And perish in our own.

– Francis Thompson, 1859–1907
'Daisy', 1893

Oh! how many torments lie in the small circle of a wedding ring.

Colley Cibber, 1671–1757
The Double Gallant, 1707

Chapter One

The girl opened her eyes. Sleep was sticky in them and she wiped it away with one small hand. She could hear her sister's steady breathing, little muffled snores that reminded her of a puppy's. The bed was warm and enveloping. She snuggled into her sister's back, the two little bodies fitted together like a pair of spoons, and drifted back to sleep.

The crash woke them both.

Susan knew she had not been asleep long because her arm wasn't dead yet and it usually was when she slept all night cuddled into her sister's bony frame.

Their father's shouting was reaching a crescendo.

Debbie giggled.

'Silly old bastard! I wish he'd go to sleep.'

Susan laughed too.

The fight, which had been going on for two days, was because her mother had got a job in the local pub. Their father was convinced she was only working there because there was something funny going on between her and the landlord.

He was always convinced their mother was having an affair and usually he was right.

That was what made the two girls smile. Even at eight and nine they knew the score and it amazed them that their father hadn't quite sussed it out yet. Their laughter stopped when they heard a loud slap, followed quickly by their mother's heels clacking down the lino-covered passage.

'You fat bastard! I'll fucking knife you one of these days.'

'Knifing, is it, eh? Always stabbing someone, you. Getting stabbed with that fucker's prick is all you're good for, lady.'

The battering was really starting now. They heard the thud as their mother's head hit the wall and both girls winced.

'You get up, Sue, I went last time.'

She sat up in bed and shook her head.

'No way. He hates me, you know he does.'

A loud smashing noise told the girls the fight had moved into the small front room.

'There goes the new lamp – that'll send Muvver off her trolley.'

Debbie was right. June McNamara screamed at the top of her voice: 'You fucker! You rotten bastard. Why must you always destroy everything?'

The fight was in full swing now and they knew their mother was holding her own. They could hear their father saying, 'Give over, you stupid cow, for fuck's sake.'

He was laughing now, and his laughter was infuriating his wife even more. Which was exactly what he wanted.

The girls sat up in bed, eyes wide.

They knew the next step would be Joey McNamara beginning the real hammering that would blacken his wife's eyes and possibly break some bones.

Debbie leaped from the bed. At nine she was tall for her age and very pretty. In these scruffy surroundings she looked too beautiful for the life she lived. Opening the bedroom door gingerly, she stepped out into the hallway.

June was on the floor of the lounge, her face a bloody wreck. Her husband was leaning over her, his breath coming in deep gulps as he ripped clumps of hair from her head. Susan followed her sister nervously. They both breathed a deep sigh of relief as the police banged on the front door.

'Come on, Joey. Open up, mate. We know you're in there.'

Susan ran down the hallway and opened the door. Sergeant Simpson bowled in with two other uniforms, knocking the child out of their way. She watched as they pulled her father off her mother while he tried unsuccessfully to kick her in the head.

'Calm down, man. You're already nicked for a D and D. Do you want to add assaulting a police officer to that as well?'

'She's a whore . . . an old whore! Shagging the fucking landlord of the Victory now, if you don't mind. And him as black as nookies fucking knockers. You bastard!'

Once more he tried to attack his wife.

'Making a laughing stock of me she is, everyone knows about it.'

June vomited on to the orange and green shag-pile and one of the younger PCs heaved with her.

'Come on, Joey, you're on an overnight. It'll all sort itself out in the morning. Sleep it off, lad, come on.'

He nodded then but as they walked him from the room he took back his booted foot and crashed the heel down on his wife's hand.

June screamed. Getting rapidly up off the floor, she attacked him once more.

The two girls watched it all round-eyed.

Sergeant Simpson looked at Susan and shrugged.

'Get your arse round your granny's. Tell her the score and come back with her. Your mother needs to go to the Old London, he's hammered her senseless.'

She nodded and went back into her bedroom. She pulled on her wellies and an old coat. Because she was heavier than Debbie and not as pretty she got all the shit jobs. Everyone always assumed she was the eldest too.

When she came out of the bedroom her mother was sitting on the sofa, nursing her injured hand, and Debbie had one arm around her shoulders trying to comfort her. Susan saw her mother shrug the arm off and sighed.

Debbie never learned to leave things well alone.

She slipped out of the front door into the coldness of the winter night and began the walk along Commercial Road to her grandmother's.

It was four in the morning and Ivy McNamara was not going to be pleased to be dragged from her warm bed. Quite frankly Susan didn't blame her.

11

Her feet were numb by the time she arrived at her granny's and tapped on the front door gently. Hopping from foot to foot, she waited for the inevitable shriek.

'Who's that at this time of night?'

Susan didn't like Granny McNamara. No one did. Ivy was a vindictive, mouthy old bitch – and that was what people said when they were being nice about her.

The front door was thrown open and she stood before her granddaughter in all her splendour. Bright yellow rollers surrounded her head like a crash helmet and her toothless mouth had spittle in its corners. She had lines of age and sleep in abundance and her hands were dirty claws, hygiene never being one of her virtues.

She was only fifty-seven years old.

'Come on in then. You're letting out all the heat!'

Susan followed her into her bedroom where Ivy pulled an old fur coat from the wardrobe and slipped it on.

'Find me teeth, I can't go without them.'

Susan looked around the bedroom until she saw the teeth in a glass by the bed.

'Here you are, Gran.'

Ivy slipped the teeth into her mouth and immediately years dropped off that caved in face.

'What's happened now?'

'The police took me dad. He was belting me mum.'

Ivy laughed loudly and broke wind at the same time.

'Found out about her and the macaroon from the Victory, 'as he?'

Susan nodded.

'Fucking whore she is! I don't know why he married it, but he wouldn't listen to me, would he? Oh, no. Had to have her – the biggest slapper this side of the water. You'll rue the day you poked that, I told him. And he did.'

Susan went on to autopilot. Her granny ripped her mother to pieces regularly and she had heard it all before. As her grandmother ranted the girl stood by the bedroom door and watched her.

Ivy put on her stockings then a pair of socks and her fur-lined ankle boots. A large knitted hat finished off the ensemble. Picking up a huge black leather handbag stuffed with everything from old ration books to her children's birth certificates and special offer vouchers, Ivy nodded to let her granddaughter know she was ready.

And without a warm drink, a decent jumper or a scarf, Susan walked all the way back home in the crippling cold of an icy London winter.

Back at the house Debbie was making tea. Their mother's face was destroyed and both girls avoided looking at it. Granny McNamara immediately took over and that made them feel even worse. She gripped her daughter-in-law's face tightly and moved it from side to side.

'You'll live. Though one of these days he'll fucking do for you, and who could blame him? Everyone's talking about you and that black mushy from the pub.'

The two little girls made faces at each other. Mr Omomuru, as they called him, was nice. He gave them lemonade and crisps and made them smile by telling them about Africa and his family.

Once the blood was washed away June's face didn't look so bad but it was still very battered. Getting up unsteadily, she walked to the mirror propped up on the windowsill and groaned.

'That rotten bastard! Look what he's done.'

Ivy laughed raucously.

'Your soot won't want to see you for a while – not with a boat like that. Anyway Joey will finish you when he gets back.'

She seemed to relish this thought and, fortified with tea and brandy, June turned to face her and shouted, 'Bollocks to you, you dried up old bag!'

Her hand was swollen to three times its usual size. Emptying the bowl, Susan refilled it with icy cold water. Her mother plunged in her hand and sighed.

'That feels better. Time you fucked off, ain't it, Ivy? Or will you hang around for your darling son to be released and see the end of the drama?'

Ivy shut up. She knew when she'd pushed things too far. June was quite capable of slinging her out of the house so Ivy kept her own counsel for a while. There was no way she was missing her son's return from prison; it would give her something to talk about at bingo.

'You in, Junie?'

Maud Granger's voice was loud as she walked into the tiny flat later that morning. She stepped into the kitchen and, seeing Ivy, nodded in her direction.

'I seen the Old Bill taking him – it's a fucking disgrace the way that man treats you. Look at the state of your face.'

June put the kettle on once more and winced as her hand throbbed.

'He'll be home soon, they normally kick him out about lunchtime, then it'll all start again. He's convinced I'm having an affair. As usual.'

'And as usual you are,' Ivy chipped in.

June turned to her and sighed heavily, trying hard to keep her temper. 'I am not having an affair. If you must know he pays me, Ivy, and without the money I couldn't survive as your darling son drinks anything that comes into this house. So now you fucking know, don't you?'

June quickly wished she had not been so outspoken because her friend Maud's mouth was like the Blackwall tunnel and that remark would be all over the estate by two o'clock.

Maud's eyes were like saucers as she breathed, 'Oh, Junie, you are a one.'

Ivy mimicked her.

'Yeah, and a right one at that, eh, Junie? My boy will boil your eyes, love, when I tell him this.'

June sat at the kitchen table and felt the sting of tears. Her face was decimated, swollen and black. It would take weeks before she looked even remotely like her usual self. Her hand was killing her and her back felt as if it was going to break. Her whole body was sore. But she was used to that. It was knowing that her husband was not going to let this one go for a good while that really bothered her. She liked her new man. He was lovely, gentle and kind, treated her with respect. He was generous as well.

June had been moonlighting as a prostitute for years, as did most of her neighbours. It was part and parcel of their lives. Kids needed new shoes? Off you went and no one was any the wiser.

What you didn't do was mouth off about it, and you certainly didn't open your trap when Maud was about. She could find gossip at a prayer meeting.

Susan and Debbie came into the kitchen as their grandmother started her tirade once more. According to her June was totally useless. Susan asked her mother if it was okay for them to go out and play.

Before June could answer, the front door nearly came off its hinges under a mighty banging.

She sighed.

'Get that for me, will you?'

Susan opened the front door and saw the biggest black man she had ever laid eyes on standing there.

He smiled at her gently.

'Is your mother there?'

Susan was nonplussed. She liked this man, he was nice. But she knew his presence would be like a red rag to a bull so far as Granny McNamara was concerned.

Debbie ran into the kitchen, squealing, 'It's the black man, Mum, he's at the door.'

June rolled her eyes to the ceiling and stifled an urge to scream against the injustice of it all. Pulling herself from her seat she said sarcastically, 'Close your mouth, Maudie, you might miss something juicy.'

As she walked out of the kitchen her heart was pounding. Jacob Omomuru was basically a very kind man as she well knew. That was what made it all so much harder. The chances were her old man was going to kill her over Jacob, and deep down she knew that if she had an iota of sense she'd run off with him. But she also knew she wouldn't. She couldn't cope with real life, couldn't cope with Joey hot on her trail because that would be the upshot.

Jacob was standing on her doorstep in front of all the neighbours in a smart navy blue suit with toning shirt and tie. The gorgeous crinkly hair that she loved was cropped close to his head; his wide almond-shaped dark eyes were pleading with her. Jacob Omomuru loved her and secretly that knowledge made June a very happy woman. But her life was set and nothing would change it.

He was folding her in his arms, exclaiming over her face. She winced as he pulled her against him. She could smell his special scent of sandalwood soap and cigarillos. She pushed him away just as her mother-in-law came to the door, her face like a white mask, mouth set in a large and ugly O.

'Leave her alone, you black bastard! My boy will cut your throat when he finds out about this lot.'

Jacob stood there, a large and intimidating figure among the women and girls. Maud was nearly wetting herself with nervous excitement. This was better than the telly, as she would inform people later in the day when she dropped in on anyone she could think of for a cup of tea and a fag. She had never heard of the expression 'keeping mum'.

'Come on, June. Come with me now, darling. Let me take good care of you and the girls.'

June looked up into his handsome face and shook her head.

'You better go, Jacob. Joey's home soon and if you're here there'll be hell to pay.' Her voice was low, no emotion in it whatsoever.

Another neighbour walked past, a young mother of twenty-three with four kids, enough stretch marks to be used as a railway timetable and more mouth than a cow's got udders.

'Here, Junie, you bringing work home now or what?'

June ignored her.

Jacob stared down into the face he loved so much. He knew June McNamara's reputation, everyone did. She was a 'sort' as the East Enders called it. June used the only asset she had. 'Sitting on a goldmine' was the way he had heard other women refer to their bodies. But nevertheless he had fallen for her heavy soft breasts and the accommodating moistness between her legs.

He was pussy whipped and he knew it.

He also knew that the chances of a mixed race relationship working out in 1960 were practically impossible. Especially in their neck of the woods.

But June had given him something he had never expected to find in the coldness of London. She had given him a little happiness. He took so much working in the Victory – he took their insults dressed up as jokes, and he took their money – but he knew that each and every day he walked a fine line. It was only his size and the fear factor that kept him alive and well in East London.

Jacob used his dark brooding looks to good effect in the pub and knew that was the edge he had over the white men. The women liked him. In London, especially the East End, powerful men were sought after. It was a trophy thing. 'My man can batter your man's brains out.' It was almost tribal. He allowed himself a secret smile at the thought.

June was pushing him towards the stairs as her mother-in-law screamed at the top of her voice, making sure she called people to their doors.

Turning from Jacob, June screamed back at her, 'Shut up, you dried up old bag! Will you shut your trap and give your fucking arse a chance for once?'

Then, turning back to Jacob, she pleaded with him.

'Will you go? You're just making things worse. He'll swing for me when he finds out you've been round here. Just go away and leave me alone!'

Her voice was husky with emotion and Jacob felt the sinking sensation of a man who realises that he has not only lost the battle but the whole war as well. He looked down into her battered face.

'You're a fool, June. I'm offering you a way out. I'm offering you a life.'

She laughed nastily.

'I've already got a life, Jacob, and it's fuck all to do with you and your kind.' She knew she had hurt him and whispered more kindly, 'Let it go, mate, just let it go.'

He tried to put a hand around her waist. She shrugged him off.

'Look at me, Jacob. This is it for me. It can't be any other way. If my old man comes home and finds you here, one of you will be doing time, okay? And quite frankly I ain't worth it. Now will you go?'

Before he could answer, a bucket of cold water hit the pair of them.

Ivy was in her element. All the neighbours were out and her boy was due home so she could really let her hair down now. If June slung her out she knew one of the neighbours would gladly take her in so she was guaranteed a cuppa and a ringside seat while she waited for her son's return.

June turned on her mother-in-law like a demented cat.

'You vicious old bitch! What did you have to do that for?'

She chased her back into the little flat, could hear laughter from the neighbours as Ivy screamed with fright and excitement. If her mother-in-law would just drop dead her life would be so much easier. Susan and Debbie watched wide-eyed as her mother set about their granny. June gave her a few resounding slaps around the mouth and head. Ivy dragged at her daughter-in-law's hair.

'You whore! He'll fucking paste you round the estate when I tell him about this. A wog, is it? Bleeding coons now, is it? By Christ, you're lower than the dock dollies you – you'd take on anything. Even they think twice about a black man.'

Dragging her mother-in-law by the hair and throwing her into a chair by the TV, June bellowed, 'He's a decent man! A bloody decent man. Too good for the likes of me. If I had half a brain I'd go on the trot with him, I would. But I know that between you and that ponce of mine we'd never know a day's peace. Your son has taken everything from me – everything. Look around you, look what we are, then pat yourself on the back, Ivy. You did a fucking great job with your boys. A really great job. We've got nothing, even less than you.'

Both women were worn out now, by the fighting and the screaming. The room went quiet, the two protagonists staring at one another like trapped vixens.

'Shall I make another cup of tea?'

June turned to her friend and neighbour and barked, 'Oh, fuck off, Maudie. Ain't you seen enough today? Go home and look after your kids. You'll hear it all through the wall, love, you normally do.'

'I'll make the tea, Mum.' Susan's voice was low and her mother stared into her daughter's face sadly.

'I'll put a drop of Scotch in it, shall I? Clear your head.'

She closed the front door after Maud had left then put the kettle on. Five minutes later she took two large steaming mugs of tea in to her mother and her granny.

Both women were whacked out though neither would admit it. Now that Joey was due home even his mother had gone quiet. No one ever knew what mood he would be in. He swung from laughter one minute to searing anger the next.

The flat was so quiet they could all hear the ticking of the clock on the Belling cooker in the kitchen.

Chapter Two

It was an hour later when Joey put his key in the front door. As they heard him fumbling, Ivy looked at her daughter-in-law and whispered, 'Now don't wind him up, right? Just agree with him. Whatever he says, just agree.'

June didn't even bother to answer her.

Joey walked through the door quietly, his narrow dark face closed and impassive. Picking up Debbie, he kissed her on the lips.

'How's my best girl, eh?'

Debbie snuggled into him, kissing him back. Susan watched. He winked at her and then walked into the kitchen. Looking at his mother, he sighed.

'Hello, Mum. Come round to pour trouble on oily waters, have we?'

Ivy kept her body still, her mouth firmly closed. Joey turned his gaze to June, taking in her battered face and hand. He blinked a few times as if unsure whether he was seeing right.

'What happened to you then, June? Had a tear up with a bus, love? You look rough, girl.'

No one said a word.

This was par for the course with Joey. He could go either way and enjoyed making the women in his life wait to see what he was going to do. Was June going to get a kicking, or was he going to forgive and forget and make long-winded declarations of love? It was a good game, one he enjoyed.

Ivy's eyes were shining with expectation and excitement. This was more like it. This was exactly what she had waited for. Suddenly she was a young woman again and Joey was his father.

What a man! Her husband's namesake was just like him.

Susan put on the kettle again, quietly this time. A loud noise could cause all sorts of trouble when her father was like this.

He grinned at her.

'Good girl, make the old man a cuppa. Calm him down after your mother had him nicked.'

Still no one said a word.

Joey looked at them all individually, drinking in the fear, the excitement and the tension. He sat at the kitchen table and lit a cigarette, taking a deep drag on it.

'I reckon a cup of tea and an egg sandwich and I'll be right as the mail.'

The two girls let out a sigh of pleasure at the sound of his calm voice. Disaster had been averted, Dad was going to let it all go and they could relax. 'Then, after my brekker, I'm going to go and shoot the coon. I nipped into Jonnie Braithwaite's on the way home and got a nice little handgun. I'll shoot his nuts off and be home for lunch.'

Joey pulled an ex-Army revolver from the pocket of his bum freezer jacket. It was large, shiny and looked menacing.

The girls' eyes widened. Ivy's face paled and June slumped in her seat.

'Don't be so bloody stupid, Joey. They'll bang you up good and proper, then what will you do, eh?'

Joey, who until this moment had not considered the possible consequences, stayed quiet.

His little pig's eyes gleamed.

'I'll worry about that afterwards. The soot is dead, mate.'

Everyone in the kitchen kept quiet.

'I put up with a lot from you, June, but fucking soots is one step too far. A big hairy-arsed wog now, is it? What's wrong with everyone else then? Had your fill of white blokes, have you? Fancied a bit of black pudding?'

He caressed the barrel of the gun then placed it under his wife's chin. The metal was cold, icy cold. June closed her eyes.

The tension in the kitchen was palpable.

Joey was quite capable of shooting her then dissolving into

tears of remorse. He would play the wronged man, the husband cuckolded by a flighty wife who had a penchant for black men.

As usual he was living in his own fantasy world.

Everyone in the room waited, breath held, eyes trained on the gun.

Susan went to her father and put her arms around him gently.

'Don't shoot me mum, I've got me school play on Wednesday and I'm the Angel Gabriel.'

Joey stared into his daughter's face.

But was she his daughter? Was either of the girls his?

That was somewhere he definitely didn't want to go.

He looked at his golden child, his Deborah, the elder girl with whom he always felt a special affinity. Mostly because she had the same selfish streak as him, the same lazy way about her. Everyone loves seeing themselves in their children, and the more of their parents' failings they have the more they are loved.

It was human nature.

Deborah was her father from head to foot. Pretty in a petulant way, she always made sure she got the lion's share of everything that was going. She would hold out her hand and take all her life, never once giving anything back. Deborah, like her father, faced a very lonely existence as an adult.

Even now, she was more worried about what would happen to her if her father shot her mother than the fact that June was in mortal danger from a man who didn't understand that human life was for enjoying, for giving and for loving. Not for making everyone do exactly as he wanted.

Being a weak man, Joey made a point of threatening, fighting and hating because he thought that made him look strong. He hated June and Susan at times because he knew they saw through him. Saw him as he really was: a loud-mouthed bully.

And that was why they were all so worried.

He would not shoot the black man. If anyone was getting shot it was going to be June because she was an easy target and today's events would give him more creds with the neighbours, the people he thought were important.

It never occurred to Joey that there was a big world beyond

Roman Road market and that people outside the area cared little if he lived or died.

He wanted to be a big fish in a little pond.

People would be wary of him coming around their houses. He would get lots of drinks in the pub. Old whores and local slappers would give him the adoration he craved. But June, his June, would still look at him with those empty eyes and laugh at him behind his back. Because she knew him for what he really was: a coward, a storyteller, a liar.

Deep down Joey was nothing. He knew it, and worst of all his wife did too. She was his Achilles heel because deep inside he loved her, really loved her, and he knew that once she had loved him. Adored him even. Until she had sussed him out.

He cocked the trigger, the noise shocking in the quietness of the kitchen.

June swallowed noisily, her voice dead as she said, 'Do it, Joey! Fucking get it over with, I've had enough.'

He stared into her ravaged face, saw the swellings and bruises that would have put a normal woman into the Old London for a week, and felt the sting of tears. He envisaged blowing her face away once and for all. Blasting off the top of her head. But the moment was gone.

She was standing up now and making more bloody tea.

'I'll do your breakfast and then you can get bathed.'

He stared at her, the gun still aimed at her, only now it was at chest level.

June smiled sadly.

'Get it over with, Joey. You'll do it one day. Might as well be now while I don't give a flying fuck.'

Susan took the gun from him gently as Debbie cuddled into her granny's arms. Ivy's face was a white mask. Not because her son was going to murder his wife but at the thought of him going down. Joey was what gave her licence to be the vindictive old bitch she was. People allowed her access to their homes and lives because they were too frightened not to.

Susan quietly took the gun to the bathroom and dropped it down the toilet bowl. She had seen a film once where a gun had been immersed in water so it didn't work.

She hoped that was true.

As she slid it into the toilet the trigger went off. The gun was totally silent. She sighed heavily.

It wasn't even loaded.

Her father had put them through all that for nothing.

After putting the toilet lid down, she went back to the kitchen. Debbie was on her father's lap now and her granny was pouring him a large Scotch. Hair of the dog, they called it.

The kitchen was full of good-humoured camaraderie from the release of tension. Putting on her old coat and wellingtons, Susan slipped from the house. She was supposed to be the Angel Gabriel in the play this week and she had no real costume, nothing. Her teacher had made her some wings and she had promised to make herself an angel costume.

What she really needed was a sheet . . .

As she walked down the steps to the street she saw the lines of washing hanging out even on a crisp winter's morning. There before her was a lovely white sheet, pristine and shining.

Susan smiled to herself.

She sat it out all afternoon, watching the sheet, making sure no one took it in. As soon as it was dark she whipped it off the line and under her coat. One last glance to see whether anyone had clocked her and then she ran like the wind back to her house.

Inside, everything was rosy. Her mother was on her father's lap on the settee, her granny had gone and Debbie had the right hump because she had been chief tea maker and sandwich filler for the afternoon.

'What's that under your coat?'

Her sister's voice was loud. She tried to pull the sheet from Susan who pushed her away heavily.

'Piss off, Debbie, it's mine.'

Debbie ran into the lounge, her petulant voice at full pitch.

'Mum, Dad, our Sue's stolen someone's washing. It's under her coat. I saw it and she won't let me have it.'

Joey looked at his daughters.

'What you got, Sue?'

His voice was bored-sounding.

'I nicked a sheet, Dad, to make me angel costume for the school play. I told you, I'm the Angel Gabriel.'

'I thought angels were supposed to be good-looking? What's the matter, they run out of kids up the school?'

She didn't answer him.

'Whose fucking sheet was it?'

Susan shrugged.

'I dunno, but no one saw me take it or nothing.'

June sighed.

'Leave her alone, she nicked it fair and square. It's hers.' She smiled at her daughter. 'You go to your room and I'll come in and make you a toga, like the Romans wore. That will be like an angel costume, mate.'

Susan grinned.

'Thanks, Mum.' Lying on the bed, she lost herself in dreams of being an angel, albeit an ugly one.

But, as Susan reasoned to herself, you couldn't have everything. What she had at the moment was enough for her.

Chapter Three

Susan McNamara was laughing, really laughing, and her form teacher Miss Castleton was watching her, amazed at the change in the dour, quiet thirteen year old she was used to.

It was Christmas and the class were watching cartoons. They had started with *Snow White* and were now finishing with Tom and Jerry. All the children were laughing but Susan's face, for once open and displaying enjoyment, held the teacher's attention. She looked radiant, or at least as radiant as someone like Susan could look.

Although well dressed, the girl had a forlorn air about her all the time, as if she was constantly waiting for something. What she was waiting for was unclear, but it was as if she got dressed, brushed her hair, then went about the serious business of the day: waiting.

For what? Karen Castleton asked herself over and over.

Every time a door opened Susan turned a half-frightened, half-eager face expectantly towards it.

Especially lately.

In the last few weeks she had been quieter than usual, and Susan McNamara was already quiet to the point of silence. Only today had she been even remotely animated.

Miss Castleton put that fact down to the Christmas holidays approaching and the change in routine. A solitary child, she usually kept to herself, lost in the library, in books and music. The librarian, a rather masculine-looking woman called Gloria Dangerfield, thought the girl was a frustrated academic, suffering from some kind of word blindness.

Everyone else thought she liked the library because no one else in the school could be brought near it without threats or as a punishment. It was just another place for her to hide, to bide her time until she had to go home.

Karen Castleton was middle-aged, pretty in a severe way and hampered by her privileged upbringing. St Jude's Secondary School had been a shock to her. A big shock. Until then she had not been aware that children swore and cursed as part of their everyday language, that telling a child off could result in a big burly-armed woman threatening to rip your lungs out, or that spelling a simple word could be like climbing a mountain for the majority of her pupils.

In short, Miss Castleton was herself being educated and it was doing her the world of good. Which she admitted to herself. Seeing this all first hand had been a boon. One day she would write about it all, she quite fancied herself as a novelist. But until then and the statutory two point five children, the house and the big fluffy dog, she decided to watch and learn about this strange East End environment where girls were simply told to bide their time till motherhood or marriage (whichever came first), and boys were taught they could work either in factories or warehouses.

It was all so depressing.

Miss Castleton looked at her class of thirteen year olds and instinctively knew that most of the girls were sexually experienced in some way. They plastered themselves with make up, they smoked and they drank if they could afford a bottle of cider, which most of them could by all accounts.

As they packed their few belongings into well-worn carrier bags the teacher watched Susan McNamara take her Christmas cards from her desk. She herself had given out no cards, overlooking the cardboard box on her desk.

She knew Susan's home life was considered deprived even by East End standards. Her mother lived with a notorious villain and her father brought up his two daughters aided by his wizened mother and monetary help from the mother's new amour.

As the class emptied Miss Castleton saw Susan pretending to sort through her bag while wishing everyone Merry Christmas.

When the classroom was empty she called to the girl, 'Merry Christmas, Susan.'

'Merry Christmas, Miss Castleton.'

Her voice was low and husky.

'Are you looking forward to it all? The celebrations and the jollity?'

Susan McNamara looked at her as if she had just appeared in a puff of green smoke.

'Are you?'

The question coming back at her like that threw her and she struggled to answer. Then, smiling, she said honestly, 'Not really, no.'

This seemed to cheer the girl up. Sitting on the edge of her desk, Miss Castleton said to her, 'I have to travel all the way down to St Ives where my parents retired a few years ago. They both paint, it's a sort of painters' paradise. Neither of them is very good, mind, but they enjoy it. For myself, I find the place boring and full of ancients. What will you do?'

Susan thought about this for a second before answering.

'I'll go to me mum's and me Uncle Jimmy's on Christmas Eve for a few hours, then I'll go home and have to start preparing everything for Christmas Day. I do all the veg and that now. Me granny says she's too old to be chasing around after us two.'

'And what will your day be like – Christmas Day?'

'Well, I'll go to midnight mass, and when I get back I'll make sure everything is going how it should. You know, the turkey in the oven to cook all night, the parsnips steeped in brandy to give them a bit of a zing. Then I'll get up Christmas morning, open me presents and read, I suppose. I'm hoping to get *The Hobbit*. Me mum promised me she'd track down a copy for me. I love that book. I borrow it all the time from the library. How about you?'

'I'll be waited on hand and foot actually. My parents miss me so much. I'll let you into a small secret: they hate the thought of my working here. They saw me as one of the mistresses in *Bunty* instead. You know, all jolly hockey sticks and lashings of ginger beer!'

Susan didn't smile with her but nodded solemnly.

'You can't blame them, can you? This place is a bit of a shit hole. But then, you choose to be here, don't you? None of us had a choice. I quite fancy living like the girls in *Bunty*. That would do for me all right.

'Merry Christmas, Miss. Hope you have a good journey to your parents.'

Karen Castleton realised she had just been dismissed and the knowledge unnerved her. She watched the dumpy little girl with the enormous breasts walk from the room. Mr Reynaldo, who had been watching the proceedings from the doorway, walked in and laughed.

'You'll never get close to any of them, love, they see us all as the enemy. I've been forcing my knowledge on these kids for ten years and it's a waste of time. They know more about life than we ever will. They can't help it, all human existence is around them from the word go. Anyone in authority is an enemy, whether it's us, the police or a shopkeeper. It's how they're brought up. She was putting you in your place. You described the type of parents she'd cut off her own arms for and you mocked them. In her eyes you're a spoiled mare, as they say in these parts. See, I've even picked up the lingo.'

Karen's dark hair and merry blue eyes had attracted him, as they had attracted most of the male teachers, but her reserved nature and failure to see a joke had eventually put them all off. He was enjoying her humiliation and she knew it.

Karen felt defeated and more out of place than ever. He walked from the room without saying goodbye.

She opened her desk and saw an envelope. Opening it, she found an expensive Christmas card, all glitter and robins. It was from Susan McNamara. Her rounded laborious handwriting stated: *All the best for Christmas and 1966, Susan McNamara and family, xx.*

Looking at the card Karen felt an enormous lump constricting her throat. He was right, Mr Reynaldo, she had ridiculed something Susan McNamara would have given her eyeteeth to possess: a normal family.

She had a feeling she would not be back in the New Year.

Suddenly St Ives seemed a lovely place. Saving the world by working in an inner city environment had lost all its glamour. Closing the desk, she put the card in her bag and left the room. She would never come back here again.

Patronising bitch! was all that kept going round in Susan's head. She had really liked Miss Castleton, liked the way she kept herself to herself, the way she dressed. Had thought of her as an ally, a friend.

Instead she was just like the others. Saw Susan as this deprived little girl with big knockers and no brain. Well, bollocks to her and all.

Two and six, that card had cost. Half a bloody crown. The woman in the shop had checked the money carefully, as if she knew that people like Susan would only buy a card of that calibre once in a lifetime.

Well, bollocks to that old bag as well.

The swearing in her mind was getting worse and she knew she had to stop it, but it released the steam from her brain, released the anger in a small way.

She was well aware of what she was but reading had shown her another world and Susan wanted a part of that other world so badly . . . but she knew it was just a pipe dream.

'Penny for them?'

She turned at the sound of the harsh Scottish accent and saw Barry Dalston. He was a new kid in town. His mother had recently arrived with him and his brothers back from Scotland. A gang there had murdered Barry's father; it had been the talk of the neighbourhood for weeks.

All the girls liked Barry because he was a hard man with the rep of a nutter. Susan liked him because he always smiled at her. Now he was actually speaking to her and it practically made her swoon with shock, embarrassment and gratitude.

'I just tipped old Castleton bollocks, I was just thinking about that.'

Barry grinned, impressed.

'I'd have no trouble giving that one myself, but I'd have to tape up her gob first. All those long words would be very off-putting.'

Susan laughed at the picture he had conjured up. Him and Miss Castleton? People like her didn't have sex, they made love. Susan wasn't sure what the difference was between these two things, she just knew there *was* a difference.

She knew it wasn't what her father did to her. Sweaty grabbing of breasts, biting and whispers of: 'There's a good girl. Daddy's girl knows what he wants,' somehow didn't fit in with Miss's skirts and jumpers. Or her crappy sensible shoes.

Susan turned her thoughts away from the teacher and she and Barry walked together in silence for a while.

'Do you fancy a bag of chips?' he asked.

Susan nodded delightedly.

'I'd love a bag of chips, I'm starving.'

Barry grinned, a feral little grin that heightened his good looks. And Barry Dalston was good-looking, everyone knew that. He raised his eyebrows and said gently: 'Have you any money?'

Susan nodded. She always had money, thanks to her mother.

He laughed.

'Well, put it away, these are on me. And I think we might swing enough for maybe a nice saveloy too, eh?'

Susan nodded; her cup was really running over tonight. As they made their way to the high street they chatted about their lives. Actually, she realised, Barry did most of the chatting but that suited her down to the ground. Every now and then his eyes would linger on her breasts and she would pull her coat tighter around herself as if warding him off. This made him laugh.

'You'll no hide them away, my little love. How old are you by the way?'

Susan stared into his face.

'Nearly fourteen.' This wasn't true, she had just hit her thirteenth birthday a few weeks before, but she knew it was a lie any woman would have told to keep the interest of the likes of Barry Dalston.

'I'm eighteen . . . nineteen in the New Year. I always think its better if the man is older than the girl, don't you?

Susan nodded. Her heart was banging like a ceilidh in her chest. He was talking as if they were a courting couple. Susan thanked God, Our Lady and every other saint she could think of for bringing her this boy.

Barry for his part stared down into that plain face saved only by her nice teeth. She looked clean, she looked ripe, and she was really a child, he knew that deep inside. Yet she intrigued him, with her snooty ways and her book reading. He had heard from the other kids about her family set up and there lay the real reason for his interest. Her Uncle Jimmy and those big breasts were the beacons that drew him to her.

She was in with the real villains, and that was what he was after. An in with the real gangsters.

He smiled at her and Susan smiled back. He actually liked her in a funny sort of way. She looked at him with utter adoration and who could resist that?

June was over the moon to see her daughter smiling and laughing on Christmas Eve. Though Debbie was always a happier girl, in her own way Susan had a quiet sense of humour and a good appreciation of a joke.

Over the last few years this seemed to have deserted her and June had blamed it on the girl's not having her mother around. Now she seemed to be full of it.

June herself was not having the time of her life as she had first thought she would. Jimmy, her Scottish laddie, had turned lately, driving her hard, criticising her dress, her hair, everything. June was kicking thirty and had the distinct impression that he was trumping something younger, something different.

She was waiting for the bad news but until she got it would sit it out.

As she walked through East Ham market, her usual Saturday jaunt with the girls, she saw an old friend, Bella Tambling. Bella was big, loud and brash but such a laugh you couldn't resist her. Today she was wearing a wide blanket coat and a woolly hat. She looked fifty, talked like a navvy and had a laugh that could cut through dense undergrowth.

'Hello, Junie me old mate, long time no see.'

June smiled at the effusive greeting.

'Come and have a cuppa in the pie and mash shop. Me feet are fucking strangling me and me mouth feels like the bottom of a budgie's cage.'

The two girls laughed as they followed their mother and Bella inside the steamy shop. Susan hated seeing the live eels in a bowl on the counter even though she ate them. Sitting down, she let Debbie get the order and listened to her mother and Bella catch up.

'Got seven kids now, but I had two misses. That was His Lordship and his fucking great boots. But in a way it was for the best – they're a crowd of little bastards. I gave them all money and dropped them off at Crisp Street this morning. Hopefully the lot of them will be run over by a fucking bus come tonight.'

June laughed, knowing that her friend loved her kids really, it was just the East End way of going on. As she removed her long leather coat she saw two men looking at her in appreciation and this cheered her.

June knew she had to sort out something with Jimmy and soon. He wasn't even bothering to come home nights.

As two steaming cups of tea were placed in front of them Bella began to talk and for a few seconds June didn't realise she was talking about her Jimmy.

Wiping her mouth with a tissue, June asked her politely to repeat what she had just said.

Bella looked at her friend sadly.

'You don't know, do you, mate?' She wiped her nose with a well-used hankie and began again. 'It's some posh sort he's took up with – everyone's talking about it. Though what's posh about a nice motor and a few good suits, I am fucked if I know. She runs the Dynamo Club. Fuck me, June, I'm sorry, love. I assumed you knew. It's common knowledge around these parts. It's my big fucking trap again, ain't it? I open me gob and stick me foot straight in it, boots and all. I take oath I wouldn't have sprung it on you like that.'

June smiled.

'I had an inkling, Bell. Just tell me what you know – and I mean, just tell me. I don't want the whole place hearing it.'

'It's Maureen Carter, her who lived over the back of us as kids.'

June's eyes widened.

'But she's older than me. Are you sure?'

Bella blew out her lips loudly.

'Of course I'm sure. And in fairness she do look good, Junie. She must be forty if she's a minute but she's like a man in a lot of ways. She earns good wedge and does what she wants. That's most likely the attraction. Men like these new-fangled birds, don't they? Even my eldest, Marie, was saying she wanted a career the other day. I slapped her fucking face for her and all, little whore. I says to her at first, "Good on yer, girl, get a life." And you know what she says to me then, quick as a flash? "Well, I ain't ending up like you, Mum, more kids than handbags and never driven a car." "I have driven a car," I tells her, "one your dad stole when we was kids. I crashed the fucker and your father banned me from even getting in a driving seat again unless it was me old bike."'

Bella's scream of laughter burst from her mouth and even June laughed, though inside she was shaking.

The dirty stinking bastard! Maureen Carter . . .

Maureen who was a force to be reckoned with in her own right.

Maureen who knew everyone and lived by her own set of rules.

Maureen who dropped the takings from the bookie's round every Saturday as a favour to Jimmy.

Maureen who came and drank coffee with June . . . who'd had absolutely no idea she was shagging her old man.

Closing her eyes, June felt devastation wash over her. She was truly on her way out.

Jimmy had had a dabble before and she'd cocked a blind eye to it, knowing it was the nature of men to pursue anything that breathed and looked remotely shaggable. But she also knew that Maureen was serious competition.

Maureen would be talking with him, having conversations about business and life. That was what nicked men away from their women, not sex.

Sex was relative. Men fucked, wiped it, bought the old woman a bunch of flowers and gave her one to compensate. But if it was someone like Maureen and he was staying out nights then it was serious.

Jimmy felt he was going up in the world and wanted a partner he could take with him, one he could respect. One who would give him a run for his money. And Maureen would do that as well; she could fight like a fucking man when the fancy took her. She already thought like one and talked like one.

Only the other day she'd been saying how she had just bought herself another house and like a prat June, Jimmy's live in girlfriend, had congratulated her.

She must have been laughing up her sleeve.

June swallowed down the last of her tea and stood up.

'Thanks for telling me, Bell. I do appreciate it, mate.'

Bella grasped her hand.

'What you going to do, give her a dig? I hear he's already moved clothes and that into her drum. I heard that from old Cathy Davies. She does Maureen's cleaning so as you can imagine it will be all over the place by now. Always the last to know, eh, girl? I'm so glad my old man's an ugly fucker – no one else would want him. His breath would put off a two-bob whore, let alone a normal person!'

Once more Bella was laughing and June, watching the gaping mouth, with the missing teeth and the yellow-coated tongue, envied her friend at that moment.

Bella's life was her kids and that was it. Why couldn't June herself have just been happy with that? Why did she always want more?

Debbie and Susan had listened to it all in silence. As they left the warmth of the shop Susan placed her hand in her mother's. June squeezed it tightly, holding back the tears of frustration and rage that were welling up in her eyes.

Flagging down a cab, she kissed the girls and told them to get along home, she would give them their presents tomorrow. The cab pulled away and she watched them go with a heavy heart. This had to be sorted and as it was Christmas it had to be sorted delicately.

As she stood on the pavement Bella came out, puffing and panting as she did up her coat and pulled on her hat.

'If it's any consolation, mate, I've always got a bed for you at my place if you need it.'

The kindness was too much and now the tears started.

'The rotten bastard, Bella! The rotten, filthy, stinking wanker.'

Bella, laughing as usual, cried with her.

Jimmy watched as June put his meal on the table. He sighed.

'Not for me, hen. I grabbed a bite earlier. Listen, why don't you go out tonight, eh? I'm tied up, really hard at it . . .

June looked at him and smiled.

'You're a lying bastard. You're tied up all right but not with work – though trumping Maureen could be classed as manual labour, I suppose. What's the matter then, cat got your tongue?'

Jimmy had the grace to look ashamed.

'Who told you?'

June sighed.

'You're not denying it then?'

'Even I cannae deny the truth.'

'Why not? It never stopped you before.'

'Come on, June, you know how it is. I never thought it would be serious. But it is – I love her.'

June sat at the table and shook her head.

'So where does that leave me, eh? You love her and you live with me. Or, more accurately, I live with you. I left my husband and children . . .'

Jimmy flapped his hand at her.

'With respect, Junie, you'd have left your husband for anyone. And as for those poor lassies . . . Christ, I think you'd have left them with Battersea Dogs' Home if they'd have taken them, so let's not go too over the top here.'

'I loved my girls.'

Jimmy took a deep breath before continuing.

'Listen to yourself, June. You loved them. And you dinnae love them now, is that it? I thought you were the bee's knees once and that's the truth. But not any more, sweetheart. My tastes are running a little bit higher than you these days. Christ almighty, you barely clean the house, you cook this shite constantly and you've no conversation. Please, June, don't make this harder than it already is by asking me what went wrong and all the rest of it. Let's just say you and me are over, hen, and I'll see you all right. I was going to tell you after Christmas anyway.'

'That was big of you, but there's one thing I need to know. Why Maureen Carter? What's she got that I haven't?'

Jimmy wiped a hand over his face, irritated. She had put him on the spot and he didn't like it one bit. Annoyed, he retaliated.

'A fucking brain, Junie, and she has nous, a mind of her own and doesn't need constantly looking after. How's that for starters or would you like me to carry on?'

June felt as if she had been punched in the solar plexus.

'No, I get the picture now, thank you.'

Picking up his plate of steak and chips, she emptied it into the bin.

'So when do I go? Or should I say, where do I go?'

Jimmy was sorry to the heart but the feeling he had for Maureen was like a cancer, constantly eating away inside him.

He wanted to be with her all the time, wanted to watch her, see what she was doing. He knew that men liked her, that she attracted them, especially well-to-do men with businesses and careers. He couldn't quite believe she had chosen him. Now she had he intended to keep her just for himself.

He admired, respected, loved her.

Really loved her.

Poor June couldn't compete with that.

'I'll leave, sweetheart. You can stay here until we arrange something for you, okay?'

June nodded sadly, unable to talk she was so upset.

'I love you, Jimmy.'

The words forced their way out of her mouth despite herself.

'I know, Junie, and believe me I'm heart sorry, lassie. I really am.'

'I could change, try and be different . . .'

Jimmy shook his head at her.

'You're lovely as you are, Junie, and someone will love you for that, you'll see.'

She grinned sadly.

'Like you did, you mean? What a thrilling thought.'

He walked from the room. She heard the front door open and ran after him, calling his name. As he looked into her face she smiled and said, 'Merry Christmas, Jimmy.'

Without answering her he left the house. June collapsed on the doormat and cried until she was aching.

The tragic thing was she was telling the truth. She did love him. Still.

Debbie was out, her granny was out and her father was out. Susan savoured having the flat to herself.

As her mother let herself in with her key her heart stopped in her breast.

'Hello, Mum. What's brought you here?'

She knew already but she would never say so. It was up to her mother to sort it all out and then tell Susan what she wanted her to know.

'I thought I'd pop round and see me girls, and give them a cuddle.'

Susan hugged her tight.

If all Bella said was true then she might be able to go and live with her mother somewhere. That thought had been keeping her going ever since it had entered her head. To be away from her father was such a wonderful prospect that she felt as if she was having all her Christmases and birthdays together.

As her mother sipped a Scotch Susan prepared the vegetables and they chatted about nothing in particular. An hour later Joey walked in.

Seeing his Junie sitting at the kitchen table made him start. He looked around hastily in case she had brought Jimmy with her and it meant trouble.

Slipping Susan a fiver, June asked her to go out and get her some cigarettes. Susan went with a heavy heart. She already knew what her mother was going to do and it grieved her. Grieved her and destroyed any hope she'd had of getting away from the man in the kitchen. June was going to try and re-enter her husband's life and if she succeeded all Susan's dreams would go out of the window.

As she walked from the house she heard the peculiar note in her mother's voice that meant she was after something. It wasn't exactly a whine, more of a low gurgling sound that made her seem girlish, childish even.

Shutting the front door Susan sighed once more.

Life was never what you wanted, Susan McNamara already knew that much.

Joey looked his wife over and smiled. She was all right, his June, he should have looked after her; she was a one off in many respects.

No other woman seemed to want him these days; his drinking, his temper or his lack of money seemed to put the kibosh on everyone he spoke to. He accepted that his June must have cared about him to put up with all that. Fuelled by drink, it seemed a logical as well as a romantic assumption.

Ever since he had first laid eyes on her, she had affected him like no other woman. He knew she was a whore and that bothered him but also excited him. In a strange way, it was half her attraction.

June's personality and body were overtly sexual and that was the nub of all her man problems. It was what had attracted Jimmy, until he had seen her for what she was. Villains didn't have to have molls hanging on their arms any more. This was the sixties and people like Johnny Binden and his ilk could take any kind of woman they wanted. Jimmy Vincent wanted this too.

June knew she was now an also ran and she had to salvage something. If it meant that she had to take back her husband then all the better really. At least she would be in an environment she knew, with people who knew her and accepted her for what she was: June McNamara, slag extraordinaire. Battered wife, haphazard mother and Jimmy's ex-bird.

As her husband made them both tea and toast and they chatted about the girls she felt herself relax. When Joey was like this she loved him. This was the man she had fallen for, this was the man she had wanted more than anything once.

Now she knew that if he took her back there would be a subtle shift of position. After all, she had crossed into the real world of villainy and her husband was aware of that.

She would let him think that she had left Jimmy. That she had gone off him. Joey would believe her, would want to believe her.

She began to talk to him, her voice soft, her eyes moist. As he responded with shy smiles and little gestures, lighting her cigarettes, pouring her more tea, she relaxed.

This was going to be easier than she'd thought. But she would miss her Jimmy, miss him very much. After all, he had shown her another way of life and for that alone June would always be grateful to him.

Jimmy walked out of his new amour's house a happy, happy man. He was glad Junie had taken it all so well. He'd hated hurting her but what could a man do?

She was old news, like a newspaper read from cover to cover. Why keep it?

He would see her off with a couple of grand and promise he would keep an eye on her. And every now and then, when he felt the urge for a bit of strange, he would call on her.

Junie was like that.

He realised now she was as mercenary as him. You didn't make respectable women out of the Junes of this world. You shagged them, used them, had a few laughs then tossed them aside when the next one ambled into the pub.

But he had loved her, at least for a while he had, until he had seen a different way of life, a better way of life. Realised that women could actually think as well as shag.

As the baseball bat hit him on the back of his knees Jimmy was nonplussed for a few seconds. He thought for a moment he had fallen over. As he hit the pavement and the gun was shoved into the back of his head he realised he had been set up.

And who better to do that than his new woman?

His last conscious thought was that, if he survived, he would take a baseball bat and crack it over Maureen's head until it was smashed to pieces.

Maureen Carter watched the commotion from the bedroom of her house, grinning to herself. Jimmy really thought she would want him? It was laughable.

The phone rang. She picked it up, her heavily varnished nails glinting in the half-light.

'Yeah, just now. It's over.'

She replaced the receiver. Then, deliberately smudging her mascara, she walked sedately down the stairs and into the street. Her screaming and carrying on brought everyone to their doors. In a respectable area, the murder of a known villain was unheard of. Maureen was hysterical, the police left her alone, and afterwards her son made her a nice stiff drink. All in all not a bad day's work.

Jimmy's death had earned her thirty grand.

Maureen sipped her drink and planned a nice holiday with the money the Davidson brothers had promised her for setting up her new boyfriend. It looked like 1966 was going to be her year.

Chapter Four

June was in shock, complete and utter shock. Even though he had been leaving her, she still couldn't believe her Jimmy was really dead.

Inside she felt glad, and that frightened her.

The police had knocked just after she'd arrived home from Joey's, full of Scotch and camaraderie, fuelled with the knowledge that if push came to shove she was home and dry with her husband. She had let him cop a quick feel while pretending she was still staying faithful to Jimmy.

She had reminded him that walking out on a big-time villain was not something she could do lightly, and even Joey had had to concede that one. Finally she had hinted that Jimmy was playing around on her and that maybe she had made a big mistake . . . With a parting shot about how she missed the children, she had left.

Though she knew and Joey knew that the part about the girls was pure fabrication, while they were still getting on friendly terms he wasn't about to pull her up on it. All in all June felt it was a good night's work.

Now Jimmy was dead, murdered in the street. And she could hold her head up, tell everyone he'd been giving Maureen the elbow and was still her beau. After the police had left, June set about the serious business of the night.

Looking for his money.

Jimmy always kept large amounts around the house and June knew where most of them were. She had arranged to identify his body in the morning, saying she was too distressed at this time.

She was hoping she could pick up his effects at the same time then she would have the key to the safe and that was what she really wanted. In there he'd kept his address books, everything. They would be worth a pretty penny to the right person.

Smiling, June poured herself a large Scotch, for her shattered nerves, and then after a long hot bath set about tearing the house apart.

By Christmas morning she had found over two thousand pounds in notes bundled up and stuffed in wardrobes, drawers, even the electric cupboard. She placed it all on the bed and looked at it for a long time.

It was a small fortune.

Stretching like a long-limbed cat, June looked at herself in the mirror. She could do with a make over really but that would have to wait.

Going to the safe, she was amazed and euphoric to see that the key she had found in the bedroom drawer fitted perfectly.

The shock caused her to start trembling all over.

Inside was more money, a few pieces of jewellery she knew she couldn't pawn in the usual way and his address books, account books and a gun.

Settling herself on the bed, lying on over three thousand pounds, June began to read his books and his simple system was so easy to understand she realised even she could have run it if she'd wanted to.

Jimmy had lent money out then dragged it back with violent threats and intimidation. He'd kept a book with all the debtors' addresses, phone numbers, and details of family members.

As she lay on the money she began dreaming about what she would do with it. And Joey was in the equation now, only not as he would like to be. That was something she would sort out as time went by.

What she really needed now was Joey's reputation for violence. After all, no man but Jimmy would have dared to take her on under normal circumstances.

It was all about front and June knew this.

If Joey had had even a bit of nous he could have been a Jimmy himself. God knew he had the other attributes. But Joey's biggest failing was his complete lack of any ambition or brainpower. He was a thug, simple as that. People paid him to do their dirty work.

As an armed robber he'd been a disaster. He had actually gone into a local bookie's in the sweltering summer heat to rob them. He had put on a balaclava but forgotten to hide his tattoos, so everyone knew it was him.

Wearing nothing but a pair of trousers and a string vest he had displayed tattoos saying 'Junie and Joey' in a large red heart, and 'ACAB', meaning All Coppers Are Bastards, on his hands. On top of this he had a large dragon on his belly which he liked to make dance by moving his stomach as a party piece.

Everyone had sussed him immediately, especially the bookie who had given him five hundred pounds and told him to go away.

Joey had taken the money but that night had had a visit from the Davidsons who were paid to protect those particular premises and had had to swallow his knob and go round and apologise.

Even Davey Davidson had laughed.

For weeks afterwards every time Joey went in there to put on a bet everyone fell to the ground as if he was robbing them and laughed their heads off. Even Joey had seen the funny side of it, and that said it all about him as far as June was concerned.

He was as much use as a chocolate teapot.

Still, she would sort out Joey because now she had the money, she was in charge, and if she looked after him then he would look after her.

Finally she hid the money and went to bed.

Susan took communion at midnight mass and prayed again to Our Lady to make her father be asleep when she got in. If possible, she beseeched, could he please be paralytic and unconscious too?

She didn't ask for him to be dead because that might be too much even for Our Lady of Perpetual Succour.

After mass she walked up to look at the nativity scene. It was lovely. As she admired it a hand came down on her shoulder and, turning, she saw Father Campbell smiling down at her.

'You're a grand child, you know. You never miss the mass, do you?'

Smiling radiantly, she nodded.

'Only if I'm very ill. I love coming here.'

'And how's your mother? It must be a terrible night for her, God love her, what with the murder . . .

Susan looked into his face in shock. Was her father dead at last? Her heart constricted in her breast. She could hear her pulse hammering in her ears.

'What murder?'

As she looked into the priest's face and he informed her that her Uncle Jimmy had been shot in the street Susan sighed.

Life was so bloody unfair.

Poor Uncle Jimmy. She had always liked him, he had been kind to her and Debs. Giving them a few minutes of his time, asking them about school, their lives. Things it would never have occurred to June to ask.

Now he was dead and it was inevitable her mother would take up residence back at home. Susan didn't want that.

She didn't want that at all.

Bowing to the inevitable as usual, she smiled sadly.

'He was a nice man, me Uncle Jimmy. I'd better get home and see if me mum needs me.'

'You do that, child. Sure you're a boon to your mother, a boon.'

The priest watched her hurrying from the church on dumpy little legs and smiled sadly. She was a lovely little thing, plain as a pikestaff but with a huge heart that was crying out for a bit of affection.

Now the man was dead, God rest him and keep him, perhaps that whore of a mother might get herself home and take care of her children as nature intended.

Davey Davidson was over the moon. He knew his biggest rival was finally off the scene and that pleased him.

What wasn't so pleasant was the knowledge that a lot of people would now be after his blood.

He would deal with that when it came up.

What he wanted now were the notebooks and ledgers of the man he had killed. To get them he needed access to the house and that was where Joey came in. After all, his old woman was the bird in the know, as he had explained to them when he had set all this up.

Joey was shrewd there, very shrewd. He'd wanted that woman off his back and had laid the foundations for this night's work with the Davidsons. Davey wondered idly if Joey would tell his wife that he was the reason her new boyfriend was lying on a mortuary slab.

He had wanted to do the actual murder but had been clever enough to see that he was going to be the prime suspect. So he had arranged to be at home with his children when it took place.

Where any decent man would be on the night before Christmas.

He had also paid a big mouth called Bella to collar his wife in East Ham market, where he knew his wife would be that Saturday with her two daughters. In effect he had masterminded a murder and had got what he wanted from it. His wife would give up the man of her dreams and he would get back a woman most men would have hung, drawn and quartered.

Davey shook his head sadly at the way some people lived their lives.

Maureen Carter was up and out early on Christmas morning. She was dressed in a blue Oscar de la Renta suit with matching shoes and bag, her hair expertly set. She looked calm and collected as she knocked at the door of Jimmy's house.

When June opened it she nearly died of shock.

'It's six o'clock in the morning, for fuck's sake!'

Maureen wriggled past her, smiling.

'I'm well aware of that but I need to pick up a few of Jimmy's things.'

June, annoyed and still half asleep, sneered at her.

'And what things would those be?'

Suddenly her mind was as clear as a bell. She knew exactly what this woman was after and she also had an idea why Jimmy was dead.

Maureen looked sadly at her. Changing tack she said quietly, 'I have a few things here. You know, things Jimmy was looking after for me. After all, we were in business together.'

June laughed outright at this then said sarcastically, 'You were in bed together, I know that much. Tell me then, what are you after? If it's within my power I'll give you just what you want, lady.'

Her words were loaded and Maureen knew this. She looked June up and down, considering whether she would have to fight her at some point. Maureen could fight like a man. It was one of her assets and she knew it. She also knew that June was smarting at this particular moment in time and the chances were she would be angry enough to give Maureen a real up and downer.

She changed tack once more. Standing in the lounge, she looked her adversary in the eye and said honestly, 'Come on, June, he was a wanker. A good-looking Scottish wanker who kept the two of us for months.

'Now I don't know about you, but Old Bill will be sniffing around soon and I don't want to be implicated in anything. So let's have a cup of Rosie Lee then get to work sorting out all his stuff.'

June nodded without a word. She made the tea. As they sat at the kitchen table, Maureen lit a cigarette with a gold lighter. Her nails were long and painted a delicate shade of pink like her lips.

She looked gorgeous.

Taking in her hair and her clothes June could see the attraction for Jimmy but that didn't make it hurt any the less. In fact it just depressed her because she knew she would always be second best in any comparison with Maureen and knowing that didn't make her life any easier.

But she had a trump card and she knew it even if Maureen smart-car Carter didn't as yet. Lighting a Number Six she sighed heavily.

'What are you after then?'

Maureen waved one well-manicured hand.

'Just his address books, things like that. Things that could incriminate us, really.'

June nodded solemnly, her expression unreadable as she smoked.

'His little black book, eh?' She smiled. 'I've always wanted to say that to someone. Sounds like one of them old films, don't it?'

Maureen stubbed out her cigarette impatiently.

'It sure does. So where does he keep it?'

'Up his arse so far as I know. That book was always with him. Never let it out of his sight.' June sounded convincing and she knew it.

Maureen sighed heavily.

'Don't fuck about with me, June. I'm warning you, some very heavy people want that book and I intend to get it for them. I have a lot of money riding on this and neither you nor anyone else will stand in my way. Do I make myself clear?'

'Loud and clear. But, be fair, what would I know about anything like that, eh? Unlike you I was strictly for shagging. Whereas you, as I understand it, were for talking to as well. I bet that was thrilling after sex – a good old chinwag about his business dealings! Beats a graphic description of what he was going to do to me the next time we was at it. The nearest I got to his business was him asking me to pass him over the phone. So there you have it. The book must be with his effects at the hospital, unless the filth or someone else has got their hands on it.'

Maureen's face drained of colour.

'I understood from Jimmy that the book was kept here in his safe at all times. It isn't good business practice to carry everything around with you . . .'

June laughed as she interrupted.

'What Jimmy said and what he did were two different things, as we *both* know now. So all I can say is, have a look about if you want. The safe is locked and closed and he had the keys. Unlike you, I had no idea what he was up to half the time.'

Maureen was livid and she didn't try to hide it.

'The Davidsons will be after you, Junie, you realise that, don't you? And unlike me they'll literally stop at nothing to find out what you know. I am not threatening you, mate, I am just stating a fact.'

June looked into her eyes.

'So that's who was behind it, is it? Davey Davidson, the poor man's friend, Jimmy's mate and business partner to be or so I understood. You set Jimmy up, didn't you? You never wanted him, you just blew my life apart on a whim. Because you, Maureen high and fucking mighty Carter, wanted something he wasn't prepared to give anyone. You were after his business. Poor Jimmy. He thought the sun shone out of your arse. And me? Well, I was just good old June. Use and abuse her, give her a couple of grand and then forget she ever existed. Well, girl, looks like you fucked up this time. Should have got your hands on his dewberries before you had him topped.'

Maureen's face was hard, her cheekbones standing out like beacons in the whiteness of her skin.

'Looks like you've dropped the proverbial bollock, girl.'

June enjoyed the other woman's discomfiture.

'I bet Davey Davidson will love you, won't he? Murder done, Old Bill all over the place, and no one any the wiser so far as Jimmy's contacts are concerned. I'd say this was an almighty fuck up. Well, the safe's in there and you can tear the place apart if you like, but I tell you now, you'll find nothing.'

'You seem very sure about that, Junie. Is there something you're not telling me?'

June shrugged.

'What's not to tell? All I know is, Jimmy's tucked you all up by the sound of it. And I'm glad he has. Because for all he dumped me, Maureen, he still deserved better than *you*.'

Fifteen minutes later Maureen had trashed the place. June had watched her, drinking tea and smoking all the while. She'd allowed herself one or two little grins as she saw Maureen becoming more and more desperate as time went by.

'Found anything yet?'

Maureen pushed one sweating hand through her now unkempt hair.

'Nothing. Nothing at all.'

June grinned.

'Well, I did try to tell you. Jimmy used to say, "You can trust everyone but still trust no one, June. It's the only way to get on in this world." I didn't really know what he meant till now.'

'If you're lying to me, June, I'll find out and then you'll wish it was the Davidsons coming after you because when I get annoyed I can give anyone a run for their money. You should listen to what they say about me and take heed, girl. I'll rip your fucking heart out and laugh while I'm doing it.'

June shrugged nonchalantly.

'I can't tell you what I don't bloody know, can I?'

Maureen leaned across the table and sighed.

'Listen to me, June. Half of me believes you, but I tell you now – if you're lying you'll be sorry. And that is no idle threat. There's money to be pulled in and it has to be pulled in soon, right? The Davidsons want their bunce and so do I. There'll be no auction of Jimmy's stuff because we've already paid a high price for it. Remember that, keep it in the forefront of your mind. If you keep information close to your chest, there'll be more than one unhappy punter looking for you, June.

'It's not just the Davidsons and me involved in this, it's also the Bannerman family. Now Mickey Bannerman wants what Jimmy had and so do the Davidsons. You think about that and if and when you want a chat, come and see me, okay? Because I know what the score is and I walk in these circles every day of my life. They respect me, understand me, and want to work with me as much as Davey Davidson does. If you take anything to Mickey Bannerman, even through word of mouth, you're a dead woman, June. So have a little think, and if you come up with anything, knock on my door.'

Maureen walked from the house, shutting the door quietly behind her and feeling the urge to cry.

This was too complicated now, far too complicated.

Even she was frightened.

June looked at the clock. It was just after nine on Christmas morning. But that would not bother the Bannermans or the Davidsons. It would be a normal working day for them. Going into the bathroom, she stood on the toilet seat and pulled open the heavy lid of the toilet cistern. Taking out the water-soaked plastic bag, she removed the documents inside and placed them inside her panty girdle.

After she'd finished dressing she plastered her face with make up. Then she picked up the rest of the kids' presents and began the long walk to her old home. Inside she was trembling. The Bannermans were the most terrifying family in London and she had something they wanted.

Inside her bag was a huge amount of money and she knew that if she had any sense she would walk to the train station and disappear.

But she also knew that wasn't an option.

Wherever she went they would find her.

What she had to do now was think clearly and decide what to do next. Damage limitation was on her mind now, not money.

Mickey Bannerman had practically beaten to death a man who had complained about his dog barking. Mickey lived in a nice road in North London, the man he had beaten was a banker. He had walked away from the Old Bailey on a charge of attempted murder because the victim had refused to give evidence.

Even a well-heeled banker had seen the error of his ways, so where would that leave June McNamara? Up shit creek without a paddle was her final decision and June knew that it was the right one. She would talk to Joey, see what he knew. He worked for the Davidsons, he might be able to sort it.

All along the roads Christmas trees stood in windows, their coloured lights cheerful in the darkness of the cold winter's morning. Children were opening presents and women were preparing breakfast and Christmas dinner.

June felt ill with worry now, a physical sickness inside her because she realised she had taken on something she could not hope to pull off.

There was no escape and nowhere to hide.

Susan was so pleased to see her mother she nearly cried. After two hours spent with her father she felt fit to scream. Joey was still in bed and the stench in his room of stale sweat and alcohol had made her feel sick.

When he had finally fallen into a light sleep she had attempted to move from the bed but an arm like a steel band had pulled her back. Lying there in the early-morning light she wondered what had happened to him to make him do these things to her.

By focusing on Barry Dalston, schoolwork, and finally just blanking her mind completely, she managed to get through the night. In her mind's eye she kept thinking of poor Jimmy being shot and the picture affected her, made her want to cry. He had been kind to her, had Jimmy. Had always given her a bit of his time.

No wanting her to sit on his lap or give him kisses she didn't want to give. He'd treated her as an older man should treat a girl.

As she had finally slipped from the bed at five-thirty she had felt a terrible urge to go into the bathroom, run a bath and slit her wrists while lying in the warmth. Then Debbie had woken up and started her usual morning moans and it had taken all Susan's will-power not to slam a fist into her sister's face. With the arrival of her grandmother, she'd felt as if God Himself had turned His back on her.

The old witch had driven her hard for hours: preparing more vegetables, making a trifle and cups of tea. It was a never-ending spiral of work.

Debbie as usual was asked to do nothing but look pretty and chatter about her little life. When June arrived it was as if the light infantry had knocked on the door to save Susan. She was kissing and hugging her mother for ages until June, laughing, said, 'All right, Susan. Relax, love. I'm here now so stop your carrying on.'

Deep inside June loved it, loved all the attention after her night of worry.

'I'm sorry about Jimmy, Mum, really sorry. He was a nice man.'

Joey heard this just as he emerged from his bedroom.

'Fuck Jimmy! Good riddance to bad rubbish, I say.'

He walked into the kitchen and shouted, 'Merry Christmas to one and all.' He kissed his mother and his daughters then taking his wife in his arms, cried gleefully, 'You coming home then, girl?'

The kitchen was quiet now as the three other occupants waited with bated breath for her to answer.

'Of course I am, I told you that last night.'

Granny Mac screamed with derision.

'You'd take on that Scottish ponce's leavings? You would and all, wouldn't you? Where the fuck I got you, Joey, I don't know. Any other man would take the teeth from that whore's head with his fist after all she's done over the years.'

June bowed her head. Her hair was mussed, her make up smeared. She looked like a smudged painting about to dissolve in front of their eyes.

Turning on her mother-in-law, she bellowed, 'Right, that's it. Out! I want you out – now.'

She looked at Joey then, her face hard, and he realised the change in his wife. Gone was the old June. Here was a much stronger character.

'I want *that* out of my kitchen unless she can keep a civil tongue in her toothless old head.'

Joey looked at his mother and suppressed a smile. Inside he knew it was time someone put the old bat in her place and if it was June who did it then so much the better.

He knew that his wife's coming back after all that had happened would be a nine-day wonder in the street and he would have to front it out. But he wanted her back; Junie was in his blood somehow. No matter what she did he still wanted her.

He looked at Susan's devastated face and felt shame creep over him. If June found out about her there would be murder done.

Inside he knew he'd been wrong but his daughter was there, she was available. He could dominate her.

Debbie would have screamed the place down. She was too spoiled, too sure of herself, whereas Susan was born to be used and used she would be all her life. He was as sure of that as he was of his own name.

With a face and countenance like hers, there wasn't much else in store for her. Not around these parts anyway. She did what she was told, did Susan. It never occurred to her not to. He attempted to smile at her and she froze.

His mother was still in her chair, her face white with anger and incredulity. Her son was taking his wife's part in this and the knowledge made Ivy doubly aware just how precarious her own position now was in this household.

She hoisted up her bust with her forearms and snarled at them.

'After all I've done for you, you treat me like this?'

June laughed gently.

'Sit down, you old hag, you can stay. But you keep your mouth shut and your head down, you hear me? One word out of place and you'll go out that door like nobody's business, do you get my drift? If, and I mean if, I come back there've to be a lot of changes here. And you, lady, are among the first of them. No more coming round here giving out with your vicious tongue. No more interfering in my business or the girls', right?'

Joey gleefully watched the changing expressions on his mother's face. If this new Junie was going to shut her up, he was all for it.

Susan and Debbie were watching closely too, both as interested as their father to know whether their granny would swallow this lot, especially as for once she had a point.

Their mother had abandoned them and their granny had looked after them as best she could. Or at least as well as someone with her nasty outlook and nasty tongue could look after someone. They'd had clean clothes and meals. Even if Susan had done the lion's share of the work.

Debbie's eyes were bright with interest to see whether her mother was going to be the victor. She hoped she was, her granny got on her nerves. Unlike Susan, when her granny picked on her Debbie told her in no uncertain terms to get stuffed and it worked. Susan was different, she would do literally anything for a quiet life.

The old woman was in a quandary. She didn't want to go back to her flat. Everything she wanted was here. Company, food and drink, and most of all her precious son. Her Joey whom she loved in her own way more than life itself.

She wanted June out of the way so she could take over again

but guessed correctly that her son would put her out the front door without a moment's thought if June made him.

So Ivy swallowed her pride and sat down again. Her eyes were bleak, her mouth was downturned and her stance that of a prizefighter who has just found out he's won the fight but won't be paid.

Swallowing down her natural aggression she dropped her eyes and was quiet.

It seemed as if the whole place had gone still, so deep was the silence as everyone realised there had been a major shift in power and for once it was on June's side. She was finally the winner.

Realising she had to lighten the situation, and feeling just a bit sorry for her mother-in-law, she shouted loudly, 'Did you hear all that, Maud, or has the glass slipped off the wall with the shock?'

Everyone laughed, even the old woman.

June put the kettle on, then turning to the girls, said gaily, 'It's Christmas and whatever else has happened we'll have a good time, right?'

The two girls nodded.

She gave them the bags with their presents in.

'Go into the front room and have a butcher's at what I got you, eh? I'll make a start out here and we'll have the best Christmas ever.'

The girls nodded. She saw the shadows under Susan's eyes and swallowed down her own guilt.

There was something radically wrong with her daughter and June didn't know what it could be. Later she would talk to her, but at the moment she had too many other things on her mind.

Half an hour later she was in the bedroom with her husband. Joey looked shaken by her revelations.

'What the fuck have you done, June? You stupid, stupid cow!'

She swallowed down the rising panic inside her breast and said calmly, 'I have what they all want. We can make out of this, Joey. Just once we can come out on fucking top. Can't you see that?'

Her voice was husky with exasperation and annoyance. He

could never see the big picture, that was his worst failing. Joey looked bewildered, frightened and sick. It was this that was scaring June so much. She realised that maybe she had done something stupid but she didn't tell him about the money. She wasn't *that* stupid.

'The Bannermans and Davey Davidson will cut your throat, Junie, when they find out what you've done. Jimmy was topped for what you've got and he was a hard nut to crack. What makes you think they'll treat you any different? They'll guess you've taken the goods and come looking for you. That means they'll be looking for me as well. I am after all your husband, though you forget that when it suits you, eh?'

June saw the logic in what he said but still felt they had a good case. She was entitled to some compensation. That was the term used when a woman's husband or partner was topped. The perpetrator always saw the woman all right, it was the villain's code. You took their breadwinner so you gave the widow compo. It was the only decent thing to do.

'I am entitled to compensation, Joey, you know that.'

He shook his head in consternation.

'You're entitled to nothing. They'll see you right only if you play the fucking game. What are you, June, mental or something? This is the Bannermans we're talking about here, not the fucking Kray twins! The Bannerman brothers are raving fucking lunatics. They ain't got no old-style righteousness like everyone else. They're violent wankers. They told Maureen Carter they'd booked her an appointment with a plastic surgeon. Why else do you think she went with Jimmy in the first place? She was told to.

'I know everything about it. I would, wouldn't I? Davey had to tell me because of you. He did the decent thing. If Bannerman knew what he'd done, he'd cut his ears off. What you dragged us into now, eh? Like we ain't got enough trouble, you bring us more.'

'But I thought the Bannermans and the Davidsons were enemies?'

Joey sighed.

'They are, love. They set Jimmy up and now Davey is going to take what they wanted. Maureen put her oar in with the Davidsons because of the threats from the Bannermans. She ain't going to take that lying down, she's a dangerous woman. You know who her son's father is, don't you?'

June shook her head. No one knew so far as she was aware and it wasn't for lack of trying to find out either.

'Her son's father is a man called Willie Dixon.'

June's mouth dropped open.

'You're joking?'

Joey shook his head.

'He's due out in about two weeks. He's done sixteen years on the island. Now he's out and wants what is his due. That means the Bannermans are up against not only the Davidsons, who they don't give a toss about, but the Dixons though as yet they don't know that. When they find out they'll retire gracefully from the fray. But now you have what everyone, including Dixon, wants. Maybe you can see why I'm shitting hot bricks at this moment in time?'

June shook her head in amazement.

'How come no one knew about Maureen Carter and Dixon?'

Joey laughed scornfully.

'Because, unlike you, she kept her fucking mouth shut. That's why she runs with the big boys. Maureen has a good rep, she keeps her trap shut and her eyes wide open. Unlike you whose mouth goes like the clappers and whose legs are spread at the drop of a hat. Now do you see what Jimmy saw in her?'

'Did he know about Dixon?'

Joey shook his head.

'I have no idea and frankly I don't care. All I care about is trying to get us out of the shit you have plunged us into, all right? Now I'd better get dressed and find Davey, see if I can salvage anything.'

He stuck a finger into his wife's face.

'I could cheerfully murder you, Junie, and that's the truth. You have no brain for business. You have no brain, period. In future you keep out of the big boys' games, okay?'

She nodded.

A loud knocking on the door made both of them start with fright.

'It's started, June, Christmas or no Christmas. You let me do the talking, all right?'

The bedroom door burst open and two men stood there. Both June and Joey breathed a sigh of relief that it was not a couple of thugs armed with baseball bats.

That is until the men opened their mouths.

'I am Detective Inspector Harry Knapp and I am arresting you on suspicion of murdering James Vincent. You are not obliged to say anything. Anything you do say will be taken down in writing and can be used in evidence against you.'

'What you on about?'

Joey's voice was loud in the small bedroom.

The two girls watched as their father was marched from the house.

Chapter Five

'Dad didn't kill Jimmy, did he?' Debbie's voice was low with fright.

June shook her head impatiently. 'Of course he didn't.'

She watched as the two girls looked at each other. She knew they believed their father had murdered their mother's boyfriend. That was how it would look to everyone.

Ivy had been silent since they had taken her son out of the door.

'You caused this, June. My boy will get a great big lump and it will be over you. The sad thing is, you're not worth it. All you ever did is take my boy's name and trail it in the dirt.'

The bitterness in the older woman's voice was like a red rag to a bull and June turned on her.

'What name you talking about then? The name of a family that's looked on as the lowest of the low in this area, even lower than the Clancys, and they're all interbred. Your son is a stupid ignorant wanker, but I did love him once for all that. If we had been left to our own devices we would have been all right. But, oh, no. I had to have the mother-in-law from hell poking her nose in, opening her big trap. Now as I told you earlier – keep fucking stumm or piss off. I ain't in the mood for you, all right?'

They were all amazed to see two fat tears fall from the old lady's eyes.

'What will I do without him, Junie? He's me life.'

June hugged her, afraid herself now she had seen real fear in her husband's mother.

'They can't pin nothing on Joey, he ain't *done* nothing.'

'You better baste the turkey, Mum, or else it will dry out.'

Susan's voice was calm and June looked at her gratefully. Taking a dishcloth, she pulled the huge bird from the oven and began to spoon the fat over it. Everyone watched her as if it was the most fascinating thing they had ever seen.

'Go and play with your presents, I need to think.'

The two girls left the room then and June looked at her mother-in-law in distress.

'He never topped Jimmy. He might have threatened it, but that's as far as it would have gone. Joey would never have dared take on Jimmy, we both know that. Anyway, they have to prove he was there, don't they?'

Ivy laughed blackly.

'The Old Bill have to prove nothing. You have to prove them wrong, and you know that. If they want my boy they'll have him, June. Look what they did to the poor Krays, then talk to me about justice.'

June didn't bother to answer. She had all the facts but what could she do with them? She certainly couldn't talk to her mother-in-law. If she did it would be all over the manor within hours.

Joey was sitting in a holding cell. He was livid. As the door opened he stood up and his rage turned to fear as he saw who was walking in.

Detective Inspector Harold Hitchin was small, just making the height requirement for the police. He had a thin wiry body and thin wiry hair. His eyes were an odd almost colourless grey. He looked slightly distant, not quite all there, his bearing and countenance giving the lie to the shrewd analytic brain and vindictive character beneath.

He smiled slowly, displaying overlarge discoloured teeth. His nickname among colleagues and villains was UB.

Ugly Bastard.

His wife was a very attractive woman whom he adored. Word was she was one of the brasses from his stint on Vice and she was his only known companion.

He had reached DI status with hard graft and even harder

collars. If UB was after you, you grassed up everyone you could think of, even your own mother, because you knew he would not let anything go until he had what he wanted. Not that he was averse to taking a few outside payments now and again to leave certain people alone.

He'd often drunk with Jimmy and seeing the man standing there, Joey knew he was up for a big lump of time, and hard time at that. UB would see to it personally.

'Hello, Joey, long time no see. How's the longshoring these days?'

He licked his lips nervously.

'I ain't done nothing, Mr Hitchin, this is all wrong. I don't know nothing about Jimmy being dead, I swear it.'

'On your mother's life, eh?'

Hitchin's voice was high-pitched, even womanish, but no one ever dared to laugh at it.

'On me mother's life, on my girls' heads, I take oath.'

Hitchin stared at him for over five minutes and it seemed to Joey that the man did not blink once. It was a frightening stare, a heavy-lidded look that reminded him of a snake about to strike.

Then, moving quickly, Hitchin said in friendly fashion, 'My wife is very upset with me. I had to leave a perfectly good dinner to come here and see you, so as you can imagine I'm rather annoyed. I like Christmas, don't you? Goodwill to all men and all that old fanny. But, you see, my goodwill has aimed itself out the window now. Because of you I have no feeling towards anyone except animosity and aggravation. Do you get my drift?'

Joey nodded.

He watched in sick dread as the man before him took from his pocket a long piece of metal pipe. It was covered with masking tape and he stood there tapping it against his palm.

'I have decided, Joey, after long and careful deliberation, to break open your head. This is not a personal thing. Though I have never liked you, I am not a vindictive man. You could be anyone today. You do understand that, don't you?'

Joey felt the tears welling up in his eyes. This was all he needed, Hitchin on his case. He had taken it upon himself to play the avenging angel. He kicked and punched confessions from people. But every now and then he beat them with a weapon, normally because someone else wanted the job done.

In the East End it was called backing.

Joey would lay money that either the Davidsons or the Bannermans had backed Hitchin with a few grand to make sure Joey was rendered senseless and disabled. It was in effect two warnings in one.

The police were doing their job and in the meantime they were telling him he was a marked man.

The tears flowed now. Joey was really terrified.

'Have you anything to say before I start? Because after I've finished with you I'll have worked up an appetite, see, and I will want to get home and have me dinner like normal people.'

Joey looked into the reptilian face before him and bowed his head. As big a nutter as he was, he knew when he was defeated.

He looked Hitchin in the eye for a split second.

'Who's this for, the Bannermans or the Davidsons?'

Hitchin laughed then. A low heartfelt sound.

'It's all for you, Joey, all for you.'

Maureen Carter was worried. Her son was watching television and as she placed the sliced turkey on a platter she was jolted back to earth by the ringing of her doorbell. Instinctively she looked at the clock on the kitchen wall. It was nearly five-thirty. Going to the door, she undid her apron and tidied her hair. She was more than surprised to see June standing there.

'What can I do for you?'

June smiled sadly.

'It's more a case of what I can do for you.'

June followed her through to her kitchen, smiling a hello at Maureen's son on the way.

'Good-looking boy. Like his father?'

Maureen stared at her for a few seconds before saying sternly, 'Cut the crap, June, and say your piece. You and your old man have caused a lot of people headaches today, and believe me the people you've crossed aren't going to forget it easily.'

June took a deep breath and began to speak.

'They've arrested my Joey.'

Maureen laughed gently.

'Joey? What, for the murder of *your* Jimmy, I suppose?'

She ran a well-manicured hand through her hair.

'God, but you're a dog, June. Even more amoral than I am. My Joey? You're having a tin bath, ain't you?'

June was annoyed.

'This is nothing to laugh at, Maureen. He is the father of my children . . .'

Maureen interrupted her. 'Let's face it, June, we only have your word for that. Now say your piece and piss off. If you're round here for a bleeding hearts session you might as well go now. I ain't interested. Neither is Davey Davidson, who incidentally knew all about your Joey's nicking before the police did. Now do you get my drift?'

June swallowed down the urge to begin battering the woman before her. However amoral she was, it was nothing compared to Maureen's behaviour. June consoled herself with the fact that whatever she had done, she had not set Jimmy up to be murdered as this woman had. He had thrown his oar in with Maureen and had paid a high price for it. As bad as June might be in the eyes of the world, she would never stoop that low.

'Suppose I could help you in your quest for Jimmy's books and everything . . .'

Maureen stared at her now, bright eyes hooded.

'This ain't the Holy Grail, love, we just want what's ours.'

June laughed, a deep rollicking sound.

'You mean, you want what's Jimmy's? Let's not beat about the fucking bush, eh? Now do you want his stuff or not, and if so what's the price?'

'I think the price is down to you and I'll see if we all think it's fair. Now sit yourself down and I'll make us both a drink and we can chat. I warn you, though, don't go getting too ambitious for what's mine, June. I can be a very tough adversary.'

June looked into the cold eyes before her and didn't attempt to argue. Instead she smiled and sat at the kitchen table, eyes drawn to the platter of succulent turkey and the well-baked ham. She knew in her heart that she was going to get the tucking up of a lifetime, but it was what she had to do. For all Joey's faults, and they were legion, she could not let him take the kick for everyone else. Because Joey would, he wouldn't *grass*. Joey would take the big lump dished out, probably fifteen years, and do his time with as much aggravation as possible. It was in his make up. The Davidsons would see her all right and then forget about them. June knew it all so well, knew what could easily happen.

She had to do a good deal here today, the deal of a lifetime.

Her husband's lifetime.

Ivy had a face that could curdle milk at the best of times. Today both her granddaughters felt sorry for her because for once she had good reason to be worried.

Susan was folding up the wrapping paper from her presents and putting it away neatly in her bedroom drawer. It was so pretty she wanted to keep it all just to look at it sometimes. She loved nice things, loved owning them.

Debbie worried about her father for about an hour and then got fed up. Nothing was happening so she decided to go round and see a friend.

Left with Ivy Susan tidied up, made her granny a hot toddy of milk and Bushmill's, and then went to her room and dreamed.

As she cleared up the mess left by Debbie she hoped and prayed that her father was given twenty years. At one point she imagined him being hung, but as she knew hanging was over now she couldn't get into it somehow and instead went back to picturing him in a cell for years and years.

It made her feel so much better inside.

She would never have to have that man's hands on her again, and by the time they let him out she would be grown up and able to tell him where to go.

Susan sighed with happiness.

Please God the police had enough on him. Please God they made the charges stick. A knock on the door broke into her reverie and she opened it expecting to see a neighbour. Instead she was confronted with Barry Dalston.

Her heart was beating so hard she was sure he could hear it. She felt as if her head was filling up with warm air and that her arms and legs had become leaden, so aware of herself did she become.

She was glad now she had put on her new clothes and had made herself up. She knew she looked as nice as she was ever going to look.

Barry for his part was dressed as usual, scruffily, and wearing his wicked lop-sided grin.

'Merry Christmas, darlin'. Do you think maybe I could come in or you could come out – whatever?'

She opened the door wide and he walked into the flat. He placed a small package in her hands and Susan smiled with delight.

'For me?'

Barry grinned.

'No, it's for your sister.'

Seeing her face drop, he hugged her to him.

'Of course it's for you, who else?'

She took him through to the lounge, glad now that she had cleaned up. Her granny was asleep in the chair by the gas fire, a Capstan cigarette dangling from her lip.

'You better come through to the kitchen, me granny can't half snore.'

Smiling he followed her into the kitchen. Going to the gas cooker Susan put the kettle on. She could feel her hands shaking. Then, turning to him, she looked into his face.

To her Barry was beautiful in every way. She loved everything about him.

The sneering look she perceived as a man-of-the-world expression. The cruel mouth was an object of intense desire to her. She wanted to kiss him until he was unconscious. The hard eyes she saw as playful and dreamy.

Susan saw what she wanted to see, and like most women in love she saw the man of her dreams.

He pulled her into his arms and kissed her hard on the mouth.

She responded to him, knowing that she needed his arms about her to make her feel safe. Barry Dalston made her safe. Safe from her father. From everything.

As his tongue explored her mouth she pulled away from him. The kiss frightened even as it thrilled her.

'Got anything real to drink?'

Susan was still half dazed.

'What, beer, you mean?'

Barry grinned.

'No, whisky. I'm a Scot and we drink whisky on special occasions though New Year is our real celebration, not Christmas. Christmas is for the kiddies.'

She opened the kitchen cupboard and took out the Bushmill's. She knew if her granny caught her she would be skinned alive but didn't care any more. She didn't care about anything except the vision before her. Barry Dalston was in her house on Christmas Day and he had brought her a present, her father was locked up for attempted murder and her mother was coming home. She was happier than she had ever been in her life before. What more could a girl want?

After she'd poured him a generous measure Barry picked up a glass from the draining board and poured another one. He put lemonade in it and gave it to her. Then, toasting her, he said playfully, 'Drink it down in one gulp and that will be our Christmas toast, eh?'

Susan poured the drink down her throat and nearly choked. Her eyes were streaming and her carefully applied mascara was stinging her. Barry was laughing and trying to pull her against his chest to stop her noise waking the old woman in the living room.

'Quiet, Susan, you'll have the old one in on top of us.'

She stifled her giggling and leaned against him. The drink went straight to her head. A warm glow was coursing through her and she felt as if she had grown two inches taller and more attractive in a few minutes.

She stared up at him.

Barry looked down at her, his mind detached from what he was doing. He studied her face. She was plain but her eyes were nice, and flushed with the drink she seemed to have become almost pretty. He could see the look of utter adoration in her eyes and decided he liked that.

Unlike the prettier girls who played games and made him chase them she was like a pliant doll, waiting for him to take her out of her box and play with her. Her enormous tits made him want to play with her even more than she knew. They were a pivotal part of her attraction. But not as much as her father and his rep were.

'I heard about your dad, I'm sorry. It's no more than any man would have done.'

Susan felt the elation seep from her body. She pulled away from him. Picking up her present she opened it and, mood changing once more, turned back to him in delight.

'Oh, they're lovely. Beautiful.'

The earrings were gold hoops, what the East Enders call gypsy earrings. The bottom of the hoop was heavier than the top and they shone in her hand, taking her breath away. Barry must be serious if he was buying her presents like this.

He grinned at her obvious delight, and hoped against hope they were a good investment. He had stolen them on a burglary a few nights before, had unwrapped them and decided they would do for Susan. He had even used the same paper to wrap them back up. Barry had no qualms about taking other people's things, even from under their Christmas trees. He had known they were worth a few quid and seen himself as a very generous individual for giving them to Susan and not pulling in money for them.

He kissed her gently on the mouth again and Susan slid into his arms. As he pushed her against the draining board she allowed him to pull up her jumper and grab at her breasts. He kneaded them with his rough hands, feeling the softness of her skin and the heaviness that would one day pull them down to her stomach.

Pushing them together, he looked down at them. He was harder than he had ever been and knew then that this girl was going to play an important role in his life, if for no other reason than these huge breasts between his hands.

'They're gorgeous, Susan, fucking fantastic.'

She wasn't listening, she was on auto-pilot. She knew that to keep him she had to let him do this to her and like her father before him he was only after what he wanted. He wasn't even trying to make it good for her. It would never have occurred to either of them that she herself might want to be a part of the sex act. She was to be taken, and allowed herself to be taken there and then in her mother's kitchen with her granny asleep in the room beyond.

As Barry entered her she was dry. He forced himself into her, making her cry out gently against his chest. He thought he was the first, he really did, and this made Susan strangely depressed. The knowledge that her father had done this to her many times before was like a vivid sore inside her mind.

She concentrated on the earrings and what they meant. They were a beacon which told her Barry cared for her. He had bought her gold – in her world that meant a lot. Gold was symbolic of commitment, a forerunner of a wedding ring. The earrings told her that he was serious about her, that he wanted more than just friendship. So to her way of thinking it was quite acceptable she should allow him to take her body. After all, she was more or less his now.

The fact that she was still a child didn't enter Susan's head and certainly didn't enter Barry's. So far as he was concerned, with tits like hers she was up for all he had to give her. He looked on the maturity of her body to be his guideline, not the maturity of her mind. As he slumped over her, his semen wet against the inside of her legs, she sighed heavily.

At least with Barry she had some power over what he did, and that alone was a heady feeling. He kissed her on the forehead and smiled at her – and with that one kind action tied her to him for the rest of his life.

Joey woke up in the Old London. His face was sore, a few teeth were missing and his legs felt like they had been amputated without anaesthetic.

But he was glad of the pain; it told him he was at least in the land of the living.

A stiff-faced nurse was looking down at him and Joey nearly

screamed with fright. She was even uglier than Hitchin, he reckoned. But the dark blue of her uniform told him he was in a place of safety and that made him feel better.

His biggest fear as he'd seen the metal bar descend on his forehead was that he would never see another Christmas.

Closing his eyes, Joey sighed to himself.

He was alive and so far not in prison, but instead of trumping June and getting her back into the fold he was lying in bed with a fierce headache and the knowledge he could still be looking at a fifteen- or twenty-year lump!

Life was unfair at times, it really was.

Opening his eyes again he saw Davey Davidson standing by the bed, his expression genial, carrying a basket of fruit.

Joey didn't know whether to laugh or cry.

Instead he stared steadily at his employer and waited for Davey to let him know what he had decided was going to happen to Joey.

'I bet your bonce is screaming, ain't it, mate?'

Davey's voice was low and sympathetic. Joey looked up at him and said dolefully: 'Well, Davey, I have felt better, know what I mean?'

Mickey Bannerman was smiling.

He had eight children by his wife Layla, a big heavy-breasted girl with beautiful teeth, rich red hair and a nose that would easily fit on to four faces instead of one. Her father was a known East End criminal called Billy Tarmey. Mickey had married her to get his hands on the old man's manor. He had easily slipped on the mantle of most feared man in London and on his father-in-law's kudos had prospered in North and South London, leaving the East End to the bullyboys.

Now, however, he wanted the lot.

As he watched his wife with his children he felt glad he had married her. Layla was an excellent mother; the girls were learning dancing and the boys all played musical instruments. They spoke properly and had exemplary table manners.

Mickey also kept a one-time stripper called Monet whom he visited with urgency and feeling up to fifteen times a week. Layla knew about it and accepted it. Mickey Bannerman was known as the horniest man in London. His prowess was legendary and in his youth hostesses were known to leave as they saw him walk through the doors of their club. He tired them out and left them unable to work for days.

One old lag said once on hearing Bannerman was after him: 'Fuck me, I hope he wants to give me a good hiding. I'd rather that than he shagged me to death.'

Hearing this, Mickey thought it was so funny he let the man off with just a punishment beating. Such was the mentality of Michael Bannerman.

Today he was happy, deliriously so. Sitting in his large lounge with his youngest daughter on his knee he smiled amiably at all the people in the room. In a few hours he would have in his possession all he needed to make him the King of the Hill. That was what he had been aiming for since he had married the horsey bird with the nice teeth, as he'd always referred to Layla before she became his wife.

When the doorbell rang he got up and welcomed in Maureen Carter and June McNamara.

He liked June. He always had. The few occasions he had seen her with Jimmy she had been all a woman should be. Quiet, compliant, and with her Bristols on show. A typical villain's whore.

Unlike Maureen he felt she was going to be a pushover.

He settled them in his office and made them both a drink, indulged in a bit of small talk and introduced them to his kids. The von Trapps couldn't have faulted him for courtesy.

Then, ushering his kids from the room, he sipped his own drink and smiled nastily at June.

'You've given me a headache, you know. But I'll overlook that fact in honour of the friendship I had with Jimmy.'

No one answered though the two women privately wondered how he could lay claim to friendship with a man he would have shot if Davidson had not got there first.

June stared down into her glass of port and tried to stifle the fear inside her.

'I'm sorry, Mr Bannerman, but I was scared. I knew Jimmy was going on the trot and I tried to save meself. I've two daughters to bring up and a husband who's about as much use as a spare prick at the Queen Mother's birthday party.'

Mickey laughed as she knew he would. If you could make Mickey laugh you were half-way home.

'Your old man's a wanker, ain't he? But thanks to you he's now in the Old London with a head that's more swollen than a virgin's knob. But I digress. Have you got the relevant paperwork, and if so what's your price, love? It's Christmas and I'm in a good mood. How lucky can you get, eh, girl? Any other time of the year I'd have ripped your tits off and laughed while I did it. But I like Christmas, always puts me in a happy frame of mind. New Year on its way, new deals to be done, new people to stomp on at some point. A very enjoyable season, I always think.'

Maureen saw the colour drain from June's face and stifled the urge to laugh. Mickey knew his audience and he played it well.

She coughed, taking the onus off June, and said gently, 'I have told her she can keep the few grand she took as compensation for losing Jimmy but she has to give us the books. I have them now in my handbag so I think today's just a formality really.'

Mickey looked at the only woman he could ever say he truly respected and liked. Maureen was a diamond in many respects. Look what she had done for him now. Got the books without its costing him a penny.

June thought she had got off lightly, and in fairness she had.

'I've told her we've called off Hitchin since her husband is now in hospital. We'll call it quits and forget about the grave error of judgement they both made.'

Mickey hadn't a clue what Maureen was on about.

June was none the wiser either.

'So what you saying then?' she asked fearfully.

Maureen grinned.

'The bottom line is, love, you keep Jimmy's money and we keep the rest. Simple really.'

June smiled widely.

'Thanks. You've both been more than generous.'

Mickey stood up happily. He had what he wanted, he could afford to be magnanimous.

'Another drink, ladies? Then you'll have to excuse me. I have my family visiting and can't keep them all waiting too long for their tea. My Layla won't serve them until I arrive. She knows a man's place is at the head of the table.'

Maureen grinned.

'Personally I think a man's head should be on the table, but I suppose I see your point.'

June watched the other two make jokes at each other's expense and wished they would shut up and let her leave. But she knew she had to sit it out until they let her go. That was how things were done in these circles and she wasn't going to try and change that.

Ivy was impressed by Barry Dalston. He took her mind off her sick son for a while and she was grateful for that. As Susan made a pot of tea Ivy rabbited on.

'What a lovely young man, and so handsome! How the fuck you managed to crib him I don't know. Now if Debbie had come home with him, I wouldn't have been surprised – but you! Well, all I can say is whatever he sees in you it's invisible because no one else will ever see it, girl. You hang on to him.'

Susan ignored her.

She was just thankful that Barry had left so she could revel in the thought of his generous gift to her. The other stuff she placed in the back of her mind as she always did with anything troubling or unpleasant.

Ivy kept giving her the benefit of her opinion. Susan listened to her with half an ear until she heard something that made a red mist of fury descend on her.

'Just like your father at that age. Same stance, same look, the same easy way with him . . .'

Susan made the old woman jump as she screamed at her across the kitchen, 'Barry is nothing like my father! Don't you dare say things like that, you old witch. Why don't you go home? Why must you always be here, ruining everything? He's not like my so-called dad. In fact, you yourself point out at every opportunity that

Joey ain't me real father and, believe me, that suits me right down to the ground.'

Ivy was stunned speechless, but not for long. Pulling herself from the chair, she raised her hand and slapped Susan across the mouth.

'Don't you talk to me like that, you little bastard. After all I've done for you, to talk to me like that!'

As her hand came up again Susan grabbed it and pushed the older woman none too gently across the room.

'Oh, piss off, you old bitch. You ever say my Barry's like *him* again and I'll kill you, do you hear what I'm saying? He is *nothing* like Dad. He's nice, lovely in fact. He isn't like your son at all so stop trying to say he is.'

Ivy was now in such a state of shock she was having trouble breathing. Her heart was beating erratically as she looked at the young girl before her. Susan had never challenged anyone before, always taking whatever was dealt out to her.

Suddenly Ivy was frightened of her.

Susan, however, had not finished.

'You come here day after day and make our lives hell. You cause endless trouble with my mum and expect us all just to take what you dish out. Well, I've had enough. You're nothing but a vindictive, vicious-mouthed old bitch and I wish you and your son would both drop dead. You're nothing to me. I call you Granny because I have to but I can't wait until I'm old enough to change my name to Smith or Jones – anything other than bloody McNamara!'

June stood at the front door and could not believe what she was hearing. Susan was shouting. Susan, the quiet one, the good girl, the daughter she knew was the mainstay of this household. The cleaner, the cook, the gofer.

June suppressed a smile. If she was shocked, she'd love to see her mother-in-law's face. She waited for a few seconds before making a noise as if she had just walked through the door, then stepped into the kitchen with a big smile on her face.

'Everything all right?'

Ivy was white-faced with anger and terror.

'She hit me! You wait until my Joey hears about this. Raised her hand to me she did, June, slapped me one and kicked me.'

It never occurred to the old woman to tell the truth. Susan, however, was too annoyed to care.

'I'm telling you, Mum, I've taken all I can from her over the last few years. I'm sick of listening to her. Make her go home. Please, Mum, make her go or I might just do her a bloody damage, a real one this time.'

She stepped towards the older woman and June got between them. She was worried now. Her daughter was not normally a violent person and in many respects that was her trouble. Living in a household like this it paid to be more aggressive, as Debbie was. She had made herself heard from the day she was born but that had never been in poor Susan's nature. Whatever had set her off today it must have been serious and her daughter was more than likely in the right.

June decided there and then that she would start as she meant to go on. This was a perfect opportunity to get rid of the old woman once and for all.

'I think you had better get your coat on, Ivy, and get yourself home.'

Ivy looked at her as if she had never seen her before.

As she screwed up her face into a mask of temper, June said quietly, 'This is no time for fighting, Ivy. Joey's in hospital with terrible head injuries. I've managed to get him out of the Bill shop and to stop all the madness of the last few days. I'm in no mood for listening to you an' all. As for Susan, she's probably worried by what's been going on, and knowing you, you wound her up. This is my house and if you ever want to enter it again I'd advise you to do as she says and piss off.'

'My son would never refuse me . . .'

Susan shouted, 'Well, your son ain't here, is he? And my mum is. Until he comes back you can go and take a flying fuck!'

Even June was shocked now.

'Susan, for Christ's sake, love, calm down. What on earth is going on here?'

She was nearly crying with frustration and anger.

'I mean it, Mum. Either she goes or I do. I have had her up to my back teeth. Half the trouble in the past has been over her. Winding him up when he's drunk, giving him gossip and making everyone's lives a misery. I hate her nearly as much as I hate him. So now you know, don't you?'

She stormed from the kitchen, leaving June and Ivy alone together. Ivy knew in her heart when she was beaten. She also knew that the girl was right. It was this that hurt more than anything, the knowledge that a young girl could see through her so easily.

'After all I did for that child . . .'

June shook her head sadly.

'Go home, Ivy. For crying out loud, will you just for once piss off back to your own house? She's right and you know it. You picked on her from the word go. Well, shall I tell you something? When Joey comes home you'd better change your tune, lady, because like Susan I've had enough of you.

'One thing you have never allowed for is the fact that Joey can't function without me. No matter what I do he always takes me back. Remember that, won't you, because if I throw you out now he won't do a thing to stop me. And if I choose to, I will.'

Ivy walked from the flat a few minutes later, a defeated old woman. Susan stayed in her room and June counted the money and planned what she was going to do with it.

All in all, she reasoned, not a bad day's work.

Chapter Six

Joey was pleased to see June at his bedside. She was dressed in a nice red dress and her make up was not too obvious; her nails were a pale pink instead of scarlet and her perfume not too strong.

'You look nice, June.'

She smiled gently.

'Well, I wish I could say the same about you, mate, but I can't.'

Joey grinned.

'I had a look at me boatrace this morning so I can hardly argue about that, can I?'

June didn't answer.

'Thanks for getting me out of the shit, I know you didn't have to.'

She sat on the bed and took his hand in hers

'Listen, Joey, I did that because I care about you, I really do. But I can't live the way we did before. It's too much like hard work. If we're going to make a go of it then things have got to change. Jimmy knew how to treat me; he gave me a new outlook on life. Whatever he was, he gave me more than anyone ever did before. Do you understand what I'm saying?'

Joey nodded.

His mind was working overtime. He had got the full SP off Davey Davidson. He knew that Jimmy had just dumped June, he knew everything by now. Like the fact that she also had three grand stashed.

'I know that, love, and I will change, I promise. Even aim me mother out of it, I know she was a trial over the years . . .'

June laughed.

'You'll never guess what? Our Susan had a right go at her.'
Joey was intrigued.

'What, she had a pop at me mother?'

June nodded.

A shadow of the old vindictive Joey crossed his face for a few seconds, then he smiled. 'Who would have thought that, eh?'

'She got herself a bloke, and Ivy being Ivy had to go and insult her.'

'What do you mean, she got herself a bloke? Sue's too young for fucking blokes.'

Joey pulled himself up in bed, the action making him wince. His legs were sore and he was still delicate, or at least as delicate as Joey McNamara could ever be.

'I'll fucking lay her out, the whore!'

June was nonplussed.

''Ere, calm down, he's a nice little fella. Who's rattled your cage, Joey?'

He took a deep breath and sighed.

'She's too young, June, and she ain't streetwise enough to land herself a bloke. I'm putting a block on it and you can tell her that from me. You can also tell her that I'll be home soon and things will be back to normal. Tell her that, right?'

June was surprised by his reaction. Debbie had been talking about blokes since she was ten and he had just laughed, telling her to keep them on the run, make them sweat, make them spend money on her.

Now poor old Susan had got herself a bloke, a nice one and all – June would have given him the come on herself a few years ago – and Joey was acting the big wronged husband. There was something fishy going on.

'You sound jealous, Joey, what's the scam?'

He felt a burning urge to punch his wife but knew he had to bide his time. He wanted her back and couldn't push his luck for a good while. She held all the cards at the moment. So he sighed once more and assumed the mask of concerned father.

'Listen, June, Debbie is a girl's girl, right? She knows the score. Whereas poor old Susan . . . well, be fair, she's got a face like the back of a bus and Bristols that would encourage a fucking monk out of his celibacy.

'You know what I'm saying. This little fella's probably gone to her head and she's vulnerable. I mean, when was she last complaining about being asked out all the time like Debs, eh? I'll tell you when, shall I? Never. And I have seen a lot more of her over the last few years than you have. Her and me got quite close, as a matter of fact, and I know how ignorant she is of men and their ways. If she meets a wrong 'un now, before we know it she'll be in the club and that will be it.

'I have great hopes for that girl, she has a brain on her. She even reads, for fuck's sake. How many people we know do that, eh? Real books and all, not just the usual old crap Debbie reads, true confessions and that. Our Susan reads real books, I've seen her.'

June was practically fainting with shock.

'That must have been quite a bang on the head from Hitchin – I can't believe what you're saying. This chap is quite a catch for Susan and seems genuine enough. He bought her gold earrings for Christmas and comes round all the time.'

Joey closed his eyes and tried to keep a lid on his temper.

'Listen here, you, I want Susan to have a bit of a chance in life, that's all. I want her to get an education. If I had the money I'd advise her to go on to college or wherever it is people go on to from secondary modern. Her face will never be her fortune but her brain might be. She could be anything, anything at all. A lawyer . . . whatever.'

'Fucking hell, Joey! You feeling all the ticket, love? If I didn't know better I'd think you'd had a head transplant instead of concussion and two broken legs.'

Joey shook his head sadly.

'I've had time to think, June, and I'm a changed man, I tell you. Be honest, wouldn't you like to see one of them put the McNamara name up in the right place for a change? It's a new world now and women can do all sorts of things. It's accepted that they'll work until they settle down and have a few chavvies. Some even work afterwards, though personally I think that's stronging it a bit. But you get the gist of what I'm saying, don't you?'

June looked nonplussed.

'I do and I don't. Our Susan has a brain on her, I admit that. But only in comparison with the people we know. I mean, outside our world she's probably a bit thick, and I mean that in a nice way.

'I love that girl, I always have. But I don't want her setting her heart on something she'll never be able to have. A couple of kids in a few years and she'll be happy as a sandboy. She ain't really cut out for all that education stuff, not deep down. And if she went on to higher education she'd meet people other than her own kind and then she'd start looking down on us. I tell you, I've seen it on telly. Kids who've gone on to better things, they leave the rest of their family behind, mate. They have to.'

'You're wrong, June . . .'

June was miffed and didn't really know why. Suddenly his being so interested in Susan was bothering her and she felt bad about that.

'Bring her in to see me tonight,' Joey told her.

She laughed gently.

'You're a funny fucker, Joey. One minute you're one thing and then the next minute you completely change.'

'That's what makes me so interesting.'

June looked into his face. It was battered and bruised but she could still see what had attracted her to him all those years ago. She pondered why she was going back to him. She had a few quid and could run away if she wanted to. But he was her life in a lot of respects. He accepted her for what she was and who else was ever going to do that? Jimmy had been a nice diversion and now it was over.

With Joey, what you saw was what you got and you'd be a fool if you thought you were getting anything else. Though there were plenty of women of her ilk who would not kick him out of bed. In their world a reputation as a hard man was a well-respected thing. Now he was believed to be Jimmy's killer it would enhance his standing locally.

She wondered if he knew about it all yet. She knew Davey had been in to visit him.

'What did Davey have to say?'

Joey laughed.

'I'm thought to be behind Jimmy's killing. That should give me reputation a boost! For the breaking jobs and that I'll get paid extra because of the added fear factor. I tell you, June, that Davey has got it in his bonce, girl. That's what hanging about with the Bannermans has done for him. He's learning all the time and now I'm going to go up with him. What a touch, eh?'

She nodded, wondering whether Joey was really as thick as he made out. Surely he didn't really believe that taking the rep for someone else's actions would do him any favours?

'What about Old Bill, what they got to say about that?'

Joey shrugged.

'They say what Davey and Bannerman want them to say, of course. It's still an ongoing enquiry.'

'What if there's comeback from Jimmy's family or something?'

Joey shrugged once more though he seemed less assured this time and June realised that the thought had not even entered his mind.

'I'll cross that bridge when I come to it, but I reckon it's all sorted. Davey ain't stupid, and Bannerman is definitely on the ball. I'll take me chances as I always do, girl. But the added bunce can only be for the good.'

June laughed then.

'What, for university fees for our Susan? I can just see her face when I tell her what you said, it'll kill her.'

June was rolling with laughter and Joey smiled as he watched her. He had no intention of letting Susan go anywhere.

Susan was a bundle of nerves. Her father was due home from hospital and she knew she was expected to be pleased to see him.

Her mother had cleaned the flat from floor to ceiling and cooked his favourite meal, a large roast beef dinner with Yorkshire puddings that stood up in the oven like diddymen. Susan was to make the trifle and Debbie was to make the Welcome Home cake for him. Ivy was once more allowed in the house, and was at least on her best behaviour which gave Susan some respite.

But she knew that once Joey was home everything would

return to normal in a matter of weeks. She only wished her mother could see that far ahead.

In fact June was getting on her nerves lately. She was acting as if she and Joey had never been parted and whenever Susan brought up the subject of Jimmy there was a row, with her mother telling her to let sleeping dogs lie. It was as if he had never existed and this bothered Susan more than anything. June had also told her that her father was not at all happy about her having a serious boyfriend. He felt she was too young and on her visits to him in hospital she had been banned from seeing Barry at all.

But Susan was seeing him, and would continue to see him whatever her mother said or her father did.

Maud from next door tripped into the flat with a bunch of flowers and some grapes. 'For the invalid, June. I hope he's better soon.'

She stifled a grin. Maud would do anything to be in this flat today. She wanted to know exactly what the score was between June and Joey. The estate had been rife with talk for the last two weeks about Joey killing Jimmy and claiming back his wife. He had been arrested and then battered in the Bill shop, everyone knew that. They assumed he had taken the beating and not cracked, therefore he was doubly a man in everyone's eyes. Jimmy was a nice bloke but at the end of the day he had taken a wife away from her husband and children. Everyone chose to forget June's past record for the time being and they were all firmly on Joey's side.

He was a bit of a hero.

June was loving it. Debbie was revelling in it. His mother was over the moon. Susan wished they would all drop dead.

Maud felt as if all her Christmases had arrived at once when Joey walked into the flat with Davey Davidson who had picked him up from hospital, but June soon hustled her out.

Davey was in a good mood and June was dressed to kill in low top, short skirt and leather boots. She bent down to pick up a small stool for Joey to put his feet on. He graciously agreed to have a cup of tea.

Joey was laughing inside. He knew what June was really like

and in all honesty he had missed her. He was glad to have her back, and pleased that he was seen as the maniac who had taken out a Glasgow bully-boy to reclaim his wife.

Already he was getting offers of work from local debt collectors, legal and illegal. His next big step would be to go up West, around the clubs. He would be raking in a grand a week at this rate and was determined to make sure he got his due.

He smiled at the two girls and Debbie threw herself into his arms. She was enjoying it all as much as Joey was, and knowing her like he did he was pleased for her. She knew how to play the game did his Debs. It was the other miserable bitch he had to take down a peg, and he was determined to do just that.

Opening his arms, he said jovially, 'Come on then, Sue. No kiss for your old man?'

Susan went obediently towards him and kissed his cheek. June had arrived with the tray of tea and watched the little scene with interest. Susan was pulled into a bear hug and dragged on to her father's lap. Davey laughed as she squealed loudly.

Then, pulling her round on his lap, Joey grabbed at her breasts. Holding them tightly in his grip, he shouted, 'See them, Davey boy? You don't get many of them to the pound.'

Even Davey was shocked though he didn't say anything. He knew his wife would have ripped his heart out if he'd attempted that with one of his kids. Not that he ever would have, he assured himself, he wasn't that way inclined.

June slapped Joey none too gently on the side of his head and pulled Susan away from him. She ran from the room, face burning with shame.

'You're a bastard, Joey. You know how touchy she is about her knockers. Now in future leave her alone.'

There was a warning in those words and everyone was aware of it, even Joey. The small room went quiet and Ivy decided this was the time for her to speak up.

'Funny little mare she is that one, not like Debbie at all. But blood will out, I suppose.'

Joey looked at his mother and snapped, 'Button your fucking mutton, Mother, we have got guests.'

Ivy's face was a picture of indignation.

'I was only saying, son . . .'

Joey turned in his seat and looked the old woman straight in the eye.

'Well, don't. I ain't interested in your opinion and neither is anyone else, all right?'

June poured the tea then went to her daughter's bedroom. Susan was lying on the bed, curled up into a ball. June sat beside her and stroked her hair.

'He didn't mean it, love, you know what he's like. It's only his way of being affectionate.'

Susan looked into her mother's face.

'I hate him, Mum. Hate him and everything he stands for.'

Her words were low, but the feeling in them was obvious.

June smiled sadly.

'It's your age, Susan, you hate the world at that age . . .'

Susan interrupted her.

'I don't hate the world, Mum, I hate him and only him.'

June didn't know why but she really did not want to get into a conversation with her daughter about Joey. Somehow she knew that if she did it was going to cause trouble for them all.

'Don't talk about him like that, Susan. He is your father.'

She snorted with contempt.

'Is he? That's not what I've heard all me life. I think you'd better have a chat with his mother. According to her I should be renamed Heinz – fifty-seven varieties and all that. I'm a mongrel according to her – and him when he's had a drink. Even you have queried my parentage over the years. Trying to remember who you fucked who looked like me, are you? Put a face to a name, eh?'

The slap on her cheek was like a gunshot in the quiet of the room.

'You little whore! You always have to cause hag, don't you, Susan? Always got to have the last word. It's all that reading, it's turned your bleeding head. Well, listen to me and listen good – I ain't in the mood for you and your fucking hysterics today. One more word out of you and I'll rip your head off, do I make myself clear?'

'Crystal clear. I think we both realise that much, don't you, Mum? If you don't talk about things then they never happened, did they?'

'What you on about now?'

Susan shook her head sadly, the red handprint burning on her cheek.

'Think about it, Mum, just think about it.'

June looked down into her daughter's face. She regretted hitting her already, but it was preferable to the alternative. She didn't even want to contemplate that.

Joey looked at the dinner on the table and sighed happily; smiling at the two girls he scooped up a whole roast potato and shoved it in his mouth. It was too hot and he made a great pantomime of trying to cool it down. Everyone laughed except Susan but no one mentioned the fact.

Ivy was in her element. Her golden boy was home and he was well. That pleased her more than anything. Joey was all she had in the world, and she was terrified of losing him.

She looked at June's gaping mouth as she laughed at something he said and grudgingly decided that her daughter-in-law wasn't that bad really. If Joey had married a different kind of woman Ivy was sensible enough to know she would have been shown the door years before. Unlike most East End women, June had a casual and relaxed attitude to everything to do with the home and her kids, whereas most of the women Ivy knew ruled their husbands and families with a rod of iron.

Oh, the men might be hard cases and the women might look downtrodden, but the truth was often very different. These women used their position as mother and wife to keep their men in line.

June never bothered. With her and Joey it was a strange mish-mash of a partnership. June did what most men did; she slept around, blew all their money and spent her time in and around the pubs. Joey did the same but on a smaller scale.

Ivy grinned, happy in the knowledge that once the honeymoon period was over she could stick her beak into everything once more and they could all get back to normal.

She looked at Susan and her grin faded.

That little mare wouldn't know what had hit her once Ivy stuck her claws into her. Raise her hand to her granny, would she, and expect to get away with it? Well, God was good, as her own mother used to say. He waited until it was time then He made sure people paid for their sins.

Ivy would see that little cow paid and paid dearly for her tantrum.

'What you thinking about, Mum? You got a face like a wet weekend in Brighton.'

Ivy looked into her son's shrewd eyes and smiled.

'I was thinking how lovely it is to have you home again, son. I missed you.' Then two fat tears spilled over her cheekbones and she was bawling her head off.

Joey raised his eyes to the ceiling incredulously. Ivy was genuinely distressed and even Susan felt for her. The old woman was visibly shaken by her son's ordeal and it had laid a damper on the party atmosphere. Susan instinctively reached across the table and grasped her grandmother's hand.

'Come on, give us one of your songs.'

She was soft-hearted enough to try and make Ivy feel better. Ivy, though, had other ideas.

'Don't you come the old mucker with me, you rotten little mare. What I've had to put up with from you would make your father's blood boil if he knew.'

June closed her eyes. Taking a deep breath, she cried, 'Oh, for fuck's sake, can we just for once eat a meal without a flaming row starting? If you cause any hag, Ivy, you're out the door and I mean it.' She pointed at Susan with her fork. 'And as for you, lady, take the miserable look off your boat before I knock it off, all right?'

Joey looked at Debbie who rolled her eyes to the ceiling.

'I get the right hump living here. All it ever is is fighting and arguing, morning, noon and night. Don't you get the ache with it, Mum?'

June grimaced.

'Yes, I do, Debbie, as it happens. So I tell you now: if it all kicks off again I'll walk out that door and I ain't never coming back, I take fucking oath on that one. You remember that, Ivy, and you, Susan. I have had all I can take in the last few weeks and I can't hack it any more. I want a bit of peace for once in me bleeding life, a meal in peace, to sit in me own home in peace. To talk to my bloody husband in peace without you two at each other's throats. Do you get my bleeding drift, eh? Think you can manage that, do you?'

Ivy hung her head. She knew she was on distinctly dodgy ground at the moment. Susan swallowed down the lump in her throat and concentrated on the food in front of her.

No one spoke a word for five minutes; the air in the room was heavy with malice. Ivy kept looking at Susan as if she wanted to say something but daren't. Susan looked at her plate. Anywhere but at her mother, father or sister. Ivy she didn't even think about.

Joey watched them all as he ate.

His mother was a case, really. Any other man would have chinned her before this but he knew that he was her whole life and at times was grateful for that. At the end of the day your mum was your mum.

'What time are your painkillers due, Joey?'

He shrugged, glad the silence had been broken.

'I don't know. Anyway I've got some stronger ones off Davey's mate Georgie Dixon. He says they're the dog's gonads as far as killing pain goes, and they give you a high. Gotta be better than the crap they doled out at the hospital. They wouldn't kill the pain of a gnat bite!'

June grinned.

'When you're ready, mate, get a couple down your Gregory then I'll tuck you up in bed, eh?'

Debbie rolled her eyes to the ceiling once more. Her parents' constant sexual gymnastics made her feel sick. You could hear them at it at all times of the day, and it made her feel queasy. But she loved telling her friends about it, it made them laugh.

'You make sure you've taken them, though, son. A painkiller is a wonderful thing. Best invention after alcohol, if you ask me. That was the poor man's painkiller years ago, you know. A bottle of Scotch and they'd cut your bleeding leg right off with a hacksaw then put tar on the stump to stop the bleeding. And I mean bleeding. The blood would spurt out into the air . . .'

Debbie almost shouted then, 'All right, Nan, we get the picture.'

Joey laughed and swallowed down his wine.

'Trust you, Muvver, when we're eating really rare beef to bring up something like that. Mind you, remember what's his name? The torturer for the Daleys. He used to remove people's toes with a pair of secateurs.'

He pointed at his wife with his knife.

'Rose fanatic he was, had a lovely garden. Anyway he's in Broadmoor now and tends the gardens there, I heard. Well, he told me once that he cut their toes off to stop people having any balance, see. If you lose your big toe then you fall over all the time, something like that. But he said he did the toes mainly because the thought of it was so terrifying that when he turned up on their doorstep they would literally give him anything to get shot of him. It's psychological. The thought of something is much worse than it actually happening. Or something like that. Anyway he was a nice bloke really.'

Ivy grinned. She loved conversations like this, they excited her.

'So long as you didn't upset him.'

Even June laughed now, and Debbie.

'Of course, he cut off Alfie Archer's ears with a broken glass because he grassed up Harry Petersen. Remember him, Mum? Big Harry the Scandinavian docker?'

'That's right, his wife was a nice woman, felt sorry for her I did. That Harry was a right nice-looking bloke and all, white-haired with icy blue eyes. He was a looker all right. Ended up doing an eighteen for armed robbery after Archie grassed him. So he had his ears removed. That used to be a warning then, in the forties and fifties like, not to grass up what you heard. It was a kind of message to others when you saw him ear-'oleless walking about the place. I remember his name – Jacob Daniels. That was it, weren't it, son?'

He nodded dreamily.

'Yeah, Jacob Daniels. Christ, Mum, you've got a memory, you have.'

Ivy preened at the compliment.

'Well, they was the good old days, weren't they? It's a different world now. Villains ain't got the class no more. I mean, even the Davidsons and the Bannermans don't really belong to the upper echelons, not like the old-style manor bosses. They looked out for their own they did. I remember during the war they made sure we had a bit of whatever was going, you know. Bacon, a few eggs, whatever. Consequently people kept stumm, respected them. Not like nowadays when you have all these young kids dealing drugs and that. Like that Barry. He deals drugs, I heard.'

She looked pointedly at Susan, who answered her through gritted teeth.

'You want to get your facts right, Ivy, he don't deal drugs. He leaves that for the likes of Georgie Dixon who Dad got his from.'

Joey laughed at the two women trying to score points off one another. But Ivy wasn't impressed.

'That's different. They're for medical reasons, ain't they, son?'

Joey nodded.

'But she don't go out with Barry any more, do you, love? You took your old dad's advice, didn't you, Susan? And if me mother's right, you got out of it just in time. Them drug dealers are heading for a fall. Davey's got his eye on them, and Bannerman.'

Susan looked into her father's face.

'What's that? After a cut, are they?'

Joey looked full at his daughter. His voice low and angry, he snapped, 'That's right, love, they're after a cut, and that cut is what will put food on this table in future so you keep that in mind.'

The pure loathing in her eyes made him angry and he could feel it spiralling through his body to his head. But he would not lose it today. Today he was on his best behaviour.

'Well, I can't sit here listening to you lot waffling on, I have a hot date.'

All eyes turned to Debbie who was trying in her own way to make it easier for Susan.

'Who you going out with then?'

Joey's voice was mild now.

'Micky Shand. The son, by the way, not the father.'

They all laughed.

'Good on you, girl, they're a nice family. His dad out now then?'

Debbie nodded happily.

'Yeah, he got out about ten days ago. They had a lovely party for him, pearly queen and everything. It was a right laugh.'

June smiled.

'I heard about it. Wish I could have gone meself but with all that's been happening . . .' She left the sentence unfinished.

Joey grabbed her hand in his and squeezed it.

'Well, everything's okay now, love. We'll be riding the pig's back now, girl. We're on our way up. I want to buy a house next.'

Ivy's face was a picture of joy.

'Imagine that! My son owning his own drum.'

Susan grinned and said nastily, 'What you gonna call it – Dunrobbin?'

Joey looked at her for a split second before his fist shot out and caught her on the side of her face. June and Debbie leaped from their seats and pulled her away from the table.

'Leave it, Joey! Just leave it, mate. She was out of order and she's been punished, don't let her ruin the day.'

June pushed Susan from the room and dragged her towards her bedroom. Inside she shut the door and pushed her none too gently on to the bed.

'I am *sick* of you, Susan. I am so sick of you today you would not believe it.'

Susan rubbed at her face and felt the lump swelling already from the blow.

'You asked for that, winding him up. You know what he's fucking like.'

'Yeah, I do, and so do you, so why are you back here with him? This will be you soon. A punch here, a kick there. You know it as well as I do.'

'He don't mean the half of it, you wound him up deliberately, but I tell you now – you push him too far and he'll break your neck.'

Susan closed her eyes, the throbbing of her cracked jaw penetrating into her brain.

'As soon as I'm fifteen I am out of here.'

June laughed then.

'I think we can safely assume that one, Sue, but in the meantime you really have to learn to keep your trap shut. I don't want to see you any more today unless you can keep a civil tongue in your head.'

She pulled her daughter's face round roughly and looked at it.

'You'll live. But I warn you, don't wind him up and don't wind me up either. I have enough on me plate as it is without you causing more hag for me.'

As June walked from the room Susan let the tears fall. She hated Joey McNamara; hated him with a vengeance. And she was beginning to dislike her mother. She already knew that any respect she had ever had for her was gone.

Today had been the beginning of the end for mother and daughter. It was to be the start of a long-running battle between them that would last almost the rest of their lives. The rough love June had doled out as and when it suited her would be all but withdrawn over the next few years until they literally hated one another.

Chapter Seven

Barry Dalston had nice eyes and he knew it. He would look straight into a woman's face and smile at them and was always amazed by the reaction, especially from the older ones.

He knew he wasn't exactly good-looking in the conventional sense, but he had something about him. Something the women liked. He guessed rightly it was his devil-may-care attitude and physique.

The night before, he had been to a pub in Bethnal Green with his mates and had met a woman there called Sophie. She was thirty-five, with a nice car, a nice flat and great tits. She was married to an insurance broker called Alfie who was boring. According to Sophie if boring the arse off people was an Olympic sport, her Alfie would get the gold.

She was a little overweight but her plumpness made her feel sexier to him, and if her hair was just a tad too bright to be real and her dresses just a little too tight to be comfortable, Christ, she was a laugh.

In her car she had climbed over the back seat as if she did it every day of her life, flashing a pair of black lacy knickers and plenty of flesh above her stocking tops.

Barry had had an erection like a policeman's truncheon in five seconds flat, and as she caressed it and giggled he had nearly come there and then.

It was a new experience for him. Sophie expected to enjoy herself. The fact that some women actually did enjoy sex had until that moment passed him by.

Looking into his eyes, she'd exclaimed happily, 'Well, boy, am

I glad I didn't wear me glasses. I'd have screamed with fright.'

Barry had loved it, every second of it. From her breasts spilling out of her dress to her straddling him and holding his arms behind his back as she made herself come. He felt as if he had died and woken up in a shagger's paradise. It was all his schoolboy dreams come to life in front of his eyes.

Afterwards she had smoked a cigarette and then started again, something that had frightened Barry as much as it exhilarated him. Never would he have believed a woman could want it like that, like a man did. When her tongue had snaked around his erect penis the second time he had had to name the whole of West Ham football team in his head to stop himself from screaming out.

Sophie loved the effect she had on him and told him so. Barry sat in the back of the car, dazed and knackered, but up for whatever she wanted to do next. They had arranged to meet twice a week, and he was looking forward to it more than he had ever looked forward to anything in his life.

He was whistling as he walked up the Mile End Road on his way to meet Susan. It didn't occur to him that he was two timing her because Susan – his Susan as he thought of her – was thick in many respects. She fancied herself a bit because she read books, but as far as the real world was concerned she didn't have a clue. And that suited Barry right down to the ground. Who wanted a bird with more up top than themselves? was his reasoning.

If Susan ever found out about Sophie he would talk her round because he knew in his heart of hearts that Susan needed him a damn' sight more than he needed her. It was six months now since her father had come out of hospital and at nearly fifteen she could soon start to see who she liked and her father could get fucked. Barry wanted her with a belly full of arms and legs. That way he was in, even Joey McNamara would have to swallow him then, anything being better than the shame of a little bastard arriving.

Barry smiled as he thought about it.

Joey was a Number One man now, a real face with real connections, and Barry wanted a bit of it: a bit of the glory, a bit of the limelight. As Joey's son-in-law he would get it.

Plus, he liked Susan in a funny sort of way. Her eyes looked into his constantly and it was like having a really devoted dog that could chat to you and tell you how much it loved you, how great it thought you were. And she let him have what he wanted, when he wanted – and for a boy like Barry with a libido that went up and down like a whore's drawers that was a bonus.

So, all in all, he was happy with life. If only he could get an in with Susan's family he would be okay.

He had already started on the granny. If he saw her round the shops or the market he always made a big fuss of her, and the silly old bitch loved it. She even let him and Susan use her house while she was at bingo, and considering she and Susan used to hate one another Barry put it down to his natural charm.

In fact Susan and Ivy had become quite pally over the last few months, now they had a common enemy: Susan's mother June.

Susan loathed her and Barry found that strange as she had loved her so much once. He had warned her a couple of times about rowing with her mother over nothing. It was bad enough she hated her father without causing hag with her mother and all. The few times he had seen June he had made a point of letting her know he thought Susan's attitude to her left a lot to be desired at times.

He was that determined to get himself an in.

Once he married Susan he could give her a right hander and sort her out once and for all, he decided. He slipped into the Londoner for a quick drink and saw Joey McNamara sitting at the bar. Smiling, Barry walked up to him and nodded.

Joey ignored him and carried on talking to the woman beside him, a dark-haired half-caste with eyes like pieces of coal and non-existent tits. Barry wouldn't have given her the time of day.

He ordered a light and bitter and smiled to himself at the conversation taking place beside him. This was more like it, this was what he wanted a part of.

'I am telling you, Joey, the man is loaded. He's a regular customer and always has about five grand on him. All you need to do is make sure you see him before I do, right? I can't roll him, he's been using me too long and he's the type of bloke who wouldn't be scared of Old Bill knowing he tommed it. But if you take him as he's coming to see me, you have the money and I have a great alibi. You see, the customer before him is a man called Josh Gold, the little Jewish bloke from the market. He'll be my witness, see? What do you say?'

Joey sighed. Turning slightly on his stool, he shook his head.

'Five grand? Fuck off, Babs, and find someone else to take the shit. I can't be bothered.'

She shrugged.

'Fair enough, Joey, it was just a thought.'

As she walked away he pulled her back roughly.

'If you do roll him, I want my twenty-five percent, though. That's my cut these days.'

She nodded, resigned to the fact that opening her mouth had cost her money.

'Of course. I'll let you know if it happens, okay?'

Joey grinned, displaying his none-too-white teeth.

'Oh, Babs, I'll know if it happens. Ain't nothing happens on this turf without my say-so any more, you remember that.'

Barry followed her out of the pub. As she tried to walk fast on impossibly high heels he grabbed at her arm. She faced him and smiled, showing large white teeth.

'Hello, and what can I do you for?'

The Caribbean lilt was strongly in evidence even though she was more cockney than many around her, having been born on the Bow Road.

Barry was both annoyed and flattered to be taken for a punter.

'There's nothing you can do for me, love. I ain't never been a lover of black pudding myself.'

'Then you don't know what you're missing, boy.'

He grinned.

'I have a good idea. Listen, Babs, I overheard your little chat with Joey Mac in there. Maybe I can help you out?'

She looked him up and down. Her voice insolent now, she said nastily, 'I want a man, not a boy.'

'I'm man enough for what you want, lady.'

Babs laughed then. She admired his guts and his self-confidence.

'My pimp is Jonah. You ready for that, boy?'

'I'll sort out fucking Jonah if needs be. Now do you want to have a chat or not? I can guarantee you a nice little earner for ten minutes' work. What do you say?'

'Look, you're Scottish. I mean, your accent isn't going to do you any favours, is it, not on a rent man?'

Barry laughed.

'You're black but it ain't done you no harm, girl. Listen to me. I'm going to cosh the fucker and rob him, not have a conversation with him. Now do you want to talk or not?'

Babs looked him over once more.

'I drink up West in the Crown and Two Chairmen. I'll be there at eight tonight if you're still interested. Think about it before you commit yourself, and think about Jonah too. He might swallow me tucking up a punter but not an outsider.'

Barry grinned again, and she grinned back. She liked him.

'Fuck Jonah.'

Babs laughed out loud.

'Oh, I have boy, many times.'

As she sashayed away on her high heels Barry felt a burst of happiness. His first real kill and he had got it himself. He felt his balls tingling with the thought of what he would do and then he was hurrying to meet Susan. He could get round her nan's, give her one and still make it for eight up West.

All in all, life was good.

'All I'm saying is, if your father finds out there'll be murder done.'

'I don't really care, Mum, it's none of his business. So stick that one up your pipe and smoke it.'

June sighed heavily as she battled an urge to smash her daughter's head in with the heavy ashtray beside her make-up bag. Putting on her make up and arguing with Susan was becoming a bit of a habit.

'You're not going out in that, surely?'

Susan looked down at her new jumper. Ice pink, it buttoned up the back with little pearl buttons and went over a black pencil skirt. It also emphasised her already considerable bosom. High heels finished off the outfit. With her eyes made up and a new feather cut, Susan thought she looked nice.

'You look like an old whore!'

Susan laughed.

'Well, you should know all about that, Mum, you practically invented that look on your own.'

'Bollocks!'

Susan looked at herself in the mirror.

'No, Mum, tits.'

She cupped her breasts and jiggled them.

June felt like laughing but she didn't. This new Susan was a different kettle of fish altogether. Fighting and arguing at the drop of a hat. This was the first time they had spoken even remotely civilly for weeks.

'They are a size, girl, ain't they?'

'I like them, they make me special. And, Mum, believe me when I say Barry adores them.'

June sniffed.

'I'm sure he does, but if your father sees you dressed like that Barry will be looking for his nuts all over the East End.'

'Mum, I only dress like this when I'm seeing him, and with me blanket coat over the top no one sees nothing they shouldn't. Even in me usual sloppy gear they stand out like beacons, so stop worrying.'

June looked at her daughter's face. It was lit up from within. She envied her in some ways. To be young and in love with your whole life ahead of you. She also knew that she should help her more with Joey, but she couldn't. Joey had a thing about Susan and deep inside June guessed what it was. The same two things that attracted Barry Dalston.

'All I'm saying is, be careful. There's more to life than a pair of tits and a bloke.'

Susan laughed then, a nasty sound.

'And you would know all about that, would you? The trollop of London giving me advice? Shove it, Mum. What's the matter? You jealous you got a bit of competition, is that it?'

At that June lost her temper and gave Susan a stinging slap across her freshly made up face.

Susan's fist went back and she had planted it firmly between her mother's eyes before she realised what she had done.

June staggered backward, trying to grab hold of the dressing table. Instead she fell in a crumpled heap on the bed. Susan rushed to her, trying to help her up and apologising over and over again.

'Mum! Christ almighty, Mum, I am so sorry. Mum, please let me look at you.'

'You little bastard! Fucking punch me, would you, you whore?'

The fight started in earnest then. Mother and daughter were clawing like wildcats. Susan was defending herself and then she was winning.

The fight took her over. As she punched her mother all the pent-up frustration of the last few years rose to the surface. Everything June had done, turned a blind eye to or encouraged seemed to crowd into Susan's mind.

Leaving them with her father to shack up with blokes; always pretending that she knew it all when she knew nothing; never doing anything to help either of her children. Always knowing it all, always letting everyone down.

Susan heard Debbie's screams as if from far away. Dragging her off her mother, Debbie was shocked and incredulous at what had occurred.

'Are you off your fucking trolley, Susan? Look what you done to her.'

She looked down at her mother's bloody face and didn't feel a thing. That shocked her more than anything she had done. She felt nothing except relief.

Susan helped her mother up and then left the room.

In the hallway she repaired her make up as best she could and straightened her clothes. Putting on her blanket coat, she picked up her bag and slipped from the house.

Barry watched Susan surreptitiously as she strode along the road. Her coat was open and she got about five bibs in the space of twenty-five seconds. His face darkened. He looked into the cars to see if he recognised any of the men daring to bib his bird.

He stepped out and as he opened his mouth to berate her,

hesitated. Susan didn't look like her usual self. She lit herself a cigarette and he saw her hands were shaking.

'What's wrong, Sue?'

Susan sighed and answered him sharply, 'What's fucking right, you mean?'

He linked arms with her and walked her up to her granny's flat. She puffed nervously on her cigarette and he kept silent, knowing she would tell him in her own time.

As they walked up to the door Ivy's face was at the kitchen window.

'You little bastard!' she greeted her granddaughter.

Susan sighed.

'The jungle tom-toms must be in overdrive.'

'What's going . . .'

The door was flung open and Susan was dragged over the step.

'That right you hammered your mother, Susan? Debbie's in a right state. I just had her on the trombone. Battered the fuck out of Junie, did you?'

Susan nodded.

'Yes, I did, and she asked for it.'

Ivy was caught between wanting to hear all the facts and the usual urge to stick her oar in and cause more hag. But even she knew that her son would go ballistic over this one. He could kick June till she was unconscious but no one else would be afforded the privilege. Plus there was something going on between him and Susan, something she could not quite put her finger on.

Barry looked into Susan's red face.

'You beat your mother up?'

'Too right I did. She hit me so I hit her back.'

Ivy's face was a picture of glee.

'That's not what I was told. She slapped you for mouthing her off and you knocked seven bells of shit out of her according to Debbie. Your father's been called from the pub and that will cheer him up no end, mate. Bashing up your mother's one thing. Interfering in Joey's social life is something else altogether. You're for it.'

Susan bit her lip.

Ivy was right about one thing: Joey would annihilate her and would enjoy doing it. Now he had a legitimate reason to give her a good hiding and all the different insults she had given him over the last few months would be remembered and count against her too.

'I ain't going back, I don't want to live there any more.'

Ivy raised her eyes to the ceiling.

'You're fourteen. Where the hell you going to go, Susan? Get a flat, will you? How will you pay the rent and stuff? Get a grip, girl. You're trapped until time tells you different. Now you get yourself into that front room and I'll make a cuppa. Your dad will be here in a minute and then Gawd help you.'

Barry looked at the old woman.

'What do you mean, Joey's coming here?'

Ivy snorted.

''Course he is. I told Debbie you was coming here like usual.'

She smiled then and Barry saw her as Susan did: a nasty, vindictive old bitch.

'He'll brain you and all, son, so if I was you I'd piss off out of it. Leave her to it, son, she deserves all she gets.'

Ivy tutted loudly.

'I'll miss me bleeding bingo now an' all. Little cow you are, Susan, causing all this trouble.'

Susan looked at Barry numbly.

'You better go, Bal, he better not see you.'

Barry was in a quandary. He didn't want to leave like a kid afraid of her dad, but he didn't want to fall out with the man either. After all, Joey was the reason Susan and he were an item.

Now she had caused all this trouble he could gladly have given her a slap himself. The front door was being banged on now and Joey's voice was loud as he shouted through the letterbox.

'Open up, Mother. I'm here and I want that bitch now!'

'Quick son, get in the bedroom. Joey will kill you stone dead if he sees you here.'

'Fuck off. I'm not hiding from him . . .'

Susan, forgetting her own fear, pushed him roughly towards the bedroom door.

'He's mad enough to kill us both. Now just for once do as I ask you, Bal, please.'

The fear in her voice communicated itself to him and he went into the bedroom. Shutting the door firmly behind him he waited and listened, his whole body tense with fear.

Ivy opened the front door and was pushed roughly out of the way by her son. Joey looked mad enough to kill all right. His eyes were red-rimmed and his whole body exuded menace.

He looked at his daughter for a few seconds.

'I'll brain you, you bastard. I'll fucking brain you.'

Susan looked into his eyes and didn't flinch.

'Brain me then, Dad. There's nothing else you can do to me that can hurt as much as what you've already done.'

The words were loaded and Ivy picked up on them quickly.

'What you on about, girl? Smack her one, Joey. Don't let her talk to you like that. No wonder she's gone off the bleeding rails . . .'

He turned on his mother and bellowed: 'Fucking shut it! Now get out and leave me and her alone.' He was spitting, his anger was so acute.

Ivy slipped her coat off the hook and turned on her heel. As she closed the front door behind her she felt immensely sorry for herself. Forced from her own home like she was no one, by the son she worshipped and adored. She stood outside in the cold and waited to hear what was going on inside.

Susan stood facing her father in the narrow hallway.

'I'm going to bust your face open, girl, and I'm going to enjoy it.'

She stood before him, quietly self-contained, watching as if she was a witness to everything instead of the victim.

'Of course you'll enjoy it, Dad, you're a fucking bully boy.'

In the bedroom Barry closed his eyes at her words. She must be off her nut was all he could tell himself. Grown men with a rep wouldn't dare say that to Joey McNamara.

She slipped off her coat and stood before her father in all her new finery.

'Look at you, dressed like a fucking slag! Walking the streets like a fucking whore!'

The first slap hit her full across the face and knocked her into the wall. Barry heard the thud as she was punched and wiped one sweaty hand across his face.

Joey punched her eight times until she was on the floor. Then, pulling her by the hair, he dragged her into the lounge. As Susan tried to get up and away from him he dragged at the pink jumper, tearing it open at the back, the tiny pearl buttons flying all around the room as they were ripped from the material.

Dragging it off her, Joey held it in front of her face as she tried to cover her body from his prying eyes. Bruising was already coming out all over her arms and face, her eye was closed and her nose was trickling blood.

'This what you parade about in, is it? Dressed like an out of work fucking dock dolly – my daughter. I've seen whores with more on than you. But then you've got the mouth to go with it, ain't you, Susan? That great big mouth you open all day without a second thought. Well, after today, lady, you don't shit without my permission, you hear me? I will watch you morning, noon and night.'

'I'm not your daughter.'

As soon as she said those words his fists rained blows down on her all over again.

Joey stood over her panting. His chest felt like it was going to explode with anger. She was below him, legs splayed, breasts free. She was looking up at him and he knew what she was thinking, what she was expecting, and decided he would not disappoint her.

Unbuckling the belt on his trousers, he laughed down at her.

'What you after then, Susan? Your usual, eh?'

'Fuck off.'

All her hatred and secret knowledge of him were contained in those words. The intensity of them reached Barry even through the bedroom wall. Susan had forgotten about him in her granny's bedroom, had forgotten everything except the fact she hated this man with all her heart.

Barry, however, would never forget what he was hearing now.

'I hope you die screaming of cancer. I hope you never know a day's peace, you bastard . . .'

Joey kicked her viciously in the stomach, shutting her up. Desperate to breathe, Susan was panicking at the pain that shot through her abdomen. As he forced himself on her she could not even begin to fight him off.

His mouth was clamped on hers and he was touching her all over. She could feel him, feel every part of him, and as the vomit rushed from her mouth and sprayed them both he was too far gone to know what was happening. He rode her hard, forcing himself inside her, and as she clawed at his face he punched her once more in the chest, winding her again.

He collapsed on top of her then and, laughing, whispered in her ear. 'I can do what I like, Susan, and you remember that. When you hit your mother you made an enemy for life. You gave me licence to do what I want, and I will, young lady, I will. I'll lock you up until I have had my fill of you. Remember that, girl. I'll break you in mind and spirit and laugh while I do it.'

Kneeling over her he felt an urge to urinate. Reading his mind, Susan rolled away from him just as the stream was about to hit her face. Pulling her up by her hair, he stared down into her eyes.

'Get dressed, you're coming home with me.'

Standing, he adjusted his trousers and looked in the fly-spotted mirror above the tiled fireplace while he tidied himself up. He watched Susan trying to get up on all fours.

'You're a fat ugly whore, ain't you? Who else would fucking want you? Look at the size of your arse. Look at yourself. You're a dog, and like a dog you turned on your master. Well, that's the last time you ever go against me, girl. From now on you earn your privileges and no prizes for guessing how you're going to do that, eh?'

Taking off his belt he set about her once more. The buckle hit her open skin and made her scream but he carried on regardless. There was no one who was going to ring the Old Bill about him, not in this quarter anyway.

In the next room Barry sat on the bed in a state of shock. He knew exactly what had just occurred and was still trying to take it in. Joey McNamara was a beast, the worst kind of beast. He was guilty of incest, the worst crime in working-class communities after rape and paedophilia.

And he, Barry Dalston, knew about it. He wished he didn't. But his business brain was telling him that this knowledge could be of use to him.

He heard Susan getting up, could hear moans from her as she tried to dress herself. A small part of him was sorry for her, but another part was angry with her for keeping this from him.

He had thought he was the first, the first man to touch those great big tits, but he wasn't. Her father was already well into her when he came along. Who else had had a touch? he wondered. And how the fuck was he going to find out if she didn't get out of the house ever again?

He glanced at the small travel clock by the bed. It was twenty to eight and he had to get up West. He wished they would all piss off so he could sort himself out, sort his head out. Decide what he was going to do. How he could use this information for his own ends, because he had a feeling that somehow this was going to come in useful one day.

Very useful indeed.

Susan was shocked by what she had done to her mother. Although she herself had taken a much worse hiding, she knew her mother couldn't cope mentally with the humiliation she'd suffered. June had looked at her with hatred, and she had aimed that hatred right back. Your mother was supposed to take care of you, stop things happening to you, but not *her* mother. She had turned a blind eye to everything and Susan would never forgive her for that.

As Susan walked into her bedroom Debbie was waiting for her, a nasty smile on her face. 'You've got some front, Susan, doing that to Muvver. I could hammer you meself.'

Susan looked at her and answered in a tiny dead voice.

'I wouldn't if I was you, Debbie. I might decide to go for the double and then where would you be, eh? If I do the old man, I'll get to keep the match ball!'

Debbie was shocked by her answer. Where had Susan McNamara gone? Her sister wasn't violent, in fact she was too easy-going if anything. But not any more by the looks of it. Susan was still aggressive even battered to bits.

As she stripped off Debbie saw the cuts and welts all over her body and against her better judgement felt sorry for her sister. Going to the kitchen, she came back with a bowl of warm salty water with Dettol in and started to help her clean herself up.

'That was some hiding, Susan. I'm amazed you're not in hospital. You'll be scarred for life.'

Susan didn't answer her.

All she knew was that Barry had heard what had gone on and had not helped her. Part of her was pleased about that but another part was telling her he should have interfered, should have tried to help her.

The shame of it was inside her like a black cancer, eating her from the inside.

Joey had it all ways. He had her and her mother. Both of them. He treated her with contempt and enjoyed doing it. Barry had listened to the rape of his girlfriend and done nothing.

Did her father really wield such power?

It seemed he must, it seemed that he could get away with anything and no one would attempt to stop him. Even Barry wasn't going to help her now.

Yet she had believed that with him she would be safe. Wrong again. Knowing he knew her secret was just about the worst thing that had ever happened to Susan and she knew all about bad things happening. He would not want her now, she realised. She was used news, already tarnished by her father and his actions. Barry was probably pleased he didn't have to dump her himself.

This realisation made the tears slip from her eyes, big fat tears that were salty on the tongue and fast-flowing. Her shoulders began to shake as the shock set in. Everything was wrong, everything was over.

Barry would not touch her with a barge pole now, not once he realised that her father, her own father, was using her sexually.

Debbie, sorry for her sister and her obvious hurt, tried to cuddle her, but the bruising and cuts made that impossible. Instead she placed a blanket over Susan's naked body and held her hand as her sister cried as if her heart was breaking.

Then June came into the room. Debbie left at a nod from her mother. She looked down at her daughter and felt nothing. No sorrow, no shame, nothing. All she saw was a child who had all her life made June feel as if she had done something wrong.

Susan was a child born of pain, her very conception had been in pain, and now she was the cause of yet more pain.

Looking down at her, June saw Joey's square jawline, the same round face and piercing blue eyes. The heavy-boned body that had no grace in it whatsoever, no style at all. Yes, Susan was her father's daughter all right. She even had his mean streak inside her. She had proved that with the hiding she had given her own mother.

But June had decided now she would change her. Or let Joey change her. He was right, Susan had had it all her own way for too long. Pulling the blanket back, June looked at the marks on her daughter's body and smiled. She hoped the little bitch was in agony as she herself was.

It never occurred to her that the reason for the change in her daughter was the way she had been treated, the fact that her life so far had been led in a home devoid of love or normal comfort. That June's way of life had rubbed off on her girls, making them unfit to be with decent people. That her father's taking her in lieu of his wife had made the girl mixed up and aggressive, unable to see things from the correct standpoint.

June, as usual, saw only herself and what had happened to her.

'I hope you realise what you did today, Susan, because it's going to come down on your head for the rest of your life.'

She did not answer her mother. She had nothing at all she wanted to say. Barry, her Barry, was gone from her and it was all this woman's fault.

'You should have looked after me, Mum. You know you should.'

The words came out eventually and June felt an urge to rip her daughter's face off her body because to her shame she knew that it was true.

Instead she turned and walked from the room.

Chapter Eight

Babs had a different look about her and Barry found he quite liked it. Instead of her usual heavy make up and sluttish clothes, he was surprised to find that at home and without the prospect of customers she looked like a regular person. In fact she seemed both young and very appealing.

Babs was seventeen and had been on the streets for four years. She was a hardened whore and knew it, but still she liked to go to church now and again and spent all her money on her small daughter Bianca who was looked after by her maternal grandmother, Ruth.

She poured Barry a Scotch and he sipped it.

'You sure you know what you're doing, mate? Only this bloke's all right, a good customer. But I need a few grand sharpish and he seemed like the only viable way of getting it.'

Barry grinned and Babs began to like him. He had a funny charm she couldn't resist, a bit like a white Jonah.

'What time does he normally get here?'

Babs sipped at her drink. Barry watched as her full lips caressed the glass. Painted a deep red, they were suddenly very interesting. All of Babs was interesting. From her small pointy breasts to her tight high arse, she was suddenly very interesting indeed.

'At nine on the dot. He's a funny little bloke really, a nice man in a lot of respects. Some of the punters are right arseholes. Flash, you know. They think because they're paying for it they own you. Pushing you around, making you do things they haven't paid extra for.'

She held up one finger as she spoke. It had a long red nail and Barry was mesmerised by it.

'I had a bloke yesterday, about fucking sixty he was – ugly as sin and he smelled. A lot of them smell. Funny that, ain't it? Anyway in he comes all sweetness and light and then he wants me to put on these shoes. So I put them on and walked about a bit. Then, right, he wants me to give him a blow job in the window – in the window, if you don't mind – while he wears a balaclava!'

She roared with laughter then.

Barry looked at his watch. It was ten past seven.

'Listen, Babs, I'll be back at nine, all right? I'll have him before he even gets here so don't worry.'

She nodded.

'Well, I thought you didn't want to know before, when you didn't turn up. What did happen, Barry, because I've seen you every day since.'

He sighed heavily.

'I told you, something came up, love.'

She bent over to pour herself another drink and he saw the track marks on her arms.

'You should keep away from that shit, it'll kill you one day.'

Babs laughed again, a real belly laugh.

'Barry, you fool, I'm already dead, mate, from the neck down.' She pulled her little top down and showed him her breasts. 'See these, boy? They take on average seven men a day, six days a week. Now over four years that amounts to . . .'

She rolled her eyes up to the ceiling, trying to work out the exact amount.

Barry answered for her.

'That's one hundred and sixty-eight men a month. Times that by twelve and then by four.'

Babs pulled back the top.

'Don't bother. I think we both get the picture, don't you?'

He was shocked by the thought.

'Fucking hell, Babs, that's a lot of blokes.'

She laughed again.

'I don't just take on men, I have a couple of women customers too. We whores call it having a bit of soft. It gets you like that in the end. Men have no mystery for you, see, so you tend to gravitate towards other women.'

Barry was even more shocked now.

'Don't you ever feel the urge to have a bit then?'

'I'm always having a bit, Barry, that's the fucking trouble.'

They both laughed and the atmosphere was defused.

'You'd better go, I have a punter due in ten minutes. A nice man with a wrinkly cock and wrinkly balls, but he's quiet and it's all over in ten minutes. Give me the olds any day of the week, they ain't trying to prove nothing.'

Barry finished his drink. He was looking forward to rolling the punter. He saw them all as perverts now. How could any man sleep with someone who was a stranger and had been sleeping with strangers all day?

The thought depressed him, and after he left he found himself walking, walking, and thinking about how Babs and people like her became what they were.

As usual he found himself walking towards Susan's flats. He stood outside and looked up at the windows.

The anger was back. Anger at himself, anger at Susan for having him over, and anger at Joey McNamara who was trumping her and getting away with it. Barry wondered what all the hard nuts would think if they knew that Joey was a beast, and the worst kind of beast at that. He fucked his own kid. And how long had that been going on? Barry would find out.

But Susan was grounded and it looked like it was for life. No one had seen her. Not at school, not anywhere.

He noticed Debbie tripping up the road. This was a whore in the making, with her make up, her fag and her provocative clothes. He watched her surreptitiously from the cover of the flats opposite.

As she walked towards her own entrance he called, 'Oi, Debbie, over here.'

She looked through the gloom and smiled radiantly to see him.

'Hello, Barry, how are you?' she asked, walking over.

She was pert as usual. The heavily lipsticked mouth wore a practised pout and her breasts were thrust out on display. He knew she liked him, knew she would do the dirty on her sister at the drop of a hat.

She disgusted him. Give him Babs any day of the week. At least she didn't pretend to be anything other than what she was.

But he smiled at Debbie.

'How's Susan?'

Her face dropped.

'Susan is in shit so deep it would take ten paddies with shovels to get her out.'

She laughed at her own words.

Barry didn't laugh and his expression told Debbie she ought to go easy.

'She's still grounded, still laid up in bed. No one can go in there now except me dad. He takes her her meals and that. It's awful. Can you imagine what it's like for me?'

Barry smiled briefly. Trust Debbie to see only her own troubles and no one else's.

'She's always hated me dad, but now her and me mum are at it it's even worse. Me mum acts as if Susan ain't in the flat. I tell you, it's terrible. I can't get in to see her unless they're both out and that's not often. But she always asks if I've seen you so I can tell her now that I have and that will cheer her up, I can tell you. Do you want me to give her a message?'

Barry wasn't sure whether he wanted it or not now he had the opportunity.

'Tell her I said hello.'

That needn't mean anything. He would decide what he wanted to do once Susan was back on the street.

'So your dad is the only one allowed in to see her? What about the doctor?'

Debbie's eyes narrowed.

'What do you mean?'

'Well, he flayed her, didn't he? Beat the shit out of her.'

Debbie realised she was on dangerous ground. Everyone knew that there had been trouble but no one knew the extent of it, her father had made sure of that.

'He gave her a dig, yeah, but she asked for it.'

Barry grinned.

'A dig? Well, that's not too bad then. I heard he'd hammered the fuck out of her.'

'And where did you hear that?'

'From your nan's bedroom actually. I heard everything, Debbie. Everything.'

His words were loaded and she knew it, but loaded with what?

'Don't let me dad find that out, Barry, or you'll be the next one getting flayed as you put it.'

Realising she had let him in on too much she turned from him and he watched as she teetered across the road. Her confident gait was gone, he noticed, and was glad. She was a slag.

Barry began the long walk back to Babs's. He had work to do and this must not interfere. He had a plan already forming in his mind and wanted to make sure he got it just right before he made it happen.

Susan's eyes were red-rimmed and the weight seemed to be dropping off her. It was three weeks now since the showdown at her granny's and she was still imprisoned in her bedroom. Her father and mother seemed set on keeping her here for the rest of her life and this scared her more than anything.

The school had been told she had had an accident and had sent work home for her. Susan had nearly laughed at the irony as her father had given her her schoolbooks and told her to get on with it all.

She was still not allowed to get dressed, not even to comb her hair. She knew she looked dreadful, even worse than usual. She also knew it was a psychological thing. Joey wanted to break her, and she was pretending that he had. She knew it was the only way out of her situation.

In her world the authorities were kept at bay with bullshit and aggression. It had always worked before and it always would. She knew that as clearly as she knew her own name and address. It was the reason her father walked the streets instead of being locked up and her mother lived her lifestyle.

They were the scum of the earth in everyone's eyes so no one expected any different from them. 'The underclass' they were called by sociologists. Susan knew all this, and she also knew that nothing would ever change it. It was inbred in them, too much a way of life to be changed by anything. Any government who thought they could change things should read the classics. There had always been families like the McNamaras and there always would be. They were a law unto themselves.

Debbie slipped into the room and Susan was glad to see her. Even though they did not really get on, she had come to rely on her sister's visits to keep her sane. Even Debbie's chatter was better than nothing.

'I just seen your bloke, Barry Dalston.'

This was said in a low voice and Susan felt her heart race at the words.

'What did he say?'

Debbie snorted nastily.

'He said to tell you hello. Not much of a conversationalist, is he? Even the blokes outside the pub could do better than that.'

It was more than enough for Susan in her isolated state, it was like a ten-page letter. He had not abandoned her, he knew the worst and still wanted to see her! She felt the pounding of her heart as it quickened. She had to get out of here, had to get back to some kind of normality.

'He's a wanker and if you have anything more to do with him you'll be sorry, Sue. If Dad knew there'd be murder done and you know that. Just let him go.'

Susan looked into her sister's painted face. All panstick and cheap mascara, she looked much older than her years, sounded much older too.

She sighed at the futility of their lives.

'How did he look?'

Debbie curled one pink-painted lip in a gesture of contempt.

'Well, put it this way, he didn't look like he was pining for you if that's what you mean.'

Susan knew that he had annoyed Debbie and was sorry for the fact. She could have been a go-between, but now it was out of the question and that depressed her even more.

'Have a nice time?'

Debbie shook her head.

'Nah, not really. The pub was fucking empty and Dave was with that slag Lynda from the buildings. What he sees in her I don't know. All tight skirts and make up.'

Debbie looked at herself in the mirror as she said this and Susan wondered how she didn't see that she was just like that herself.

In fact she was more made up than poor old Lynda, a good-looking girl who had to live down the fact that she was from an even worse family than their own. At least they had some cachet as the daughters of the local bullyboy. Not much to brag about, Susan knew, but in their world it afforded them a small amount of respect.

Lynda's father was an Irish drunk who beat their mother in the street and had got the two elder daughters pregnant before they were thirteen. But then, everyone knew about him. Pity they didn't know about Joey. That would put a stop to his gallop in more ways than one. Even the Bannermans and the Davidsons would balk at employing him then.

You could do a lot of things in the East End: murder, steal anything, inflict violence. But touch children, especially your family, or rape and you were on your own. It was an unwritten law.

'Did he look nice then – Barry?'

Debbie took pity on her sister and smiled.

'Yeah, he looked lovely. But listen to me, Sue, he reckons he was in Nan's when it all happened, and if that's true there'll be murders. I mean, if he was there why didn't Ivy say anything?'

Susan rolled her eyes to the ceiling.

'Why do you think? She likes him. Thinks he's all right. If Dad knew, imagine what he'd do to the old cow.'

They laughed at the thought of Ivy getting one over on the son she professed to adore.

'All the same, Sue, Dad wouldn't be a happy bunny if he knew.'

'Fuck him. I'm sick of thinking about him.'

The words were loaded and Debbie was quiet for a moment. The two girls looked into each other's eyes.

'He might not be your dad anyway. At least you can console yourself with that much.'

It was the first time Debbie had hinted at such a thing and Susan was grateful to her.

'If he ain't me dad, then who is?'

Debbie laughed gently.

'Well, not being funny, mate, but with Mother's track record that's a question that may never be answered.'

They laughed then, girls together, finding humour in the darkest of secrets and circumstances.

Sitting upright in bed Susan looked prettier than she had before. She was much slimmer and her dumpy legs had fined down.

'You look better than you did, Sue. Try and keep the weight off and you'll look great in no time.'

She shook her head.

'I don't really care what I look like, not any more. With my face and figure what chance have I got anyway? Barry liked me the way I was, or at least he told me he did. Not with words, of course, more with actions. You know.'

Debbie nodded. She knew Susan meant he wanted to sleep with her so ergo he must like her. Susan, she reasoned, for all her book reading knew nothing about blokes. They would sleep with anything at Barry's age, it was the law of youth and hormones.

'I'd better go. Mum's snoring off the lunchtime sherry and the old man's due in soon. I'll try and pop in later, all right?'

The phone started to ring and Debbie rushed from the room. She knew it would be for her.

Now their father was a gangster they had a phone. It was used by all the neighbours and the number was given out to relatives to ring if there was a problem, such as a death or a birth.

Susan found it laughable.

Debbie loved it, she felt as if she was the queen of the street now because of it – giving out the number to everyone and anyone with her eyebrows arched and her pert bottom arranged expertly to look the picture of the sophisticated phone owner.

Susan heard the front door open and sighed. Joey was home. Her life could only get more difficult now.

Joey had the raving hump. It was in the way he walked, the way he closed the door and in his face as he saw his eldest daughter curled up on the new Dralon telephone table-cum-chair.

He had been drinking, that much was evident, and he had also lost a lot of money on the horses. That much would not be evident until later in the day. Sufficient to say that one look at her father told Debbie to cut the call short. The sensible part of her brain was telling her this, but the stupid part of her wanted to talk to Dave who had apparently dumped Lynda from the buildings and had now rung her.

He was trying to talk her into going back down the pub. She was going to go back down the pub but her womanly instincts told her to make him beg first. If her father had the hump then that was his look out, not hers.

'Get off that fucking phone, I'm waiting for an important call.'

Debbie put her hand over the receiver and whispered, 'Two minutes, Dad, that's all.' She put the phone back to her ear and carried on talking to Dave.

Joey watched her and in his drunken state his daughter's heavily made up face and tight clothes registered on his brain.

It could have been June sitting there twenty years before. For some reason this annoyed him. Debbie annoyed him just by looking like her mother. Everyone annoyed him tonight.

'Get off the fucking phone, Debs, or I'll rip it out of the wall.'

As he spoke he took the phone from her and slammed it back on to the cradle.

Debbie jumped up from the mock Tudor love seat and bellowed, 'What you fucking think you're doing? I was talking to someone.'

She had no fear of her father, he always let her get away with everything. She picked up the phone again and started to dial a number. Ripping the phone from her hands, Joey threw it against the wall. It crashed to the floor in pieces.

Debbie's eyes were like saucers as she looked at her father.

'Well, that was clever, weren't it? No fucking phone now for you, me or anyone.'

She dragged her coat off the hook by the front door and started putting it on.

'Where are you going, madam?'

Her father's voice was dangerously low but Debbie was too angry to care.

'Out. What does it look like?'

Joey stepped towards her.

'You ain't going nowhere, lady, you hear me? And you talk to me with a bit of respect. I'm your father not some kid off the street.'

'Piss off, Dad, you're drunk.'

Her dismissive words were like a knife through his brain. June had woken up at the noise and come into the hallway.

'What's going on now?'

Joey looked at her. She looked terrible; her make up was smudged, her clothes creased.

'What's going on, June? I'll tell you what's going on. Your daughter is talking to me like I am a piece of shit. Now I wonder where the fuck she could have got that from, eh? Not you and that other fat cunt in the bedroom by any chance?'

He dragged Debbie roughly towards her mother and pushed the two women into the lounge.

'You,' he pointed at Debbie, 'are going nowhere. And you, lady,' he pointed at his wife, 'are not going anywhere either. What the fuck am I in this house, eh? I earn the wedge, I put the food on the table and clothe the lot of you, me mother included. And you two treat me like I'm the local fucking nonsense. Well, not any more.'

He was bellowing now, his face red with temper and fists clenched ready to strike them.

He looked at them in disbelief, his anger so acute he felt capable of taking on the whole Metropolitan Police Force and winning the battle if he did. He had had a day that would make anyone upset and the family he provided for, looked after and cared for, were mugging him off.

Today he had lost not only his own money but a debt he had been paid to pull in. Consequently he was three grand down and had no way of getting by that night when he was supposed to give the money to Davey Davidson.

The worst of it all was it wasn't a debt he could go and collect again, which he had done numerous times over the last few years. People paid up twice if you frightened them enough. Davey knew this man and he was sound. Joey knew he could not trounce him, Davey would not allow that.

'Who's rattled your cage then? What you done to make you like this?'

June, ever the voice of reason, opened her mouth before thinking twice. Joey looked at her for a full minute, then answered.

'I have lost three grand over you, that's what I have done.'

She was stunned.

'Over me? How could you lose it over me?'

Joey shook his head as if he could not believe what she'd said.

'The horse was called June's Surprise. I backed it because I'd heard it was a good earner, but like my dear wife it was left at the fucking starting gate. It was useless – fucking diabolical in fact. I have seen fucking hamsters with more go in them.'

June stared at him. Then, her voice as incredulous as her husband's had been, she screamed: 'And so it's my fault, is it? The horse lost and it's *my* fault. You're a fucking head case, Joey. Now piss off back out and leave us alone.'

Debbie started to button up her coat.

'I'm going out, I ain't staying in listening to this lot.'

Joey looked at his wife and daughter through hooded eyes.

'Make her take that coat off, June, or I take oath I will rip it off her fucking back and everything else the little slag is wearing into the bargain.'

He shook his head again as if clearing it.

'What you doing letting them walk about like whores anyway? Look at her, like mother like fucking daughter. A pair of slags together here.'

He pointed at June.

'Go and get the other one from the bedroom then I can look at the three whores in my house at once.'

'I ain't a whore, Dad, don't you dare call me that.'

Debbie was upset now as she realised her father was not going to let her out of the house and Dave was going to be down the pub by himself.

'Even my poor mother would have done a better job of raising these girls than you, June. I must have been off my rocker to have you back after your stint with that Scottish pimp.'

'You didn't have me back, mate, I came back . . .'

Joey interrupted her, raising his fist to quieten her.

'I had you back, you two-faced cunt. I took you back after you'd shagged that ponce and all his mates, I bet. Why change the habits of a lifetime, eh? Not good old June the margarine legs of fucking Bethnal Green. Spreads easily does June. Your mother should have named you Marge.'

Normally Debbie would have laughed at her father's words but tonight it was not the usual fighting, it was more serious. Both she and her mother guessed as much and were careful of him.

'Please let me out, Dad, I have to see someone.'

Joey mimicked her.

'Let me out, Dad, I have to see someone. Who the fuck you got to see? You're only a little kid. You should be in here doing what kids do, not hanging round a fucking notorious pub. That's your mother's job, love, not yours.'

'Let her go out. Your mother's coming round, she'll keep an eye on her if need be.'

Joey looked bitterly at his wife and daughter.

'That's right, take advantage of my poor old mum. At least I can depend on her, even if she is a silly old bag at times. At least she's loyal to me and mine. Not like you lot, you grasping bastards.'

As he spoke Debbie was once more trying to do up her coat. She had had enough of her father for one night and was going out whether he liked it or not.

'Talking of your mother, Dad, did you know that the night you went round after our Susan her boyfriend Barry was in Nan's bedroom, listening to everything that went on? I know because he told me. Tonight actually. So your mother's not as loyal as you thought, eh?'

When Joey's hand caught her by the throat Debbie knew real fear for the first time in her life.

'What did you say, you cunt? What did you just say? Who was there . . . are you trying to tell me Barry Dalston was in my mother's flat that night? Is that what you're telling me?'

He was shrieking with rage.

'Jesus fuck, Jesus fuck, are you telling me he heard everything?'

June was trying to drag him off her daughter and she was frightened. Frightened because in her heart she knew what was scaring Joey so much. He had been found out.

She didn't know what she was going to do.

'Leave her be, Joey. Leave her be, for fuck's sake. You'll kill her.'

As Joey let go of his daughter she fell back against her mother and they both collapsed on to the settee, Debbie gasping for air.

Joey, who'd had enough problems for one night, was literally terrified now. Barry Dalston knew his business, knew what he was. Exposure was the one thing he dreaded above all and he wanted to kill the boy stone dead.

'I'll fucking kill him! I will, I'll kill the ponce.'

Debbie was crying with shock and fear. She knew that she had opened up a can of worms that could never, ever be closed again. They would wriggle into everything from this moment on, defiling everything they touched.

'The ponce! The bastard! I will fucking take his head off his shoulders and bury it in shit.'

June stood up. Taking Joey's hands in hers, she walked him to a chair.

'Sit down, Joey, sit down. Think about it. Who'll listen to him anyway?'

Debbie listened to her mother calming her father down and resisted the urge to vomit. June was sorting everything out once more, but what she was doing was wrong and even Debbie knew that.

'Who is he anyway? A kid – a silly kid with a crush on our

Susan. Though what he ever saw in that bitch I do not know. Let it go, Joey. After all, what did you do, eh? You did what any other father would have done. You sorted her out after she had beaten up her own mother, the woman who gave birth to her. That's all. What else can it be, eh?'

The voice of reason was penetrating the drink and Joey started to calm down. No one would accuse him of anything. He just had to make sure the boy kept his trap shut, that was all. And he had not actually *seen* anything, thank Christ.

'As for the money, I have it. I have enough to give to Davey so stop worrying.'

Joey looked into her face.

'No, you don't, June. You don't have any money at all.'

Her eyes narrowed.

'What do you mean?'

He wiped a hand across his sweating face. The gesture was like admitting defeat to June. 'I had that away. I knew what you had done with it and did the bet today to try and recoup me losses. Believe me, June, this fucking horse was a dead cert . . .'

She was stunned.

'You're having me on, Joey? Tell me you're joking, please?'

She knew as she spoke that the money was gone. Gone for good.

'You stupid, stupid man! You took our stake, you took our little bit of security and fucking blew it on a bastard horse? Now you'll have Davey Davidson knocking for a debt you ain't got. He'll go fucking ballistic. Three grand is three grand, Joey. What the fuck was you thinking of?'

But she knew he would not answer, there was nothing he could say.

'Me tom will have to go to pawn, I'll go round uncle's now and see what I can salvage. He might loan us the rest anyway – our credit's good enough these days with you working regular. Whatever, Davey must have his poke. If he thinks you're unreliable then we are up shit creek without a paddle. Without his good will you're nothing, Joey, and the sooner you realise that the better off we'll all be.'

She pointed at Debbie.

'You, get that fucking coat on and come with me, right? I need a hand with this, I ain't walking the streets on me own with three grand in me bag.'

Then she pointed at Joey.

'You, get yourself in a cold bath and fucking sober up before Davey comes for his dosh. Tell him anything but keep him here until we get back with the money, okay? Are you listening to me?'

Joey nodded.

Storming from the room, June went in to Susan.

'Get up, get dressed and sober your father up. Make him coffee and something to eat, whatever he says. Force him to eat something even if it's only toast, right? You've heard enough to know we're all in the shit so my advice is, get yourself in there and maybe, just maybe, you might be out of the place in a day or two because of your help.'

Susan nodded. She had heard every word and would do anything at this moment to forget what had taken place tonight. She needed to get out now more than ever. Barry would have to be warned, and warned well. Her father was capable of murder rather than being found out and Barry needed that point impressed on him as soon as possible.

Susan started to dress.

Marcus Stein was a nice man. He was short but stocky with a kind smile and the sad brown eyes of his ancestors.

On Tuesday nights he liked to visit his little girl, as he thought of Babs, and then to have a drink in the pub with his cronies before giving his takings to his nephew Jacob. Jacob was the son he had never had, his sister's son, everything a boy should be. Strong, handsome, industrious. Marcus would leave him his business one day happy in the knowledge that he was leaving it in good hands. His wife Rita was bedridden and had been for most of their married life.

The market was a good screw but the real earner was acting as an unlicensed uncle to the Jewish community. He loaned money

– small amounts at first. Now he pulled in between three and five grand a week. All in all his life was good.

As he approached Babs's house Marcus straightened his tie and slicked down his wispy grey hair. It was important to him to look presentable even for a girl he was paying.

As the iron cosh came down on the back of his head he felt only the first sting of pain. Barry kicked him five times in the head; he wanted to make sure the old man was not getting up and calling for help until he was well away. It was so easy he was amazed.

Marcus Stein was not about to call for anyone. His heart had given out in an instant; he was dead before he hit the ground.

Barry did not even bother to see how he was. Instead he riffled the man's pockets, took everything he had including his watch and diamond ring, then pushed him into a pile of rubbish waiting to be collected on the pavement, covering the old man with empty boxes and old food. Then, whistling, Barry tripped down the road towards his home.

Marcus was as far from his mind as an elephant's trunk as he planned what to do with his ill-gotten loot. He decided to go home and think about the next step in his life. The one that would take him into the world of the Davidsons and then hopefully the Bannermans.

Life was indeed good if you constantly pushed to better yourself. He was up for whatever was going, and he was going to get whatever he wanted.

As he walked he passed June and Debbie. Crossing the street, he studiously ignored them. Time enough to upset that little lot later, and time was something he had a lot of. He smiled at the thought and kept on walking home.

Marcus Stein was dead and gone but Barry Dalston was still alive and kicking. Kicking being the operative word in Barry's case.

Chapter Nine

June realised that her husband was very worried and that annoyed her. Joey always got himself into trouble then expected it to sort itself out without actually doing anything himself.

Like the money. He had taken *her* money and used it, the money she did not even realise he knew about. Now she had had to pawn her gold jewellery to try and salvage her husband's so-called career.

Davey, as luck would have it, did not arrive at the flat until after her return with the money, and the trouble she had had getting it was unbelievable. Uncle had insisted on her signing a loan form that guaranteed repayment in twenty-one days or he would ask Davey Davidson to have the money collected. It was laughable really because Davey would normally get Joey to pull it in and that would be the height of embarrassment. Not that he would be embarrassed, he would find it hilarious after a couple of drinks – and then decide to kill whoever dared to try and pull in his debt.

It would not occur to him that someone like Davey might not find it as funny as he did. That Davey might see it as a right piss take and therefore decide that his Number One had to be taught a lesson, one that would need to be very violent as befitting someone with Joey's rep.

Plus, unlike everyone else, Davey Davidson knew that Joey had not murdered Jimmy. Joey himself now believed that he had killed him, such was his mentality. He really believed he had shot and killed Jimmy and consequently told everyone in a roundabout way how he'd planned and executed it without actually saying outright he'd done it.

Yet he knew people believed it was him, knew what he was doing in that respect.

Now it was down to June as usual to sort everything out, keep everything going. What on earth had possessed her to come back to him?

But in her heart of hearts she knew the answer to that. It was easy and it was what she knew.

June knew she thrived on aggravation, on constant trouble and excitement. It had been ingrained in her as a child and now she had got the habit. Unless she was in pieces inside, June did not feel really alive. Did not feel real. The worse her life was, the more vindicated she felt, as if she deserved all the trouble she accumulated through the course of an average day. There were times when she actively sought trouble from Joey, upset him to cause the explosion of violence she needed to keep her adrenaline levels up.

In reality, Joey was all she wanted. He was such a scummy, devious, violent criminal that whatever she did he would swallow because he wasn't sure anyone else would have him. They wore people out. They wore each other out. That was the secret they shared, and what kept them together.

If June thought about it too much it frightened her.

Barry looked at Babs and smiled. She smiled back, happy with the two thousand pounds he had given her and pleased that there were no comebacks from anyone. She did not know as yet that Marcus was dead, knew only that Barry Dalston had given her the money to pay off her fines and some over for enjoyment and some bits and pieces for her daughter.

As she counted the notes again Barry marvelled at the toms' disregard for the money they earned. It was easy money to them, a bottomless pit of men paying for the use of their bodies.

He would never understand it in a million years.

'Listen, Babs, I could get us a good little earner if you wanted me to.'

She frowned.

'Doing what exactly?'

Barry smiled and winked.

'Doing fuck all, Babs. That's the beauty of it really. I wait while you bring the punters, then I roll them.'

Babs started to shake her head before he had even finished talking.

'Sorry, Barry, but no way. I ain't getting involved with all that. Anyway Jonah would skin me alive if he knew about last night. Thanks, mate, but no thanks.'

There was a finality in her voice that annoyed him.

'What do you mean, no? You could pull in a fortune . . .'

She interrupted him.

'Last night was a one off. I would have asked Jonah to do it but I knew he would keep the money for himself or lie and say there wasn't as much as usual.'

That barb hit home and Barry nearly blushed.

'At least with you I got a percentage, Bal. Other than that I'm not up for any more scams. I do me job, I get me poke and that's it really. I ain't ambitious otherwise I wouldn't be a tom. I don't even want to work in the clubs like most girls, couldn't be bothered with all the dressing up and the competition. But I do appreciate the offer, thanks.'

She smiled to take the sting out of her refusal and Barry knew he had to swallow it.

'Not only that, Jonah would skin us both alive – and I mean both of us. Don't be misled by his friendly manner and the act he puts on. He's a vicious bastard, all pimps are. They have to be.'

Barry shrugged.

'It's your loss, Babs. There's plenty would snap me arm off for a chance like this.'

'I'm sure there are, Barry, and I wish you well. But one last thing. How much did you collar in the end?'

He grinned. 'Never you mind. Enough for what I wanted.'

When he left ten minutes later he felt strangely depressed. Not just because he knew Babs had sussed him out and had known he was having her over, but because she'd expected him to do it.

All in all he had four grand, four thousand lovely sobs to spend. He had already given his mother a ton, and a hundred quid had cheered her up no end. She had not asked where he had got it, and she wouldn't.

Now it was time to put his plan into action and he was nervous about it. The night before he had not been able to sleep. Not because he had mugged an old man – that was nothing, just work – but because his actions today would either bring about the dream he cherished or would once and for all slam the door in his face and make him an enemy for life.

But, he reasoned, he would have an enemy either way. It was just he could keep his eye on the enemy if everything worked out the way he wanted it to.

He made his way to the Victory, a small drinking club in Bethnal Green where he knew Joey McNamara would be until lunchtime. As he tapped on the heavy wooden door Barry was sweating. He could feel the sweat trickling down his armpits and made a conscious effort to compose himself. A small grid was exposed as the top of the door was opened.

'What you want?'

The voice was abrupt.

Barry took a deep breath before answering. He was pleased that his voice was not quavering in the least.

'I need to see Joey McNamara. Tell him it's important.'

'Who wants him?'

Barry sighed.

'Never you mind, it's private. Just tell him he's needed out here, all right?'

The grid disappeared as the shutter was forced back into place, and now that he had started Barry felt a surge of uncertainty again. Joey might decide to kill him stone dead. After all, he was hardly Joey's favourite person. He might even roll Barry, perish the thought. Suddenly he was glad he didn't have the dosh on him.

He was kept waiting for five minutes and it seemed like hours. The sweat really was taking hold now and he was convinced he could smell himself.

Fear made his heart race and his legs feel weak. He was regretting everything, and wondering whether he could sneak off and forget the whole business. Then the door was unbolted and there before him stood Joey.

He squinted out into the gloom then his face set into a snarl.

'What the fuck do you want?'

The doorman laughed. 'Shall I evict him for you, Joe?'

Walking towards him, Barry saw what made people wary of Joey McNamara. It was his stance, his very movements that were intimidating.

'Nah, Colin, I'll evict this cunt meself.'

Barry raised his arms as if in self-defence even though nothing had as yet happened.

'Hang on, Joey, I have something I think will interest you. All I'm doing is paying my respects, that's all. I had a tickle and I'm just bringing your due. No more, no less.'

Joey's eyes screwed up and he said incredulously, 'What are you – a fucking brief? Bringing me me due . . . you sure?'

He turned to the doorman and laughed.

'Did you cop that lot, Colin? I have been accosted by a fucking dictionary.'

The big man laughed loudly.

'Well, rip out his index then.'

Barry listened fearfully.

Joey began to push him none too gently towards the street. The street and people. People who would see him beaten to within an inch of his life if he wasn't careful.

'Look, Joey, like I say I have just had a bit of a tickle and I'm bringing you your twenty-five percent, that's all. I was told I had to do it. Everyone had to do it. I know you don't like me, but this is business.'

Joey stopped dead.

'How much you get?'

The money was always the angle with Joey and Barry had banked on that.

'Four grand. I rolled someone last night.'

He was unsure whether he should tell the truth but decided he ought to in case Joey knew more than he was letting on.

Joey was impressed.

'Four grand? How you manage that, Sonny Jim? My daughter been teaching you the tricks of her father's trade, eh? Along with everything else. I know all about you sneaking around me mother's house, boy, I know all about it. Debbie grassed you up, sonny. Now I reckon it will cost you that whole four grand to keep me sweet.'

Barry knew that this was the make or break time.

'I was there, I admit that, Joey . . .'

Joey's fist hit him in the jaw but he was ready for it and stayed on his feet.

'He's a game little Jock, ain't he, Colin?'

Turning round Joey bellowed, 'You get back inside, this is private. Family business.'

Colin disappeared.

'So what did you hear, eh? A father giving his daughter a hiding, teaching her a lesson.'

Barry nodded.

''Course. What else?'

He frowned as if wondering what Joey was talking about. They both knew it was an act but that did not matter at the moment.

Barry brought out a pack of cigarettes and offered them to Joey. He took one and they lit up in silence. But it was an act of reconciliation, they both knew that. Each in their own way knew they were going to strike an unlikely bargain and neither knew where it would lead.

'So where's me grand then, boy?'

'I've got it whenever you want it.'

Joey nodded.

'That will be sooner rather than later, mate. Where did it come from? No one I'm minding, I trust.'

Barry shook his head.

'I done an uncle, a money-lender off the market, late last night. Marcus something or other. A front wheel skid. I had him as he went to a tom's house, sweet as a nut. Got six grand in all, two for the tom, three for me and one for you. I intend to make it a regular thing, I have the contacts now.'

He was ribbing and they both knew that.

132

Joey drew deeply on his cigarette.

'What about the money to the tom? That's five hundred sobs she owes me.'

Barry was nonplussed for a moment, until he saw Joey's grin.

'Fuck the tom. A grand is a grand as my old dad used to say.'

Joey was over the moon. He had recouped a thousand of the three he owed the uncle.

'Actually, I have a little earner for you meself, if you're interested?'

Barry nodded so hard he nearly took his own head off his shoulders.

'If you like killing uncles, then I have the perfect man for you. Come in and have a drink and we'll talk about it, eh?'

Barry felt as if God Himself had finally realised he was alive and had decided to bestow everything he had ever wanted on him in one day. As Joey put an arm around his shoulders and led him into the Victory, a place he had never thought would be open to him, Barry swelled with pride.

All he needed now was an in with Susan once more and he was set like a jelly.

Murder did not bother him at all; his own father had been murdered. In their world it was just an occupational hazard, a chance you took, a chance you used if you had to.

Joey wanted another uncle trounced and for completely selfish reasons. If the man he owed the three grand to was dead, then all debts died with him. Another very handy unwritten law of the turf.

All in all he was beginning to think that his Susan had better taste in men than he had at first thought. He could like this boy, if only because he was a lamb going to the slaughter. Unable to see further than his own nose and impressed for all the wrong reasons, Barry could be moulded into something, used for Joey's own ends and then left to take the rap.

Joey would set people up and Barry execute the acts of violence and robbery, leaving Joey with the wedge and the kudos of being number one bailiff to the criminal community, while at the same time earning off the people stupid enough not to have him as their protection.

Something he would offer them after the first attack.

Davey Davidson was going to love him, and it was all because of this young man. Life had a funny way of making you rich. His own father had always said that and now Joey understood what he'd meant.

June looked at Susan and sighed. Her daughter looked better than she had in ages. The bruising was gone and with her weight loss she looked quite attractive. But the closeness they had once shared was gone for good.

June was jealous of her daughter, and inside knew that she had failed to protect her as a real mother should. But how could she have done? There'd been no precedent in her own early life and June's mothering instincts had long ago withered and died.

It wasn't as if Joey had hurt her or anything – Christ, she was quick enough to jump on that Barry's bones, so what was the difference really? Anyway, Joey had sworn to her that he had not really done anything and June chose to believe him whatever the truth of it all. As he said, he had her. What would he want Susan for anyway, ugly bitch that she was? He could have the pick of the local women with his creds and his rep.

Ever since she was a small child Susan had caused trouble and now she was growing up she had to face the consequences of her own actions. To attack her own mother was a disgrace and she had to be taught a lesson.

'You finished those potatoes then?'

Susan nodded and started to clear the peelings from the sink.

'You chipped them yet?'

She nodded once again and started to clean out the sink and wash down the draining board. The slump of the girl's shoulders made June feel angry, and at the same time she felt a surge of sorrow for her daughter. Pouring herself another drink, she swallowed it down in one gulp.

Ivy let herself in at the front door and June swore under her breath at her mother-in-law's loud voice.

'Only me, thought I'd come and see me family.'

As she walked into the kitchen Susan nodded hello and June said nastily, 'What do you want?'

Ivy ignored her and put the kettle on for a hot toddy. She had seen the whisky bottle as soon as she walked in and she had another cold.

Ivy had had a cold all her life.

No one spoke. When the kettle boiled, Ivy poured hot water into a mug. She sat at the kitchen table, her hand hovering over the bottle until June allowed her to pour herself a generous measure.

'I been down the market. Guess what? Marcus Stein was found dead last night. Beaten to death he was by a thug. What is the world coming to? Lovely man, for a Jew. I remember during the war, he made sure we all had a few bob if the old man was away. Had no kids of his own, see, so he liked everyone else's. His sister's boy was the apple of his eye. He'll be worth a few quid now. I reckon Marcus must have been worth a bit. Uncles always are.'

June listened with sadness. She had used him a few times herself over the years. The reason she had not used him last night was because she already owed him from years ago. It was only Joey's rep that had stopped Marcus from calling in the debt. Unlike the other uncles he was not under the protection of the Davidsons and consequently got mugged off now and again.

'Poor man. He was ever so nice, Ivy. Never tried to get you to pay the debt in kind and a lot of them do that. Remember old Isaac? Dirty old fucker he was.'

Ivy nodded, eyes shining with whisky and malice.

'You know who was one of his best customers, don't you? Mary Hanson. Christ, she used to keep us in fits when the kids was small, telling us all about what he wanted her to do and everything. Her old man knew, encouraged it even. She was into Isaac for a small fortune when he died. We all joked he would leave her something in his will – and he did. He left her a bracelet her mother had pawned years before. Ain't that a weird one!'

June roared with laughter.

'I remember him.'

Ivy stopped laughing.

'You never, June!'

She topped up their drinks and said jokily, 'Well, you'll never know, Ivy, will you? Give you something to think about on the long winter nights in bed on your own.'

Susan rolled her eyes at their talk and looked out of the kitchen window at the estate gardens. As she looked out she got the biggest fright of her life.

'Mum! Mum, you'd better come and see this.'

June went to her daughter.

'What now, Susan? You're getting a right fucking nose bag, just like your granny.'

Ivy joined them at the window.

'Oh, for fuck's sake. What are them two doing out there?'

She was amazed to see her son and Susan's boyfriend crossing the grass together.

June laughed. 'Oh, by the way, Joey knows you had Barry in the flat the night he give Susan her justs so I'd be careful of your beloved little soldier today, Ivy. He's out to hang you from the rafters.'

She was terrified.

The two men went out of sight and they could hear them coming up the stairs. All three women felt their breath stop at exactly the same time. Then they heard it. The noise was deafening and they looked at one another in shock. The two men were singing. At the top of their voices, they were singing. 'I'm Forever Blowing Bubbles' was blaring out all over the estate as they vied with one another to sing the loudest.

They came along the balcony towards the front door and heard Maud next door cry, 'Give us another shot of that, Joe.'

Joey and Barry did as they were asked and stood outside the window, grinning like idiots and singing their hearts out.

'Now I have seen fucking everything.'

June's voice was amazed.

Susan ran from the kitchen to the bedroom to repair her make up and try and look pretty She did not know what had occurred and did not care. Barry was coming into her home and she was amazed, excited and jubilant.

The front door was opened and the two men fell into the hallway.

'Junie, get me and my friend a drink and some grub in that order, please.'

June looked at her husband as if she had never seen him before and he smiled. Taking the thousand pounds out of his pocket Joey threw it at her, the money going all over the place.

'There's a grand there and plenty more where that came from. Stash it in your drawers, girl, keep it safe from prying hands.'

'That's the last place you want to put it then.'

Ivy's voice was jocular but nasty.

Joey turned on her.

'Shut up, you. You're still in me bad books.' Then he hugged her. 'You know me mother, Barry? Dirty, smelly, full of cobwebs but she's good with the kids.'

Barry laughed uproariously as they all did. Ivy loved it, even the insult. It was a sign that she was forgiven.

'Eggs, chips and tomatoes and a nice little drink, June, pronto. For me and me new partner.' Joey looked around him. 'Where's our Susan then?'

'Making herself presentable.'

He grinned. 'Fuck me, we ain't got that much time, we're going out again at seven.'

Everyone laughed again. Especially Ivy and June. Barry laughed but hollowly.

'Go in the bedroom, son, and drag her out. Once you marry them they look more frightening than a fucking Hammer Horror in the mornings. I should know. Look at June. Someone asked me once if I would rent her out for scaring crows for the summer.'

Ivy roared now but June did not find it at all amusing and showed it by pursing her lips.

'Very funny, Joey. What's your next trick, dropping down dead?'

He looked at the ceiling in mock fear.

'I have upset her who must be obeyed. Now the fucking eggs and chips will be cooked to within an inch of their lives.'

June grinned.

'Go through to the lounge and we'll get you something to soak up the drink, all right?'

'Christ Himself knows they need it, June. I'll give you a hand,' Ivy offered.

Susan came out of the bedroom then and Barry smiled at her. Joey felt a flicker of jealousy and swallowed it down. He could have his cake and eat it if he was clever, and he was clever. No one knew as yet just how clever he was. The drink was making him unstable and he decided he needed to sit down. He dragged himself into the lounge and collapsed on the sofa.

Susan looked better than Barry had thought she would. She was slimmer and that emphasised her two major attractions. Barry was quite happy to let Joey take the piss, he knew he would have the last laugh.

Susan watched her mother as she observed the two of them getting acquainted after so long and hoped against hope that Barry would not do or say anything to cause dissent.

He did not as yet understand the vagaries of McNamara family life. Joey could change in a split second and then Barry would be unceremoniously thrown from the flat. Things like that had happened before and Susan was hoping against hope they would not happen today.

'Ain't he a lovely little fella, June?'

Ivy's voice was wistful and June snorted.

'He's just like Joey, but she won't see that, silly whore that she is.'

She walked into the kitchen. Despite herself she was annoyed with her daughter. Susan had got herself a handful, as the East Enders would say, and June herself wished she was young enough to be embarking on life once more. At least, she wished she was younger while knowing exactly what she knew now. Susan's bright eyes and happy expression made her feel old and tired.

'I like that young Barry, I think he's a nice boy. Too good for that madam. Now if it was Debbie, I could understand it.'

'Debbie, love her heart, is lacking in the two things that make

Susan interesting to all men. And I don't have to spell out what they are, do I?'

Ivy nodded sagely.

'Down her knees after the first kid, then round her ankles after the second. You mark my words.'

This cheered June up and she laughed.

'He'd better make the most of them, girl, before he has to chase the fuckers round the bed!'

It did not occur to either of them that Susan was fourteen years old and should not even have been contemplating sex, babies or anything else.

They both knew the score. It was the way they all lived and it would never change as far as they could see. Sex kept their world going, kept them interested and kept them amused. It was free, it felt good, and at times it gave a woman great power.

Because Susan looked older they treated her as an adult. What she had seen and witnessed all her life made her seem like an ancient in comparison with most of her peers. Neither woman saw anything wrong in how they behaved towards the girls or around them. As far as they were concerned Susan and Debbie were already women. Susan was expected to learn earlier because she was so well developed. It did not occur to either of them that her being so well developed at such a young age might be a good reason to protect her from men. They saw it as a natural progression. You grew up, you got a body and you used it, which was exactly what they had both done. They did not think in terms of emotional development, that was beyond their comprehension.

The girl talked as they did, knew what they knew, because they talked about and let her see things that most people would hide from their children. Therefore they'd assumed Susan must understand it all, which she didn't. She let Barry do what he did because that was how she would keep him. That was what she had been taught all her life.

She did not even expect his fidelity, that was not something within her experience.

As the women made the meal they chatted about past times

and reminisced about their respective youths. Susan was just another victim of careless people. People who lived careless lives.

In Susan's bedroom Barry was trying to kiss her and she was nervous about her father.

'Come on, Susan, I didn't go through all this for nothing, girl.'

His Scots accent sounded sexy to her as did everything he said.

'Me dad's only outside the door, he'd go mad if he came in.'

Barry grinned.

'He ain't coming in here, lassie. Now will you pull your top out of your skirt before I have to go and find someone more available?'

The words were said jokingly but the threat was there nevertheless. He pinched her breasts hard.

'I've missed these, Susan. The other girls' are nothing in comparison.'

She basked in the compliment.

He kissed her hard on the lips.

'I have your father eating out of my hand so stop your worrying, girl.'

Susan kissed him back with all the feeling of a young girl in love for the first time.

Barry knew he excited her even though he also knew she got nothing from the sex. He knew Susan would never, ever like it. It was not in her nature. She expected him to be in charge and would concentrate on keeping him happy.

'In future you're mine, you hear what I'm telling you? No one else can come near you, right?'

He looked down into her eyes and she knew he meant her father and nodded solemnly.

'No one else, Barry, I promise you. I ain't like that, honestly.'

She was apologising as she would all her life with him. Telling him that her father took her whether she liked it or not and that in future she would fight him, make him fight her for it.

But that meant she would be half murdered. So she decided there and then that she would go along with them both and keep them both sweet so she could have what she really wanted.

Barry Dalston.

He was like a shining light to her, a beacon to guide her. He would not know what was happening because she would not tell him. Her father would never stop. Because he did not want to stop, she knew that.

She would do anything for Barry Dalston. To have Barry Dalston. She thought he was worth it. More than worth it. She loved him. Really, really loved him. And all because he was nice to her, was presentable and someone everyone of their age respected.

He was a Jack the lad, a villain, a lovable rogue. He was the sort all girls in her environment wanted to hook, a man before he was supposed to be a man. A bloke who looked after you just by being with you. He gave you kudos and respect.

She did not see him as a younger version of Joey, a younger criminal with a selfish streak and a vicious temper. A coward really who conned people and tried to control them by fear and intimidation.

She saw only a handsome boy who cared about her in his own way. And for Susan McNamara, that was more than enough.

As he lifted her up the wall attempting to enter her she closed her eyes and imagined they were in a nice little flat with nice furniture and nice kids.

As he pushed inside her she winced and stroked the back of his neck, a caress that seemed to spur him on because he came almost immediately. He sagged against her. She felt the warmth as his semen trickled down her legs.

Barry looked down at her and smiled. Kissing her on the lips he bit into them, making her wince, and she knew he was leaving a mark for her father, a little reminder of who she really wanted. This depressed her momentarily until, seeing her expression, he pushed her head against his chest and whispered, 'I love you, Sue.'

Overcome with joy, she nearly shouted out with glee.

'I love you too, Barry, more than anyone in the world.'

He poked one finger gently into her cheek.

'You see you do, girl, or you'll know all about it, mate.'

As he pulled away from her to tidy his clothes she watched him. He was like a god to her and she felt he really was godlike. From his broad shoulders to his gorgeous eyes, Barry was everything a young girl could want.

Especially a young girl from her background and environment. As they left the room Susan was glowing. Her face looked almost pretty and her skin was radiant with health and vitality. June noticed it as did Ivy. Joey saw the change in her at once and decided that until the time was right he would lead them both on.

This young man would collar for him, take the heat and do the real work. Joey knew that opportunities like Barry Dalston came along only once or twice in a lifetime. If it all went pear-shaped it was young Barry who would do the bird. Then Joey would groom someone else.

He smiled at the lovebirds, noticed Susan's swollen lips and the smile disappeared. But there was plenty of time to put a spoke in there; all Joey wanted at the moment was money.

Plenty of money.

And young Barry seemed to think he could provide it.

June smiled at her daughter for the first time in weeks and Susan was grateful. But only because she didn't want Barry knowing too much about the family set up. He would in time, of course, if he had not already sussed it all out.

As Ivy put another fried egg on his plate Barry looked up and smiled at her. Then he began to tell a story about his dead father and they all laughed in the right places. Susan felt as if her heart would burst with pride as she listened to him.

For all the pain she had experienced in the last few weeks, Barry was more than worth it. She was absolutely sure of that.

After all, Susan McNamara was in love.

Chapter Ten

'Oh, Mum, you look lovely, really lovely.'

June basked in her daughter's praise. She was glad now that she had listened to Susan and not Debbie. The pale blue fitted suit did wonders for her figure and brought out the colour of her eyes. It was the sort of suit a real lady would wear, someone who appeared in the pages of a magazine. With it she wore a pillbox hat of the same shade with a half veil that made her look mysterious and interesting.

For the first time in her life she felt like a million dollars.

Debbie sighed.

'Well, I preferred the trouser suit but it docs look nice, Mum. You look too posh for us lot to be honest.'

June ignored the barb. Debbie was getting to be a right sarcastic little mare and it was beginning to get on her nerves.

'You're not wearing that, Debs, surely?'

Susan's voice was high.

Debbie turned in front of the mirror and shrugged.

'What's wrong with it?'

Susan shook her head sadly.

'What's right with it? You look a right whore. Wear the dress I bought you. I want this day to look lovely in all me photos. Please, Debs. Just for me.'

'Fuck off, Susan. Anyone would think no one had ever been married before. I ain't schlepping round in a lemon cotton short-sleeved dress for no fucker. I'd never live it down. All me mates would be laughing at me.'

'Yes, you fucking will, Debbie, or you ain't going.'

No one was more surprised than Debbie at her mother's words.

'Susan's right, that dress looks classy and you'll wear it, lady. You'll also get that make up off. This is a church wedding, not a fucking disco.'

Debbie sighed heavily.

She looked at herself in the mirror. She was wearing a denim dress that fitted where it touched and a pair of high platform shoes. Her short fat legs were exposed to their utmost and she looked ridiculous.

Her make up was thick as usual, and inexpertly applied, too much being the order of the day. Fashion was very important to Debbie, whether the current fashion suited her or not.

'I ain't telling you again. Get changed and have a bath, you dirty little whore.'

Debbie was fuming now.

'How could I have a bath with Fatty in there all morning, and then you until now?'

Susan and June laughed.

'Come off it, Debs, washing's never been one of your favourite pursuits, has it?' Susan teased.

'Why can't you speak fucking English like everyone else?'

Debbie stormed from the room.

June sighed.

'She's a right ponce her, always arguing. I don't know where she gets it from, I really don't.'

Susan raised her eyebrows but did not answer. She wanted her wedding day to go without a hitch.

'Your hair looks beautiful, Susan. Mind you, you always had nice hair even as a kid.'

June's sixteen-year-old daughter turned awkwardly in the chair because of her heavy pregnancy and smiled.

'I'm glad I had something going for me, Mum. Me boatrace left a lot to be desired.'

Today Susan's face had been made up by a beautician and her hair had been professionally styled. It was piled on top of her head with curls all around the outside. A halo of paper flowers had been woven through for the veil to be attached, and with her skin glowing from her pregnancy she looked almost beautiful.

June stared at her.

'Pity Barry didn't get out of prison earlier. You're big, girl. There's no hiding that lump.'

Susan patted it happily.

'I don't really want to hide it, Mum. Barry loves it. He kisses it every day.'

Ivy came in then. She was dressed in a light green dress and coat with a straw hat and pale gloves and shoes, looking every inch the mother of the father of the bride.

'It's fucking roasting outside, girls! What a glorious day for a wedding. Your hair looks lovely, Susan, you look really special.'

Susan smiled at her.

'So do you.'

She knew her grandmother was only fishing for compliments.

'Put your fucking teeth in, Ivy, your face looks like a collapsed paddling pool.'

'Up yours, June, I will when I'm ready. They're killing me, these new ones. Me gums are bleeding with them.'

Ivy's teeth were a bone of contention and everyone avoided talking about them if they could.

'Where's the men? Has anyone checked on them yet?'

June snorted.

'They left here yesterday at nine in the morning, fuck knows where they are now. They'd better be ready and that Barry had better be in a fit state to say his fucking vows because it was him and his mother who pushed for a church do. Scottish Catholics in the family, Jesus wept! And him the biggest thief this side of the water. Mind you, that's why the Bannermans like him, they're all religious fanatics.'

Susan sighed.

'Barry's mum is the one who really wanted it but I did an' all. It seems fitting somehow to do it in the eyes of God.'

June shook her head sagely.

'But marrying him and being lumbered for life is a foolish thing to do, girl, you mark my words. He's already unfaithful, he treats you like a nothing, and more importantly he doesn't give you much money. Just exactly what are you getting out of this except a new name?'

Ivy was annoyed and it showed.

'She'll get what you got, June: a man. Someone to take care of her and look after her and her kids. Now will you shut the fuck up for two minutes and stop putting the kibosh on everything? I reckon you're just jealous.'

'Jealous of what? Her? Don't make me laugh. I can see what her life's going to be and so can you.'

June stormed from the room and Susan dropped her head on to her chest. 'She's been funny all morning, Ivy, take no notice of her.'

Her grandmother nodded.

'Remembering her own wedding day and realising she's over the hill, that's what's eating at her.'

'Maybe, but don't antagonise her today, I want it all to go really well.'

'You're getting a good man there, I hope you realise that, Sue? I bet he's good in the kip, eh?'

Susan laughed despite herself.

'You're terrible you are.'

Ivy laughed.

'In this get up I might even pull meself. Who knows, eh?' She roared with laughter and Susan laughed with her. 'How's the house coming on, love?'

Ivy was impressed that they had already been given a council house. That was because Barry had dropped a few quid on the housing officer and he had arranged it all for them. The house was lovely and just down the road from her. A double pleasure so far as Ivy was concerned.

'It's been decorated and the furniture's in. It looks lovely. Barry's even had someone in to dig the garden. Oh, and guess what? He bought me a vacuum cleaner and a washing machine.'

Her grandmother sighed with happiness.

'You are a lucky girl, you know. He'll go places him. You mark my words.'

'I do love him.'

Ivy grunted her agreement.

'Of course you do. What's not to love about him, eh? He's a bundle of manhood him. I wish I was you tonight, I ain't had a bit since the old King died.'

She roared with laughter once more.

June came back into the bedroom with a bottle of champagne and some glasses.

'Come on then, get this down you. Barry left it yesterday, said to get you half pissed so you looked in a good mood.'

They all took a glass and Ivy held hers up in a toast.

'To Susan and Barry.'

They chinked glasses and drank the cold bubbling wine. Susan finished hers and laughed. This really was the happiest day of her life. In a few hours she would be Mrs Barry Dalston and she could not wait.

Barry opened his eyes and squinted. His mouth was dry and his eyes felt as if they were glued shut. He could smell himself, a mixture of sweat and alcohol so strong it made his eyes water and helped to open them properly.

He was in the new house, he knew that much from the wallpaper. In his bedroom, the one he would share with Susan.

A movement beside him made him look round. To either side of him a woman lay asleep and Joey snored at the bottom of the bed.

Memories assailed Barry as he tried to remember what had happened the night before. He saw fleeting images of strip clubs, a gambling den and a brothel in Paddington. He felt the bile rise inside him and swallowed it down.

His head hurt and his face was aching. Then he remembered the fight. Sitting upright he felt his face over and sighed with annoyance. He had at the very least a black eye and a swollen mouth. His mother would slaughter him if he didn't look perfect for the priest.

Joey stirred and sat up slowly. His eyes were red-rimmed but his face was unmarked.

'All right?'

It was his usual form of address.

'What's it fucking look like, Joey? They'll kill me. Me mother, Susan, June. All of them.'

Joey shrugged and rubbed one of the women's legs to wake her up. 'Come on, you, up and out of it. You've had the best, now leave some for the rest.'

'Where the fucking hell did we get this pair of old dragons?' Barry said peevishly.

One green eye opened and a voice that could crack concrete said stridently, 'You weren't fucking complaining last night, sonny.'

He kicked her from the bed until she fell on to the floor.

'I was fucking paralytic last night, darlin', that's why I never complained. Who in their right mind would fuck either of you sober?'

The woman stood up and with as much dignity as she could muster said nastily, 'Same same, mate, same same.'

'Go on, fuck off, and take your twin with you. I assume you're related because no two people could be that ugly by accident.'

Joey laughed at the woman's outraged expression and so did Barry.

'You still owe us money.'

Barry was out of the bed, making the woman wince.

'Are you telling me you expect us to pay?' His voice had risen about five octaves with shock.

The other woman began to wake up. She stretched out her arms and yawned, her breath sour as her body.

'Where did we get you two from, if you don't mind my asking?' Joey put in.

As they began to dress the two women ignored him. He watched anyway. They were about thirty with heavy legs and flat chests, but the taller of the two had nice hair and eyes.

'Come on, girls, where did we get you from, eh?'

The taller one answered him.

'The Valbon if you must know, and we're not transvestites. We were on our night off and you talked us into a night's work. So pay up.'

'Bollocks! Get dressed and piss off.'

Barry walked from the room, his head splitting.

'Get them out, Joey, and I'll make us a cup of tea. Me mother stocked us up yesterday.' Then, running back into the bedroom, he glared at the small clock on the bedside table. 'Fuck me! She'll be here soon with me cousins to lay out the food for the reception. If she sees this pair she'll do her fucking pieces.'

'Relax, boy, we're nearly dressed. You just give us our dosh and we'll go quietly as little mice.'

It was a threat and Barry knew it. Taking the taller woman by her hair, he began to drag her from the bedroom. At the top of the stairs he bellowed, 'Do you want to walk down them or shall I fucking kick you? The choice is yours, darling.'

The blonde prostitute came out of the room like a bullet. Holding their shoes and bags and coats she forced her friend down the stairs. At the front door she looked up at Barry and cried, 'We were off work with the clap so happy wedding day, you wanker.'

He was halfway down the stairs after them before he realised he was naked. Taking his cock in his hands he groaned.

'It looks all red, Joey.'

Joey laughed his head off.

'I ain't surprised. You nearly wore them two out, son. That's old tom talk. Now make the tea, for fuck's sake. Me mouth feels like the bottom of a bird cage.'

Joey started to tidy the bedroom. The sheets were smeared with everything from lipstick to semen, but still he made the bed. After a couple of minutes the urge to pee was growing strong and he lurched towards the toilet. As he peed he felt a stinging sensation and swore under his breath.

That was all they needed now, a round of applause. Last time he'd had the clap June had gone mental. When he'd finished he put his head under the cold tap to liven himself up. As he finished dressing he heard Barry's mother, Kate, coming in with the food.

'Are you all right, son?'

Her voice was pure cockney. She had married a Scotsman and after his murder had returned to her roots. She worshipped her son as his mother worshipped Joey. He really liked her.

Kate was loyal, decent, and kept her ears and mouth shut. She was everything a woman should be so far as he was concerned. Barry had confided that before and after his father's death there had been no other men for her.

Kate went to mass daily and prayed for him and his father, and that was about it. She saw no wrong in her son and took his part against anyone with a different opinion from her own. All in all she was an honest to God cockney, one of the old school.

Her home was spotless, her food exemplary and a warm welcome assured. Joey wished she was his old woman, he would love to have married someone like that. She was still good-looking and all. For her age, of course. But he wouldn't kick it out of bed if he got the chance, and Christ knew he had tried enough times. Kate always acted as if she didn't know what he was trying to do.

He shrugged as he tidied his hair before going down to her. Maybe she didn't. Not all women were like June, up for whatever was going.

As he thought of his wife he sighed. She was only trumping a bleeding Indian stall-holder off the lane! He had a big Jag, a turban and a set of gleaming white teeth that had cost a small fortune.

Joey smiled. Well, let him make the most of them because Joey was going to knock them out of that bastard's head soon. All he wanted to do first was find out if the bloke had anything worth nicking then find an opportunity to pinch whatever he could while teaching the Asian ponce a lesson he wouldn't forget in a hurry.

Fucking June! She did her bit for race relations all right.

Kate smiled at him as he came into the kitchen.

'I'm making eggs and bacon, do you want some?'

Joey grinned happily and rubbed his hands together.

'Please. We could do with something to get us back to normal.'

Barry, he noticed, looked suitably shamefaced in front of his mother and this cheered Joey up. The boy had been getting a right little rep for himself recently, and although Joey was still the mainstay of the operation, Barry could well take it into his head to work alone. Which was why this marriage was a godsend in more ways than one.

When Joey was too drunk or stoned to finish off a deal, Barry would automatically take over. He had been nicked already, done his bird and kept his head down and his trap shut. Three months he had been banged up and it had done the boy some good. He didn't want to go back and that was an encouraging sign.

Now he would do anything to stay out of clink, and anything was a big threat to the world.

The church was packed, the smell of polish overpowering in the heat of July. Susan was already sweating like a pig and her hair was sticking to her forehead in damp tendrils.

'I wish they'd bleeding hurry up. I'm supposed to arrive late, not him.'

'He's a ponce like your father. That shit head was late for our wedding,' June said sourly.

Susan's voice was high.

'Will you stop swearing in church?'

Her mother rolled her eyes to the ceiling.

'Like we come in here all the time! Bleeding waste of time and energy this. If there ever was a God, love, He forgot about us a long time ago.'

Susan ignored this and concentrated on trying to look out of the small window beside the church doors to see if Barry and Joey had arrived.

'I'll string that bastard up if he's got nicked today, I take oath on that.'

June's voice was hard and Susan's belly twinged. The child was lying heavily inside her. It kicked, a strong hard movement that nearly doubled her over.

'Here, love, you all right?'

She nodded and took a deep breath, rubbing her swollen belly as she did so.

'Yeah, I'm all right. I think the baby is as fed up as we are, that's all.'

Ivy lit a cigarette and took a deep draw on it.

'Here you are, love, puff that. It will calm you down.'

Susan took the cigarette gratefully and puffed on it hard.

'Where are they?'

'They could be anywhere. Up jack's arse and round the corner for all we know.' Ivy's voice was resigned.

Susan was beginning to panic now. Barry was nearly half an hour late.

'He is coming, Mum, ain't he?'

The fear of being left at the altar entered her head then and she felt a sickening lurch in her stomach as she realised that, with the hump, Barry was quite capable of deliberately 'forgetting' to turn up.

June looked into her daughter's white strained face and felt a moment's pity for her.

'Get used to this, love. He's like your father though you can't see that yet. All his life he'll do only what he wants, darlin', and there's fuck all you can do about it. I hope he don't come in a way. Do you a favour though you won't see it like that, not for a long time.'

Susan felt tears sting her eyes and tried to stem them before she began to wail out loud. If Barry shamed her in front of everyone she would kill him, kill him stone dead.

Where was he?

'Here, flag down that Old Bill car!'

The two women watching the fight were mesmerised. One of them ran to the kerb and raised her shopping bags in a signal for the squad car to stop.

'What's going on, ladies?'

The two young PCs could see the fight for themselves but it looked a bit vicious and they wanted to call for back up.

Betty Tomlinson pursed her lips.

'From what I can gather that blue car was cut up by the black one and now the four occupants are having a tear up. But from the looks of the two men winning, I'd say a bride somewhere is tearing her hair out. Look at the ribbons on the car. What a disgrace, eh, fighting in the street on your wedding day? This didn't happen in my day, I can tell you.'

The policemen weren't listening. They had already clocked Joey and Barry battering two middle-aged men all around the road.

Five minutes later two more panda cars arrived and the young PCs decided now was an appropriate time to get out of their motor.

'Look at them, they've been going at it ever since we got here.' An older policeman sighed.

'Come on, let's break it up. That's Joey McNamara – his daughter's marrying today. We were warned about the reception two weeks ago. Half the criminal underworld will be at the church.'

The six policemen dragged Joey and Barry off the two men they thought had cut them up. In fact, Joey had cut them up then decided they were taking the piss and needed teaching a lesson.

The men were battered but not senseless. One, a large man with a balding head and a large beer-gut, was sitting on the kerb when the older policeman asked if he wanted to press charges. He said no, as did his passenger, a market trader from Covent Garden.

They were not stupid. They knew the fact they'd been asked meant the Old Bill didn't want to do anything. It was the law of the pavement and they acknowledged it.

Five minutes later Barry and Joey were in a panda car on their way to church. The car darted in and out of traffic and they loved every second of it. The kudos of arriving at the church in a police car was too much for them to resist.

A bottle of Scotch downed while they dressed had put them in the mood for the ceremony. It had also put them in the mood for aggravation. Two flash gits in a nice new Daimler had given them just the boost they needed to add to the excitement of the day.

As they screeched to a halt outside St Vincent's they saw the shocked and wondering expressions on everyone's face and were full of themselves.

The priest however was unimpressed.

Father Stewart Munro was legendary for marrying the criminal fraternity, no awkward questions asked. But he would not countenance any trouble whatsoever. At six foot four and eighteen and a half stone, he was a man many listened to. He spoke good sense, but also had a fist on him could down any man, and who would raise his hand back to a priest?

Father Munro had another wedding in five minutes and he was annoyed. Seriously annoyed. He had only agreed to marry these two because of Kate Dalston, a good woman and a devout Catholic, and this was how they repaid him. He had half a mind to cancel the ceremony.

But as he looked around him at the Davidsons and the Bannermans, criminals spanning the whole of London, and the countenance of the pregnant bride, Father Munro relented.

But it would be a quick service, it would have to be.

Barry stood waiting for his bride, spattered with blood that was not his own and with a ripped jacket and muddied trousers. He was over the moon at his own antics and assumed everyone else was too. He could hear whispering and laughing in the church and knew he had made this a day no one was going to forget.

Least of all Susan Dalston.

He loved the thought of her being called by his name. It was as if he had stolen her from Joey and now owned her. After today Joey would have no say whatever in her life. It gave Barry a thrill.

Smiling at her as she stood awkwardly by his side, he made his vows in a loud, firm voice, making everyone laugh once more.

Listening to him, Susan forgave him everything. He was here, they were married and she was now his wife. What more could any girl want?

She could smell the polish, the flowers and the scent of Midnight in Paris, a perfume worn by most of the women in church. She felt the thrill every bride feels, knowing she is embarking on the adventure of a lifetime.

Even though his shocking appearance had upset her, she was determined to enjoy her day, remember it as a happy occasion, make herself laugh at what he had done even though she inwardly knew she should be condemning him. Hating him for the humiliation he had caused her in front of everyone.

As he placed the ring on her finger she saw the blood drying on his hands and a small shiver passed through her body. The baby lurched inside her once more and she felt slightly sick.

The whole place seemed to recede before her eyes and all that was left was the crucifix above the altar. Christ looked down on her and Susan knew she needed Him, needed her God, and would need Him all her life after this day.

The sweat was plastering her dress to her body and her head felt light and as if it would burst.

But she loved Barry so much. For all he was, for all he did, she loved him. That love, she decided, would have to be enough for both of them.

Barry felt the tremor in her hands and hugged her close, a rough embrace that made everyone laugh again and Father Munro sniff in exasperation.

At least he cares for her, was his only thought. Even if it was a rough sort of love, it was something.

For if ever anyone needed his prayers it was this poor child before him, with her sad eyes and her hope-filled belly. Suddenly the priest felt depressed.

The child would be fêted for a few weeks by the father who would then lose all interest. Stewart Munro knew this as he knew his catechism, as he knew the parables. He had lived in the East End for many years and had seen Barry Dalstons come and go. He had christened them, he had married them, and he had buried them.

Barry, for his part, thought himself wonderful. He had made sure no one would forget this day. He looked at his Susan, as he now thought of her, and imagined her naked later, her huge belly hanging down as he took her from behind. He was getting hard already thinking about it and tried to control his thoughts.

She was a good old girl was Susan. She had the house lovely and she cooked well. He knew he could have done a lot worse. His mother liked her, that was the main thing.

He felt his insides rebelling against the alcohol and then a moment's dizziness as he swallowed down the vomit ready to be released. He realised then he was seriously drunk and held his breath to stem the sickness and keep himself on his feet. He wished the priest would hurry up and shut his trap now, he was getting bored with it all. He wanted a drink, some food, to be with his new wife.

His wife.

His Susan Dalston.

As soon as the service was over, Barry turned to bow to the congregation in a display of mock bravado. Unfortunately he knocked his new bride flying.

Susan ended up on her behind at the bottom of the altar steps. Barry was laughing so much he could not even help her up.

Susan Dalston endured the indignity of having a drunken bridegroom in the church, a man so drunk he knocked his own heavily pregnant wife over then laughed. Barry genuinely thought it was hilarious.

Some of the people in the church laughed too, but nervously because they could see the look on Joey McNamara's face. Davey Davidson, renowned for his own sense of humour, found it difficult to smile.

Looking at his beloved wife, he whispered, 'Scum, darlin', fucking scum. Let's get to the reception fast and off home early. I've had enough already.'

'What you doing, you little shit? That's my daughter you're knocking all over the place.'

Joey's voice was loud and June and Ivy immediately went to him to stop the row they knew was going to start at any moment.

'Leave it out, Joey. It was an accident and Susan isn't complaining. Let it go.'

Joey pushed his wife off.

'Please, Joey, not here in front of everyone.'

'Let it go? That wanker knocks my girl over and I'm expected to let it go? I'll rip his fucking head off.'

June sighed heavily.

'Come on, Ivy, let's leave them to it. I've had enough.'

Joey turned on his wife.

'*You've* had enough? *You* have had enough? You taking the piss, June? If anyone has had enough it's me, mate.'

He pushed Kate Dalston and her son none too gently out of his way and hauled Susan up off the floor.

'That's it, you're coming home with me right now.'

She dragged her hand from her father's grip. Her voice was thick with tears and humiliation as she cried, 'Let it go, Dad, it was an accident. Please don't ruin everything, make it even worse than it already is.'

Joey grabbed her none too gently by the arm.

'You're coming home with me and your mother. I must have been fucking mad to agree to all this crap. He's a ponce and the sooner you realise that the better off you will be.'

Barry listened to all this in incredulous silence. Father Munro listened in anger and disbelief.

As Barry angrily pushed Joey away from Susan, Joey swung his fist back. Before it connected with Barry's jaw, Father Munro had laid him out on the steps of the altar with one almighty punch.

'Would you all get out of my sight? May God forgive you because I certainly won't.'

Kate put her arm around a weeping Susan as Barry rushed out to empty his stomach all over the gravel outside. His retching could be heard all over the church as if amplified. The wedding party due in after them watched it all, horrified.

Inside people began picking up presents, looking at each other and wondering what the protocol was for a disaster of this magnitude on a wedding day. Would the reception still be going ahead?

Susan, her make up running and her face red, cried like a baby into her new mother-in-law's arms. Kate tried to soothe her while June shook her head in dismay as her husband lay unconscious on the floor of the church.

'I'll fucking kill him, I take oath on that. The rotten bastard!'

Ivy knelt down by her son's side and shook her head. Even she knew it had gone too far this time. The hope and happiness that had heralded the wedding were replaced now by a quiet desperation to try and salvage something from the day.

Two of Ivy's oldest friends came up and took her arms.

'Come on, love, let's get you back to the house.'

She nodded, for once speechless.

* * *

Joey opened his eyes and the first thing he saw was Bannerman's face. Dropping a gaily coloured parcel by Susan's side, he said sadly, 'We got to go, love, but we wish you all the best.' He smiled and then added jokily, 'I reckon you're going to need it.'

He kissed her gently on the cheek and left, his wife stiff-backed with indignation at the fracas she had witnessed.

Joey saw himself then as everyone saw him. A foul-mouthed thug who did not even hold a church sacrosanct from his foul language and his violence.

It was an insight of such stunning clarity that he started to cry. He sobbed and even his mother ignored him. No one, it seemed, wanted to make him feel better, wanted to excuse what he had done.

Getting to his feet unsteadily, nearly falling, he implored his daughter with eyes and words.

'Sue, I'm sorry, love. It was the drink . . .'

Susan shook her head and walked away from him. Her bouquet was ruined. Debbie picked it up and tried to rearrange it.

Joey was crying loudly now, all inhibitions gone. He hated it when people shunned him, when he knew he had gone too far and ruined things and people made him aware of the fact.

He needed to feel valued, needed to feel he was above everyone else.

'SUSAN!'

His voice was an entreaty.

But Susan and Debbie carried on walking from the church and the guests followed them outside like sheep. No one spoke to Joey or offered him a word of comfort.

Kate Dalston waited until everyone else had left, then looking at him with hate-filled eyes, she whispered, 'You rotten, filthy bastard! If my husband was alive today he'd take you out and destroy you for what you've done here. Getting my Barry drunk and into a fight before his wedding, then abusing him and your own flesh and blood before the eyes of God Himself.'

She looked him up and down. Shaking her head, she whispered, 'You disgust me.'

Finally he saw June. She was standing at the back of the church.

Even from that distance her eyes were condemning him and he knew that no matter what he did or said he would be blamed for this day all his life.

Wiping a hand across his eyes he realised he was still crying. June turned her back on him and walked from the church. Joey McNamara had never felt so alone in all his life.

Chapter Eleven

Barry was drunk but contrite. Everyone could see that much. Kate Dalston had made sure everyone had a drink and some food and had tried her hardest to make the day a success. The ceremony was not mentioned by anyone and that suited all concerned.

June and Ivy were in the bedroom at the new house, changing the sheets and tidying everything away. Ivy, for the first time ever, had a downer on her son.

'Mind you, June, they was each as bad as the other.'

She nodded.

'All that money, all that time and effort. Poor Susan, she really tried and all.'

Ivy shrugged.

'Well, at least she understands now what she's taken on. I never thought I'd say this, June, but that Barry is as bad as Joey in a lot of respects.' She shuddered. 'Every time I think of that scene in church I feel ill.'

June shook her head in consternation.

'How do you think Susan feels? She's a pain in the arse at times but even I have to admit that today's antics were totally out of order. Did you see Bannerman's face, him being religious and all?'

Ivy sniffed the sheets suspiciously and sighed.

'They've had a shagging session in this bed and all, dirty pair of fuckers. Look at the colour of that lipstick, and it'll never come off these sheets. Candy stripes are always fuckers for stains.'

June rolled her eyes to the ceiling. She heard Susan's voice from the garden and walked to the window so she could see what was going on. Joey had come in at the back gate and she lifted the sash window as quietly as she could to hear what was being said.

He was trying to put his arm around Susan who was pushing him away, gently trying to make him leave.

'Please, Dad, ain't there been enough trouble today?'

Joey, it was evident, had stocked up on more drink for Dutch courage. June looked down on husband and daughter as if she were a stranger, watching them like an impartial onlooker. She could smell the heat of the day, the familiar odour of exhaust fumes, cooked food and grime that denoted the East End in the summer. She saw her husband place one hand on his daughter's belly and try and rub it.

'Come on, Susan, you know I didn't mean it. I was drunk, just drunk.'

Susan pushed him now with greater force as if his touching her had clicked a switch inside her.

'Keep your fucking hands off me! I ain't nothing to you now. I'm a Dalston not a McNamara, okay? You can't ever touch me again.'

June was aware of Ivy standing quietly beside her. Neither woman said a word.

'I was trying to stick up for you, love. He knocked you over in front of everyone.'

Susan moved away from him once more, though in the narrow confines of the walled garden this was difficult.

'You ruined my wedding. You got him pissed and into a fight. You ruined it all. I know what your game is. You're fucking jealous. You need him because you're so fucking useless you can't even keep a job as a paid thug. Well, it all stops from here, Dad. I have had it up to my back teeth. Barry is my husband and I am his wife. You can't touch me now, not ever again, because if you do I'll tell him.

'He knew what you did to me round me nan's, and he knows what you really are. A nonce, a beast, whatever you want to call it.'

June and Ivy watched in stunned silence as Joey started crying again.

'Please, Susan, I only did it because I love you. You're my best girl, you always was.'

There was a pleading note in his voice that broke June, made her realise just what he was.

'What's going on? What's this all about?'

Ivy's voice was querulous.

June looked at her mother-in-law and shrugged.

'What do you think it's about, Ivy? Your golden boy has been shagging his daughter. Has been for years by all accounts.'

Ivy was shaking her head in denial.

'No, no way. He ain't like that. He might have a few strange habits but not that. Susan's probably got him wrong, you know what she's like. All that reading, a fucking drama queen her . . .'

June interrupted her.

'You know what, Ivy? He takes after you in a lot of ways. Selfish, opinionated and thoroughly nasty. He first took her when she was twelve, and he's been taking her ever since. I've known about it for ages.'

Ivy looked at her daughter-in-law in stunned silence.

'You *knew*? You knew and you didn't do anything?'

Even she found that difficult to believe.

June smiled thinly.

'Don't you think we all had enough problems without that getting out? Imagine Davey Davidson or the Bannermans finding out about that, eh? We'd have been run out of the East End, you know that as well as I do.'

Ivy was prevented from answering by a scream below them in the garden. Barry's mother was pulling her son away from Joey and Susan was trying to push her father through the small gate out into the alley.

'Just go, Dad. Will you just go? Please.'

Her voice was pleading now. She had had enough of the day, the heat and the company. All Susan wanted was to lie down and try and forget any of this had ever taken place. Joey left the garden and she sighed with relief.

'What did he want then?'

Barry's voice was hard.

'What do you think he wanted, Bal? He wanted to come to the so-called reception.'

Kate Dalston left them to it. She thought it would be best for them to clear the air. Ivy and June watched from the bedroom, both quiet as they listened to what was being said.

Barry pushed Susan against the gate and tried to put his arms around her. She could smell vomit, whisky and red wine on his breath and turned her head away in disgust. He sensed what she was thinking and pushed her more forcefully against the wooden gate.

Susan could feel a nail digging into her back and tried to twist away from his grasp.

'Let go of me, Barry, I'm sick of being forced to do what everyone wants.'

He grinned.

'Oh, you're sick of doing what you're told, are you? Well, let me spell it out to you. When I married you today, I gave you respectability, mate. I took you from that pair of scumbags who raised you and turned you into my wife. So please do me the honour of remembering that at all times. If I tell you to jump, Susan Dalston, you jump and you jump as high as you can, lady, because I expect the best from you. Now, do I make myself clear?'

He was holding her face in his hand, squeezing her jaw until she winced with pain.

'I can't hear you, Susan, was that a yes?'

She nodded painfully and he released his grip.

'You're getting like your mother. You think I'm going to put up with all the crap your father put up with, don't you? Well, listen to me. You are mine and no one else's. Understand that now, Susan. And that includes your fucking father. If I hear he's been sniffing round you, I'll kill him.'

She nodded again, frightened now.

'Then I'll kill you. If that baby comes out even remotely resembling that cunt, I will rip you to shreds. You hear what I'm telling you, woman?'

Susan licked cracked and sore lips.

'Please, Barry, not today, eh? The day's been ruined enough as it is . . .'

He wasn't listening to her. He was dragging her out into the alleyway and thrusting her against the opposite wall. He was pulling up her wedding dress, all the while biting her neck with vicious little nips that hurt and distressed her.

'Leave it out, Barry, not out here. Not in front of everyone.'

He was ripping at her underwear now. She felt the cheap fabric tear in his hands and closed her eyes against the glare of the summer sun.

'You're me wife, Susan. I can do this when I like, love. It's the reason people marry, see? I fuck you rigid, you let me. But I can also fuck other people rigid and you still have to let me do it. It's the difference between men and women, see.'

He was lifting her off the ground with the force of his thrusts; it was excruciatingly painful. But Barry had got his rhythm now and was pounding away at her as if his life depended on it.

Susan looked up and saw her father watching from the garden alongside. He was partially hidden behind a broken down fence covered in weeds and accumulated rubbish. She saw his drawn face. His eyes were dark with emotion and his hair was plastered to his head with sweat.

A wasp was buzzing around. She could hear it loud in her mind. It seemed at odds with what was happening to her at that moment. The distant drone of traffic and the occasional tremor in the ground as a heavy lorry passed by were all normal events, yet nothing was normal about this time or place. She realised that Barry was Joey, even though her mind shrank before this notion.

Barry loved her, she was sure of that.

At sixteen, heavily pregnant and after a childhood most people would not believe, she had to believe that he loved her. She *wanted* him to love her.

Wanted somebody to love her.

All her girlish dreams dissolved then, and as she relaxed, just wanting the punishment of his assault on her body over with, she felt him ejaculate. His whole body tensed and then sagged and he held on to her buttocks for dear life. Then, as the lust left him and he realised how heavy she was, he lowered her to the ground and buried his head in her chest, cuddling her close, murmuring what to him were endearments.

'That's the best, Sue, the best it's ever been. You're mine now, love, all mine and no one else's.'

She stroked his head and nodded, wanting it all to be over. She wanted it finished and done with, wanted to forget it had ever happened. Wanted to move away from her father's gaze.

If Barry realised Joey was watching them he would be incensed, would go ballistic . . .

But turning from her, he looked over at her father and, zipping up his trousers, cried out: 'Get a good look, Joey? See what your lovely daughter got for herself, eh? A real man.'

Susan closed her eyes in distress.

'Oh, please God, make this fucking day be over.'

Joey stumbled out of the garden and started down the alleyway behind the mean houses. He looked defeated, and Susan felt a moment's sorrow for him.

Then Barry was walking after him, pulling him round, and Susan felt the breath leave her body as she heard her husband's words.

'Come on, Joey, let's have a drink to today, mate. We all know where we stand now, don't we?'

Joey looked at his daughter and imperceptibly she nodded her head. There was nothing else she could do. Barry Dalston had spoken and now she had to do what he wanted.

Her life had not changed one iota. All that was different was the name of the person who now controlled her. What she did, what she thought, what she said.

As the men walked back into the garden together and made their peace in front of everyone she watched them, her heart breaking inside her at the unfairness of a life that replaced Joey with Barry.

Susan grew up in those fifteen minutes but it was too late. Barry Dalston now owned her lock, stock and barrel.

The wedding reception was going with a swing. It was eleven-thirty at night and the warm summer weather made it even better. The stars were glittering in the heavens and a cool breeze whistled among the guests as they spilled out of the kitchen into the garden and alleyway behind the house. Music was playing, and people were dancing inside and out.

Susan was absolutely shattered. Her belly felt as if it was hanging down to her knees and her head was thumping from all the noise and the tension of the day. She watched Debbie dancing with all the men, and flirting with them. She saw her mother and Ivy talking together, saw friends and relatives drunk and without inhibitions, dancing, kissing and disappearing with partners they had not arrived with.

Debbie danced over to her.

'All right, Sue? Turned out a right blast in the end, eh?'

'You taking the piss, Debbie? It's been a fucking nightmare.'

Her sister shrugged.

'I admit the church was heavy, but all in all I think it's gone quite well. That was just Dad getting Barry pissed. Mum's already had him over the coals about it and he's suitably shamefaced as you can see. She bollocked the life out of him actually, I heard her.'

'All that money and time, Debbie, getting everything right for today, and they ruined it. I'm a laughing stock now. I heard Auntie Violet telling Grace that it was because of me trying to be flash. Getting us all dressed up and pushing the boat out with a big white wedding. Her exact words, of course, were, "It all went wrong because God don't like people getting above themselves. And who's she think she is? The fucking Queen?"'

Debbie laughed.

'I can just hear her saying it. She asked me earlier if I was gonna be next. I told her to fuck off. I ain't getting tied down, mate, there's too many men and too little time. I never learned much off the old woman but I learned that. This ain't for me, taking the first one to come along. I want to have a nose about, see what I want out of life before I commit meself.'

Her words depressed Susan even more.

'Is that what you think I done then, took the first one that came along?'

Debbie looked at her sister and Susan realised she was being honest.

'Ain't that what happened then? Christ, Sue, you wanted him so much it was painful to watch you at times. The last couple of years you've been like an old married woman. Never going out, never doing anything, just waiting until your lord and master told you what you were allowed to do and what you weren't. Name me one place you ever went without him? Come on. A club, a pub, even the pictures? You can't, can you?'

Susan shook her head sadly.

'Well, there you are then. You got what you wanted, Sue, you got him. So why ain't you happy, eh? All right, I admit the wedding itself was a fucking shambles, but you got what you went to church for. You got Barry. What else did you expect? Instant happiness or what?'

Susan looked into her sister's eyes. She saw the real sadness there as well as the little gleam of pleasure Debbie was deriving from the day. In a way Susan could understand that. Her wedding had been talked about and mulled over for months. It had overshadowed everything and everyone.

As she went back into the house to get a drink from the makeshift bar in the lounge she saw Barry trying to grab her cousin Frances's breast as he sat beside her on the stairs. She noticed Frances only pushed him off because she saw her and Debbie walking towards them.

The worst of it was she knew Frances was more bothered about Debbie seeing it than Susan herself. Debbie was the one with the mouth, the one with the aggression. Not good old Susan who turned a blind eye or pretended to misunderstand everything because it made life easier.

Swallowing down a large gin and tonic she felt the alcohol as it hit her brain and relished the feeling of carefree abandon it gave her.

She was married, wasn't she?

As Debbie had pointed out it was all she'd ever wanted. Now Susan Dalston had finally got what she'd wanted.

What was the old saying? 'Be careful what you ask for, you just might get it.'

The words whirled around in her brain and she pushed them

away. She was a married woman now, Mrs Susan Dalston. She had her whole life ahead of her.

She could make her marriage work, try and change Barry, make him more of a family man. The baby would fix everything, she was convinced of that. He was mad keen about it, convinced it would be a boy, just like him.

Perish the thought!

If it was a boy Susan would bring him up with respect for himself and the people around him, especially the women. She wondered what life would dole out next, then had another large drink and was soon dancing and singing as if this was a real wedding reception. Which it was.

And if Barry was dancing with her cousin instead of his wife Susan knew she would have to let it go, just this once. She did not want any more trouble today. There had already been too much as it was.

'Fucking hell, Susan, it's like being in bed with an elephant. Move over, you fat whore!'

Barry was laughing as he tried to shunt her across the bed and on to what would be her side in future. She rolled over to help him and he laughed again.

Then, looking down at her in the moonlight, his face softened.

'I'm sorry about today, love, really I am. It was nerves. I drank the Scotch to calm me nerves, see. I wish I'd listened to me mother and left it till the reception.'

He was dragging her out of her dress as he spoke.

'Life your arse off the bed, Susan, this is hard enough as it is.'

She allowed him to strip her naked. He knelt in front of her and rubbed her belly gently.

'My little boy is in there, swimming about getting brains and everything, ready to face the world. Bless him, I want to give him everything a boy should have.'

'It could be a girl, Bal, there are two sexes in the world.'

He laughed.

'Nah, no way is it a split-arse. It's a boy, I made sure of that.'

Susan smiled. She loved Barry when he was like this. This was the man she wanted, not the other Barry, the one she was ashamed of, scared of even.

'I'll take him up Upton Park, show him football at its best. And I'll take him to the park and play with him, make him into a man. Teach him to fight, to defend himself, be his own person. Learn him not to take shit off no one without forcing it back down their fucking throats. I will do all that for my son, Susan, because I'll love him and I know what the world is really like.'

'I hope he's a gentle person, Bal, a bookish person. I want him to have an education, be someone. Not like us. You know, taking what we can to survive. I want him or her to have a choice in their lives. Be a good person, better than us and what we come from.'

Barry was quiet for a few moments, thinking about what she'd said. Susan was pleased about this. She wanted him to want what she wanted for their child.

Finally he spoke.

'Listen, *Mrs Dalston*, if you think you're turning my son into a fucking poofter then you had better think again. Now you're getting away with murder here because I fucked up at the church and I know I owe you one. But if I ever see my son with a book or anything remotely resembling one I will take your fucking head off your shoulders. Do you understand me? Fucking gentle! You'll have him playing fucking netball before he knows what's going on.'

He turned her over on to her belly then and forced her up on to all fours, even though she was trying to stay on her back. Eventually he dragged her around roughly. Digging his fingers into her shoulders, he whispered, 'Don't fucking push it tonight, Susan, okay? I ain't in the mood.'

By the time he entered her she was on auto-pilot and ten minutes later he was finished. Her legs were aching, her shoulders were sore from his rough treatment and her belly was tight and uncomfortable.

Two minutes after he withdrew from her he was asleep. His arm lay across her and it felt like a steel band pinning her to the bed.

Lying there, white, drawn and exhausted, Susan cried again,

only this time it was for her unborn child and for a life she realised she had thrown away. The little house was seen now through eyes unblinkered by love as the scruffy dump it really was, even if it was a step up from her mother's flat.

The rest of her life rose before Susan and the fear it engendered set the child rolling inside her belly as if it too was rebelling against the fate that had sent it to the two people in that poky bedroom.

Caressing it gently, Susan tried to calm herself and the child. She was trapped and she had trapped herself, that was the worst of it. Susan Dalston, as she now was, had sentenced herself to life.

'I mean it, Joey, what's going on with you and Susan?'

He was drunk, but not so drunk he did not realise he was on dodgy ground here, very dodgy ground.

He decided he would front it out as usual.

'What you fucking on about now? Me and Susan, what about us?'

June walked across the bedroom and stuck a finger in his face.

'You heard me. Are you giving her one? I warn you, I was listening today at the window with your mother so remember that before you say a fucking word.'

Joey felt the fright in his chest. He was trying to remember what he had done and said but the drink had had him in its hold and he couldn't remember much.

'What did you hear then? A father talking to his daughter on her wedding day. Big deal.'

'We, that is your mother and I, heard you apologising to her and trying to get your leg over again, that's what we heard. You know I know, Joey. Why do we have to go through all this pretence? What I want from you is your word that you will leave her alone in future. No more and no less.'

He was silent still and June began to mock him.

'"I love you, Susan. You're me best girl, you know that."'

Joey sat himself down on the bed and put his head in his hands.

'Rubbing her belly . . . What's wrong, Joey? You think it's yours, do you? I suppose it could be. Then it would be your son and your grandson. That's one for the record books, eh?'

Joey looked up then, into his wife's eyes.

'You're jealous, ain't you, June? Because I don't love you like that and you know it. But is Susan mine, that's what we have to sort out once and for all, isn't it? Is Susan McNamara my daughter? I mean, she could easily be someone else's, couldn't she, June?'

June shook her head and grinned, showing yellow teeth.

'You've always thought that, haven't you, right from day one?'

She picked up her drink from the dressing table and gulped it down. 'She's yours all right, Joey, don't you worry about that. It's Debbie you should be wondering about, not Susan.'

Joey shrugged then, an irritating gesture that made her want to kill him.

'Maybe I should start giving her one then?'

'Debbie has too much sense to fall for that with you, mate. Did Susan give in gracefully or did you force her? Only from what she said today, I think you made her, Joey. I think you enjoyed making her do it, to get back at me for leaving you for Jimmy.'

'Fuck off, June, you're a pain in the arse. For your information she loved it, it was her who came to me. It's only since Barry Dalston came on the scene that she's changed towards me. It was her who started it all off actually. She missed you so she turned to me, we turned to each other . . .'

June began to undress.

'If this was other people I might believe that. I know what it's like to be sad, unloved and unwanted. I know that can cause things to happen. I remember someone saying once it often happens after the death of a mother. The husband and daughter turn to each other for comfort and it gets out of hand. But you're not noble enough to do it for those reasons, Joey. People like that realise what they have done and they stop. You would enjoy doing it to her *because* she was your daughter. You try and pretend you think she isn't because it makes you feel better. Well, she is yours. All yours. She is totally yours.

'Only after today, of course, she's Barry Dalston's. He's giving her one now, as you know. You watched them at it today. Me and your mother watched you watching them, so to speak. You've broken Ivy. I only hope you can repair the damage you've done to her because you could have murdered and she would have stood by you. But not for this. She was in a terrible state, terrified people would hear about it, find out and we would all be labelled child molesters.'

Joey stared at his wife. She was down to nothing but her bra and knickers now and was lighting a cigarette.

'Do me a favour, June, please.'

His voice was small, quiet.

'What's that, Joey? Keep it all quiet, eh? Brush it under the carpet, what?'

He laughed nastily.

'Give us a call at about eleven in the morning. Some of us have to go to work, okay?'

He jumped into bed and turned on his side.

'Tell who you like, June, I don't give a fucking toss. It's your word against mine and let's face it, if I lose me rag there ain't many people going to say it to me face, is there?'

June sat on her side of the bed and looked down at him.

'Only the Davidsons and the Bannermans.'

Joey laughed again.

'You wouldn't tell them, June, you know you'd only be cutting off your own nose, love. Now are you coming to bed? If not, turn off the light and piss off, I'm tired.'

June turned the light off and left the room. She dragged on a cardigan and went to sit in the front room. It was dark but she did not bother to put on the light. Her mind was reeling because she knew this was all her fault really.

She had guessed for a while and she had done nothing. She had found him out and still she had done nothing.

It had made her life much easier, to tell the truth. Plus Susan had made her jealous though she did not know why. She wasn't pretty in any discernible way, she wasn't anything really. It was her wanting to be so much better than her mother that really grated. Every time she had picked up a book and become lost in another world she had more or less made June's life seem unimportant somehow.

Even though she knew her daughter was right, it hurt. Or maybe that was why it hurt. Because she was right.

She had never once cared that Joey was doing things to Susan that a father had no business doing to his own child. Well, she admitted to herself, she *had* cared but for the wrong reasons, always the wrong reasons.

She was jealous in case Susan affected the part of him June herself could never affect: his heart.

She was frightened he loved Susan properly. Cared for her more than he cared for his own wife, the mother of his children. The child he was taking to bed she had given birth to for him.

Why did she not care what he was doing to that child, their daughter? What was missing inside her that she still did not really care, was just glad that Susan was out of the house, out from under her roof?

All the other women had been nothing, she knew that, had always known that. Until Susan she had been sure she was the only person Joey McNamara had ever really cared for or needed.

Now she was not so sure.

Susan was not a bit of strange, as he referred to his other amours. Susan was his daughter, his child. His own flesh and blood. Was that the attraction?

June curled up on the sofa and lit another cigarette, its red spark the only light in the room other than the subdued shadowy glow of the street lamp outside.

It was chilly now, the treacherous cold that summer brings at the start of a fine day. She heard the dawn chorus, the little birds chirping away. Their noise would be drowned out soon by the traffic.

It was Sunday, the day of rest. People would sleep off hangovers, go up the pub or cook huge meals no one really wanted to eat.

She heard the clack, clack of her other daughter's shoes as Debbie walked along the balcony towards the front door. Heard her key in the lock and her footsteps stumbling through the doorway. Getting up, she helped Debbie, who was drunk and practically incapable, into her bedroom. She stripped her off and Debbie fell asleep.

June looked down on to her sleeping daughter's profile. She was pretty in a funny, cheap sort of way, but her body was stumpy and heavy like her father's. She looked pretty only because people always looked at her then Susan, and compared them with each other.

As June gazed down at her she was aware that her husband had come into the room. Looking at him, she whispered. 'Fancy some of Debbie now, do you? Or is there something else I don't know?'

Joey pulled her from the room. Shutting the door none too gently, he bellowed, 'Get your arse in that bed, woman, and shut the fuck up.'

June did as he said.

Not because she wanted to do it but because she was cold and tired. When he reached for her she was amazed at how she responded to him. It was as if they had been parted for years and had just come together after all that time. After missing one another, wanting and needing one another. They made love till the sun was high in the sky and their bodies were slippery with sweat. Yet not once did either of them utter a word.

Afterwards they slept in each other's arms, something they had not done for years. June was at peace with herself and did not know why. All she did know was that she was glad. It was as if Susan had lost out somehow and she had won.

Though what exactly she wasn't sure.

Chapter Twelve

Susan felt tired and irritable, it had been a long day. Married for only a month, and eight months pregnant, she was beginning to realise the extent of the work involved in keeping the house nice, cooking her new husband meals and having a heavy weight dragging her down from the moment she woke to the moment she went to bed.

But, all in all, she was enjoying herself.

Their wedding was now part of East End folklore. People had talked about it for days, all laughing and joking and making remarks. Susan had taken it all in good part and endeared herself to neighbours and friends alike. Her home was spotless, her washing was done regularly, and her step and her windows shone like beacons before the passing women.

Unlike her next-door neighbour, Doreen Cashman, who lived like a pig, let her kids run in the street and spent her days smoking fags and gossiping, Susan was accepted by the older women and taken to their hearts.

Susan, though, liked her new neighbour.

Doreen was a slut with long bleached yellow hair, a cigarette permanently dangling from her lips and a mouth like the Blackwall tunnel.

But she was funny, hilarious even, and Susan found her a good sort.

Barry, however, couldn't stand her and made that fact very evident. Doreen did not care a hoot. She gave as good as she got, which did not endear her to him at all. She was the type of woman he referred to as a brass, and she was a brass in that she did moonlight as a prostitute now and again then told the world what she had done. Even the older women laughed at her antics when they were in the mood. Susan thought her a character, someone with personality, life pouring out of her.

After only a month, Susan had grown to rely on Doreen. Her wit, her outlook on life and her crazy lifestyle made Susan envious of her at times.

But all in all she was happy enough with her marriage. After the disaster of the actual day they had settled into their new home and made it like a little paradise for the two of them. Kate Dalston was thrilled to bits with Susan's aptitude for housework and cooking that matched even her own high standards. Consequently she came round every day and they were getting quite close. Susan loved having a real mother figure in her life, and if sometimes Barry did not come home, she didn't berate him. She just cooked him some food and asked him how everything was going when he finally did arrive, and acted as if everything was normal.

Barry, realising that she was a diamond, gave her peace and quiet and affection. So long as Doreen was not in the house everything was fine.

Doreen for her part made sure she disappeared as soon as his key was heard in the door.

This morning the sun was out, the heat was growing and the council had arranged for standpipes in the road because of the water shortage. In the East End this was common in summer and Susan was grateful to Doreen's two elder boys as they saved her the job of filling buckets then carrying them all the way home. She was making them both a cup of tea when her cousin Frances arrived without warning and with an expression on her face that told both women something bad had happened.

'Where's Barry?' Frances asked tersely.

Susan shrugged. Sweat was trickling down her neck and back, making her itchy and uncomfortable.

'How do I know, Fran? He could be anywhere.'

Frances looked lovely and Susan poured her a cup of tea while admiring her dress and shoes.

'You look as fresh as a peach, don't she, Doreen? You always had the figure, girl. Make the most of it, I say.'

Frances looked ashamed. Without a word she walked out into the tiny garden. She looked in a state, as Doreen put it to herself, and she had an idea it was over Barry Dalston.

'What do you want to see him for, Fran? Only he normally comes in about sixish, if you want to come back then?'

Frances was still feigning interest in the garden.

'Does he still drink in the Londoner?'

Susan shrugged. 'I don't know, he's all over the place these days with me father. Can I give him a message?'

Doreen picked up the anxiety in Susan's voice and leaning on the wall by the back door called out, 'What do you want to see him for anyway?'

Her tone of voice brought Frances back into the kitchen. Susan had just sat herself down on a chair and was pulling at the neck of her dress to fan her skin and try and cool off. Her belly was huge. Looking at her cousin, Frances felt the first stirrings of regret for what she had done and what she had to say.

'You been up the hospital lately? What did they have to say?'

Susan laughed. 'Not a lot. I have to wait now – the last few weeks are always the hardest or so everyone tells me. Trust me to be in the fucking club through the hottest part of summer, eh? Just my luck.'

She patted her belly happily and sighed.

Frances smiled sadly.

'It must be hard, mate. Still, at least you ain't bothered by Barry, are you? I mean, him wanting his leg over and that. You give it up at six months, don't you?'

Doreen and Susan both roared.

'You're joking, ain't you? He's still at me like anything. I could do with the rest to be honest.'

Frances looked dismayed and this made the other two women laugh even more.

'Listen, Fran, you feel randier when you're pregnant for some unknown reason and Barry says it's good for the baby too. He read it in the paper.'

'I bet he did! I didn't even realise he could read, to be honest.'

Doreen and Susan laughed at that, assuming it was a joke.

Frances took Susan's hands in hers and sighed heavily.

'Listen, Susan. I need to talk to you, mate. What with the baby and everything . . .' She turned to Doreen. 'Would you mind leaving us alone, please?'

Susan pulled her hands from her cousin's and shook her head. 'Whatever you're going to say, you can say it in front of Doreen, I'll probably tell her anyway.'

She didn't want to hear this, somehow she knew it was going to cause trouble.

'Listen, Susan.' Frances knelt down in front of her and gripped her hands, an action that for some reason really irritated Susan.

'I don't know how to tell you this, but I have to . . .'

'You slept with Barry on my wedding day? I already know about it.'

Susan's voice was low, heavy with menace, and Doreen sighed in annoyance. She knew her friend was feeling under the weather and that something like this was not conducive to a peaceful lying in. As she saw the hurt in Susan's eyes she felt an urge to punch Frances in the face.

The girl dropped her eyes and stood up unsteadily.

'That's not the worst of it, Susan.'

She was baffled for a moment. Suddenly she knew what her cousin was going to say and, heaving herself from the chair, felt her hands make contact with Frances's hair. Susan was dragging her across the kitchen the next minute and attempting to throw her out of the back door.

'You bitch! You're in the club, ain't you?'

She could feel her baby struggling as she strained with exertion and pushed the unwelcome guest from her home. Her home, the one she shared with Barry. Barry Dalston, the lying, cheating, two-faced bastard.

Doreen was pulling her away from Frances, using all her considerable strength to separate the two girls.

'I'll kill you, Frances, I take oath on that.'

Frances was crying now. She stood in the garden and cried like a baby, big fat tears that ran down her cheeks and made her make up run. Yet still she stood there, unable to leave until she had divulged all the news she had to tell the woman before her.

'I ain't pregnant, I wish I was. Anything would be better than this, Sue, anything.'

Susan heard the pleading note in her voice and relaxed, made her body calm down as she waited to hear something even worse than she'd imagined.

'Well, what is it then? Is he leaving me, is that it, and ain't got the guts to tell me himself?'

Her world was broken in two. She felt as if someone had taken a meat cleaver and sliced through her breastbone then straight to her heart. The pain could not be worse than this hatred inside her, this feeling of inadequacy, of being nothing once more.

Doreen held her as a mother might hold her child, in an embrace that was loving and caring. Being more streetwise, more worldly, she had already guessed the worst.

Frances looked into her cousin's eyes. Shaking her head, she whispered, 'He gave me a dose, Susan, a dose of the clap.'

At first she thought she had not heard Frances correctly, that she had somehow misunderstood the simple statement.

'You what? He gave you a what?'

She realised she was screaming the words now. That the neighbours would hear if she wasn't careful. She knew they all liked her, thought she was a respectable girl whatever they might think of her husband. Yes, she was a good girl, a clean girl, a decent person.

Now her cousin Frances was standing in her little garden, the garden she had carefully swept not two hours before, and telling her that she was diseased, that she had VD. That she was tainted, dirty, full of some dreadful illness.

'You treacherous slut. How could you do this to me, Fran? How could you do this to your own?'

Frances was sobbing now.

'I'm sorry, Sue. Honest to God if I could turn the clock back . . . I was drunk and you know what he's like. He could talk the drawers off a French dresser. Please try and understand . . .'

Doreen laughed then, a booming sound that seemed to be amplified by the tiny kitchen.

'You're fucking unbelievable! You stand there and tell a heavily pregnant woman her husband has given you a round of applause – and you expect sympathy? Jesus, girl, what are you? Some kind of fucking nut?'

Frances was still crying.

Picking up her bag and throwing it out into the garden, Doreen shut the door on her, all the while shouting at her to go away in language that left no one in any doubt what would happen to her if she disobeyed.

She grabbed Susan by the arms and looked into her face.

'Listen to me, Susan. Calm down, love. I'll take you up the hospital meself, all right? No one will know about this, I swear. I can keep a secret, love, you know that. Now listen to me – everything is confidential at the VD clinic, no one will ever know, all right? But you have to see what they say because of the baby.'

Susan was nodding now, like a child, grateful that Doreen was taking over.

'Will it be born blind? I know it can make people blind . . .'

Doreen pulled Susan towards her once more. Whispering gently, she tried to calm her again.

'Listen, this only happened a month ago. There hasn't been much time for it to affect the baby. Also, that little whore could have got it anywhere for all we know and Barry might not have it at all. That means you might not have it, so let's only start worrying when we know the score, okay?'

Susan nodded, grateful for something to hold on to.

'Yeah, you're right, she's probably trying to cause trouble.'

The hope in Susan's voice made Doreen want to cry.

'She always liked him. All the girls do, see? I feel sorry . . .'

Doreen nodded, wisely keeping her own counsel.

'Come on, mate, let's get you up Whitechapel Hospital and see what they have to say, eh?'

Susan was in shock and Doreen guessed as much. She helped her put on a cardigan and locked up the house for her. Then, warning her own children that if they started anything she would murder them in cold blood in their beds, she walked Susan to the bus stop.

All the time her mind was working over and over, trying to remember what happened when you caught VD while heavily pregnant. But it was something no one knew about unless it had happened to them personally.

Barry and Joey were the best of friends again, working together to collect debts and strong arming for whoever needed a 'touch', the term for paid-in-the-hand threats. Sometimes a debt might be owed by a friend who, taking advantage of that friendship, might then tell the lender they could wait a while, etc, etc. The lender then became upset, seeing their money thrown down the drain, and would employ the likes of Joey and Barry to make sure the debtor understood the correct procedure for returning monies borrowed in good faith.

Joey turning up also protected the lender, because he would collect a percentage and that percentage guaranteed that if the person owing got upset, the lender had the added protection of Joey sorting it all out once more.

All in all a very lucrative and interesting business, as Barry was finding out.

On this bright August afternoon they were collecting a debt for a woman from Barking. She had lent her estranged husband two thousand pounds which she had been left as a legacy. When she had given him the money to open his new café on the Barking Road, she had believed they were happily married and that the café was going to make them a fortune.

Two years later he was living with her friend and she was not only without a husband but also without the couple of grand she had been left. She needed the money because her errant husband was also being difficult about giving her money for their six children. Consequently, through Ivy, she was introduced to Joey and Barry who assured her there would be no comebacks from her husband as they would make sure he knew the score from the outset.

The husband, a large man of Greek origins, was well known in

Barking for his size and his temper. He was just the type of face Joey loved humiliating. Plus they were doing the deserted family a service – six kids unfed and unclothed!

Joey and Barry's hypocrisy knew no bounds.

As Stefano Skarpelis was cooking his all day English breakfasts he did not feel any fear as the two well-known breakers came into his café. It was two in the afternoon and a beautiful day. The café was hot and the door stood wide open. Two heavy electric fans were working overtime. The place was nearly full, as Joey had known it would be. The two men sauntered in and found a seat.

Stefano came to their table. He knew they would not want to queue up like everyone else and wanted to show the respect due to them.

'What can I get you, gentlemen?'

His voice was jovial. He was pleased to see them. Everyone was watching, as they'd known would be the case.

'Nice place here, Skarpelis, I like the décor.'

Stefano nearly burst. His pride and joy were the murals of Greek village life painted on the walls.

'Thank you, Mr McNamara, it's a pleasure to have you here in my café. The weather today is like my homeland – hot and exciting.'

He laughed and Joey and Barry laughed with him.

'Where'd you get the money from to open this place?'

Barry's voice held just the tiniest hint of menace and the big man was unsure how to answer.

'I borrowed it, of course, like everyone does.'

'Must have cost a couple of grand at least, eh?'

Stefano nodded, suddenly unsure where this conversation was going and aware that there was a hidden agenda he would rather not think about.

'How's that lovely wife of yours? A great favourite of me mum's, she is,' Joey cut in. 'And them kids of yours? Imagine, six fucking kids all by the one bird. Don't bear thinking about. My mum reckons you never fired a blank in your life, mate.'

Their conversation was being listened to by everyone now and

Stefano's new woman, a thirty-year-old blonde with heavy make up and an even heavier chest, stood watching warily from behind the counter.

Joey started talking in a sing-song voice, as if he was telling a story to a bunch of little children.

'Funnily enough, Stefano, my mum had to give your old woman some dosh the other week, to help pay the rent and get some grub in for that bunch of daughters and sons of yours. "Funny," I says to me mum, "ain't he just opened a café in Barking? I heard he was raking it in." But she informed me that you had had it on your toes and left the old woman, the kids and your own mother in fucking stook. "So," me mother says to me, "you go and see him and find out what he's doing, because poor old Angela is boracic lint." That being due to the fact that you robbed your old woman of the two grand she'd been left by her grandfather.'

Barry shook his head solemnly.

'What a ponce, eh? I can't believe I just heard that, can you?'

He looked towards the five workmen at a nearby table for confirmation.

'Don't you think he's a ponce, leaving his kids in the fucking lurch and his old woman potless while he reaps the benefit of her couple of grand?'

The men nodded vigorously. They knew exactly what was expected of them. If the Greek was going to get a hiding they wanted to make sure they were on the winning side. He might make a blinding sausage sandwich, but that was as far as their loyalty went.

'Fucking terrible, ain't it? Unbelievable. I was shocked, shocked and appalled by my mother's tale of woe. "Get your arse down there," she said, "and sort that foreign ponce out."'

Joey held out his arms inviting general acclaim.

'So, Stefano, here I am, and I want your old woman's dosh, plus my expenses, and your word you will pay your old woman a regular amount.'

Stefano looked into Joey's eyes and saw how much he was enjoying this.

'I understand what you're saying, Mr McNamara, but let me assure you . . .'

Barry interrupted him.

'Shut your trap and bring the food. Once we've eaten we'll explain it all to you in simple terms in your flat above this lovely café. Unless, of course, you want to discuss it here right now? In which case, that suits us down to the ground.'

Stefano Skarpelis knew what was going on, and he knew he was defeated. News of this visit would be all over by late afternoon. He was worried about it affecting his business.

East End people were strange. They would hide a murderer yet string up the same man for leaving his wife and children without support. Yes, they were weird, and he knew when he was cornered.

'I'll make you both a full English breakfast then we'll sort this out.'

He walked away with as much dignity as he could muster, face pale and wearing a smile that did not quite reach his eyes.

'See, Barry, sometimes you don't have to raise a hand. A right slagging off in public does the job better than a firearm or a cosh.'

Barry laughed.

He had a twinkle in his eye because in the corner sat two little birds who looked right up his street. They were smiling and simpering at him. One was short with fat legs and breasts but the other was better: red-haired, with full lips and shapely legs that she crossed and uncrossed at an alarming rate.

'You ain't winking at the two dogs over there, surely? Fucking hell, I'm going to buy you a lead for Christmas so you can take them out in public.'

Even Barry laughed. One good thing about Joey, he did have a sense of humour. Five minutes later the food was still not on the table and, leaning back in his chair, Joey shouted across the café to a workman and his friend by the door.

'Oi, mate, how much for a bite of your sandwich? I'm fucking dying of starvation here. Hitler invaded Poland faster than it takes this Greek ponce to make breakfast!'

Everyone cracked up laughing and Stefano Skarpelis closed his eyes and asked God what the fuck he had done to deserve this?

* * *

Susan had been examined by a doctor and now he was helping her to get off the high table. She was so ungainly she could not get up without help. The doctor was young with wide brown eyes and a broad nose, but was saved from ugliness by his curly black hair and the merry twinkle in his eyes.

'Did you know you were in labour, Mrs Dalston?'

Susan shook her head in amazement.

'No. I have had a bit of a back ache for the last couple of days but everyone said it was all the weight I'd put on. Fuck me, I'd better get home quick smart.'

She tried to stand and he kept her seated with a wave of his hand.

'You are not going anywhere, Mrs Dalston, except up to the labour ward. I think if you have contracted gonorrhoea you should be okay, but we need to keep an eye on you and the baby just to be on the safe side. You say you contracted it nearly a month ago, yes?'

Susan nodded, humiliated.

'I might have got it sooner but he certainly gave it to my cousin on my wedding day. Mind you, that Frances is such a dog the chances are she gave it to him.'

Daniel Cole looked at the woman before him with sadness and resignation. During his time at the Whitechapel he had met many women in her position and it always amazed him how resilient they were. How they took all life threw at them and managed to rise above it.

'Will the kid be blind and deformed, doctor? That's me biggest worry.'

Dr Cole smiled.

'I'm sure everything will be okay. Now, the worry of today has probably brought on labour – a fright or a shock can do that. So let's just concentrate on getting your baby into the world, shall we? Then we can worry about anything else if it proves necessary. Okay?'

Susan nodded, unsure what exactly he was saying to her.

'But it's a month early. Is that because of the disease like? Has the VD made it come out too quick because there's something wrong with it?'

Dr Cole sighed heavily and made himself smile.

'Like I said, let's just wait and see. Mrs Dalston, no one knows anything at the moment except that you are in labour and the child will be delivered within the next twenty-four hours. It's pointless worrying yourself and risking making things worse. Now, let me get a nurse to take you up to the ward and we can proceed from there.'

Susan nodded.

His voice was low and reassuring, exactly what she needed at this moment. Someone to take over, take the pressure, take the strain.

Doreen accompanied her up to the ward with the nurse. Susan held her friend's hand like a life-line. She felt that if she let it go she would fall into some great abyss and that would be the end of her life, her child's, and her sanity.

The redhead's name was Sonia. She had a flat near the Heathway in Dagenham, and a little boy called Luke. He was living with her mother apparently because she found it hard to cope with him. Luke, it turned out, was five. She had given birth to him when she was fourteen. Not that that bothered Barry Dalston. He didn't want a virgin, he wanted a good time.

Sonia's friend's name was Abigail but she liked to be called Abby. After tearing up Stefano's flat and giving him a good hiding, the two men took the girls to the Bull for a drink and a bit of a crack.

'In fairness, he does do a blinding breakfast,' observed Joey.

The two girls laughed.

'Not for a while, though, by the sounds coming from the flat. Everyone could hear it going on, it was great.'

Sonia, it turned out, liked a man who was a bit of a face. Like most of her ilk it would never occur to her that she was in the predicament she was because of her taste in men. One little boy and three abortions along the way had taught her nothing. Sonia was an accident waiting to happen.

She'd been unsure at first whether she wanted young Barry as he had laughed at his friend's crude joke about them, but being a girl who never held a grudge she'd decided to go along to the pub and see what developed.

The way his hand was sliding up her thigh now told her things were developing very well.

'Another rum and Coke, girls?'

Joey's voice was loud in the confines of the pub garden.

The two girls nodded.

'Fuck me, Bal, the way these two put it away we'd better go and knock over the fucking local Post Office in case they want something to eat as well.'

He grinned at Abby.

'You could do with missing a couple of meals, darlin'. I ain't seen thighs like that since I caught my old woman in bed with the window cleaner.'

Abigail laughed delightedly, happy with the attention.

Joey went into the pub and up to the bar.

'Two treble rum and Cokes and a couple of pints, mate.'

The barman laughed.

'What time's Cinderella turning up then? I see you got lumbered with the Ugly Sisters. Be careful, mate, the little fat one lives with a black bloke off the market and he is handy.' He tapped his nose. 'Just a word to the wise like. No offence, but I don't want me pub torn up.'

Joey was grateful for the nod.

'What are they, a couple of wog lovers then?'

The man nodded. 'In a word, yeah. So long as they're worth a few bob, of course. They're dogs, mate, and if that's what you want for an afternoon, good luck to you. But just keep out a beady, they ain't worth fighting over.'

'Too fucking right! Have one yourself and give us a couple of brandy chasers, large ones. I need a drink after a shock like that. I was gonna give it fucking plenty and all. Now, though, I might have to have a rethink.'

The man laughed with Joey.

'Fucking daughters! Who'd have them, eh? I remember my old

mother used to say: "Be careful where you plant it, boy. Always remember that the biggest dogs in the world are someone's daughter, mother or sister."'

Joey laughed at that. It had never occurred to him before and he liked the way it rolled off the man's tongue. He would nick that little homily and use it himself.

In the garden Sonia was allowing Barry to take right liberties, as the more liberal of the East End women referred to being titted up in public.

He could smell her, all of her, the heat was so strong. It was a mixture of sweat, perfume, deodorant, and underlying it all was the smell of her sex.

He knew he could have her on the wooden bench if he pushed it and the thought turned him on.

Joey returned with the tray of drinks.

'Have I got a bit of a tan, girls, with all this sun we've had? Do I look a little bit like a macaroon, eh?'

Barry saw the two girls look at Joey without laughing.

'What's the matter? Don't tell me two young girls like you are prejudiced against our Caribbean brethren? I mean, how would we run the buses and trains without them, eh?'

Abigail lit a cigarette and puffed on it hard.

'Or the Health Service, come to that.'

Barry realised she was defending black people and tried not to laugh.

Joey was warming to his theme now.

'Like a bit of black pudding do you, Abigail? Come to think of it, the barman told me you live with a lemonade from the market. Is it true what they say about black men then – hung like horses and can last all night?'

Abigail nodded.

'Yeah, it is, actually, and they have softer skin and nicer manners than white blokes. Especially white old blokes. Funny that, ain't it?'

She picked up her cigarettes and bag and stood up to leave. Joey grabbed her arm and she winced.

'You ain't going nowhere, lady. I have paid out a heavy portion of wedge on you and you'll come through for me. If your soot turns up I'll give him the hard word, OK?'

Sonia was pissed, but not so pissed she didn't realise they were both in trouble. Bad trouble. The two men were looking menacing now, scary. They had been found out and that frightened them.

They knew the score. With men like Joey and Barry you had to play the game or you were expected to pay a forfeit.

Joey forced Abigail back into her seat. Smiling nicely, he continued, 'So, ladies, whose place are we going to after the next few drinks, eh?'

Sonia smiled grimly.

'Looks like it will have to be mine, don't it?'

Joey laughed again, displaying all his teeth and a fair amount of his gums as well. His nicotine-covered tongue was dancing in the gaping hole of his mouth.

Sonia, drunk and feeling brave, looked at Abigail and trilled, 'I don't think much of yours girl.'

She looked at her friend and answered sarcastically, 'Really? Well, I have a feeling you'll be seeing a bit of him and all, Sonia. These two looks like they do a double act.'

Barry grinned. He was enjoying himself now. It was so much easier if you had them down on the floor with a metaphorical foot right on their windpipe. It added to the game, the excitement and the jollity.

'We certainly are. What's his is mine and what's mine is his.'

As soon as he said it his expression changed and the three other people round the table knew he had said something profound.

But only Joey understood what he had really said.

Raising his drink, he smiled at his son-in-law.

'In more ways than one. Cheers.'

Susan was pushing with all her might. Her hair was plastered to her head and her body felt as if it was being ripped in two.

'Come on, love, one more good push then you can have a rest.'

She nodded. Taking a deep breath she pushed again, harder this time, but she felt as if she had achieved nothing.

The nurse smiled and listened to the baby's heartbeat once more.

'It's coming along lovely but I think you might need a bit of help. Relax, and let me talk to the doctor.'

Susan lay back gratefully, supporting her head on the pillows and trying to fan herself with an old copy of *Woman's Realm*. She had never dreamed it would be like this, the constant pain and the dragging feeling in her back. She had only ever visualised the baby all dressed up nice and in a pram with everyone admiring it. Even Ivy's stories of the terrible births she had witnessed over the years had seemed miles away from real life.

Now, though, she believed them.

Susan was praying again, not for the pain to stop but for the child to be all right. Not blind or deaf or twisted up. It was terrifying, the thought of what could be inside her.

One part of her wanted this baby to emerge so much, but another part wanted it to stay where it was, safe from the world, safe from Barry and his disease.

The disease he had given to her, and through her his innocent child.

She swallowed down the tears and fanned herself harder. Then she felt it, an almighty pain that tore through her like a hot sword, making her feel her body would be rent in two.

The shriek she gave brought in two nurses and the doctor.

'Christ, she's crowned!'

As Susan gave birth in Whitechapel Hospital at eleven-thirty-five p.m. on 22 August 1968 Barry was tucked up in bed with Sonia and Abigail. Joey was asleep on the sofa in the lounge after too much drink and overindulging in fish and chips.

The earlier arguments were forgotten. The two girls had turned out to be a right laugh and a right handful. Especially Abigail, who seemed actually to enjoy it all which made a change. Most of the women they picked up did it just because they were asked to. It never even occurred to them that they might have the option of saying no now and again.

Their attitude was that if a man bought them drinks and a meal he should be repaid in kind, whether they wanted to or not.

Joey and Barry were blissfully unaware of what was going on while they romped, drank and ate to their heart's content. Not once did it occur to either of them to let someone know where they were or what they were doing.

While his wife was grunting and groaning so was Barry Dalston.

As his wife lay bathed in sweat so did Barry.

The only difference was, while she was thinking about him, wondering where he was, what he was doing and who the hell he was doing it with, she was the farthest thing from his mind.

The child finally born, Susan lay back in relief. All she wanted now was to see it, touch it, hold it and make sure it was all right. For the first time that day, Barry was the farthest thing from *her* mind. The child took precedence.

That in itself was a relief.

Not to think about him was a wonderful thing, but she didn't realise it at the time. It would not be until afterwards that Susan thought back over that day and clearly understood the truth about Barry and herself.

The pain, the anger and the humiliation she suffered then would stay with her for many years, hidden away in her subconscious, waiting to erupt.

For the moment, though, her only thought was for her child.

Chapter Thirteen

Ivy looked down at the baby and felt tears prick her eyes. He was beautiful, the image of Joey when he was born. The same impossibly long eyelashes, rosebud mouth and deep blue eyes. The sturdy little body fitted into her arms perfectly, as if he was meant to be there.

Tears in her eyes, she looked pityingly at Susan. At that moment she hated men, all men, but particularly her son and her granddaughter's husband.

Putting the child gently back in the bassinette she took Susan into her arms for the first time since childhood and embraced her, pulling the distraught girl against her bosom in an attempt to ease the horror and pain of the situation.

Susan was sobbing, her body heaving like a rogue wave as she cried out all the hurt inside her.

'The bastard! The rotten bastard.'

She could not talk properly; hiccoughing sobs made her words incomprehensible, only the tone made any real sense.

Ivy stroked her back and murmured endearments, tried to comfort the girl she had always taken pleasure in baiting. She felt suffocated by guilt as she looked down at her great-grandson. Realising what she had done, what she had allowed to be done.

'There will be others, love. These things happen in life.'

The words were lame even in Ivy's ears. How could anyone even attempt to make a disaster of this magnitude better? It was impossible. So they drew on every cliché, every old saying, every piece of crap they could get their tongues around.

Susan, though, would not be soothed. She blamed her father

for everything. Not Barry, her husband, who, in fact had had a choice in what he had done. She chose to see him as the victim of her father's excesses. She knew Barry wanted to be like Joey. Have the respect her father commanded in the area where they lived and beyond. That his aim in life was to be a bona-fide breaker, a man people came to when they needed help of a violent nature.

Barry copied Joey in everything, from his walk to his way of life, that way of life including taking any woman who looked 'up for it'. Who would have thought that one of those one night stands could be the cause of her child's death?

Susan looked at her mother, sitting silently in the side ward with her head in her hands. The three women seemed at ease with one another for the first time ever. June looked up into her daughter's strained face.

'He was beautiful, Susan, a beautiful little boy. He would have been a real man.'

Her words struck a chord inside her daughter somewhere. She wiped her face with her hand, snot and tears mingling.

'It's a good job he's dead then, ain't it? I don't want to bring any more men into the world. I don't want anyone to go through what I have been through at the hands of so-called men.'

Her words were so raw, so obviously heartfelt, neither woman attempted to stop her. Both of them knew the girl was in a state of shock, not herself. Would need time to heal, physically and mentally.

Doreen came in with four cups of tea.

'They want to take the baby, Susan . . .'

Her words were cut off as the girl bellowed like a market trader.

'When his father has seen him – when Barry has seen what he has done! Then they can take him and clean him up and dress him in something nice for us all. Make us all feel fucking better. But not until then.'

Doreen didn't argue with her. Instead she moved the child to one side of the room in his bassinette and put a cup of hot sweet tea into Susan's hands.

'Drink that up, mate, it will make you feel better.'

Susan laughed then, a deep rollicking sound that was so out of character it made the others frightened.

'Have a cup of tea, Susan, then we'll bury the baby in the back garden and all get some sleep.'

She started to laugh again only this time she couldn't stop.

The tea was going everywhere – over Susan, the bedding, the floor. Ivy left the room and two minutes later Susan was being wrestled down in the bed by three nurses while they injected her with a relaxant.

Susan felt her eyes growing heavier, her body limper, and tried her hardest to fight the effects of the drugs. But the drugs won. As she relaxed into a nightmare world of babies and coffins, the three other women breathed a sigh of relief.

'That will ease her, sleep is a great healer.'

Ivy's words sounded hollow even in her own ears.

Nothing was going to ease the suffering of Susan Dalston.

Barry was annoyed, Joey fuming.

The house was cold, there was no food to be seen and the milk was off. The aftermath of a night of drink and drugs had left them both with a stale taste in their mouths and an even staler smell in their underpants.

It had not occurred to either of them to wash.

Food was their priority at the moment and a cup of tea. They had been missing for two days and neither of them wondered where the pregnant girl was.

Joey looked around the neat front room and said admiringly, 'She keeps the drum nice, though, old Susan, I'll give her that.'

Barry raised one clenched fist.

'And I'll give the cunt that when I get me hands on her. Fucking real, ain't it, Joey? Married a month and already she's tripping off here, there and everywhere, without a fucking thought for me. I come home and there's fuck all in the house. No milk even for a cup of Rosie Lee.'

The back door opened.

'Here she is, all sweetness and light, I bet. Wait till I get my fucking hands on her!'

Barry stormed out of the sitting room, followed closely by a grinning Joey. He was looking forward to seeing Susan get a mouthful, seeing the perfect marriage come down to the level of everyone else's. Especially his own.

Barry was surprised to see his mother standing there.

'Hello, son.'

The words were brief but loaded with meaning and neither man knew what to say to Kate. Her eyes looked a bit red, Barry noticed, and she didn't seem to want to look at him, glancing over his shoulder as if she couldn't bear the sight of his face.

'Hello, Mum. Bit early for you, ain't it?'

He kept his voice elaborately casual but his body language told her he knew what she was going to say before she said it.

'Susan had the child last night – a boy.'

Barry's face lit up like a beacon.

'A boy? What a touch. Susan gave it the large then?'

Joey and he were ecstatic. Rushing into the sitting room, Joey came back with a half bottle of Scotch he kept in his coat for occasions like this.

'Fuck the tea, get the glasses, let's celebrate! A boy at last. I thought all they were capable of was split-arses.'

He thought, as did Barry, that Kate's sombre air was because they had gone on the missing list for a few days when Susan was heavily pregnant.

'He died, Barry. The little child died, son.'

Both Barry and Joey looked properly at her then and recognised the ravages of crying and loss of sleep.

'What do you mean, he died? What's she done now, fell over or something . . .'

Barry looked devastated. He had enjoyed waiting to see what he had made. The thought of another life existing thanks to him had given him a feeling of power.

'Susan did nothing. The child died of gonorrhoea, a venereal disease given to her by you, Barry. You also gave it to Susan's cousin at the wedding. No one is sure yet if it was Susan's fright and shock at finding out or the disease that killed the child, but he's dead. A beautiful strong boy is dead and you are to blame. By

Christ, I could take my fist now and batter your brains out on this kitchen floor – a floor I saw your poor wife wash only two days ago, on her hands and knees, with that big swollen belly hanging down in front of her.'

Kate began to cry then, real tears of shame and loss.

'You are a dirty, filthy animal, and I'll have no more to do with you, boy. No more at all. And if that girl has any sense neither will she.'

She walked out of the back door, a small hunched figure who seemed to have aged overnight.

Joey and Barry stared at one another in shock.

'Mum! Come back, Mum – listen to me.'

Barry was down the garden now and pulling at Kate's arm.

'Don't touch me! Don't you ever touch me again. She won't let them take the child until you have seen him. Be a man for once, a real man, take your responsibilities seriously and get to that hospital. Try and repair the damage you've done to that young girl and her poor baby. Put her at peace if you can.'

She walked away and left him standing in the little garden that Susan swept so meticulously every day. She left him crying.

Joey stood watching in the kitchen, his face blank and his conscience pricking him. He took a tumbler of whisky out to Barry who was still standing shell-shocked in the garden.

'Drink that up, mate, get over the shock. Then you'd better get up the hospital – get it over with.'

Susan looked at the little coffin. It was white with a beautiful gold cross on it and the child's name on a brass plaque. It had cost Barry a small fortune and had gone some way to assuaging his guilt.

Susan looked at the name on it again and felt an urge to scream. JASON BARRY DALSTON.

She had not wanted Barry's name on there, but his grief, so real that it was almost painful to witness, had made her relent. If ever a man was sorry, that man was Barry Dalston. It made Susan sad, but also happy to see it. She wanted him to hurt like her, hurt as much as she did. Wanted him to feel the emptiness she felt in her arms and body. All that time she had lived with the child inside her, feeling him kick, move and swim.

She missed the lump. Missed the feeling of hope it had given her, the feeling of being in on a really exciting secret that only women experience. It had made her feel, for the first time ever, like a whole person.

Now she was burying Jason, giving him to God and the Virgin Mary. She hoped someone would take good care of him for her up there in Heaven.

She looked around the graveyard. Her mother, Ivy and Kate all stood by her side. Debbie stood apart from everyone, her pretty childish face awash with tears. But Susan knew that was all an act with Debs. She was too selfish ever to understand another's suffering. In fact, to hear her, you would think *she* had lost the child and not Susan. All today was to Debbie was an excuse to be part of a drama, a big exciting drama that made her the centre of attention with friends and their families. Made people listen to her for once, instead of wishing she would piss off and leave them in peace.

Susan knew the score, she had always known the score. That was part of the trouble.

Looking at her brand new husband she felt the first stirrings of sympathy for him. This bothered her, bothered her a lot. He was genuinely devastated by the tragedy but Susan knew, as Barry didn't because he was too thick, that he was feeling more guilt than sorrow. Barry was like her father, and Debbie, and her mother and Ivy. They only felt things for the way they affected them personally, not understanding the full implications. They felt sorry for her because she had had the baby, given birth to it. But their real sympathy was for themselves.

Barry's biggest sadness was that he was out shagging while 'his' boy was dying. He referred to his boy constantly, saying how good-looking he'd been, how he would have become a 'real man'. He'd have broken some hearts had he been allowed to grow up. Even the dead child's penis was brought into the equation. It was big, apparently, and he would not have had any worries in that department.

Susan knew this was the only way he knew how to grieve. How he came to terms with it all.

But it did not make her hate him any less.

She still had not spoken to him. Even in the funeral parlour, where they had chosen the expensive coffin with the real gold cross on it, she had just nodded her head at his suggestion.

Susan felt someone take her hand and knew it was Doreen. What would she have done without her friend? She was the only person Susan would speak to, and then only when they were alone. Then the words poured out of her in great torrents that made sense to no one but Susan and, she liked to think, Doreen.

Because she seemed to feel it all with Susan, seemed to understand the enormity of what had occurred in a way that her mother and poor Ivy could not. The boy had been dead only three days when Ivy advised Susan to 'pull herself together', and told her that 'these things happen' and she should 'get on with her life'.

The funny thing was, she didn't feel resentful of Ivy's words. In fact, they had endeared the old woman to her. At least she and Kate acknowledged that something truly appalling had happened. Both had refused their sons sympathy or consolation. Both had taken Susan's side, if that was the correct way of putting it. She wondered about that for a while, trying to blank out the service with thoughts.

Debbie's up-to-the-minute flares made her want to laugh. With her fat legs she looked like a sawn off dancer from Pan's People. Susan felt the ghost of a smile on her lips and bit them hard, reminding herself that she was at her own child's funeral.

Susan studied her father. He at least was sombrely dressed. His suit pressed, his hair newly cut and his face neatly shaved. Joey saw her looking at him and smiled sadly. She realised she must still be smiling and put her hand over her mouth.

What was wrong with her?

How could she find humour in this terrible situation?

What was the bloody joke anyway?

That Jason had escaped it all, she realised. She was thinking that more and more as the days went on. He had escaped Barry and Joey and their making him a man because she knew that if he had lived they would have tainted him with their views.

Barry had already talked of his becoming a boxer, a fucking hard little nut to crack. But Jason, her beloved child, had had the sense to escape, she saw that now. He had taken one look at them all and made his exit.

This thought pleased her even in her grief.

She had felt dirty in church, knowing she was still suffering from that filthy disease, one only filthy people got. Standing there, under the gaze of Our Lord, she had felt the poison rushing through her veins as it had done before and into her child's body.

Courtesy of Barry Dalston, wanker extraordinaire and father of the dead baby.

She wanted to laugh again.

Four of the people at her son's funeral were undergoing treatment at the VD clinic. She wished now that Frances had come, that would have made five.

The famous five.

She wanted to laugh out loud thinking about it all.

The coffin looked so small and lonely that Susan felt an urge to scream at the priest and tell him Jason wasn't going down there in the dark all on his own. He needed his mother with him, in case he was frightened. He needed someone to take proper care of him, love him, and make sure he was not left to cry with no one to answer him.

Why didn't she go with him? Surely God could have taken her too, given her something to look forward to, eternity with Jason and no one else.

Just loving him, caring for him, keeping him safe.

Her father said they would have to watch the grave for a while because of the real gold cross he had told all and sundry was on his grandson's coffin.

'Some ponce will dig him up and chad it. You know what they're like around here.'

Even her mother had shut him up when he had come out with that gem. Yet Susan knew he meant to comfort her. It was Joey's way of saying how well they had done for the child. They had spent money on him, given him what Ivy called 'a good send off'. But to where? Where the fuck had they sent him? All alone, without his mother.

What kind of God did things like that?

Her face relaxed.

But this was the same God who had given her Barry Dalston, wasn't it? And how she had prayed to get him, fool that she was.

It was over now, she knew by the expressions of relief on everyone's face. Barry came to her side and put his hand around her shoulders. He was crying. She could see all the neighbours watching them, Maud next door and all her cronies, gathering like rats around a dead body.

'Fuck off, Barry.'

Susan's words were softly spoken but clearly audible because of their intensity. Then the real tears started, and all because of Barry's smell. The smell she had loved so much once: Old Spice and fags mingled with Brylcreem and fish and chips.

Once his nearness had been everything to her, made her feel safe, made her love and want him. Now she was crying for her child and for the lost youth she would never again remember with happiness. Barry had been the one thing she had had that was good after life with Joey and June. He had been a beacon to her for so long, something she had wanted to attain so much, and now she knew she had longed all the time for fool's gold.

But she let him hold her tight to him. Her son's funeral was not the time or the place for hysterics, however much she was tempted to shame him. After all, the neighbours were watching and didn't need to know her business.

Disillusioned and sick at heart though she was, old habits died hard for Susan Dalston.

She awoke in the night. The street-lamp outside the house bathed the bedroom in a warm soothing glow but all she felt was the furnace inside her breasts. Milk was still seeping out of them and it made her feel hot and sick.

Barry was kneeling down by the bed and she realised then that it was he who had woken her, taken her from blessed dreams that made the pain disappear for a short while. Sleeping tablets were a wonderful invention.

'Surely you ain't after a bit of the other?'

Her voice was flat-sounding but loud in the stillness of the house.

'I love you, Susan Dalston, I love you more than anything.'

Barry's voice was full of his own sorrow. Susan couldn't have cared a toss. She didn't answer.

'I'm so sorry, Susan, really I am. I know it was all my fault but, you see, it was that fucking Joey. He took me out, got me pissed up. I woke up the next morning with him and two old sorts in this bed . . .'

Barry was really crying now.

Susan felt strangely detached from him.

'They were here in my bed? Is that what you're telling me?'

She felt him nod, knew he was trying to make things better, trying to be honest.

'They was brasses, old whores, didn't mean a thing. Not like you and me, darlin', that's real. I love you. I don't care a fucking toss about them.'

Susan heard the humour in her own voice as she answered, 'I'm glad to hear it. Now can I go back to sleep?'

Barry pressed his head against her belly, the big rounded soft belly with its red stretch marks and loose skin.

'Please, Sue, don't leave me out. Stop pushing me out . . . I hurt as well.'

She lay immobile, eyes open in the darkness, forcing down an urge to take his head between her knees and crush the life out of him.

How she had loved to feel him down there once, how she had enjoyed the feel of his tongue inside her. She had almost let herself go then, let the good feelings wash over her once and for all. She was glad she had not succumbed. It would have been a betrayal of her dead child.

Barry had nearly made her enjoy sex; once or twice he had

nearly hit the right spot. But she had forced the feeling away, not wanting to know what it was that made people go mad, do things with total strangers to fulfil a primal urge.

Fuck 'em and leave 'em. That was one of Barry's favourite expressions. Well, he had fucked one and she had left him with more than he had bargained for. Susan Dalston had had her fill of sex and all it brought with it.

'Let me sleep, Bal, please.'

He grabbed her then, with hands that were clawing and desperate.

'Susan . . . please, Susan. I love you, darlin'. Really love you. We can make a go of it. I'll change, I promise you. I'll make you proud of me again. I promise I won't touch another woman as long as I live. On Jason's grave, I swear it.'

She was sitting up now, her face stern and unmoved.

'Don't you swear on that child's grave, Barry Dalston. You're trying to make a promise you can never keep. You're like me father – fucking is all you know. Fucking in all its forms, sexual and emotional.

'You both fucked me and you both fucked me up, the pair of you. You leave that little boy out of this. Don't you taint him any more than you have already. You killed him. Face it, face that fact, and let me fucking sleep. I just want to sleep.'

She lay back down and he lay against her, his head once more on the softness of her belly. He needed the clean smell of her to make him whole again.

Susan, he realised, was a diamond really. She was clean in herself and in the home. She was loving, she was good. Susan was a good person and she scrubbed up well. He knew he could have done a lot worse, got a Frances or a Debbie who would have married him and like June been taking on all comers by their first anniversary. Because they needed to be wanted, needed to feel sexually desired. Because they didn't have the brains to differentiate between love and fucking.

They saw themselves as nothing more than sex objects, and that made for unhappy women because once real life set in they had to look further and further afield to get the buzz they craved.

Strange men, who would use them for a while and tell them any old crap they wanted to hear.

Unlike Susan, his Susan with her ugly face and cumbersome body who gave him so much more, because she gave it without any thought of a return. He didn't have to buy her drinks or tell her a load of crap, she was just there. There, waiting for him, and him alone.

For the first time in his life he realised just what loyalty meant.

Barry Dalston, hard man, vicious thug and grieving father, grasped his young wife as if she was all that prevented him from drowning.

Ten days later Susan was dressing to attend another funeral. This time it was her cousin Frances who was being buried. No one outside the family knew just why she had topped herself.

Frances had taken herself out to Essex and hung herself from a tree in Belhus Park, Aveley. It was a place they had all gone as children to visit an old relative, long dead and forgotten.

Susan was too preoccupied with the funeral and her own mixed emotions to notice a piece that appeared that day in the *Daily Mirror*. A prostitute from the Valbon club, Soho, had been beaten to death two days before, her body dumped in rubbish in Gerrard Street.

But Barry read it, over and over. He was a great believer in paying back debts without money changing hands.

Well, Frances had topped herself over the baby and all the pain she had caused. He had had to help the other woman die, but it had been worth it.

He had paid her back for his son's death. Got the perpetrator and punished them. It made him feel much better inside. Someone had to pay, and as usual it was not going to be him.

After the funeral he grasped Susan's hand and she looked briefly into his eyes.

'You look almost happy, Barry.'

He shook his head and his face resumed its mournful expression.

'I'm happy because I have you back, darlin', that's all.'

As he pulled her into his arms he smiled. The sad part was, he really believed what he said. Such was the mentality of Susan Dalston's husband.

But as they left the cemetery, Susan, still suffering from grief and shock, felt a glimmer of hope for the future. Their future.

At least, she thought, he cares about me. That's a start anyway.

The sun was high again, the day golden. Everywhere new life was burgeoning. Children were playing, flowers were blooming and people were going about their business.

At least, Susan thought to herself as her husband gently helped her into the car, things can't get any worse. As he started the engine Barry leaned over and kissed her on the lips. For the first time in ages Susan actually smiled back.

He was forgiven.

Out of the corner of his eye he saw Doreen watching them. Pulling away from the kerb he put one hand behind Susan's head and stuck two fingers up.

'Shall I put the radio on, girl, cheer us up a bit?'

Susan nodded absently, her mind full of Frances and the funeral. She did not see Doreen, grimacing like a maniac and making wanker signs.

But Barry did, and filed it away for future reference.

Book Two

1969

There is no peace, saith the Lord, unto the wicked.

– Isaiah 48:22

Chapter Fourteen

'Will you shut that fucking baby up!' Barry's voice was louder than the little girl's. Susan was walking around the adjacent bedroom, patting the child's back and trying to calm her.

Wendy's teeth were just coming through and she was not happy about it at all. In fact the child seemed to have come into a world she did not like and had made her feelings abundantly plain ever since.

Wendy had cried since birth.

The doctor said it was colic, Susan thought it was colic, Barry was convinced the child had been given to them by the Devil himself and was not pleased at all. To make matters worse, if Wendy did quieten, all she needed to see was Barry's face looking into her cot and the Third World War started up again.

Wendy Kathryn Dalston did not like her father. Susan did not think she was a bad judge.

But Barry was becoming increasingly annoyed with his daughter's nocturnal screaming fits and made a point of letting everyone know. Susan often wondered who was the loudest, Wendy or him. Either way their voices were all she heard.

Unlike Barry, Wendy was Susan's heart's delight. She only had to look into those big blue eyes and she melted. She was convinced this child was destined to become a great beauty and adored her without reservation. In short, Wendy meant the world to her. Barry, guessing this, had felt from the moment the child was born a jealousy he knew he should suppress. But he could not help it.

Wendy took up all of Susan's time, her patience and her love.

Getting out of the bed, he went into the next-door bedroom and practically dragged the child from Susan's arms.

'Put the spoiled little fucker back in her cot. Let her cry. For fuck's sake, Sue, let's get one night of fucking peace!'

His screaming made Wendy even more upset and she began really to yell, feeling the tension in the room and the fear in her mother's body.

Susan held the child closer still, pressing her into her breasts.

'She's due a feed anyway, Bal. Give the kid a break. She's four months old, she can't tell the fucking time.'

Susan was hanging on to the child for dear life and Barry was once more trying to drag her from her mother's arms.

'I'm warning you, Barry, you'll hurt her if you keep this up and then you'll know all about it, boy.'

The words were out before Susan realised what she had said. They were instinctive, just a mother's way of defending her baby. Barry looked at her for long moments and she felt the icy grip of fear around her heart.

'Bal, listen to me – Barry, please . . .'

The fist when it hit her was so unexpected she staggered back against the cot, nearly letting go of the baby and dropping her on to the floor.

Susan felt her eyebrow split, felt the flow of blood and the onset of stinging tears. Barry watched as if in slow motion. He knew as soon as he made contact with her that he had hit her hard, as he would have hit another man. He knew, from the split second he raised his arm, that what he was doing was wrong.

Wendy fell quiet, deadly quiet, and both Susan and Barry looked down at her. Susan's blood had dripped on to the baby's face and both thought she had been injured.

'You fucking bastard, Bal, what have you done?'

It was the quietness that made Susan scared, the child's unnatural quietness. Then Wendy smiled, a big beatific smile, and Susan felt the hand around her heart ease its grip.

Barry looked down at his daughter, and there was no mistaking she was his. She looked so like him it was unnerving. He saw the smile, and the blood and mucus from her nose, and felt the relief only a guilty person can feel. He'd thought for a moment he had harmed her and that to Barry was the worst thing he could have done. Not so much because it was wrong but because in their world anyone who hurt a child was banished, abused, treated with public contempt. You could batter them black and blue once they were old enough to start school and became real people, but a baby . . . well, a baby was a thing of joy to everyone. Except, a lot of the time, to their parents.

Barry was sick of people praising Susan and her gift for motherhood. Even Davey Davidson had remarked on what a diamond she was, telling him how his own wife was always talking about their lovely daughter and spotless house. Susan, it seemed, was born and bred for mothering, though how no one understood considering June and her track record. It seemed to be a knack she was born with.

Even his mother loved Susan. Thought she was the bee's knees, the dog's bollocks. Looking at her now, plain-faced and with a fat belly in her old nightie, he felt nothing but revulsion. Her breasts were still full of milk, she was always leaking all over the place, the child was clamped there morning, noon and night. 'Feeding on demand' Susan called it; he called it ruining the fucking baby from the off, but would she listen to him?

What Wendy Dalston wanted, Wendy Dalston got. Whether it was cuddles, food, attention or even a fag, if the child wanted it, she got it.

Susan was making a rod for her own back as far as he was concerned, but the fright was still in him and taking the child from her mother he rocked her in his arms. Wendy for once was docile, as if the shock and the noise had knocked the stuffing from her. Staring up at her father she smiled again, a big gummy baby smile that defied anyone not to love her.

Barry jiggled her up and down for a few minutes, marvelling at the feeling her little body created nestled in his arms. He loved her then. When she wanted him, when she was close to him, he adored her.

Susan watched them, feeling the blood clot above her eye and telling herself it didn't matter. Babies put a strain on most relationships. And a relationship already strained was bound to split at the seams.

Walking from the room, now she was sure Barry could cope, she went to the bathroom and wiped her face. There was blood everywhere but she was too tired to care. The wound looked worse than it was, a split over the eyebrow. She wondered briefly if she should get herself down the London, have a couple of stitches, but she was bone weary.

Instead she placed a plaster over it and cleaned herself up. It would do until the morning, then she would have to explain it away to Barry's mother.

What she would have done without Kate she didn't know. The woman had become her staunchest ally. Since Jason's death Kate had been like a mother to Susan. So far as Barry went, she was less convinced. She had not spoken to him for over a year until Wendy was born. Then Susan persuaded her to bury the hatchet. But she knew her marked face would only make matters worse again between mother and son.

Kate, it turned out, had a mouth that was worse than June's in some ways. Although she didn't swear and holler, she spoke with such conviction that her every word carried the full weight of her disgust behind it. Barry was the recipient of this opprobrium so often that in some ways Susan wished his mother would stay away from them. It would certainly make life easier.

Clearing away the medical kit, she went back into the bedroom. Barry was asleep in bed with Wendy cradled on his chest. She was sleeping too. Smiling slightly at this picture of father and daughter, Susan settled herself in a white-painted wicker chair. She would doze until Wendy woke then take her and give her a feed.

She was tired, so tired.

Doreen walked into the kitchen carrying a large apple pie. It was eight-thirty in the morning and she was already in full make up with her hair newly styled. She would not bother to change out of her housecoat, though, unless she was going somewhere.

'How's my little angel then?'

Her voice was jocular until Susan turned from the sink and faced her.

'What's he done now?' hissed her friend. 'I heard him ranting and raving, Sue. I never heard him clump you one or else I would have been in. I'd phone Old Bill, mate, if I thought he'd touched you or that child.'

Susan sighed.

'He lost it, couldn't help it. Wendy was kicking up, we were both tired, I mouthed off to him . . .'

Doreen's eyes widened to their utmost.

'What did you say?'

She blushed.

'Never you mind, but it was enough to get me this.' She pointed at the swollen eye and its plaster.

'Anyway he was sorry as fuck this morning. You'll never guess what, Dor? He actually slept with Wendy on his chest all night. You should have seen the two of them. Then this morning, when he woke up and saw her there, he smiled, really smiled at her for the first time. She was so comfy she didn't even wake up for her night feed.'

Doreen smiled grimly.

'So he's finally realised that she's his responsibility an' all? A real person, not a doll.'

They both heard Barry coming down the stairs then.

'He's just given her a feed.' Susan put a finger to her lips and smiled.

Barry walked into the kitchen with Wendy in his arms. He looked at Doreen as he might a cockroach he had just found in his salad and exclaimed, 'She took five ounces, bless her. That's because *I* fed her and she didn't have to labour her poor little gob round your big fat tits. In future express the milk and bottle feed her.'

It was a command.

Susan nodded absently. 'She takes enough from the breast, it's just you can't actually see how much because they ain't got measures on.'

She was deliberately sunny, trying her hardest to make light of everything.

'With the stretch marks you've fucking got, if there was bloody measures you wouldn't see them anyway. Do what I told you and I'll feed the little fucker of a night, keep her sweet. You spoil her.'

He placed the child carefully into the Moses basket in the kitchen. Wendy kicked up her feet with pleasure and smiled again. Barry smiled down at her and felt again the sensation of power she gave him. To make her love him seemed like the most exciting thing in the world, better than a love affair.

She *would* prefer him to her mother, he was certain of that. He walked from the house without another word. Doreen felt the tension ease as soon as he closed the back gate.

'He's a wanker, Sue, I wish you'd see it like everyone else.'

She laughed and poured them both some tea.

'I do, Doreen, I just know how to handle him.'

The words made her sound much more confident than she actually was. But Barry was gone for the day, and hopefully the night, and she had Wendy all to herself now which was exactly how she liked it.

Barry was regaling everyone in the pub with his story of the 'night feed'. As the men listened to him pontificating on the best way to bring up children he felt all powerful. Susan was under the impression she was the only one in the house who could make the child happy. Well, he had proved her wrong, very wrong. Barry was in his element as he told everyone they should all have babies to make them more aware of the easy life their wives led.

Most of the men laughed and agreed with him, a couple laughed without conviction, and one man, a hard docker called Freddie McPherson, did not find it in the least amusing.

'You're wrong, Barry, women have it hard. My Jeanette had nine of them and it killed her. Forty-one when she had a fucking heart attack. You're talking out of your arse, boy. Just because you fed the child once you think you're fucking Doctor Spock. I had the nine of them to care for until my Lee-Anne was old enough to take over from me. Don't denigrate the women, boy, they do a good job.'

Barry was annoyed but he had to take the flak because everyone knew that Freddie was a marvel, undisputed king of the kids.

Feeling foolish now, he made light of it.

'It must have been hard with nine. But as they say, Freddie, you never fired a blank in your life. Probably shagged the old woman to death!'

Everyone laughed now, even Freddie who had found out the hard way just what a job bringing up nine children on no money really was.

'I shagged her all right. Miss it in fact. A bit of strange don't make up for the comfort a real woman can give you, one who knows all your secrets and loves you anyway. From your smelly plates to your sweaty armpits.'

His voice was filled with longing for his wife and the comfort she'd given him. Then Joey came into the pub and as soon as Barry saw him he knew they were in for trouble.

Nodding at everyone he ordered a large Scotch and pulled Barry into a quiet corner, forcing two men from their seats so they could have total privacy.

'What's the matter, Joey?'

He shook his head in anger.

'It's that fucking ponce Derby. He really is asking for a fucking clump and I'm just the man to give it to him.'

Barry ran a hand through his hair in agitated fashion.

'What's he done now?'

Joey swallowed his drink down and sighed.

'He won't pay, tipped me bollocks. Told me he wasn't frightened of me *or* Davey *or* Bannerman. Apparently he now works for a little firm over the water in Bermondsey. You'll never guess whose?'

Barry felt ice in the pit of his stomach.

'Not the Winter brothers?'

'The very same. He's employed by them as a debt collector so all of a sudden he thinks he's the main man.' Joey spoke through his teeth, the words almost forced out of him so great was his anger.

They were in a quandary now.

The Winter brothers were well known and had formed an uneasy alliance with Bannerman. This was common knowledge and no one wanted another war. Since the Krays had departed for their thirty-year sojourn courtesy of Her Majesty firms all over London had carved out their own turfs and defended them in any way they could. The guns were put away for now but an event of this magnitude could set them blazing again.

'I'll have to talk to Bannerman, see what he says.'

Barry nodded absently. Then, leaning forward in his chair, he grinned.

'Why don't we teach him a right fucking lesson and see what happens? I bet the Winter brothers wouldn't say a dickey bird if they thought he owed wedge. After all, they'd probably do the same, or expect him to at least.'

Joey shook his head.

'This is too big, Bal, we don't want to start any wars. Not without Bannerman's say-so anyway.'

He seemed uneasy and this bothered Barry. It was unusual to see Joey worried like this.

'Come on, have a few drinks and forget it, eh? Think about it tomorrow.'

Joey picked up his empty glass, his expression angry and defeated.

'I hate that cunt for putting me in this position. If you'd seen him, Bal, a great big gorilla standing beside him, another one in his car – I felt a right fucking greebo. But I'll have me day with him, you see if I don't.'

Barry knew he had to say something to bring Joey back down.

'As I was standing there, right, he was laughing at me, really laughing, and there was nothing I could do. I tell you, Bal, it's a good job I weren't tooled up. I'd have shot the ponce right through the fucking head.'

Barry could see his point. Being mugged off in their chosen profession was like the Queen being asked if she could provide a quick blow-job.

It was especially galling from someone like Georgie Derby, a big aggressive man with a mouth that could cut through steel and a vindictive manner to match. He was a hard man to press for money at the best of times, but a job in the debts game would make him even more of an arsehole than he already was.

Getting up, Joey picked up his empty glass and sighed heavily.

'Let's have another drink. Christ knows, I could do with one.'

As they walked towards the bar Barry was trying to think of something to say that would make Joey feel better.

'By the way, Bal, how's the baby? Still screaming the fucking place down?'

Everyone laughed and Freddie shouted out, 'Ain't you heard? He's got healing fucking hands.'

Everyone cracked up laughing. Glad as Barry was for the light relief he still felt an urge to give Freddie a dig. After all, he was taking the piss. But he let it go. He started to tell Joey all about Wendy and how she'd stopped screaming as soon as he held her. How he had told Susan not to spoil the child with constant picking up.

'At the end of the day, Joey, kids are like women. They have to know who's in charge, same as birds do. It makes them feel safe like. I mean, you can't have the old woman doing what she wants, can you?'

Joey laughed wearily and turned to his cronies at the bar before answering.

'You tell that to June. The last time she did as she was told was by the clap doctor up the Old London.'

Everyone laughed right on cue and Barry, realising he had made a faux-pas, laughed sheepishly.

'Well, June's in a league of her own, ain't she?'

Joey nodded sagely.

'That's one way of putting it.'

'Let's order some food and get some serious drinking in, eh? It's still only half-one and we have the whole day ahead of us.'

Joey nodded but was still preoccupied and everyone noticed. He was belligerent by three o'clock and in a murderous rage by four-thirty. Georgie Derby had upset him more than he'd realised, but Barry knew the score and wound Joey up accordingly. As far as he was concerned, if they wiped Derby out they would publicly prove a point.

The point being that anyone mad enough to take them on would be obliterated, no matter who they were or worked for.

Susan's eye was sore and she knew it should have been stitched. Looking at herself in the mirror, she felt depressed. In the nude she looked awful. Her face, never her best point, looked grotesque, her swollen eye and brow almost comical. The bruising coming out all over made her look even plainer than she was.

'Sod you, Barry Dalston,' she said into the empty room.

The bedroom was lovely. Susan had spent a lot of time on it, imagining Barry and herself wrapped in each other's arms loving one another in the bed or playing with the kids in there on Sunday mornings.

'You read too many books and didn't think things through.'

She had taken to talking to herself. It eased the unhappiness inside. Wendy was lying on the bed gurgling away happily.

'You talking to yourself and all, girl?'

She peered down at the child and received an answering gurgle of pleasure. Susan adored the baby, absolutely adored her.

As usual when she approached Wendy she felt the rush of milk. Barry and his bottle-feeding . . . she smiled as she thought about it.

Lifting Wendy, she placed her gently on the breast, feeling the softness of her lips as she sought her food, then the clamping down of her gums on the sore nipple. Susan held her gently, letting her feed in her own time, giving her downy head caresses, kissing the little fingers and feet.

Satisfied with her treatment, Wendy relaxed into her mother's billowing softness, reassured by the familiar smells and tastes, the enveloping love that accompanied her feeds all part of the process.

Susan sang to her softly, crooning gently as the child drank and gradually relaxed against her mother's body.

As Susan was kissing her and debating whether to change her nappy or leave her to sleep, she heard Barry come rolling in. He slammed the kitchen door, stamped up the stairs and was in the doorway before she could move.

He stared at them both for a few seconds. His eyes were like slits in his face so great was his anger.

'I waited for you, Bal, but I had to give her her feed, she was hungry.'

He stared once more, not saying a word.

Getting up, Susan placed the baby in the Moses basket by the bed. Straightening up, she turned to face her husband.

'You do it deliberately, don't you? I tell you to do something and you never fucking listen.'

His voice was angry but resigned, as if he'd known exactly what he would find when he came home.

'I left work to come and feed my daughter, but you had to fucking do it, didn't you? You couldn't wait a second . . .'

'Barry, for fuck's sake, it's two in the morning. You've been out since eight-thirty yesterday. What was I supposed to do – let her starve?'

The words were out but they were said in an apologetic tone.

He looked her over.

'Look at you, Sue, you're like a fucking great cow, all udders and stretch marks. You think I want to come home to that, do you? A big, fat, smelly, fucking hag like you. You think I look forward to coming home here? Well, I don't. The thought of you makes me puke.'

Susan closed her eyes in distress. Wendy was crying again, building up to her big crescendo. Susan automatically began to bend down towards the basket on the floor.

'Leave the baby alone. She's fucking spoiled enough as it is.'

Susan straightened and beseeched him with her eyes.

'Don't start, Bal, please. Not tonight, mate.'

He looked her over, his gaze staying on her belly and breasts. The breasts he had loved so much. She felt the milk trickling from being close to the child once more, felt it rushing in again, the heat and the uncomfortable sensation of knowing she was in for more trouble because of it.

'Christ, Sue, but you're an ugly bitch and no mistake.'

She looked down at the screaming baby and Barry slapped her hard across the face, an open-palmed slap that was even noisier than the baby's screaming. Walking over to her, he forced her face down on the bed. Shoving a pillow underneath her belly, he knelt behind her.

'I can't look at your boatrace or I'd lose the fucking horn.' He pulled out his penis, already swollen and rigid. Thrusting it inside her, he heard her grunt.

'Go on then, you fucking fat pig. Grunt away, you cunt.'

He was riding her hard now. She could feel his fingers digging into her buttocks and felt the thrusts as if they were knife wounds. Turning her face to the side she saw their reflection in the mirror of the dressing table, Barry with his trousers and shirt still on, his face a red ball of concentration as he pumped away. Her breasts were hanging down by the pillow, still heavy with milk. She could feel it leaking out.

Barry was talking, his words ragged now as he neared his climax. She felt the rhythm change and sighed with relief. The child was reaching a screaming pitch so loud as to be deafening. Susan wanted to kill him so she could comfort her baby in peace.

Barry was shouting above the noise as he rode her, voice deep with emotion and hatred.

'You're a fat, ugly whore and you should think yourself lucky I married you, girl. Who else would have you, eh? Who else would give you children?'

He was pulling on her hair now, dragging her head backwards and hurting her even more.

'You're like me mother. Think your shit doesn't stink, you do. Well, you stink all right, you stink, you're a fucking . . .'

He was coming; she felt his body shudder, felt him relax his hold on her hair, thanked God it was all over.

She rolled away from him, her body aching and tired. Wendy was still crying and automatically she went to pick her up, thinking that now he had had what he wanted he would leave her alone.

She was wrong.

The blows were heavy at first but nothing Susan couldn't

handle. She was sitting on the side of the bed, her hands over her face, trying to deflect the worst of them. Barry's fists were clenched until he was all white knuckles and gritted teeth, his handsome face stretched into a horrific mask of disgust. This more than anything made Susan frightened.

He had reached the point where he didn't care anymore. Anyone could be hurt now, even the child.

She ran into the smaller bedroom and crouched down by Wendy's cot, covering herself as best she could with her arms. He kicked her, punched and abused her until he was tired and Susan was a bloody crumpled mess. Finally the anger left him and Wendy's cries penetrated his rage. He could hear a banging noise and thought for a split second that the sound was coming from Susan, that she was banging her feet on the floor.

Then he realised it was coming from the back door. His mind registered that fact and he relaxed. If it was Old Bill they would have come to the front.

He looked down at his young wife. She was in a mess, he realised. Going to the window of his own bedroom he looked out and cursed softly under his breath. It was Doreen, in her nightie and holding a large frying pan.

'I know you're in there, you bastard. Leave that girl alone and come out here now. I'll fucking fight you, you gutless ponce!'

Wendy's cries were echoing in his head. As he walked past the baby basket he felt an urge to kick it, kick it across the room and down the stairs and finally shut the little fucker up.

Instead he pushed it hard with his foot, making it slide about two feet. Wendy was not impressed. She cried harder and louder.

Doreen was screaming now at the top of her voice.

'You give me that baby, you bastard. I can hear her. Where's Susan? What you done to her? I've phoned Old Bill, mate, they'll be here in no time.'

He went back to Susan. She was still on the floor and he saw for the first time that she wasn't moving. Suddenly fear crept into him. He thought for a moment he had killed her.

He ran down the stairs and opened the back door. Pushing

Doreen out of the way he rushed out into the night, Doreen's voice following him as he ran down the alley at the back of the houses. Fear lent his feet wings.

He saw that lights were on in all the houses and cursed Doreen for waking everyone up. It never occurred to him that it might have been him who'd woken them all. Him shouting, the baby screaming, and it was all Susan's fault.

Doreen rushed into the bedroom and picked up Wendy. She checked the child over gently as she tried to calm her. Sue's bedroom was next to her own so she'd heard everything as clearly as if she was in the room. She knew what had happened and was frightened for her friend. Once she had sorted out the child and calmed her she went to look for Susan.

When Doreen saw her on the floor, her face unrecognisable and blood sprayed all over the child's cot and the walls, she felt a moment's hatred so intense she was glad Barry had gone. She did not know what she might have been capable of doing to him at that moment.

Susan was conscious but obviously concussed. She was trying to grope her way to the wall to lever herself to her feet. She was covered in blood, some of it rust-coloured where it had dried, other cuts still bleeding.

'Oh, Susan, Susan love. What's he done this time?'

Doreen's voice was shocked.

Placing the baby on the floor by the door, she attempted to get Susan up, help her through to the bedroom, get her lying down on something soft. It took her what seemed like hours. Susan couldn't co-ordinate her movements; she was walking as if she was wearing astronaut's boots, lead-lined and heavy as a car.

Doreen picked up a now quiet Wendy. She put her in the basket by the bed then glanced fearfully back at her friend. Susan's body was one big bruise, from her face down to her feet. Doreen knew she needed a doctor, needed hospital treatment. She wished she had phoned the police now. They would have got help, maybe stopped the worst of the beating by arriving.

But that inbred East End rule had stopped her. You don't call

Old Bill in for anything. It just isn't done. People sorted things out for themselves. Though how Susan was to sort this out she had no idea.

Going to the phone, Doreen picked it up and rang Kate and then June, though why she bothered with her she didn't know. But she felt that, seeing her daughter, June might just feel pity enough to get Joey to sort Barry out. Though Doreen did not hold out much hope.

Then she phoned a moody doctor from her days on the game. He was there within the hour.

Barry had stolen a car. It was a flash one, a pale blue Zephyr with a radio and an eight-track cassette. He drove around for a while, listening to Elvis singing 'Are You Lonesome Tonight?' and feeling sorry for himself.

Then he had an idea. He stopped at a phone box and rang Joey. The phone was answered immediately.

'What you done to my Susan now?'

Joey's voice was slurred and menacing. 'June's just left in a cab to go round your fucking drum. That ponce Doreen's been on the blower.'

'I had to give her a dig. Listen, I've had a marvellous idea to get back at that wanker Georgie Derby. You want in? You want to give him some or what?'

There was a threat behind his words. He was talking as if Joey wasn't up to retaliation but, knowing the amount of drink his father-in-law had consumed earlier, he knew he would rise to the bait.

'What you talking about? 'Course I want to give him some . . .'

Barry interrupted. 'Then get ready and I'll pick you up. You're going to love this, mate, fucking love it.'

He put the phone down and made his way to Joey's flat. When they had finished tonight, no one would ever take either of them for a ponce again. Tonight was to be the making of his rep, Barry's rep. He was going to make himself into a legend.

With Joey's help, of course. His father-in-law was about to

enter into an unholy alliance tonight which would keep the two men bonded together from now on.

Barry was sure of that.

Georgie Derby was a good husband and father who genuinely loved his wife and kids. He had married late in life and his children were doubly precious to him as was his young wife.

Georgie was asleep in bed, his wife cuddled into him. The three children – Maxine, seven, five-year-old little Georgie and baby Caroline, two – were all sleeping soundly.

Georgie was dreaming about a big black dog that was trying to get to him and his family. In the dream the dog was vicious with huge fangs he knew could crush his children's heads. Then suddenly the dog began to spit out flames. He could smell the burning, hear a loud crash as they consumed him, the dog breathing more and more flames out of its mouth.

He woke then as his wife's screams became louder and saw what she was screaming about. The house was on fire – his home was on fire. It was a nightmare come true.

Leaping from the bed, he pulled his wife to her feet and tried to get her through the bedroom door. She was petrified, unable to move, screaming at him to get her children, save the babies. Rushing from the room, he clapped one hand across his face. The landing was filled with black smoke but by feeling his way he managed to get to his screaming children and carry them back to the main bedroom.

His wife Natalie had the window open and the neighbours were all outside calling up to reassure them they had phoned for help. All they could do was wait. His youngest daughter, an asthma sufferer, was coughing badly, her little ribcage heaving as she fought to get her breath.

As Georgie looked out of the window, willing the fire brigade and ambulance service to hurry, he saw Joey and Barry. Standing by a big blue car they waved to him nonchalantly.

He realised then what had happened and felt fear tighten like a steel band around his chest. They would have killed his children. They would have taken innocent lives for money. As hard as he was, and he was a hard man, he would never in a million years have done anything like that.

But he knew then that, hard as he was, he wasn't hard enough to retaliate because that would put his children and his wife in more danger than ever.

Joey McNamara was undoubtedly a force to be reckoned with. Georgie had known that, but had thought that his association with the Winters would have put something like this on to the back burner. Now it seemed they were after war, and he wasn't sure it was a war either of them could win.

He saw his little daughter collapse in her mother's arms and rushed to support her but he knew immediately that Caroline was dead. It was instinct, something he just knew without having to be told.

Caroline was a sickly child, had been since birth. Now she was dead, killed by two men with no idea how much love he'd felt for his child, how much store he set on his family and their life together.

He would kill them now, he knew that. Kill them both stone dead. He would have to. They had destroyed his child and he could not let that go.

His home was burned out, his wife would never be the same again, and Georgie lost his zest for life all in under an hour at the hands of two men who thought they were a law unto themselves.

But he would wait, and he would watch, and he would pay them back, he was sure of that. As sure as he was of his own name and what he was going to carve on his daughter's tombstone.

His wife was keening hysterically. For now he had to file away the hatred and get on with comforting her. But his memory was long and he had something on his side: time.

Susan woke up in Whitechapel Hospital, Doreen by her side and a smiling Wendy in her friend's arms. Susan could not move at all. Her body was racked with pain and her mind reeling from the knowledge that Barry had done this to her.

Barry Dalston, her husband, the man she had loved with all her heart.

'All right, mate?'

Doreen's voice was soft, concerned.

Susan attempted to smile.

'I assume I'll live?' It was a joke. A bad one but a joke all the same.

'How's me best girl then?' She tried to take the baby's hands in hers but it was too much effort.

'I feel fucking awful. Has Barry been in?'

Doreen did not answer but the flowers all over the place spoke volumes.

'He knows I hate chrysanthemums, the ponce. How long have I been here?'

Doreen smiled gently.

'Four days, Sue. Don't worry, I've had Babes. I told your mum you insisted before you passed out. I guessed you wouldn't want her going to them. But Kate's been a great help.'

'Four days! I've been here all that time?'

'Barry told them you fell down the stairs. I think they swallowed it, but I ain't sure. No one has said anything, really.'

Susan nodded. Forewarned was forearmed.

'I'll play it by ear. I can't remember everything but I remember enough.' Her voice was sad. 'I expect he'll be in later, all sweetness and light.'

Doreen shook her head.

'That's just it – they arrested him yesterday for murder and arson. They arrested your father and all.'

Susan's eyes widened, her pain forgotten in the surprise of Doreen's revelation.

'Who have they murdered then?'

'A bloke called Derby's youngest daughter. She died in the fire of smoke inhalation.'

'How old was she?'

Doreen could not keep a tremor from her voice.

'She was just two years old, Sue, a baby really.'

Susan nodded then, a sad, lonely gesture. Neither of them spoke again. There was nothing they could say. They were both filled with their own thoughts, with disgust and a terrible pity for the bereaved family. Finally Wendy started to cry and Susan looked at her as if for the first time. Pulling herself up in the bed, she took her child in her arms and held her so tight the baby cried even harder.

Through her pain Susan realised she was fighting a war, one she could not win but in which she might just carry a few battles for her child. Barry, she knew now, was capable of anything, anything at all, to further his own ends. That included sacrificing an innocent child.

Two days later he was released without any charges and a few days after that Georgie Derby was found with his throat cut. Once more, it seemed, Joey and now Barry had literally got away with murder.

Susan for her part was treated like royalty by her now repentant husband but when she realised she was pregnant again she felt an urge to kill herself. He was over the moon, seeing it as a sign they must stay together, be a family. Susan saw it as another nail in the coffin she had placed herself in.

Because she knew now that Barry was capable of anything, and anything with Barry meant just that.

Chapter Fifteen

Susan was sore, very sore. It seemed as if her whole body was screaming, even the nerve endings. She caressed little Barry's head and wished for the millionth time that Barry Senior would die.

As she watched him stalking around the little house, face red with rage, body taut as a watch spring with suppressed aggression and his mouth constantly spewing obscenities, she pictured him in his coffin. This picture had become her lifeline. Sometimes, as she hoovered or cooked or looked after the three kids and had a nice day without him, she allowed herself that pleasant daydream.

The police would knock on the door, and instead of asking her where he was and taking him in for questioning they'd stand on the step, their hats in their hands, faces solemn as they informed her that her husband, the father of her three children, was dead. Sometimes he'd died in horrific circumstances, depending on how much she hated him at the time. He was slain by a crossbow bolt through the heart or shot in the head. Once she even daydreamed he had been burned alive, that one had scared her, but mostly she imagined the police telling her he had died in a car crash. No other car involved, of course, he just drove accidentally into a tree.

If she was really in a good mood she would imagine then that he had insured himself and she came into a large amount of money. The daydream would then take on movie star proportions as she pictured herself, miraculously slim and beautiful, and the kids turned out like fashion plates. Travelling the world and being chatted up by David Bowie and Mick Jagger . . .

At this moment though the daydream was destroyed as she

realised that Barry was talking to her. Well, talking at her would be more accurate.

'Look, Bal, it ain't our fault you are in shtook. The kids are hardly to blame, are they? Let me make you a nice cuppa and a bacon roll, eh? Give you a chance to calm down a bit, think a bit more clearly. If push comes to shove you can have me tom to pawn, all right?'

He looked at her with contempt.

'Shut the fuck up, Sue. Don't start winding me up, I warn you.'

She closed her eyes in distress. She really could do without this today. Wendy was nine years old tomorrow and wanted a party. If Barry launched himself at her at any point tonight Susan would be marked and have to suffer the pity of all the other mothers tomorrow.

She knew what was wrong with him. He was skint again and owed money to everyone. Since the death of Davey Davidson, Barry and her father had been in limbo. Bannerman was retiring and going abroad to live. He had paid off his two main debt collectors who had promptly blown the money, expecting to be offered jobs by all and sundry. This had obviously not happened. Over the years they had fallen out with everybody who might have been interested in employing them. Even bouncing was out because their reps preceded them and no one wanted the hag, though Barry had been offered a door job in a hostess club. A come down as far as he was concerned.

Susan knew also that since the death of Derby's daughter and her own hospitalisation eight years ago, he and Joey had been put at a distance by the local people. They were tolerated but no longer liked. She knew this bothered Barry a lot, and that he blamed her for it.

Strange it was his beating of her that day which made people hate him even before they heard about the child. He and Joey had been attacked late one night by men armed with baseball bats. They were both seriously injured and never knew who'd ordered it though Susan privately thought it was Bannerman, his way of getting his own back on them and also of placating the Winter brothers.

Susan knew much more than her husband guessed. Her mother kept her up to date on everything, she made sure of that. She wanted to know what to expect, and if possible when to expect it. She had to defend herself and the kids as best she could.

As she made the tea and the bacon roll, she hoped he would calm down. He had already upset the kids and picked on Doreen, telling her she was banned from his house. Doreen left without an argument but the very fact she had been there annoyed Barry. He hated her because she saw through him.

Doreen was the expert on men. She should be – Christ knew she had had enough of them. The thought made Susan smile. Her friend's current squeeze was a young Greek waiter from up West, apparently. Doreen told Susan about their love life in graphic detail, making her roar with laughter. Even June had warmed to Doreen when she had seen how comical she was. Doreen could make a joke of anything and anyone. Especially men.

She was back on the game, needing the money now that the kids were getting older and because of her debts. At times Susan was tempted to live like her: take Social Security, moonlight in the Smoke, and do what she wanted when she wanted. It sounded bloody good to her.

'Are you going to take all fucking night to sort that out or what?'

Barry was behind her. She could hear the Blue Peter theme tune and hoped the kids would watch it quietly.

Wendy rushed out into the kitchen, smelling food.

'I'm hungry, Mum.'

She stopped dead as she saw her father's expression. Susan tried to lighten the situation.

'All right, babe, I'll do you something in a minute. Go and watch the telly.'

Barry blocked the child's exit.

'Didn't you eat at school then?'

Wendy, all chestnut hair and big blue eyes, shook her head.

'I didn't like it, it was horrible.' She pulled a face to show just how bad it had been.

'What was it then?' Barry's voice was friendly, conversational, but the child wasn't fooled.

'It was fish and chips, it's Friday. But it was all fatty and greasy, I couldn't eat it. Nanny Kate says it's because my year go in too late and by then it's been cooked a while.'

She brought her grandmother into the conversation because she was the only person her father listened or was remotely civil to.

'So, what you're saying is, you were provided with a meal, a perfectly good meal, and you didn't eat it?'

Wendy nodded solemnly.

'It was horrible.'

Then seven-year-old Alana came rushing out to the kitchen. She was black-haired and beautiful, looked more like her father than any of them.

'It was shit, Dad, I didn't eat mine either.' She looked up into his face and smiled and Barry smiled back.

'That bad, eh, princess? Well, Mummy will make you something soon, all right?'

She nodded, and grabbing Wendy's hand pulled her from the kitchen. Alana took advantage of her father's fondness for her and tried to make life easier for poor Wendy who could do nothing right so far as Barry was concerned. Susan guessed it was a case of the girl being so like her, albeit a better looking version.

'It's Christmas soon, Bal, I'm really looking forward to it.'

She hated herself for the forced joviality in her voice, the way she tried to pretend that everything was okay when everything was wrong, very wrong.

'Big fucking deal! You might have to get off your fucking arse and get a job if I don't get sorted soon. Might take some of that fat off you.'

Susan stared at the man she was tied to. He would never let her go, she knew that. She provided for him – his comforts, his home. She had his kids and his ring, as he reminded her constantly. My house, my car, my wife. She didn't even come first in the equation.

Barry owned her as much as he did his watch or his jumper. She was just another possession so far as he was concerned.

As she put the food on the table he dragged her over to the sink by the front of her dress.

'What's that?'

Susan looked into the sink and sighed. She had emptied the tea pot earlier and forgotten to swill out the tea leaves.

'It's tea leaves, Bal.'

Her voice was rising, she had had enough of him today. He pushed his face closer to hers. She could feel his breath on her skin, see the malice in his eyes. She closed her eyes in distress. He would love it if she back chatted him, gave him the excuse he was looking for to give her a good hiding.

'I was just going to clear it all out, I ain't bleached the sink yet anyway.'

She could hear the begging tone in her voice and hated herself for it. Sometimes she wished she had the guts to walk away, get out of it for good. He pushed his clenched fist under her chin, forcing her head back until she was straining every sinew in her body.

Just then Kate slipped unannounced through the back door. Barry turned guiltily, his face ashen as he looked at his mother.

'The big man's home then, is he, Susan? I can see you're getting the usual greeting.'

Barry dropped his fist and walked from the room. A few seconds later the front door slammed and the house along with its occupants seemed to breathe a big sigh of relief.

Kate shook her head.

'That I bred that, eh? I'd never have believed it. His father was a villain, by Christ, but he would never have harmed me. God rest his soul.'

'I wish at times he would rest Barry's.'

Susan's words came out so fast the two women laughed together.

'Here you are, Wend, come in and eat this bacon roll, love.' She looked at her mother-in-law. 'Shame to see it go to waste.' The baby started crying then and Susan sighed. 'Here we go again. Barry Junior starts as if he knows he has to take over from his father.'

She laughed again and Kate watched the big cumbersome woman go to comfort her child. She felt the full hopelessness then of her daughter-in-law's situation and the worst of it was it was Barry who was causing it. If only you could pick your kids like you did everything else, she would ask God for Susan as her daughter and feel honoured if her plea was answered.

The girl was marvellous. The house shone. The kids were well turned out and clean, had good manners and an impressive vocabulary. Even Alana, though she swore like a trooper.

How Susan managed this in the teeth of Barry's vicious temper and unpredictable moods Kate had no idea. But the girl obviously fought him, in her own quiet way. The bruises were never mentioned, the kids were protected, and Susan managed, even when he had really hurt her, to carry on with the day-to-day things that mean so much to young children.

She kept up the routine of meals prepared and baths before bed. She read to them when she could, listened to their tales of woe and loved them with every fibre of her being. Even though they were Barry's children. Barry who had burned her with a cigarette when she was carrying Luke. Little Luke had died at two days old, a tiny scrap of a child born two months early thanks to Susan's receiving a broken pelvis from her husband.

How that had hurt Kate as a mother, knowing she had brought into the world a man so evil and depraved. It was a terrible thing to hate your own son but she could not abide him near her. Despite that she spent a lot of time at this house, hoping to prevent any further harm being inflicted on this poor girl who had married her son.

Wendy pulled herself on to her nana's lap. Kate cuddled her into her ample bosom. 'All right, me little love bug?' Wendy smiled happily.

Alana laughed then. She opened the fridge and took out some ham, starting to make herself a sandwich. She looked at her grandmother and smiled as she buttered the bread in her usual clumsy way, ripping it as the hard butter refused to spread.

'What's a fat cunt, Nan?'

The beautiful face seemed genuinely interested. There was curiosity in her eyes and a little fear because she had heard the expression used so malevolently against her mother. Kate guessed this much and as she answered the seven year old, fought an urge to weep.

'That's a dirty expression used by ignorant people like your father. Don't ever let me hear you use it again, okay?'

Alana nodded, sorry now she had asked.

Wendy, all big-eyed innocence, said loudly, 'He talks like that, Alana, because he's a wanker.'

Kate closed her eyes in distress.

'That is another expression you shouldn't use, child.'

Wendy turned on her lap and looked Kate straight in the eye.

'But that's what Doreen calls him. She said it was the proper name for people like him.'

Kate felt an urge to laugh, she could just see Doreen saying it. Instead she bit hard on her lip and sighed.

'That's a joke – one Daddy must not hear about, all right?'

The two girls laughed, happy to be a part of a grown-up conspiracy they did not understand. Gathering the children to her, Kate cuddled them hard. She loved them with a vengeance, and she loved their mother too. She wished she could wave a magic wand and make Barry disappear but knew she couldn't do that. All she could do was try to limit the damage he did to them.

At that moment Barry was at the Hiltone Club in Old Compton Street. A young woman with dyed black hair and pendulous breasts looked at him expectantly.

'Can I help you?' The words were spoken in a parody of a posh accent.

'Where's the owner, Ivan? Tell him Barry Dalston's here.'

The girl picked up the phone and dialled an extension. Barry took the opportunity to look around. It was, he decided, a shit hole. All faded carpets and cheap curtains. He knew the place without even looking at it. It was like all the others. The lighting, subdued and pink-tinted, hid a multitude of sins, not least the ugliness of some of the girls. As if on cue two skinny tarts walked out from the main bar and gave him the once over. He could see they were not impressed and cursed his mother for turning up when she had. He hadn't had time to change. Tidy himself up. Even these two ugly mares gave him the elbow and walked past him into the toilets.

The girl on reception smiled properly now.

'Ivan will be down in a tick, take a seat. Can I get you a drink?'

Barry was placated. Respect at last.

'A large Scotch, and I mean large.'

She nodded and walked through to the bar, returning moments later with a large Chivas Regal. Barry downed it in two swallows but the offer of another was not forthcoming. He was standing there awkwardly with the glass in his hand when Ivan appeared.

Ivan Rechinovich was a loner but that did not make him any the less dangerous. He was a foreigner, the cockney expression for anyone born south of the water. In Ivan's case it meant Bermondsey. He was the son of Russian Jews forced out of their homeland and was now seventy years old. He had a screwed up face, a red bulbous nose and heavily lidded eyes that gave him a clownish appearance.

But Ivan was no fool. He was a violent and dangerous man and anyone who did not give him his due soon knew about it. Unlike his peers, he liked to take an active part in all his business ventures, whether it was running the hostesses or robbing a security van. His only vanity was that he still dyed his luxuriant hair black, a fierce colour that looked out of place above his lined face.

He wanted Barry Dalston because his club was under threat from a new firm out of North London, a couple of young men with guns in their pockets and Kalashnikov rifles in the boot of their car. Ivan wasn't stupid. He knew you could not keep the young men away for ever. Many of his peers had retired already. But he did not want to just yet.

Talk was that he was still scamming, but like everything else to do with Ivan, he wasn't letting on. When he was ready to move he would inform everyone and that was as much as they would ever know. If he pulled a job only the people concerned knew of it. He was very interested to meet hard man Barry Dalston.

'Come through – come through, my son,' Ivan greeted him expansively. 'Take a look at the establishment, tell me what you think.'

He was playing the genial host but Barry was not fooled. He knew this was all part of the game. Ivan came across as a decrepit old man. In fact he was as wily as a fox and twice as dangerous.

Years before, when someone had called him a Jewboy, he had personally removed their nose. Consequently when he demanded respect he got it.

'The girls are eager to see you. They think if you like them, you'll tip the punters the wink. Take my advice, son, stick with your wife. These are professional fuckers and they take men for granted. Don't get involved. Fuck them if you wish, it's a perk, but be careful. I will not tolerate in-fighting among my girls, understand? They grass, they lie and they cheat – they can't help it, it's their natural inclination. A whore is born and not made, you know. I have come to realise that.'

Barry nodded, impressed by the older man's acumen and happy that he had the green light for a marathon shagging session. He gave the women the once over.

'All right, girls, this is Mr Dalston who will be investigating the wallets for you. Be kind to him, eh?'

The women all nodded respectfully and Barry was pleased.

As they walked along to the dance area Ivan whispered loudly, 'I use the term "girls" loosely, you understand. I never call them women. Real women wouldn't have the stomach for what they do. I always find whores so depressing, don't you? They hate what they do and eventually they hate men, blame them for something they do willingly for monetary gain. A lot of them end up dykes, though of course you can't tell them that. Like all women they think they know everything.'

Barry laughed with him. He liked the old boy.

Ivan took him through to where the strippers changed and where they kept the private rooms for gambling.

'When we have the cards, I expect you to stay on and keep order. You search the punters for knives, guns, anything. I once had a man come in with a phial of sulphuric acid to throw at an opponent who had taken his money a few days before. The people who play here are serious and they expect a safe game. It's your job to ensure they get one. The women are never allowed in here, especially when a game is in place. They only try and ponce off the punters, take their mind off the game.'

Barry nodded. He liked the sound of this job more and more.

'By the way, Mr Dalston, I expect you to be tooled up at all times. You need a squeezy for ammonia, and a cosh. I also expect you to carry a piece. You may only use it once a year but you will need it. And I expect you to beat the customers who refuse to pay. That's par for the course. There's a sawn off shotgun under the counter in reception for emergencies. Don't worry about the police, I have fair warnings of any raids. So far as they're concerned we're clean as a whistle. You also get the girls cabs to the punters' hotels or wherever. You never, ever let a girl wait on the pavement. That is a no no. They can be nicked for soliciting and we definitely do not want that. There's a list of local establishments by the phone. Make sure you ask for one of those hotels, whatever the girls say. They do us a reduced deal.'

He smiled then, seeing Barry's bemused expression.

'If they argue with a punter you slap them – but not on the face. We don't ruin their main asset. Punch them in the kidneys or the belly, that's their biggest fear. I allow them to buy rubbers from me at a reduced rate. They're kept in a cupboard in my office. That's about the gist of it. Do you think you can cope?'

Barry nodded.

'And the poke, Ivan, what's that?'

He grinned.

'A oner a night and whatever tips you make off the punters. You know how to dress a wallet, don't you?'

Barry shook his head.

'It's easy, son. As they pay their entrance fee, or if you can talk them into joining as a member, you look in their wallet. Then, on a piece of paper, you write the details of their credit cards and how much money they have in cash. You'll learn how to judge that as you go along. Then you walk them through to the bar and give the piece of paper to Roselle. She has an idea then what she's dealing with and serves them accordingly.

'You'd be surprised the number of cunts who come in here with only about a ton and expect that to buy them the earth. I like the foreigners meself, they spend their poke and that's it. It's the Brits who give you the grief. Them and the Arabs. They can be bastards. Fucking cheeky buggers, some of them. I'm sure they think I'm running a charity. Oh, and before I forget, look out for the weirdos. Last year I had two girls striped up by the same fucking bloke. That's how come Tom Hanley's still talking through a wired jaw. He wasn't doing his job and he was creaming off me. I won't have that. My girls are protected. Well, as much as we can protect them, and I protect meself and all. Right, another drink?'

Barry nodded, amazed at how complicated this job seemed to be. He liked the old man, though, and was grateful for this chance.

'You won't regret taking me on, Ivan.'

The older man looked into his face and said flatly, 'If I do, son, you'll be the first to know.'

The kids were in bed and the baby was lying beside her on the sofa as Susan watched television. She was enjoying a few hours of peace and quiet. She hoped Barry wasn't going to come home now and spoil it all. She still had to make some jelly and a trifle for Wendy's birthday party the next day. She had got the money from Kate, Barry as usual pleading poverty.

Susan kissed her little son's fingers and he crowed with delight. He was gorgeous. Holding him into her breasts, she caressed his little sturdy body as she watched Starsky and Hutch, smiling at their antics on screen with Huggy Bear.

Twenty minutes later she was asleep, tiredness enveloping her body like a shroud. Barry came home at just past midnight and stood in the doorway looking at her and his son.

Barry Junior had dumped and the acrid smell permeated the room. Susan was snoring softly, her face almost pretty in repose. Barry watched them. He saw his son move, trying to get comfortable, and heard his snuffling. He saw Susan instinctively hold him tighter, moving her body as she slept to accommodate him.

Barry smiled and wished he had not hit her earlier in the day.

On the kitchen table was a ham sandwich and a cheese sandwich, covered in clingfilm. Seeing this little bit of homely care made him feel guilty. She was a good sort, old Susan really. A kindly person.

As he opened the sandwiches and the bottle of Scotch he had bought, he heard her stirring in the lounge. After putting the baby in his cot in their room she came back downstairs and into the kitchen.

'I thought I heard you. Want me to do you a bit of egg and bacon?'

'Nah, that's all right. Get up to bed, mate, and I'll join you in a minute.'

He was being nice to her and she felt like crying at this change in him. He could be so good at times, so nice, like he used to be.

'It's Wendy's birthday tomorrow and I have to get me arse in gear and start the jellies and that. I fell asleep watching bloody Starsky and Hutch.'

She put the kettle on and began taking bowls out of the cupboards.

'Do it in the morning.'

Susan shook her head. 'I won't have time. I have to do all the sandwiches and cakes tomorrow. Your mum's going to give me a hand, and Doreen.'

Barry nodded, resigned.

'I got a job.'

Susan turned towards him, beaming.

'Really, what you doing?'

He shrugged nonchalantly.

'You are now looking at the new doorman for the Hiltone Club. A oner a night.' He threw fifty pounds on the table and she looked at it gleefully. 'I got a sub from Ivan, the old cunt. Practically had to prise it out of him with a fucking jemmy.'

His countenance was dark now, remembering Ivan's warning.

'Don't try and tuck me up, Barry. I know all about you and I hear everything, remember that.'

He had swallowed it, had had to. He owed money all over, especially the bookies. He was going to have to sort out a scam at some point to clean his slate.

'Well, at least it's a start. What kind of club is it?'

Barry bit into his sandwich noisily.

'It's a hostess club of all things. But the money's good and the hours. A lot of responsibility, though, a hell of a lot.'

This was said with a great deal of self-importance.

'Can you get your collar felt, that's what I want to know?'

Barry tutted loudly.

'Why do you do it, Sue, eh? Why do you have to put the mockers on everything? I try and make a fucking living and you mug me off.'

He was spitting out food as he spoke, his anger building, and Susan felt her heart sink.

'All right, Bal, keep your fucking hair on. I was worried about you, that's all.'

He stood up and poked her hard in the chest.

'Well, fucking don't worry about me, all right? Worry about yourself and getting some of that fucking fat off your arse. You look like a fucking sow as usual.'

Picking up his plate, he smashed it against the wall. Susan stood white-faced and silent, waiting for it to be over, hoping it was.

'You've even turned me fucking mother against me, you have. Everything I do you fuck up somehow. You fucking Jonah.'

He was incoherent with rage. Susan watched helplessly as he ranted on and threw everything to the floor. She watched the jellies she had begun making hit the lino and sighed inside herself.

Then he was poking her again, hard bony finger prodding her soft chest. Hitting her milk-swollen breasts as hard as he could, making her flinch, making her nothing. She tried to disappear inside herself, go to her special place, but Barry was not having any of it. Tonight for some reason he wanted her to answer him.

She couldn't.

He pushed her with the flat of his hand and she slipped heavily on the soaked floor, face banging hard against the lino as she tried to save herself.

He looked down at her and shook his head as if in disgust before he kicked her.

'Please, Bal, please! Not tonight, mate, it's Wendy's party tomorrow. Please leave it, mate, please.'

He mimicked her.

'Please, Bal, leave me alone. You fucking wind me up and then you expect me to let it go, don't you?'

He was genuinely incredulous.

Susan pulled herself to her knees. She could hear the kids getting up and prayed they would have the sense to stay upstairs until it was all over. He punched her in the side of the head then, knocking her flying across the kitchen.

Wendy and Alana came into the room.

'Leave my mummy alone, you horrible bully!'

Alana's voice was high-pitched with fear.

Wendy stood like a statue in the doorway. Susan's eyebrow was bleeding and she could feel a lump forming on the side of her head. He had opened her eyebrow with a heavy gold keeper ring she had bought him one Christmas.

'Go back upstairs, darlin', Mummy's all right. Just go back to bed and I'll be up in a minute to tuck you in.'

But Wendy came into the room and went to help her mother up. Barry's hand hit the child as she passed him, knocking her flying. The blow was hard and Wendy screamed out in pain and shock.

The next second Susan was on her feet. She used her body weight to knock Barry out of the child's path. Then, as she went to Wendy, he grabbed her arm to stop her. The little girl was on the floor, nightie soaked from the molten jelly and her face red from the blow.

She was still screaming.

The next thing Susan was aware of was both girls pulling her away from Barry – who was on his knees in front of her now as she held a knife to his throat. The big carving knife she used to cut bread for the kids.

'Mummy – stop it, stop it!'

Alana's voice was a high-pitched scream, terror in her every word.

Susan shook the girls off her.

'Get upstairs. Now!'

Her voice was loud and brooked no argument. The girls ran

from the room. Susan looked Barry in the eye.

'You ever touch my kids again and I'll slice you into little pieces, do you hear me, boy?'

For the first time in his life Barry Dalston was scared of his wife.

'Let go of me, Susan, I mean it. If you don't, I'll break your fucking neck.'

She laughed, a small bitter sound she would have sworn she did not have inside her.

'You touch my kids again and you'd better break my neck, mate, because if I can get my hands on you, I'll kill you. I mean it, Barry. I'll fucking kill you.'

He knew she meant it and swallowed hard. He saw the truth in her eyes, heard it in her voice.

She removed the knife from his neck slowly, her whole body shuddering as she tried to draw breath.

Everything felt different somehow. Even the teeth in her head felt strange and out of place. She had a tannic taste in her mouth that she guessed was blood and imagined the tableau they must have made for the kids.

She dropped her arm to her side, still keeping hold of the carving knife.

'Get out, Barry. Get out now.'

He waited until she was relaxed before he lunged at her and took the carving knife from her grasp.

Then he laughed.

'You really meant that, didn't you, Sue? The mother hen looking after her chicks, eh?'

He sounded proud of her, friendly even. But she wasn't fooled. Picking up a tea towel she held it to her eye. She was immune to pain now. Having experienced it so often, this was like a paper cut to her. She looked him in the eye.

'I ain't joking, Bal. No one touches my kids, not even you. Now go and stay somewhere else tonight, go round one of your old sorts or something, but leave this house.'

She walked from the kitchen and went upstairs to try and calm the children. Wendy had run her a bath and was trying to soothe little Barry who had woken up with all the noise.

'You all right, Mum?' Wendy's own face was swollen and Susan knew she would be bruised.

'Are you all right, mate? Let Mummy look at your face, heartbeat, let me kiss it for you, make it better. Daddy isn't well, love. He don't know what he's doing.'

Barry stood at the bottom of the stairs and listened to her talking to the child.

'Come on, let's put some witch hazel on it, bring the bruise out, eh? Then I'll make us all hot milk and biscuits.'

Alana was crying still, her little sobs were heartbreaking.

Susan put the two girls in the bath about ten minutes later, telling them they both had Monday off school.

'Now have a little play and I'll tidy the kitchen up and make us something nice, eh?'

They nodded dutifully.

'Can I still have me party, Mum?'

Susan smiled.

''Course you can, heartbeat, don't let this spoil it for you.'

She walked slowly down the stairs, her whole body screaming out for sleep and rest. She had picked up little Barry from her bedroom and cradled him to her until he dropped off again. Placing him on the sofa with two cushions to keep him from rolling off, she went out to the kitchen.

Barry was strewing all her clean towels on the floor to try and soak up the mess. She closed her eyes in distress. More washing. As if she didn't have enough already.

He stared at her. She was wearing an old nightie and looked a mess. Her face was a mass of bruises and streaked blood. It had dried on her hair and dyed it rust-coloured in places.

'You know I don't mean it, Sue.'

It was the nearest he ever got to an apology.

'I don't want to hear it, all right? I still have to make her stuff whatever happens. I said she'd have a party and a party she will have, no matter what you do.'

Susan started to cry then, long ragged sobs that seemed to bounce off the kitchen walls.

'Look what you done to me, Barry, and with everyone coming tomorrow. I look like I've been in a fucking car crash. Little Wend's face is already bruising. Why do you do it, Bal? Why the fuck do you do it?'

Going to her, he held her in his arms for a moment, caressing her back and shoulders. Kissing her hair and her face.

'Take the fifty quid and blow it round the Jewish deli down the lane, eh? Get her what she needs and something special for the others. Some champagne or something.'

Susan didn't answer, she was still crying.

'I had the hump, mate, and I took it out on you. But you taught me a thing or two about women tonight, Susan – you can't trust them where the kids are concerned.'

He tried to make her laugh but she wasn't having any of it.

'You can't hit the kids, Bal. They'd take them away and then I'd go fucking mad.'

He held her face in his hands and caressed her cheekbones with his thumbs.

'You're a blinding mother, Sue, a fucking diamond and I am a right arsehole at times. But you got me tonight, girl. I thought me number was up then.'

He lifted his head and laughed.

'Look at the cut under me chin, girl, it's still bleeding.'

'It scared me, Bal. I really wanted to stab you and it frightened me.'

He laughed again, everything forgotten until the next time. And Susan knew there would be a next time.

'Stop making a big deal out of it. All married couples fight, it's what you marry for. Fucking and fighting, girl. That's us two, I'm afraid.'

She wiped her eyes with her fingers.

'I promised the girls some hot milk and biscuits. I slung them in the bath.'

He nodded.

'I'll clear up, you go and jump in with them, give yourself a soak. I'll make us all something nice, eh?'

She nodded, resigned now to this switch back to the Barry she could have loved. Did love once. It was pointless arguing with him.

Twenty minutes later she lay in a hot bath and listened to Barry making the kids laugh with his silly antics. She prayed that this new job worked out and that he'd like it.

But, knowing him like she did, she knew what would happen. What always happened.

Still, she reasoned, it was night work so that should keep him out of her hair and give her some peace at last.

She lay back in the bath and let the hot water do its work. Then he brought her a cup of tea and a cigarette, luxury as far as Susan was concerned.

It crossed her mind she should threaten to kill him more often.

Wendy's party was a success until Barry and Joey had an argument. Everyone left in a hurry and the police were called to the house by a neighbour. The men were both locked up on a D and D.

Susan was over the moon. She'd finally get a good night's sleep. The first one she'd had in months.

Doreen stayed late and they drank the bottle of champagne Barry had brought home with him. Susan, drunk on the wine, told her friend about threatening Barry with the knife. They both laughed their heads off. All in all Wendy's birthday had been a success.

Susan felt empowered, as if finally she was in control. She had fought back for once and it had worked. He had listened to her, respected her.

One week after Wendy's birthday bash she was hospitalised when Barry attacked her in a drunken rage.

It seemed he was not so forgiving after all.

Chapter Sixteen

Roselle Digby was tiny. Not just small, which she was, but tiny. Her hands were like a child's, stubby fingers ending in heavily painted nails like talons. She had little feet, a turned up nose, small pointed breasts. Her eyes were wide-set, giving her an air of vulnerability even though she was far from that. The biggest thing about Roselle was her heart. She had a big heart and was well liked by everyone.

She was a reader, which made her interesting to Barry because she seemed so well informed. He decided to forget that Sue was a reader until she met him, a pastime he had banned because he'd said it gave her ideas above her station.

With Roselle it was different, she was a person in her own right. As head girl at the Hiltone Club she was respected in her own little world because she did not have to flog her arse, as the other girls expressed it. And that suited Roselle right down to the ground.

She had been on the game since she was fourteen in Chapeltown, Leeds. Now in the Smoke she was respected, someone who did not have to work the trade any more for a living.

She had embarked on an affair with Barry Dalston and was loving every second of it. He had swept her off her feet: buying her flowers, taking her out for romantic meals and treating her like a normal woman would be treated.

She was opinionated, intelligent and streetwise, all the things Barry abhorred in his women usually, but Roselle had something none of the others had. She was one of the few toms who had invested her money wisely.

A natural loner, though friendly enough to everyone, she had made her money work for her by buying a small but well-positioned flat and filling it with expensive furniture and fittings. Barry had been shocked but impressed when he had seen how she lived. She even put napkins on the table just to have a sandwich. She had a son in private school and drove a top of the range car.

Roselle made money and looked after it wisely. Barry for once in his life was openly admiring. So far, if he'd had money he'd spent it on things such as drink or lately drugs. The hostesses had introduced him to the delights of amphetamines and cannabis. He also liked clothes, electrical goods, all the latest gimmicks.

Now he'd had a glimpse of how life could be lived if someone had the sense to look out for themselves. True, Roselle smoked dope, but she kept away from anything else, and in this environment that was difficult.

Now as he watched her walking around the club, talking to the punters and making sure everything ran smoothly, he felt he loved her.

Barry wiped his nose with one heavy-knuckled hand. He was as high as a kite. He had not been home for over a week and knew that Sue would be out of her mind. Not with worry, she knew he could take care of himself, but she would be skint and that would be the real bug bear.

Wendy and Alana wanted to go on a school trip to Lourdes and he was supposed to find the money. This annoyed him, and because of the speed and the drink he began to get paranoid. Felt that Susan and the kids expected too much from him. It would never occur to him that the money he was spending on Roselle and drugs could have paid for the trip twice over. He had worked for that money, he was entitled to it.

He knocked back the last of his drink at the bar and walked out to the foyer. It was a Wednesday night, a slow one for the Soho workers. As he stood by the reception desk a tall black girl approached him.

LaToyah Fielding, a twenty-year-old brass from Brixton, was on reception while the usual girl was off after a botched abortion.

'Some woman rang for you. Said she was your wife, Susan. Asked if you'd been in and if I could get you to ring her?'

She was smiling. His domestic arrangements had always been a secret in the six months he had worked in the club. Mainly because of Roselle with whom he had begun an affair almost immediately.

Now she was everything to Barry. He lived for the nights they spent together and was finding it increasingly hard to leave her and go home. He never really knew what she did when she wasn't with him. Sometimes she went out clubbing with the other toms, had what she called a blinding night and did not expect him to question her right to do this. After all, they were not a couple as such. She was her own person, as she pointed out constantly. This was the late seventies after all.

If Susan had tried to give him that old fanny Barry would have punched her lights out, but with Roselle he knew he wouldn't get away with that. She was too on the ball, too much her own person even to give him the chance to try and clip her wings. He knew in his heart she slept with other men, he just knew it. He also knew that so far as she was concerned it was none of his business.

As he looked into the black girl's pretty face he nodded, angry with Sue for intruding into his other life. Daring to ring the club and shame him like this. He decided he would brain her when he got home, because he would have to go now whether he wanted to or not.

Little Barry was teething and as miserable as sin. Nothing Susan did seemed to calm him. His cheeks were red, his ear was red and he had a hump on of Olympian dimensions. Coupled with the girls' constant demands for money for the trip to France and the fact that she had borrowed off everyone and now had nothing in her purse, not even the money for Junior Disprin, Susan was at the end of her tether.

Her mother was boracic due to her father's complete refusal to get a job so she was unable to help out any more, and Susan didn't like to keep asking Kate as it just made relations between her and her son more strained. Doreen needed her money herself, though Susan knew she would lend her another couple of quid if she asked. But she didn't want to ask Doreen again, she wanted to know where Barry was and what he was doing.

At four months pregnant she was just about fed up to the back teeth of it all. The kids were living on jam sandwiches and eggs on toast and she was behind with the rent, gas and electric. The meter would go at any time and then they would be in the dark on top of everything else.

The two girls came in with Doreen. Susan smiled wearily at them.

'You look done in, mate. Sit yourself down and I'll make us a cuppa, eh?' Doreen's voice was kind and Susan laughed bitterly.

'Still no sign of him, Dor. I reckon he's got a bird, don't you?'

Doreen, a patron of the clubs herself, knew he had a bird and just who that bird was as well.

'Probably, knowing him, Sue. It's the way he is, you know that. It don't mean nothing.'

She wanted to spare her friend more heartache and was also hoping that if what she'd heard was true Barry might leave her for Roselle and let Susan get a bit of a life.

'The electric's nearly out, the food's nearly gone, and the rent and everything is overdue. I'll have to find the fucker. I know he'll go mad but I have to speak to him, try and get something from him. It's not like he ain't got the money, is it?'

Doreen didn't answer, she knew she wasn't expected to. Susan was just sounding off to her, getting it off her chest.

'I gave the girls beefburgers and chips with my lot. Okay?'

Susan smiled gratefully.

'Fucking real, ain't it? He's walking around in the top fashions like a rock star and his kids ain't even got a bit of fucking grub in the house. He is one selfish ponce.'

Doreen laughed.

'Ain't they all? I never met a man yet with a brain in his actual head. Most of them keep it in their cocks.'

Before Susan could answer the lights went out.

'That's all I need now, ain't it, with babes teething like mad. Thank fuck I've got a gas cooker.'

The two girls ran into the kitchen.

'The lights have gone, Mum, and the telly's gone off.'

Susan laughed loudly.

'I never would have noticed if you two hadn't pointed it out.'

The two girls giggled with glee.

'Good job you got us then, Mum, if you didn't notice that.'

'Go through to my kitchen and get me purse, lovies. I've got a bit of change. See if we can get the telly back on for you, eh?' said Doreen.

They ran out of the back door and Susan had to hold back tears.

'You're too good to me, Dor. What would I do without you?'

Doreen held her close and tried to lighten the situation.

'That's what friends are for, mate.'

As if on cue little Barry started to cry, a great yell that sent Susan running from the kitchen. By the time she had taken him out of his cot and cuddled him the lights were back on. Walking down the stairs, she pondered her situation. She had to see Barry and sort something out. She wondered briefly if he might have left her, but decided that her luck wouldn't run to that. If only he would leave her she could get herself on the jam roll and sort herself out from there. At least with the dole she would have a budget, know what was coming in each week so she could spend accordingly. At the moment she never knew where she was when in fact Barry was earning a good wedge. Though Christ knew what he did with it, he was always pleading poverty.

Her gold was pawned and everything else on which she could raise a quid or two. This time she didn't think she would ever be able to get any of it back from uncle.

Putting Barry in his playpen and telling the girls to keep an eye on him, she went back out to the kitchen. Doreen had made the tea and was smoking a cigarette at the table.

Susan felt she had taken as much as she could. Everywhere she turned someone had their hand out for money and she was getting desperate. Even the few quid she'd had saved was gone. She was on her uppers and that meant literally. Her shoes had given up the ghost as well. She was reduced to wearing slippers constantly because of her swollen feet.

Now there was another child on the way and Barry was on the missing list and she didn't know what to do. There was nothing in the house for the kids tomorrow morning. Then Wendy came into the kitchen.

'I've still got three pound notes from my birthday money, Mum, you can have that if you want?'

Susan looked at her gratefully.

'That's all right, darlin', Mummy will sort it all out.'

The child held the notes out without a word. When Susan didn't take them she placed them on the table by her cup of tea. Then she walked back into the lounge and sat down by little Barry's playpen. She was making him laugh by pretending to disappear behind her hands then popping up and saying 'boo' to him. He was crowing with enjoyment and holding his ear at the same time.

Susan looked down at the money. Leaping from her seat, she said to Doreen, 'Will you watch this lot for a few hours?'

'Where are you going?'

Susan smiled. 'I'll tell you later.'

Pulling a comb through her hair and dragging on her old coat, she left the house with the three pounds safely in her pocket.

Roselle was dressed to kill in a revealing spangly dress she had bought that afternoon in Regent Street. She felt good and looked better. Barry was supposed to be taking her to a Chinese in Greek Street that catered for the night workers and did a great breakfast-cum-dinner at three in the morning. It also had a little gambling room and she fancied a flutter.

Now, though, he was telling her that he had to get home and sort a few things out. He was constantly moaning about his wife. Saying they only stayed together for the kids and how she was a spendthrift who blew all his money, etc. It just went on and on. Now he had to go home when Roselle wanted to go out.

'That's okay, Bal, I'll go with the girls. They're going to the Stage anyway. I'll tag along.'

The Stage was a blues in Brixton just off the Railton Road, or the Front Line as it was called. A blues was a disused house that became a twenty-four-hour-a-day nightclub. An enterprising person would board up the windows, put in a makeshift bar and sound system, and take money on the door. It was perfect. You could smoke dope or speed or trip all day and all night if you wanted to.

Roselle knew Barry hated her going there which was why she told him she was. Elementary female psychology.

A stripper came on stage and started to gyrate to a Slade single. The noise was deafening and Roselle walked away from Barry and over to the bar. He watched the stripper, a strikingly ugly brunette with a hook nose and acne and the biggest pair of tits this side of the water.

When he went over to the bar Roselle had gone. Smiling to himself, he walked out into the foyer and into the worst possible nightmare for a man like Barry Dalston.

Susan was standing there, large as life in her old blanket coat, with her hair looking like something from a book on birds' nests and her sagging body revealed to all the world along with the latest lump.

To add insult to injury Roselle was standing with her, looking like a magazine plate and actually listening to what Susan had to say. Then his wife spied him and, smiling broadly, gave him a friendly little wave.

'Here he is, love, thanks for helping me out.'

Susan was smiling at Roselle and Roselle was smiling back at her. Only her smile was tinged with sadness and a trace of disbelief. They both looked at Barry and he wished the ground really could open up and swallow him.

Susan looked just what she was and it hurt Barry to have her show him up in public. He saw her from Roselle's point of view: badly cut hair in need of styling, a heavy body unrestrained by anything remotely resembling a girdle; a face devoid of even the most basic cosmetics; and a huge belly denoting the fact she was once more with child. He saw her bitten nails with the skin around them chafed and red-looking. They were caked with grime from cigarettes and housework. He saw the large heavy breasts that could touch her belly button these days and needed a bra with enough metal in to armour a tank. He saw her teeth, yellowing and blunt. Saw her legs – no tights, a month's stubble on them and varicose veins already evident.

He also saw how Susan automatically deferred to Roselle, assuming she was someone of importance in Barry's working life. It would never occur to her to be spiteful or jealous of the other woman, Susan was too nice for that.

He also realised Roselle would have been expecting a right bitch with a gob like the Dartford tunnel and a self-righteous attitude. That was the way he'd always described his wife, after all.

Walking towards the two women he felt as if he was moving through heavy swirling water.

Roselle smiled at him sarcastically.

'Barry, your wife's just popped in to see you.'

She turned to Susan and smiled once more, this time genuinely.

'Lovely to meet you at last, Mrs Dalston. Do stay for a drink. I'll be in the bar to introduce you to everyone.'

Susan smiled at the glamorous woman and nodded.

'Thank you. Thanks very much. I'm ever so sorry to trouble him at work like this . . .'

Roselle interrupted her.

'Don't be so silly. See you again soon.'

She walked away, her tight little bottom wiggling in an exaggerated fashion. Barry looked at his wife, his scruffy dilapidated wife, and felt hatred boil within him for what she had done.

'What you fucking doing here?'

Susan reacted as if she had been punched.

'I had to come, Bal, I'm at the end of me tether. I ain't got a bean – you ain't been home. I ain't even got any electric.'

Barry turned and saw the receptionist watching them, an interested expression on her face. Then all the hostesses seemed to want to go to the toilet. All sashaying past on clouds of perfume, eyes alert. Checking out a legal and finding her wanting. He knew they'd all thought he had a wife like the other doormen. Nice-looking women with their cars and their houses and their holidays. What they were seeing in Susan was themselves if they weren't careful.

A defeated-looking breeding machine.

They all knew about Susan's life because they had taken the course they had, prostitution, to stop the same thing happening to them.

Grabbing her arm, he forced her out on to the street.

'Go home, Susan, fucking coming here and showing me up! Look at the fucking state of you.'

She looked at him and snorted through her nose in disgust.

'Is that all that's bothering you, that I look a mess in comparison to a load of old brasses?'

He didn't answer her.

'Listen here, you, I might not be fucking Joan Collins. How could I be even if I wanted to? I have three kids and another on the way, enough debt to keep a small banana republic going, and on top of all that I have an old man who thinks more of his work associates than his own kids. I have no food, no electric and no help. I'm sorry if I look a scruff bag, Bal, but what you give me don't fucking stretch to shopping for anything other than cheap cuts of meat and bargain basement clothes.'

She was crying now and annoyed at herself for letting him upset her so much.

Barry took a ten-pound note from his pocket and gave it to her. If he got shot now he could still go out with Roselle. After Sue's inopportune entrance he needed to see Roselle as soon as possible to put over his side of the story.

Susan stared at the money in disbelief.

'Is that all? A tenner?'

He didn't answer her. He needed the rest for his night out with Roselle. Susan was defeated already. Looking at him, she shook her head in disbelief.

'You're a selfish bastard, Barry. I ain't even had the money for Junior Disprin for the baby and you don't bother to come home and see we're all right. I'm living on a fucking shoestring and look at you. New clothes, hair freshly cut and highlighted.'

She stabbed one finger into his chest.

'Your kids have been waiting night after night for me to give them the lousy twenty-quid deposit they need to go to France, and what do you do? You go on the missing list. What about this child I'm having, Barry? What shall we do with this one, eh? Another fucking mouth to feed and you ain't feeding the three you've already got.'

He still didn't answer, just stared at her. Willing her to go away. She looked so perplexed, so baffled by his attitude, that he felt like crying. Surely she could see how it was for him, a wife who looked like a bag lady coming to his place of work obviously looking for money. She was making him look bad. Deliberately making him look bad. She was trying to blackmail him.

Then Roselle came outside and told him he was needed at one of the tables to sort out a difficult customer.

He walked back into the club and pushed Roselle through the door before him. Then, turning to Susan, he bellowed at her, 'Get home, you silly bitch. I'll see you in the morning.'

She stood outside the club. It was raining now and bitterly cold. She stuffed the ten pounds into her pocket and turned away. The road was dark and busy. People were pushing past, ignoring her.

Turning back, she looked through the glass-fronted double doors of the club and saw Barry deep in conversation with Roselle. He looked so smart. He was wearing a new suit, his hair was immaculate and she realised he'd also had a manicure. His hand had felt softer than hers as he'd thrust the money at her.

Looking at him, head inclined towards the little woman in the red spangly dress, the way he talked to her, handsome face earnest, Susan realised what all the dressing up and grooming himself was for.

He wasn't having his usual leg over.

Barry was in love.

While she was sitting at home worrying herself sick, he had been spending all his money on that little woman with the beautiful clothes. Opening the door of the club Susan stepped inside once more. Warmth hit her like a blanket. Her chapped cheeks smarted. Barry and Roselle turned towards the draft of cold air and saw her standing there once more.

Barry looked at her as if she was nothing, beneath his notice.

Walking towards her, he grabbed her roughly by the arm and pushed her back on to the street. Then he began to drag her along the pavement. People stood watching them, amazed.

Susan forced him to let go of her.

'You rotten bastard! No wonder we ain't seen hide nor hair of you. There's us lot thinking you was off on your usual skirt chasing and all of a sudden we find you've gone up market.'

He stared at her again and she could see that she had pushed it as far as she should. Barry had a short fuse at the best of times and tonight he was practically ready for blast off. He shoved her hard in the chest, his hands brutal against her soft body.

'Fuck off, Sue. I'm warning you, girl, don't make me lose me temper.'

He shoved her again and this time she lost her balance and fell into the road. A black cab skidded to a halt and a passer by helped Susan to get up. She was crying now. The cab driver leaned across from his seat and shouted through the open window, 'Sober yourself up, woman,' before driving off with a stream of obscenities floating behind him.

Susan stood forlornly in the busy street. Her attempt to get Barry to cough up some money had gone horribly wrong. All she had wanted was a few quid to tide her over, that was all. Instead she had been humiliated and abused for doing what she had every right to do. She knew she had upset him but didn't he ever think about her? Didn't she and his kids even come into the equation?

She watched him shrug and felt a moment of stunning hatred for him. It was so intense she could practically taste and feel it. It was rising inside her like a big black cloud, seeping out of her pores and into the very air around her.

'All I wanted was money for the kids' school trip, Bal, not the last two pennies off your eyes. I had to come up here on the tube using three quid I skanked off poor Wendy. If I hadn't found you at work I'd have had to walk home so I had enough to buy food. Yet you treat me like a fucking leper, like I've done something wrong.'

'Go home, Susan, before you get hurt. I ain't in the mood for all this tonight.'

He shoved her hard in the chest once more and she nearly lost her balance. Out of the corner of her eye she saw people from the surrounding buildings looking on.

A pretty girl with a long black wig and high heels watched them from the peep show doorway, a smile on her face. She obviously thought Susan was trying to get into the Hiltone and the bouncer was removing her. It would be a funny story, a bit of light relief.

'You bastard, Barry. Well, I ain't going until you give me some more money.'

The next punch caught her in the jaw and Susan felt her legs go. Like a boxer she staggered back, trying to keep on her feet, her head a blaze of white pain as she felt her jaw click back into place.

Holding it she screamed at him, 'That's your answer to everything, ain't it, Barry? A kicking. Well, fuck you. I don't care any more.'

She was crying now, snot and tears mingling on her face.

'I just don't care. My kids need money and I'll fucking go in there and do a night's work if I have to, to get it. You're not the only one who can work Soho, mate.'

Roselle listened to the woman through the glass doors. She was seeing a new side to Barry Dalston and did not like it one bit. Opening the door she walked over to Susan. Taking her arm, Roselle gently led her into the club and up the stairs to the offices above.

Hostesses had left their tables and the bar to watch the little kitchen sink drama out on the street. One of them, a large blonde in a tight black sequinned dress, passed Susan a bunch of toilet roll to wipe her face.

'You all right, love?'

Susan nodded. They were all women together now. Looking out for one of their own kind who was obviously in dire straits.

'Come on, come up to the office, I'll get you a cab home.'

Roselle looked at Barry as if he was something nasty she had found on her shoes. 'Ivan will skin you for this, boy.'

She took Susan gently by the arm again and helped her up the rickety staircase. Her bulk seemed too large for the confined space and her legs were still unsteady. She felt defeated, humiliated and cold.

In the office Roselle made her a cup of coffee and poured a good measure of brandy into it.

'I'll send you a percentage of Barry's wages every week, okay? I'll clear it with Ivan – he'll be sweet as a nut once I explain. We do it with a lot of the blokes, love.'

She was lying and Susan knew but was grateful to her for making it so easy.

'He'll kill me for this. I didn't want to come here tonight. I've never wanted to come in one of these places, not even out of curiosity. I know Barry loves it here, loves the idea of it all, but it's never appealed to me.'

Roselle smiled at her.

'It is an acquired taste, I must admit, and sometimes I wish I never acquired it to be honest. But it's a living and it keeps me all right. I wonder at times, though, what it must be like to be a married woman and sleep with one man all the time.'

Susan shook her head.

'This is certainly preferable.'

Roselle offered her a cigarette and Susan took it gratefully. She decided she liked this woman and wondered what on earth a nice streetwise girl like her was doing with the piece of shit Susan had married.

Roselle opened a drawer and took out a hundred pounds. She counted it off a roll and Susan watched enviously.

'Take this as a sub from his wages. I'll tell him about it, don't worry.'

Susan took it and shoved it into her pocket with the other ten quid.

'He'll break my neck because I came here but I had to. I'm practically on me uppers.'

She rubbed one hand across her belly.

'This poor baby's taken some punishment tonight too.'

Roselle felt a sudden urge to cry. In Susan Dalston she saw her own mother. Saw the bruised face at breakfast, the constant struggle to keep her kids fed and clothed at the expense of herself. Never a thing for her. Old before her time she had died at fifty, embracing death, happy to go. To be released from the daily grind of just existing.

Barry treated his wife the way he did because he could. Because she let him. Because she was too weak to fight him and take control of her own life. Roselle knew all about the Barrys of this world and what they were capable of, and it occurred to her then that she was practically sleeping with her father. He had been like Barry: a violent bully who saw weaker people as fair game, even his own wife and children.

'Do you feel well enough to go home?' she asked softly.

Susan's face was a white mask of pain. Taking a fur coat from a cupboard, Roselle smiled at her.

'Come on, I'll give you a lift. That way I can be sure you get home okay. Otherwise I'll be worried about you all night.'

Susan shook her head vehemently.

'Oh, no, Barry would go mad . . .'

Roselle interrupted her.

'Fuck Barry, love. He works here for me and Ivan. He'll do as he's told.'

Susan was terrified and it showed.

'There's a toilet in there. Go and wash your face and tidy yourself up, I have a call to make then I'll take you home. And I will brook no arguments, okay?'

Susan did as she was told. She always did as she was told by anyone in authority.

She had a long painful wee that made her feel as if her belly was trying to escape through her vagina. She felt a heavy pressing sensation on her pelvis, almost like labour pains, and hoped she was not in line for another miss.

She relaxed on the cold toilet seat for a few moments, forehead heavy with sweat, sickness in the pit of her stomach now. It seemed to spiral up through her body. Fear was setting in.

Barry would be livid over all this and now she wished she had stayed home and left it all to sort itself out.

Susan washed her hands in the basin and splashed cold water

on her face. She saw herself in the little mirror above the wash basin. Her eyes had black circles under them, and her jaw was bruising already. She smelled. Her coat had the shaggy dog smell of old material wet with rain. Her hands were rough. Her bitten nails and stubby fingers looked obscene to her as she wiped them with the pink towel that hung on a nail by the basin.

No wonder Barry didn't want to come home any more; he would rather spend time with the woman in the office. Susan wanted Barry to be with the woman in the office, though she guessed Roselle was too shrewd ever to take him on permanently.

But Susan needed his money, she had to look out for the kids. Stepping back into the office, she smiled tremulously. Roselle looked stunning in the fur coat, with her make up perfect and her hair styled immaculately. Susan envied her self-assurance and confidence.

'Come on then, let's get going.'

Downstairs Barry was like a man demented. Susan saw him looking at her with what could only be described as hatred.

'Where are you going?'

Roselle shrugged.

'I'm taking your pregnant wife home.'

Barry shook his head.

'Oh, no, you're not.'

The words had a finality about them that Susan recognised.

'I'll get a cab, love. Thanks for the offer.'

'I'll take you home, Susan.'

He had his car keys ready.

Roselle shook her head doubtfully.

'I've already sorted it with Ivan.'

Barry looked at her coldly.

'Then you can fucking unsort it, can't you?'

He grabbed Susan's arm and dragged her from the club, Roselle following. He ignored her and took Susan to his car, a nice black Mercedes she had never seen before. Shoving her unceremoniously inside, he drove off without a word to Roselle who watched the car as it disappeared around the corner.

Barry and Susan drove in silence until they reached the East

End. Then he stopped the car by the Roman Road, in the car park of a block of high-rise flats.

He turned to her and looked her in the eye.

'You're a cunt, Susan, do you know that, eh? You signed your own death warrant tonight. Fucking showing me up like that! I can't believe you done it. Can't believe you were that stupid you thought you would get away with it.'

His voice had the cold detachment she had learned to listen for; it was the warning of a really good hiding to come.

'I didn't want to go there, Bal. I had to, I had no choice.'

She could hear the pleading in her own voice, the fear, and hated herself for it. But she had a baby to protect and Barry had beaten one out of her before.

'I have to look after the kids, Bal. Unlike you I don't have any choice over what I do or don't do. I can't swan around and forget about them for days on end because I have to cook for them, clean for them, take them to school. Every day.'

She was willing herself to shut up, stop antagonising him, but the words spewed out of her like a torrent.

'I have to listen to their tales of woe, make sure they're smart, clean, cared for. I have to talk to them, make everything better for them when they've had a shit day.

'I have little Barry down with earache because of his teeth and didn't even have a few pence to buy Junior Disprin because you didn't bother coming home to give me any. I've borrowed off everyone, your mother included, while I waited for you to deign to turn up and pay me me keep. So don't talk to me about showing you up. I have credit in two shops and they won't give me a penny sweet till I've paid off the back. Your reputation don't gain us nothing these days, boy. You're old hat, you and me father. Bannerman saw to that.

'So short of moonlighting down Shepherd's Market, what was I supposed to do? Wait for Father Christmas? All right, do your party piece, kick me in the head. I couldn't give a flying fuck any more.'

She looked into his handsome face then and felt the pull of him again. Saw what attracted the Roselles of the world to him. He was handsome and he was dangerous. Why had she never realised that when she was a girl? She could have avoided so much heartache.

Barry stared at her for a full five minutes, feeling her nervousness. He could smell it coming off her in waves. But he wasn't seeing Susan, the mother of his kids, the woman who was decent, true, and in her own way respectable.

He was seeing her from Roselle's point of view.

Scruffy, defeated and smelly.

He had never been so ashamed in all his life as he had been tonight.

And it was all her fault.

She had shown him up for what he really was and he would never forgive her for it. He punched her in the face then, a hard back hander that was shockingly loud in the confines of his lovely new car.

A car he had bought to impress Roselle and the other hostesses. He had wanted to impress a bunch of whores at the expense of his own family.

'You think you've fucked it up for me there, don't you, eh?'

He punched her again, harder this time. Enjoyed watching her try to cover her face and body as he rained blows on her, talking all the while in his quiet sing-song voice. Finally he opened her door and pushed her out on to the wet pavement. Her cumbersome body landed like a sack of potatoes on the wet ground.

Jumping out of his seat, he ran around the car to her and started to kick her. Small kicks at first, gradually culminating in one heavy blow that moved her a foot across the pavement with its force.

The lights of a car illuminated them as if they were on a stage. Two policemen jumped from their car and ran up to them.

'Here you are, constable, have her. Have the ugly fucking bitch. You have her because I don't want her any more.'

Barry left them standing over the unconscious body of his wife, confident that as usual the police would not get involved in domestic disputes. Susan would tell them what they needed to hear and he would be safe as the proverbial houses.

Jumping into his car he reversed out of the car park like a

maniac and drove back to the West End and Roselle. The woman he would have to placate if he wanted to keep on the right side of her.

The two policemen looked down at the crumpled heap on the ground and sighed.

'Weren't that Barry Dalston?'

The older man nodded.

'It certainly was. Let's get her to the hospital, let them deal with her. I ain't in the mood for a domestic tonight.'

Susan lost her baby in the back of the police car, which upset PC Hutchinson no end.

'All that blood and gore . . . will these women never learn? The number of times we've been called to their house is unbelievable. But she'll have him back, she always does.'

It never occurred to him that Susan didn't have any choice in the matter.

Chapter Seventeen

Susan was laughing, her voice loud and drunken as she called out. Smoke from the pub's regulars was heavy and it was noisy in there, too noisy really for anyone to hear what they were talking about. Though it didn't stop drunken conversations going on all over the place.

June screamed as a stripper came on to the small makeshift stage. He was gorgeous with short blond hair and rippling muscles.

'Gis a flash, son!'

Her voice as usual was louder than everyone else's.

'I've seen bigger things crawling out of apples.'

Ivy was in her element. This was where she loved to be these days. Finally, after years of being too good for rowdy local pubs, she had embraced her nights out with a fervour that shocked everyone. Not least her son Joey who could not believe the change in her.

Susan was Ivy's blue-eyed girl these days. She saw her younger self in her granddaughter. In Susan's struggle to keep body and soul together. Even Joey was sorry for his daughter at times. Since the last ding-dong with Barry she had been left with a permanent limp. He had shattered her anklebone, but no one had realised until after the loss of the baby. Even Joey had been shocked by that and with the encouragement of June and his mother he had taken Barry aside and kicked seven colours of shit out of him. Barry had taken the hiding without a word, as if he'd expected it. Knew he had finally gone too far.

But deep inside Joey knew he had really hammered him because he had got himself a nice little earner. Joey had asked him time and again to put a word in with Ivan for him, but knew he wouldn't. Barry saw himself as being above Joey these days and that rankled. Rankled badly.

So there was an underlying animosity between them now that had not been there before and Joey was looking out for his daughter a lot more these days because of it. It was the only way he could get back at Barry and he was enjoying it.

Plus the kids were a treat. Susan, whatever her faults, was a brilliant mother and everyone praised her efforts to raise the kids in the difficult circumstances she lived under. Tonight, though, she was in her element. She was drunk and loudly enjoying herself. Joey laughed as she stumbled trying to get out of her chair.

The male stripper was gyrating before his audience, shaking his body in the women's faces, daring one of them to remove his jockstrap with her teeth.

'Come over here and I'll take me teeth out for you, son.'

Ivy made everyone crack up with laughter again.

'Shut up, Mother, stop frightening the boy.'

His music ended and the small stage was dark once more. Susan finally managed to get out of her seat and walked unsteadily towards the ladies'. Doreen followed her.

'That little Barry's a case, ain't he? Do you know what he said to me today, Sue? He asked me why the world had clouds. I said so the sky looked pretty for us all when we wanted something nice to look at. Do you know what he said then? He said, "Why don't God make the sky pretty all the time, like my mum?"'

Susan burst out laughing.

'He's only three, bless him, he ain't seen me properly yet.'

Doreen sat on the toilet, the door wide open, in full view of the packed bar if another woman came in. But she didn't care about that, none of them did. It would just be a bit of added excitement, a bit of a laugh.

'He's a good kid. How's things with His Lordship?'

Susan sighed. 'Same as usual. He'll never change all the time he's got a hole in his arse.'

Doreen shrugged. She hadn't really been expecting anything different.

Susan applied pink lipstick with a drunken hand, laughing to herself as she tried to get it within her lip line.

'I am so pissed, Dor. I haven't been this pissed in years.'

Doreen wiped herself and pulled up her knickers and tights unsteadily.

'Well, it won't do you any harm to let your hair down now and again.'

Susan staggered into the toilet after her and pulled down her pants, leaning against the wall for support. She felt the first wave of nausea and took deep breaths. She was drunker than she'd thought.

'I am drunk as a skunk.'

She washed her hands and she and Doreen made their way back to the table. Susan saw Barry then and her heart skipped a beat. She forced a smile to her face.

'Hello, Bal, long time no see.'

The sarcasm was wasted on him, she knew, but it afforded her a little pleasure. He was drinking a large Scotch and she worried that he might be staying. Her fears were soon allayed, though.

'Where's my passport, Sue? I can't find it.'

She smiled.

'You've been home then?'

He nodded.

'I seen the kids, had a laugh with them and tossed them all a few quid, like.'

He was practically apologising for not being there with them. This was a new one.

'What do you need your passport for then?'

He grinned sheepishly.

'I'm going out to Spain to collect a debt for Ivan.'

'That's nice for you, Bal, make a change from Birmingham or Liverpool, eh? Bit of currant bun, a nice bird. Sounds great. Roselle is going too, I take it?'

He nodded.

Since the night she had turned up at his place of work, Susan's life had changed in more ways than one. Roselle was now a friend to her. She made sure Barry kept his family commitments and

Susan allowed his relationship with Roselle to blossom. Not that she could have done much about it anyway. If he decided he wanted an affair, he would have one. But at least Roselle made sure she got her wedge regularly and she was left in relative peace. Which suited Susan right down to the ground.

She met up with Roselle about once a month and they had a bit of lunch together. Afterwards she always treated Susan to something: a hairdo, a dress or handbag. Little things, which made Susan enjoy herself more, made her feel better about herself. Roselle gave Susan a modicum of self-respect.

Plus the two women got on famously, seeing things in each other they had only ever seen in themselves before. Their love of films and literature, for instance. Susan looked better than she had in years and this made her happier with herself. Coupled with Barry's gradual defection to Roselle's flat, all in all life was going well for her. These days he came home just once a week or so to see the kids and show his face for the benefit of the neighbours.

'Your passport's in the electric cupboard in the hall, I hid it among all the letters and that for safety.'

He nodded, happy now he knew where it was. Getting to his feet, he looked down at her. 'You look nice. I'll get you a drink before I go, eh?'

She nodded, amazed at the way they could talk to one another nowadays. He treated her with respect.

'Mind you, Bal, I think I've had enough as it is.'

He grinned and walked up to the bar, standing out because of his clothes and his looks. Susan studied him; he really was a good-looking man. She saw the other women looking at him, saw the way he eyed them all as he walked, grading them from one to ten.

The thought made her smile. If Roselle could see him now, winking at the younger women, smiling at the older ones. Letting them all think they were in with a chance. She wondered if he played away from home with Roselle and put the thought from her mind.

If he did he was a fool. Women like her didn't grow on trees and if anyone should have been aware of that fact it was Barry. As she watched him a familiar voice hailed her loudly.

'Hello, Susan love, how are you then?'

It was Peter White, a boy from school.

'Hello, Peter, how are you? You're looking well.'

He grinned at her, displaying white teeth in a tanned face. He was a merchant seaman nowadays. He'd got away from home at fifteen by coasting on small ships and now worked the big ones, the ACT boats and the Blue Star lines.

Peter had merry blue eyes and sandy hair. He was thickset, a large man with the beginnings of a beer belly, but handsome in a rough kind of way.

'Just got back from South America. Thought I'd mosey on down here and see what the score was with everyone. Your mother looks great, don't she? I always had a crush on her at school.'

Susan laughed loudly.

'You never did have very good taste in women. Married yet?'

He shook his head.

'A girl in every port though, I bet?'

'If you can call them girls. Right ropey the foreign whores, ain't they?' Barry's voice was loud and people stopped their conversations to listen to him.

Peter took a deep breath and said gently, 'I'll see you again, Sue, take care.'

She nodded, saddened by Barry's interference.

'He was only being polite, Bal. Christ almighty, I've known him longer than I have you.'

Barry curled his lip in contempt.

'He's a fucking wanker and I don't want to hear you've been seen with him, all right?'

The old Barry was back, the possessive Barry, the one who owned her. Could dictate her life, who she spoke to and who she didn't. Susan felt depression come over her like a lead weight.

'He's a neighbour, Bal, that's all. Stop putting everyone on a downer for once and get with it. Anyway, what you got to be jealous about? He wouldn't look twice at me, mate.'

She ended on a joke to try to lighten the situation but Barry's dark brooding countenance was unchanged.

'You'd better get going, Roselle's probably waiting for you.'

He grinned nastily.

'Trying to get rid of me now so you can carry on your conversation with fucking Popeye?'

She lit a cigarette and took a long drag on it. A female stripper came on, a large girl with thunderous thighs and a wobbling belly. The men slaughtered her. Insulted her and tried to cop a feel. Barry found it disgusting. He was better than all these people now. The thought cheered him and as he saw Peter White talking to another woman, he got up to leave.

'How long will you be gone then?'

He stared at Susan. She looked quite reasonable lately. Nothing spectacular but at least she wouldn't frighten anyone any more.

'How's your ankle?'

The question caught her off guard. He never mentioned her limp.

'It's all right. The damp plays it up. They reckon I have arthritis in it, 'cos it was a bad break, like. But other than that, it's nothing I can't cope with. Why?'

He looked meaningfully at Peter White and she rolled her eyes to the ceiling.

'You don't need to threaten me, Barry. I don't want any men, thank you very much. Christ knows I haven't had much luck with the one I've got, have I?'

His hand moved quickly and she flinched away but he caressed her chin instead of hitting her.

'Don't ever ask me when I'll be back again, right? I tell you all you need to know, and that should be enough for you.'

Without another word he walked from the pub. No one said goodbye to him. Not even Joey.

Doreen came and sat beside her.

'I don't believe the cheek of him, Sue.'

She grinned. 'I do. He's a dog in the manger is Barry. He don't want me but he's still frightened in case someone else does. Well, he needn't worry. I don't want any men, thank you very much. Too much like hard work.'

But inside herself a small part of her was pleased by his reaction and this annoyed her because she didn't still want him, did she?

She didn't answer her own question, she was too afraid. But it had sobered her up all right.

Back at June and Joey's flat they were still partying. The records were on loud and the drink flowed like water. It was a typical Saturday night. Debbie was there with her husband Jamesie Phillips, a wide boy from Canning Town who was a watered down version of Barry.

Debbie was pregnant and had only just been accepted back into the fold. She had fallen out with everyone when she moved into her new terraced town house in Rainham, Essex. For a while she had seemed to think, as her mother so aptly put it, 'That her shit didn't stink like everyone else's.'

She had soon become lonely, though, Jamesie being at work all day and out drinking all night. He clumped her and all, which had come as no surprise to any of them except Debbie. She had already lost two babies, seemed to find it hard to carry them.

Susan privately wondered if it was all the abortions her sister had had over the years. Debbie had used abortion as a form of birth control and it seemed that now she might be paying the price. But Susan was sorry for her, knowing how much joy kids brought you no matter how hard they made your life. She would die without her lot, she knew that as well as she knew her own name.

Her life might seem weird to outsiders but it was a pot of gold to her in as far as she finally had what she wanted: a few quid, the kids she loved and no Barry to think about. She knew Roselle did everything for him these days, even his washing, and after years of that ponce's feet, that suited Susan right down to the ground.

She walked through to the kitchen and poured herself more gin and tonic. There was no ice so she drank it warm, revelling in the hot drunkenness that enveloped her. She laughed heartily, thinking about Barry's jealousy. He was a boy and no mistake.

She suddenly felt very lonely and wished she was tucked up in bed with little Barry. He slept with her as of right as the baby of the family, though some mornings she awoke to find the two girls had crept in in the night as well.

Susan felt tearful then, thinking of her children, nostalgic for their babyhood.

Then her mind went to the children she had lost. Jason and handsome little Luke and the baby she had felt slip away from her in a police car.

Barry Dalston was a devil, a violent devil. He had taken those children away from her as carelessly as he had given them to her. Without a second's thought. She poured another drink. This time she drank it straight down and shuddered.

An arm went around her shoulders and she turned quickly.

It was her father.

'What's the matter, girl? What you doing out here on your own?'

He saw her tears.

'Has that ponce upset you again?' Joey's voice was harsh. 'I saw him tonight, giving you verbal diarrhoea of the earhole.'

She shrugged.

'I'm just drunk, Dad. Thinking about the kids. When they was babies. I'm just nostalgic, that's all.'

She laughed to counter the sadness in her voice.

'Come here and give your old dad a cuddle.'

Afterwards Susan blamed the drink. Without it she would have been more alert. Would have heard the underlying meaning in his voice. But she was young, and she was lonely, and she was sad. As he cuddled her she felt the feeling she knew her own children must feel at the touch of a parent. She needed to feel someone was looking after her for once, that someone cared.

As Joey's hand moved up to her breast she didn't at first realise what he was going to do. She thought he was going to put a hand to her cheek.

As he grabbed at her she brought up her knee and hit him in the groin with a sickening thud. She put all her strength behind it.

Joey crumpled, his hands grasping his throbbing testicles, moaning. As he slumped before her, June entered the kitchen. Taking in the scene she started screaming abuse at both him and Susan.

'What you letting him do to you, you filthy bitch? Can't keep your own husband home so you start on your father, eh?'

The people in the living room were listening now, all loving the excitement of June and Joey about to have a punch up.

They were not disappointed.

As soon as he could move he pulled himself up by the sink and turned on his wife. 'What you on about, you silly whore? She's me fucking daughter . . .'

June was in mid-scream and refused to be shouted down. She was just starting to enjoy herself and the drama she had created.

'I know what went on, mate, you can't fucking shut me up. It ain't like it's the first time, is it?'

Joey flew at her then, fists and feet flying. Dragging his screaming wife by the hair, he forced her out on to the balcony and began beating her with every ounce of strength he had.

Debbie was screaming, Ivy was screaming. Susan hoped someone would call the Old Bill and an ambulance. She picked up her coat and bag and walked out of the flat. Side stepping her mother and father, she started to walk home.

It was always the same. No matter what they did, how happy the day was, they ruined it. Somehow they always ruined it.

She felt the tears building up in her chest, making it hard for her to swallow. Her eyes were red and hot and felt as if they had been sprayed with sand. She was overwhelmed by the realisation that nothing good could ever come of her ties to her family. The people who should be the most important in her life after her children were liars, thieves, sexual predators. Their whole lives revolved around themselves and their needs, their wants. Barry included. He was off to Spain with Roselle, without even leaving an address in case one of the children had an accident or got ill. He would see her asking for a contact address as a piss take, trying to check up on him.

But Roselle would get in touch, by a card or a phone call. She always did.

Everything had been so nice tonight, why did her father have to do that to her? Everything was sex with him. It was all he talked about, all he thought about, all he ever wanted. She was nearly home. Taking a deep breath she rearranged her face so the baby sitter would not guess anything had happened.

As Susan walked around the back of the little terrace she sighed heavily.

The hand came out of the dark and grabbed her. She tried in vain to scream. Then she smelled the distinctive aroma of Paco Rabanne aftershave and realised it was Barry.

'What you doing, Bal? You nearly gave me a heart attack.'

He grinned.

'I was just waiting to see who you came home with. I thought Popeye might have walked you home, sung you a few sea shanties and slipped the old anchor into the waterline.'

Susan felt so degraded by his words that she flew at him.

'What is it with you, Bal? You are living with another woman, you have always lived your own life, you even gave me a fucking venereal disease, and you have the fucking nerve to spy on me in case I get a knee trembler? Well, let me put your mind at rest. I don't want sex with you or anyone else. Can you take that on board? I hate sex, I loathe sex. It causes nothing but fucking trouble because no one in my life has ever made proper love with another person or loved anyone in any way. Now, take your bad attitude and your flash car and go home to your old woman. Because you ain't a part of this life any more, Bal. You went on to better things and, frankly, I don't blame you.'

She tried to walk away from him but he grabbed her arm.

'Who are you talking to? Getting very lippy all of a sudden, ain't we?'

She pulled her arm away and cried in exasperation: 'I've had enough, Barry. Enough of all this. Do you know what happened to me tonight?'

He looked into her strained face. In the darkness she seemed almost pretty.

'My father tried to give me one in me mother's kitchen.'

As she was saying the words the alcohol-free part of her brain was screaming to her to keep her mouth shut, not let Barry know what had occurred.

'Me own father. What kind of a life is that for anyone, eh?

Twenty-seven years old and my father still thinks he can take me as his right.'

She was crying again, a deep shuddering crying that made her incoherent. Stopped her from explaining how she felt, trying to let her errant husband know just how bad she felt inside. How dirty, how hateful, and how disgusted she was with them all. Her mother and Barry included.

He took her by the arm and led her into the little house. He paid the babysitter, Doreen's eldest boy, a fiver, which pleased him no end. And he made her a cup of tea.

As Susan sat on the new sofa, courtesy of Roselle and her regular payments, and looked at the spotlessly clean little home she had created for herself and her children she realised the futility of her own life. Everyone treated her as if she was a thing, something they owned and therefore had the right to use and abuse. Without a care in the world for whether they hurt her feelings or were going against her wishes.

She sipped the hot sweet tea and grimaced.

'I'm on a diet, believe it or not. I haven't taken sugar for over a year.'

But she drank it anyway, grateful for the warmth.

'So what happened with Joey then?'

She shook her head. 'The usual, Barry.'

He was seriously upset and she was grateful for that as well. His caring was very important to her. Anyone's caring for that matter.

'What? He tried to get his leg over?'

She nodded. 'It was the drink. At least, that's what he'll say anyway. I left him and me mum going at it like fucking navvies on the balcony. I expect they've both been nicked by now on a D and D.'

'I'll kill him. You make sure you keep away, right? Me and Roselle see you all right for poke and that so there's no reason to mix with them, is there?'

Susan sighed.

'Easier said than done. Me mum will be round in a few days as if nothing's happened, blaming it on the drink as usual, and then we'll all play games until it happens again. I won't let him near the girls. He knows that and all and it annoys him. But I would take a knife and cut that fucker's throat if I thought he had touched them, I take oath on that.'

'I know you would, Sue. You're a good mother, you know. A good wife. I never appreciated you really, not until I met Roselle. She thinks the sun shines out of your arse.'

He grinned and Susan smiled, pleased that he was praising her, pleased that Roselle liked her as much as she liked Roselle.

'You want to look after her, Bal, she's a diamond.'

He laughed out loud.

'I can't believe we're having this conversation, can you?'

Susan laughed with him.

'Why not? Everything tonight has been weird, you giving me a compliment being the weirdest thing of all. I thought I was a lazy fat whore who should get off her arse and lose some weight?'

Barry fell quiet.

'I'll have a word with Joey,' he said finally. 'Sort it out for you. Make sure he leaves you alone.'

Susan waved a hand in dismissal.

'A waste of time. He'll leave it now for a while before he starts again. Let it go, it causes more trouble than it's worth. Besides me mother blew his cover tonight. Her mouth was going like the fucking Lutine bell. And you know them. Keep it quiet, keep it in the family. In more ways than one!'

Barry copped a quick look at his watch.

Susan saw him and sighed.

'You'd better get a move on. What time are you flying out?'

Barry looked sheepish.

'Nine in the morning. Yeah, I'd better go. Roselle will be wondering what happened to me.'

Susan nodded, inexplicably saddened by his words.

'Of course. I'll see you to the door.'

He kissed her gently on the cheek.

'Ta ta, mate. Take care.'

She smiled tremulously.

'And you. Have a good time. Give my best to Roselle.'

She watched him walk down the path and sighed. If only she

brought out the best in him like Roselle did. They could have been happy then. Shutting the door, she felt the silence of the house crashing in her ears. Locking up, she crept upstairs and went into the bathroom to undress. In her bedroom she saw three faces on her pillows. All crashed out, dead to the world.

Susan smiled. Creeping into the middle, she put little Barry into the crook of her arm and cuddled the two girls at the same time.

She felt a moment's happiness as she loved her children. Whatever else happened to her she had these three and for that she would always be grateful. But the loneliness inside her, the want of another adult to love and care for, stayed with her until finally she slept.

When Susan came down to breakfast, Kate was already at the back door. Letting her in, Susan smiled.

'You're an early bird.'

Kate's face was grave.

'Have you not heard? Has no one been round?'

Susan shook her head. It was aching from the previous night's drinking and the subsequent events.

'What's happened now?'

Her voice was resigned.

'Your dad threw your mother down the stairs of the flats. She's in intensive care.'

Susan blinked. Her whole body seemed to be shaking.

'He what?'

'He threw her down the stairs, the concrete steps, and she landed awkwardly. She's in a terrible state, child.'

Susan wiped a hand across her face.

'Where's me dad? Has he been nicked?'

Kate shook her head.

'Everyone said she fell while drunk and they believed it. He's at the hospital with her.'

'I'd better get meself up there. Will you watch the kids?'

Kate nodded.

'With pleasure. Bring them through and I'll start the breakfast.'

She opened a carrier bag from the Co-op and took out bacon and eggs and bread.

'You know you don't have to do that any more, Kate, Barry sees we have enough.'

Her mother-in-law's voice was gentle.

'I'll not eat food that was paid for by him, you know that, child. Now get yourself ready and go and see your poor mother. Though, God forgive me, I should imagine she asked for all she got.'

Little Barry toddled into the kitchen then and seeing his nan let out a scream of delight.

Kate picked him up and cuddled him, smelling the baby sweat from his night's sleep and a distinct aroma of jelly babies from the previous evening.

Susan went up to get washed and dressed, ready for the hospital.

Debbie was doing the concerned daughter act. Susan wasn't fooled, though. She knew her sister was loving the drama.

As she walked on to the ward in Whitechapel Hospital she saw exactly how the land lay.

'How you can waltz in here after what you caused, I don't know, Susan.' Debbie was all self-righteous anger and the usual histrionic tears.

'Oh, for fuck's sake, shut your trap, Debbie, and tell me what the score is?'

She placed her hands protectively across her pregnant stomach and said dramatically, 'He threw her down the stairs – chucked her with all his strength. It was awful, Susan. I've never seen them go at it like that.'

A nurse walked into the little side ward and Debbie switched to the official story.

'She just went flying. I reckon she caught her heel, and with the drink she couldn't do much to help herself.' She smiled at the nurse, an Irish girl with hips like a steam liner and merry blue eyes. 'This is me sister, Susan.'

The nurse smiled back.

'The doctor will be in soon. Your mother seems better. Her

OBs are stable and she has no real physical injuries. Broken bones, you know. Though she will be sore when she does wake, it was quite a fall.'

Susan nodded, unsure what to say.

'Shall I get yous a nice cup of tea?'

They both nodded and smiled once more and she left the room. Debbie rolled her eyes up to the ceiling.

'I feel like one of them dogs you see in the back of cars. Nodding and smiling all the time. I wish they'd all fuck off and leave us alone. I can't be bothered to make conversation.'

'They mean well, Debs. Where's Dad?'

Debbie shrugged.

'He went off with Barry just after the police left and they took Mum off in the ambulance. I assumed they were coming here like. But knowing the old man he's out on the piss. Jamesie is fuming. He thought I should go home and leave them all to it. Fucked off, he did, and left me to cope with it all.'

Susan felt sad for her. What with the baby, she didn't need this added aggravation. Then an icy hand gripped at her entrails.

'Did Barry say they were coming here then?'

She tried to keep her voice light.

'I don't know. He called up to the balcony and me dad went down to him. Then he got in the car and I ain't seen him since.' Debbie started to cry. 'I've been here all night on me own.'

Susan felt the fear mounting inside.

Barry had been strange the night before. He had been kind, considerate. She had missed him when he had gone, and considering all he had put her through over the years that in itself was strange. Yet she had felt for the first time in years as if he cared about her, really deep down cared. Whether it was just as the mother of his children she didn't know. She assumed it was that. But whatever the reason it had felt good. Made her feel better about herself. As if it made her a proper person somehow, made her real. Proved she existed.

She should never have told him about her father and what he had done. Now she would have not only her mother on her conscience but also her father because Barry, upset and self-righteous, could easily have killed him or left him half dead somewhere.

Violence, violence, always violence. Would she never get away from it? Would her children have to live with it as she had?

Debbie watched the change of expression on her sister's face and sighed.

'Did Barry know about what happened?'

Susan nodded.

'You told him, I suppose?' This was said with the usual aggression and Susan lost her temper. Forgetting about her mother lying behind the curtains of the bed, she bellowed, 'Why shouldn't I have told him, eh? Unlike you I don't find my father trying to have sex with me remotely normal. I know that probably shocks you, Debs, but that's me, ain't it? I'm weird like that.

'I'm of the opinion you should only have sexual relations with people who ain't your relations, if you get my fucking drift.'

Debbie dropped her head down on her chest.

'Are you going to look at Mum?'

Susan shook her head.

'Not yet, I can't cope with all that yet.'

Debbie snorted.

''Course you can't. Not you, Mrs Big Brain. Mrs Analyse Everything.'

Susan didn't answer her, she knew Debbie was hurting. She only wished her sister would realise once and for all that their unhappiness stemmed from their upbringing. They had never learned to love properly, any of them. Love was always expressed by sex, a sexual act, sexual innuendo.

She remembered her father grabbing at her tits and Debbie's tits, saying how big they were getting, not his little girls any more. No one thought it was wrong, his talking about them as if he owned them. A real father would never discuss his daughter's attributes.

Now Debbie was caught up just like Susan with a man who was like Joey in every way. A man who used her and took her as and when he wanted. Gave her a slap when he decided she needed one, talked of and treated her like something he had found on the bottom of an old shoe.

It did not take an Einstein to realise they were broken people, living broken lives. Coping in their own way, giving the impression of being in control to the outside world. After all, they mixed with people who would not find their behaviour strange, they mixed with people like themselves. Other broken people who laughed at everything life threw at them, finding humour in the worst possible circumstances. And when one crisis was over, they blundered helplessly into another one.

'Debbie, I think we should ask the hospital if they had anyone brought into casualty last night. Barry wasn't pleased with the turn of events, I can tell you. For all he is himself he finds Dad's preoccupation with sleeping with me hard to take. It makes him angry, and when Barry Dalston is angry anything can happen.'

Debbie's eyes were round. The enormity of what Susan was saying was just sinking in.

'You don't think . . . Barry wouldn't . . . Would he?'

Susan shook her head.

'I really don't know, mate. I don't know what to think.'

Debbie jumped up from her seat and screamed at her, 'Why did you have to tell him, Susan? You must have known what it would cause.'

The nurse walked in then with the tray of tea and smiled at them both. Her Dublin accent was strong as she informed them happily, 'Your father's here, just talking to the Doctor. He'll be in soon.'

'Is he all right?'

The nurse shook her head.

'Well, obviously he is very concerned about your mother but he's here now. I've told him you two are here as well and that pleased him.'

She pulled back the curtains from the bed and Susan finally saw June. She looked awful, her skin livid, her breathing strained and shallow. Joey walked in. He was tidy, shaven and in clean clothes. He looked almost respectable.

The nurse decided to leave the family together. But first she looked at the two women and said gently, 'I know this is a stressful time but if you could keep your arguing down . . . there are other patients here, all very ill. And your mother may be able to hear you, you know.'

Joey looked at his wife and sighed.

'She looks rough, don't she?'

'Where have you been? What were you doing with Barry?'

Susan's voice was low now; all the fight had gone out of her.

'He wanted a hand to collect a debt before he went away. Gave me a bar to do it.'

Susan nodded. She could not avoid seeing the pleased look cross Debbie's face.

She drank her tea and was quiet. Fifteen minutes later Susan left the hospital. The concerned husband and daughter were making her stomach turn.

Inside, although she was glad Barry had not done anything to her father, she was also strangely disappointed.

'You're getting as bad as that lot.'

She spoke the words out loud and the people in the bus queue stared at her strangely. But Susan was too tired and too upset to care.

Chapter Eighteen

Roselle looked around the club. Satisfied everything was running smoothly, she decided to go up and talk to Ivan. This conversation was long overdue.

As she walked out to the foyer she saw Barry laughing with one of the new hostesses, a skinny northern girl with almond eyes and sallow skin. She had definitely been touched with the tar brush somewhere in her family line. Roselle stood observing them, and saw Barry put an arm across the girl's shoulder and cuddle her to him.

It was the action of a man with intimate knowledge of the woman in front of him and Roselle felt the anger only a betrayed woman can really feel. Especially as she knew the girl had supposedly just got over a bout of 'flu and had been off work for a week recuperating.

Roselle wondered now what form that recuperation had taken. Barry and she seemed very close.

The girl's name was Marianne. There were very rarely last names with hostesses, and the names they did give were usually made up. One girl called herself Starlight, and another, for reasons that were self-explanatory, called herself Miss Lovelace. But Marianne seemed to be catching the attention of all the men and Roselle wondered why. True, she was pretty, in a girlish spotty way, but nothing special. Roselle guessed that she offered the ultimate and that was usually a good reason for seeing a girl on her way.

S and M caused trouble in clubs. A suck and fuck was the usual menu. Once a girl deviated from it the money came in faster, but the life seemed to catch up with them faster as well. Looking at

Marianne, Roselle wondered if she took the violence on herself. She had a lot of time off and Roselle believed she might be taking customers off the roll.

How anyone could be beaten or abused for money was a mystery to her. She had given out a few good whacks for a certain price over the years, indeed she still had a couple of regulars she saw occasionally, but to be the object of someone's hatred seemed to her a mug's game.

The whore should be the one who exploited, not the other way around. If she used her brains anyway. Barry saw her watching them and moved away from Marianne. The girl walked past her and smiled smugly.

Roselle knew her type all right, she had seen them come and go over the years. She wouldn't last long because Roselle was going to give her the bad news soon, tell her she wasn't what the club was looking for. That should take the spring out of the bitch's step.

Catriona, a large-boned African girl, was on reception. She smiled knowingly at Roselle and nodded at the door. Ivan was leaving and Roselle was annoyed, she had wanted to talk to him. As he pulled on his coat there was a commotion from inside the club, a scream and then a heavy thud. Turning back Roselle went in, followed closely by Barry.

Marianne was on her knees trying to disentangle her hair from the long red talons of a black hostess called Lucille. She was the designated hard nut among the girls, renowned for knocking out a bouncer in Dean Street with one hefty punch. Her pretty face was criss-crossed with scars from fighting. She had a girlfriend called Lizzy who did as she was told, gave her case money to Lucille and rolled her joints for her.

Lizzy stood watching the fight now with bright eyes. The other hostesses were also watching, but warily.

Roselle saw Barry wade in to intervene between the two women. Picking Lucille up by her hair, he half dragged and half pulled her off the screaming Marianne. But clumps of the hostess's hair were coming out in the process.

'All right, all right, calm down, ladies.'

Barry's voice was jovial. But he was straining to keep a hold on the big black woman.

'You fucking fuck me, girl, me take you out of here and kill you. You hear what me saying to you?'

As Lucille screamed the words out she was kicking at the woman on the floor. Her high heels were hitting the mark each time and Marianne, bloody and bleeding, lay there, arms over her head to protect herself from more blows.

'What on earth is going on here?'

Roselle looked at the dozen women standing around the bar.

'What's she supposed to have done?'

As she spoke she saw two customers requesting their bills and sighed.

'Whoever is with them two geeks get your arses over there or you'll be looking for another fucking club tonight. The rest of you better get yourselves sorted and back on the meat seats in case we have any more customers. Only that is why you're all here, isn't it?'

Her voice brooked no argument. Even Lucille realised she had gone far enough. She liked Roselle who gave everyone a fair crack at the punters and had no favourites. As the girls drifted back to their seats and tried to calm irate punters Lucille pulled herself free from Barry's grasp.

'She been dealing in here. Bad stuff – you know, H, skag, whatever you want to call it. He giving it to her to sell. Now, Barry boy, don't you try 'n' deny it because the little whore tell me herself. Any dealing here is *my* territory and then it be only amphetamines or barbs. Stimulants. Plus a bit of puff now and again, to mellow them out.' She looked at Roselle, eyes wide in outrage. 'Now they all highballing – heroin and speed mixed. That be dangerous stuff. You telling me you want that in here, Roselle?'

Barry was quiet and that told her all she needed to know.

She poked a bleeding Marianne with one foot.

'You get your stuff and disappear. You too, Barry. You're both out.'

He thought he was hearing things.

Roselle already knew he did a sideline in puff. What was her problem?

Lucille laughed then, a deep man-like sound, seeing the expression on Barry's face. Marianne was pulling herself up from the floor. She looked very young and very bloodied.

'If I hear of you in any of the clubs in Soho, I'll be forced to tell them why I let you go,' Roselle told her sweetly. 'So if I was you, dear, I would find myself an alternative city and a new ID.'

Her voice was smug. She knew she could see to it the girl was blacklisted. No clubs wanted skag on the premises. Heroin was for street girls and club hostesses were supposed to be a step up from them. Though once they tried H they usually ended up on the streets. It was poison. It destroyed the girls and also the clubs themselves. People on heroin became users, thieves and liars. These girls were no angels to start with. Couldn't afford to be in their line of work. But heroin addiction gave them an added edge because the need for it became so strong. They would go case for as little as ten pounds and their lives became an endless round of fucking and scoring. Roselle had seen it so many times before.

So she had right on her side as well as a certain amount of vindictive joy at getting her own back on two people who'd thought they could get one over on her. Well, so far as she was concerned, the man or the woman had not been born who could pull a fast one on Roselle Digby.

She made her way up to her office. She had just poured herself a large brandy when Barry burst through the door. She had been expecting him. With her back turned, she allowed herself a half smile, before she swung round.

'And what can I do you for?'

It was a joking expression they had between them, a hostess expression that made them both laugh normally. Barry was seriously upset. She could see him trying to come up with an explanation for what he had done. Trying to justify himself and his actions.

She felt sorry for him. He had not even taken the time to come up with an excuse before he burst into her room. She knew he cared about her deeply and that people like Barry saw caring as ownership. She also knew he needed constant reassurance of his power over women. His power to fuck them and use them. It was part of him, an intrinsic part of him.

Roselle sat at the desk and sipped her drink, looking every bit the dispassionate observer. She knew this was what was bothering him most.

'She meant nothing to me . . .'

Roselle interrupted him.

'I should think not, Barry. If she did it says a lot for me, doesn't it? But, you see, what you failed to understand is that I will tolerate no outside dalliances. I don't care who they're with. I accept you might give your wife one now and again, but apart from that you were supposed to be mine. I don't sleep with Ivan any more, even if I have his child.'

She watched the colour drain from Barry's face.

'What you talking about?'

Roselle laughed, enjoying the power she had over this mindless, violent but, oh, so handsome thug. She moistened her lips with her pink tongue.

'Ivan is my son's father. He and I had a thing going for a long time. Why else do you think I have the position I do in this club? I assumed you were astute enough to suss that one out for yourself.'

He was flabbergasted.

'You mean, you and Ivan . . .'

She nodded, smiling happily.

'I was a prostitute, remember, Barry. It was my job. Ivan offered me an alternative and I grabbed it with both hands. In more ways than one.'

She laughed raunchily.

'He can't raise a smile these days, bless him, but we still have our child in common and our business interests. You see, unlike Susan I like to be in control of my life and my work. Even when I was whoring I always made a point of being in control. I kept a little bit of me back and that's what saw me through. It was just a means to an end with me and sleeping with Ivan, who was a nice man and a wealthy one, was certainly preferable to humping strangers day in and day out. Surely you can see the logic in that?'

Barry was staring at her with a mixture of disgust and grudging respect. He did understand what she was saying, but that did not mean he had to like it.

'I was faithful to you, Barry. I expected you to be the same to me.'

She picked up some papers from her desk in a gesture of dismissal. Scanning them as if they were the most interesting things she had ever seen in her life. Barry stood before her, a hangdog expression on his face and no idea how to get himself back into her good books.

Roselle looked up, her expression puzzled.

'Still here?'

He stared into her smiling face and felt the first stirrings of rage. Turning from her, he marched from the room.

She called out gently, 'You may as well finish the week out, I have to find a replacement and discuss it with Ivan.'

Barry's macho half wanted to tell her to get stuffed. The part of him that loved Roselle, and what she could give him, hoped this reprieve would give him a chance to sort it out with her. A few more days to get into her good books. He couldn't go home to Sue, he just couldn't. She would know what had happened as soon as he walked in.

As he shut the door carefully behind him Roselle allowed herself a little giggle. She would make him sing for his supper, and enjoy doing it. What he did out of her sight was his business, but to do it with one of her hostesses was a real piss take. She could not let it go. If she did she would be giving him licence to do it again, a red flag saying anything he did was acceptable.

And as she had said to him, she was most definitely not Susan.

A sheepish Barry returned home to his wife that night. As soon as Susan heard the key in the front door she knew it was him. Two minutes later he was standing in the bedroom doorway looking at her and the three kids in bed together.

The new baby was nearly due and Susan was heavy with the child. Her ripe body was bloated even more than usual and her face and hands seemed to have swollen.

'All right, Bal?'

He shook his head, sorry for himself. Little Barry opened one eye, saw his father and cuddled closer into his mother, uninterested in the new visitor.

'He ain't getting in here, is he?'

Susan laughed.

'He couldn't fit in, son. I'm amazed we all do.'

Even Barry laughed.

'Put the kettle on, Bal, I'll come down.'

He went back downstairs and Susan moved all the kids gently and slipped from the bed. Shoving her swollen feet into an old pair of slippers, she dragged on a stained dressing gown and quietly stole from the bedroom. At the door she looked the kids over once more to see they were well covered then made her way downstairs.

She was yawning as she walked into the kitchen, her hair a bird's nest of tangles and her belly practically down to her knees.

'Fuck me, girl, you look rough.' Barry's voice was kind.

She patted her belly happily.

'Once this one makes an appearance I'll be all right. But this baby is killing me, Bal. Taking everything from me. I'm so fucking tired all the time.'

He nodded sympathetically. As he poured out the tea Susan lit a cigarette and drew on it deeply. Barry always made her crave the rush of nicotine, it was how he affected her.

'So what brings you home at this time of night? I wasn't expecting you.'

She had picked up a hairbrush from the table and was pulling it through her hair, the fag perched precariously in the corner of her mouth. Her eyes were screwed up against the smoke, her cheeks red and rough from the late-winter weather.

Barry thought of Roselle in the silk dressing gown with the red embroidery that she had bought in Portugal. Her graceful feminine ways. Very different from Susan who was more in the class of Yootha Joyce than Ursula Andress, Ursula being his all-time erotic fantasy.

Susan sipped her tea noisily and gratefully.

'I just needed that. So come on, Bal, answer me. What brings you home then?'

He started rolling a joint on the table.

'Have you fallen out with Roselle?' Her voice was harsh now

and he didn't answer her. Telling her all she needed to know.

'Oh, Bal, are you stupid or what? You will never, ever get another girl like her.'

Barry was concentrating, getting the roach in nice and tight. He finished what he was doing and lit the joint, taking a deep puff of it.

'I fucked meself, Sue. You know what I'm like.'

Susan sighed heavily, annoyed with him. Now she was expected to take him back and she didn't want to.

'Do you want me to talk to her like, see what I can do?'

He looked at her with a strange, disgusted expression.

'You telling me you want shot then, is that it? I thought you'd be pleased.'

Susan forgot herself then and snapped, 'Well, you thought wrong then, didn't you?'

Barry shook his head in amazement.

'Fucking real, ain't it? Me old woman don't want me back. I pay all the bills, keep you all clothed and fed, make sure everything is hunky-dory – and now you've got the cheek to tell me I'm an inconvenience.'

Susan shook her head, distressed at the change in him. Like this he was dangerous.

'I never said any of that and you know I never. You was happy with Roselle, that's all, you was a good team, you two. I liked seeing you happy, Bal. As hard as that may be to believe she made you into a better person. She could give you what I never could in a million years.'

'And what was that then, smart arse? Other than decent conversation, a nice face to look at and the best sex I ever had.'

Susan hitched her belly up to get more comfortable and give herself time to think.

'She gave you peace of mind and a reason to work. Me and the kids never gave you that. You've always seen us as a millstone hanging round your neck. With Roselle you was content, happy, and if you've ballsed it all up, it's hardly my fault, is it? Don't take it out on me. I think the world of her.'

Barry started laughing then.

'You're a fucking case, you are, but you don't fool me, Susan Dalston. You live the life of Riley, you. A few quid and the kids, that's all you want from life, ain't it? I provided you with all that: kids, money, a nice drum. And what have I got in return?'

Susan looked into his face, her heart heavy. She had given him the best she had, and though he might not have thought much of it, it had been all she had to give. Herself, her self-respect, the best years of her life. She had produced his children, brought them up decently against all the odds and kept a home here for him whenever he deigned to come back to it.

Now she was ripe with yet another baby, one she loved already even though it had been forced on her like the others. She had saved and scrimped and made sure the kids had everything they should have and a little bit more on top. And he had the gall to sit there and compare her with Roselle who had a life Susan often dreamed of. Fantasised about. He beat her on a whim, took away any happiness she had by ridiculing everything she did, he laughed at her attempts to better herself and the kids, and now he expected her to take him back with open arms?

Yet she knew she had no choice.

If he wanted to come home, he would come home and that was it.

Life was shit. At least her life was anyway.

Roselle looked wonderful and Susan told her so. Roselle basked in the pleasure of a genuine compliment.

'You look fantastic, girl, like something from a magazine.'

Roselle grinned.

'I've just been and had a facial, and there's this queer in Soho who does your make up for you. I'll take you there next time, he loves a challenge.'

The two women laughed.

'Well, he'll fucking get one with me, eh?'

Roselle laughed affectionately. What you saw was what you got. That was Susan's secret though she never realised it.

'How's happy Harold?' Her voice was neutral and Susan thought for a while before she answered.

'Honestly?'

Roselle nodded.

'He'd kill me if he knew I'd told you, but fuck him. I can honestly say I have never seen him in such a state in me life. Not even when he was up on the GBH and attempted murder. He's like a little boy who's lost his best gun. Straight up, he's in a fucking dream world half the time. And the other half he's giving me and the kids serious grief.'

Roselle looked pained.

'I'm sorry, Sue, I should have realised you lot would bear the brunt of it.'

Susan sighed.

'He loves you, Roselle. You were good for him too. Made him into a nicer person.'

She shrugged slightly, her face a beautiful mask.

'He should have thought of that when he started trumping that little whore.'

Susan flapped one hand at her and shook her head knowingly.

'She was a nothing, love. I've seen them ones off meself. With Barry it's just something to *do*, it don't mean nothing. A little ego boost, that's all, and as he has the brain capacity of a gnat you have to allow for it. But he regrets it big time now.'

The waiter came and took their order then and both women smiled up at the handsome young man. Susan watched as he bent over backwards to serve Roselle and wondered at the power of a pretty face.

He didn't even realise she existed.

She looked around the restaurant. It was a nice Italian in Dean Street and she felt at home here, she had visited it so often. She remembered her first visit. Her nervousness as she wondered if her clothes were good enough, her make up applied properly. Whether Roselle would regret asking her to come to lunch. But they had had a right laugh and Susan had felt at home. This was part of the real world where people went to lunch and had conversations and fun.

Since Margaret Thatcher had become Prime Minister even the Susan Dalstons of this world realised that women could do what they wanted if they tried. Providing, of course, they didn't have a Barry hanging round their neck to stop them.

Barry hated the PM, hated everything about her, and believed Denis Thatcher should give her a 'fucking right hander' to 'sort the mare out'. Susan liked and admired her. More so because Barry hated her and was so vocal about it.

Margaret Thatcher gave hope to Susan, hope that her girls would get a fair crack of the whip one day in the workplace and their private lives. The teachers said that Wendy could make it to university. She absorbed knowledge like a sponge and was of well above average intelligence. She was also good-natured and loving, looking out for the little one and helping her mother when she could.

Now Susan shifted uneasily in her seat. This baby was huge and constantly pressing on her bladder.

Roselle finished ordering and turned to her again.

'I ordered you a nice bit of Dover sole, cooked in butter and lemon, some veggies and a big pasta salad. We've got a nice red wine, light and crisp to give that baby a bit of iron. One glass won't harm you, not the amount you smoke anyway.'

They both laughed together.

'I should give up, but since Barry's been back me nerves have been shot. I liked it on me own. No smelly feet, no aggro, no bloody tantrums. It was nice. Quiet but nice.'

They both laughed again then Roselle looked serious.

'He hurt me, Sue, doing that with a little tart like her. Especially in me workplace and all. I mean, the girls have to respect me and if they think I'm swallowing that they'll only take the piss.'

Susan nodded sympathetically.

'I can see your point, but that's him all over, ain't it? Probably the only reason he did it. See how you'd react. He's like that.'

Their starters arrived and Susan smiled.

'I guessed you'd order me this, you cow.'

In front of her was a large bowl of spaghetti bolognese dripping sauce.

'Get it down you, the baby needs the nourishment.'

Susan did not need to be told twice and began to eat.

'How are the kids?'

'The usual. Wendy and Barry are still at loggerheads. She's twelve now and thinks she knows it all. Mind you, compared to Barry she does. But she does annoy him. I tell him she's just at that age when they have opinions and he says she's not entitled to any until he's told her what they are.' Susan shovelled in more food and giggled between each mouthful. 'He's a case, ain't he? He really meant it and all.'

Roselle bit daintily on a *crostino*.

'Doesn't it bother you, having another baby?'

Susan shrugged.

'Not really. It's all I'm good at, I reckon. Having kids, taking care of them, loving them. I'm boring really. Anyway, what else is there for me? Another one won't make much difference to me, will it? I just wish he would see them as I see them, but Barry thinks they're solely my responsibility. If they're good, they're his, but if they're fuckers they're all mine.'

'My little lad, Joseph – well, I don't really see him that much. He goes away to school as you know and lives a lot of the time with another family. I love him but my lifestyle is hardly conducive to bringing up kids properly.'

Susan nodded sympathetically but deep down this was the one thing she'd never understood about Roselle. The fact that she barely saw her son. Only now and again at school or on the odd visit to the Grangers, the family he lived with.

But Susan didn't press the point. She knew her friend had her own reasons, and being Roselle they would be good ones.

Ivan would leave them well set up and that would enable her to indulge the boy as much as she wanted. She was already planning to send him abroad at eleven to be educated in Switzerland. It was her dream, a son who'd become someone. Even if she could never tell anyone in her world about it, she would know and that would be enough for her.

'I've a few presents in the car for the girls, and something for little Barry too. I couldn't resist them.'

Susan laughed. 'You ruin them.'

'I know, but they're worth it. So how's everything else going?'

Susan picked at the table cloth, an agitated gesture, and said softly, 'I wish you'd put him out of his misery. He really is in a state. It's over a week now and he's getting more and more dejected.'

Roselle laughed out loud, bringing the other diners' attention upon them.

'Good. Do him the world of good. I might get in touch on Friday, say we need him for another few weeks until we find someone else.'

Susan relaxed then.

'Thank fuck for that, Roselle! I really thought you was giving him the bad news for good.'

Roselle laughed again.

'Why I care about him, I don't know. I suppose it's having power over him. That's a lot to do with it. When I see you and hear what he's done to you, I hate him. But he isn't like that with me.'

'He wouldn't dare be, girl, and that's the crux of it all. You have his respect and his love, that's why he treats you so well. Other than that little lapse, of course, and I think we can safely say he won't be trying that on again!'

Susan felt as if all her birthdays and Christmases had arrived at once. Little Barry would be back in bed with her once more, the girls would have peace and quiet, and she could relax at night in front of the box, watching all her 'old crap' as Barry put it, and just live in peace and tranquillity.

What a touch.

She rubbed her belly and grimaced.

'I think I ate that Spag Bol a bit quick.' She burped loudly and put her hand over her mouth, grinning.

'Trust me to show you up.'

Then her face went white, drained of blood as she felt the warmth of her waters breaking and flooding the chair and floor beneath her.

'Oh, fuck, Roselle, me waters have gone.'

She started laughing, thinking it was a joke, then jumped from her chair, shrieking, 'Come on, girl, let's get you to hospital.'

Ten minutes later Susan was sitting on the leather-covered seat of Roselle's Aston Martin, gripping the walnut dashboard with her fingernails.

'Did you see those people's faces? I bet a few of them regretted ordering liver, I can tell you.'

Roselle and Susan started to laugh again.

'Can you keep hold of it until we get to the East End?'

Susan nodded.

'I reckon so, but for fuck's sake, girl, get a move on. This little git is on its way out, I can feel it in the birth canal pushing already.'

Barry and Roselle stood looking at the new baby. She was beautiful. Even Barry was amazed at the looks of the child who was exquisite. She already looked a few weeks old. There was no redness, or wrinkling, she was a peachy skinned little darling.

'How that ugly mare manages to produce such good-looking kids I will never know.'

Barry's voice was jovial. He had his Roselle beside him and that cheered him up no end.

Susan opened one eye groggily.

'I heard that, you cheeky bastard.'

Roselle held her hand tightly.

'She's a blinder, Sue, really gorgeous. Makes me feel broody!'

Barry frowned at that but let it pass. Though sometimes he wished he could keep her in the club so no one else could have her.

Susan pulled herself up in the bed and said seriously, 'Don't say that to him. He is a great believer in the old adage "well fucked and poorly shod". Otherwise known as barefoot and pregnant.'

'Well, if anyone should know it's you.'

Barry watched his wife and mistress laughing together and felt slighted. Knowing that they had been friends all along made him feel as if he'd been manoeuvred into something, though it was something he wanted.

His Roselle back and everything hunky-dory again.

Now he could see the real friendship between them and marvelled at the ways of women. By rights they should hate one another's guts. He guessed he would probably prefer that.

'I want to name her after you,' Susan was saying. 'I mean, you were with me for it all, Roselle.'

Barry stared at his wife as if she had just told him she was the mistress of Henry Kissinger.

'Don't be so stupid, Susan . . .'

She interrupted him.

'I'm naming her Rose, an abbreviation of Roselle. All right?'

Roselle smiled with delight.

'I'll take that as a great compliment, Susan, really.'

She looked down at the perfect child regretfully.

'I'd better be off. I can't leave that place to run itself and Ivan will be like a madman, wondering where I've got to. He's getting old, bless him, and the club is too much for him really. Not that he would ever admit that.'

Barry felt awkward.

'I'll walk you to your car, eh?'

Roselle nodded. Kissing Susan and little Rose she left them, promising to return the next day.

Outside the room they stood and looked at one another and Barry said seriously, 'I am sorry, Roselle, I miss you so much.'

She nodded gently.

'Susan talked me into giving you another chance today. Ain't that strange?'

He shook his head.

'Not really, Roselle. She knows the score and she's sensible enough to live with it.'

Roselle looked into his handsome face. His hair was streaked, as was the fashion, and he looked like a footballer or a pop star. His blue eyes were to die for and his bone structure was fantastic. It came out in all his children.

'You're a fool, you know, Barry. Susan is a decent person. Better than me or you can ever hope to be. There's men out there would give anything for a wife like her. She's the best thing that ever came into my life, you know. For the first time ever I have a female friend I can trust, one I can talk to and be with without worrying about what I do for a living, or being judged, or having to pretend things to make my life seem more respectable, more valid. I can discuss Joseph with her and she understands why I want more for him even though she would have to be dead herself, before she would let one of her kids go.'

She felt tears sting her eyes and Barry pulled her into his arms and hugged her.

'Be nice to her, Bal, please. Don't treat her like you normally do. Buy her some flowers or something, make her feel special, just once.'

He nodded. 'All right then, mate. Will I see you tonight?'

She pulled away from him and nodded.

'Aren't you coming back to work then?'

He grinned, that little grin that melted her heart and reminded her of the power of beauty. He was good-looking and dangerous. That was his attraction. She went up on tiptoes to kiss him on the mouth, to the outrage of two nurses and a midwife who had helped deliver the baby.

'See you later.'

Barry smiled.

'That is a definite, darling, you try and keep me away.'

He went back into his wife's room, a wide smile on his face.

'All right, girl? You done sterling work today, all over in an hour and a half. I reckon you're getting too good at this. Soon be giving lessons.'

Susan saw his happiness and relaxed inside herself. A nurse came in then with more tea and toast for her and the look she gave Barry told Susan everything. She suppressed a smile. Watching him cooing at his new daughter she awaited the visit from her mother and father, Kate and Doreen.

She was looking forward to seeing Kate and Doreen. Her mother and father she could do without. But she knew she was expected to see them, let them give the new grandchild the once over then go home and get as pissed as possible to celebrate the new arrival in the family.

And Susan, as usual, did as expected.

She was good at that.

Chapter Nineteen

Roselle watched Barry closely. In the year since the last baby was born he had become closer to Rose than he had been to any of his other children. She was his golden child, the apple of his eye. Even Alana, the previous favourite, had to take a back seat.

As he changed her and kissed her little belly Roselle felt a momentary pang, almost a feeling of jealousy, and shrugged it off as quickly as it had come over her. In fact she should be glad he had these feelings, she told herself, it proved he was human after all.

But his love for Rose was almost an obsession.

She was him, a born again Barry. From the amazing eyes to the chiselled cheekbones. She had his thick black hair and his gracefulness. Everywhere he went with the child people exclaimed over her, admired her beauty and her daintiness. She really was exquisite.

Barry had her as often as he could, for an afternoon or a morning. Roselle had watched him mastering parenthood so Sue could not put a block on him and what he wanted.

'Who's her daddy's girl then, eh?'

Rose smacked a kiss at him and he laughed loudly.

'See that, did you? She kissed her old dad, love her. She knows who the important one is, don't you, darlin', eh?'

Rose grabbed at her fat little baby feet and broke wind loudly, laughing all the while.

'Well, even you can't answer that, Barry. I think she told you exactly what she thought of you there, mate.'

Roselle's voice was strained and she tried to cover it with a smile. But having a baby around, even one as lovely as Rose, put a different complexion on things.

Barry the dad was not part of her equation and she felt awful for feeling that way. But justified it to herself with the thought that Susan didn't like his obsession with his daughter either. And that was what it was, an obsession. Rose was all he talked about and it was getting wearing.

'Don't you think you should get her back, Bal? We open in two hours.'

He nodded, his attention still on his daughter.

'Susan will be wondering where you've got to.'

'Let her fucking wonder. Rose is mine as well as hers.'

'So are the other three, Bal. Yours as well as Sue's, I mean.'

He didn't answer her, kept his own counsel, but she could see he was annoyed. Looking down at this mirror image of himself Barry finally understood the love of a parent. His other three kids were crosses to bear most of the time. They were good enough kids and he grudgingly allowed that Sue was a good mother. But Rose, his little Rosie, was something else entirely.

She really was wholly his.

She responded to him in a way the others had never done.

It didn't occur to Barry that he never gave the other three a chance to be anything other than an annoyance. He saw himself as father of the year. A man misunderstood by everyone else.

Especially the women in his life.

Thinking about the women in his life made him hurry up with the changing and dressing.

He had a little bird on the go near where Sue lived and just had time to have a quick coffee and a leg over before work. As he kissed Roselle goodbye, promising to be back by seven, he felt a trickle of fear run down his spine. If she found out she would kill him this time. But she wouldn't. All he had learned from the last time was not to get caught.

After dropping Rose off he made his way to Maggie Brittan's council flat.

Maggie was twenty-five, with a young son called Duane. She was what Susan would call a slag. Her home was dirty, her little boy ran the streets, and she drank and smoked all day to her heart's content. She bonked for England with anyone who caught her eye and wore too few clothes and too much make up. All in all, exactly what Barry needed. No real conversation, except a few of his hard nut expressions, a fuck that lasted as long as *he* wanted it to, and no crying when he left after an hour.

As he parked Roselle's Aston Martin outside Maggie's block he felt a happy man. When he walked into the flat Maggie was asleep on the sofa. He could see she had been crying. Her hair was tied up in a ponytail and without foundation her skin was spotty and red. Her nose was chapped from crying and her mouth wore the usual discontented pout.

He could smell rubbish and guessed rightly that the bin was overflowing. There was a faint smell of sour milk about her person and he smiled gently as he looked down at her.

She was a dog really.

Maggie opened her eyes and sniffed.

'Oh. It's you, Barry.'

Sitting up, she tried to tidy herself.

He leered at her. 'I've only got an hour.'

She grinned. 'That's plenty of time for what you want, eh?'

He undid his trousers and pulled out his already erect member. Pushing her head on to it, he forced it into her mouth. He watched her making a right meal of it and grinned. She was a dog but a game bird for all that.

He looked around the scruffy room, saw the dirt everywhere and smelled her body odour, a mixture of cigarettes and cheap perfume mingled with fried food and Weetabix. He could feel her tongue running over the tip of his cock and felt the stirring inside his belly as he moved his hips so she could accommodate him properly.

He rode her mouth, forcing himself into the back of her throat, hearing her gagging and laughing at her. Enjoying the power he had over her. She would take any abuse as long as it was from a *face*, a name. From someone with a bit of criminal kudos.

In her little world it made her feel somebody, made her feel she counted. She would tell all her mates that Barry Dalston, local hard case and lunatic, was giving her one. Was her bloke. Like he would be seen in public with it!

But she did the job expected of her and afterwards he zipped himself up and she made him a coffee.

'This place is like a fucking tip. Shall I get a skip so you can have a clean up?'

Maggie laughed at him, too stupid to take the insult on board. She spat into the sink, on the bowls and cups left there from breakfast.

'That's made all me throat burn.'

He laughed.

'I needed that, Bal, needed to see you. I've had a terrible day today. You know I was seeing that Peter Groves?'

He nodded. Peter was an all right geezer, very much like himself though obviously not in Barry's league.

'What? Is he giving you grief?' He had his macho stance on now and watched her watching him, pleased at the reaction he got from her.

She nodded. 'Yeah, grief is the right word. He reckons I've given him something called herpes.'

Barry felt as though an icy hand was holding on to his testicles and gradually squeezing them.

'*What* did you say?' He had to be hearing things.

Maggie faced him and sighed, annoyed he wasn't listening to her.

'I said, he reckons I've given him this disease called herpes. Says it's American, so how the fuck can I have given it to him? Silly fucker, where would I meet a Yank?'

She raised her arms in an exasperated gesture.

Barry's head seemed to be filling with hot air. He looked around the squalid little flat and felt sickness rise in his belly.

'Well, ain't you got nothing to say then?'

His hand was on his cock, feeling it through the outside of his trousers as if it might have disappeared without his knowledge.

Herpes, the talk of the hostesses, the new scourge. Jesus fuck! Even the old timers were using Durex these days. The whores were always the first with diseases, they spread them. They talked about this and tried to avoid it. Well, the sensible ones did. He felt the sweat break out on his forehead.

Roselle would denut him in a moment if she knew anything about this. Anything at all.

'What makes him think he got it from you then?'

Maggie laughed. Her teeth looked suddenly yellow and he saw her for what she was. A dirty slag. Why hadn't he seen that before? He could kick himself.

'He reckons he gave it to his wife, that's how he found out he had it. Anyway, he went schlepping up the Old London and they give him the bad news. But how does he know it was me? He says he reckons he only shagged me. Yeah, right. He'd shag his own fucking sister in a good light!'

She chewed on a fingernail, face alive with misery as she reached the climax of her story.

'He gave me a slap, Bal. I told him you wouldn't have that and he said, "Fucking tell him then. Tell him and tell him to come and see me."'

She was expecting Barry to do his crust, assure her he would 'sort that ponce out', and then she would have a story to tell all and sundry. Instead he stared at her, and as he stared she felt the fear creep over her.

'Are you going to answer me?'

He nodded, eyes cold now and fixed on hers.

'If I find out you have herpes, Maggie, I will personally take you and slaughter you. Do you understand what I'm telling you?'

She scratched at a scab on her arm and he looked at her tattoos and her grey skin and felt sick. Whatever had possessed him to shag that, he didn't know. He thought back to his wedding night, and what he had given his heavily pregnant wife, and felt the sickness sweep over him again.

Roselle would not be as trusting as Susan or as forgiving.

'Well, if you have got it, whose fault is it, eh? Not mine, Barry. I just have a laugh, that's all. It's up to you to take care of yourself, mate.'

He thought of the prostitute he had kicked to death and wondered if he could get away with it again. But everyone knew he visited here. The Aston Martin he had parked so happily gave him away. He'd loved the thought of people talking about him trumping a slag. It was part of his hard man image. Well, not any more.

The blow, when it was delivered, sent Maggie across the kitchen and into the hallway. Barry gave her a good hiding, making sure she was repaid for what she had done to him. There was blood all over the walls when he had finished. It gave him some satisfaction at least.

Her face was swollen and bruised beyond recognition and he knew he had broken her arm. But he did not care.

She had asked for it, each and every blow.

When he had finished he walked from the flat. Other occupants were out on their balconies, listening to the trouble going on in Maggie's. Older women nodded to each other sagely but no one phoned Old Bill. They watched Barry walk down the stairs and get into his flash car. Then, when they deemed it safe, they went into the flat and tried to help the hysterical girl.

Barry went straight back to Susan and told her the whole sorry tale.

'Well, what is herpes then?' Susan's voice was nonplussed. She was unsure what to say to him.

'It's like VD. Well, it *is* VD. But unlike a dose it never goes away. You keep it all your life like a fucking birthmark. It's sores around your nuptials. They hurt and weep and make you feel ill.'

'Can it kill you, Bal?'

'It fucking can if you give it to me, mate.' His voice was a bellow, a roar of despair.

'Well, who you got it off then? Surely not Roselle. I'd never believe that.'

'Of course I never got it off of her, you stupid bitch. I got it off some old fucking sort, didn't I?'

'Are you sure you've got it? I mean, have you had a test?'

'The same person gave it to Chopper Groves, and he gave it to his old woman.'

Susan's face was a picture of shock.

'You mean, that bastard's given it to poor Brenda?'

306

He nodded.

'The rotten creep. I hope it fucking drops off.'

Barry raised his eyes to the ceiling.

'I hope his knob drops off too, but it's mine I'm more worried about at the moment, Sue.'

'Poor Brenda, and she ain't long had a baby, has she? A few months after me she had her little boy, I seen her down the clinic. What a bastard.'

'I think we are both agreed that he's a bastard. Now can we drop the subject of him and fucking Brenda? Sue, I am panicking here. Roselle will launch me into outer space if she finds out about this lot.'

Susan stared at him. She wasn't sure what he wanted her to say.

'Well, you need a test, Bal. Make sure.'

He nodded, his face drawn. His whole body seemed to be shaking, his hands constantly on the move. He was like a trapped tiger and Susan felt sorry for him in a funny way. He never thought about the consequences of his own actions. He spent his whole life doing what he wanted and not worrying until something awful happened.

Then, when it did, it was everyone else's fault.

'Who did you get it off?'

He couldn't look her in the face.

'Come on, Bal, who's the culprit?'

'Maggie Brittan.' His voice was so low Susan thought she was hearing things.

'Not tattooed Maggie!' Her voice was incredulous.

Everyone knew Maggie, she was a legend in her own lunchtime. She went with anyone, and that meant anyone. She took them on mob-handed after a few drinks and laughed about it afterwards.

The Brittans were even lower in the food chain than her own family and that was saying something.

'Oh, Barry, what have you done? She's had everything from crabs right through the card. What possessed you to sleep with her?'

He shook his head, bewildered. He didn't know why now.

'She was there, that's all.'

Susan answered him sarcastically.

'Like Everest? Jesus, Barry, you don't half get up my nose at times. Suppose I was to go out tonight and see a nice bloke. I fancy him and he fancies me, so I bring him home here and give him a right seeing to. What would you think of me then? Because there are men who would go to bed with me, Bal, you just proved it by sleeping with Maggie Brittan. If she can pull, I'm fucking sure I can.'

He took a deep draft of Scotch and didn't even attempt to answer her.

'Do you see how people might judge your behaviour now, Bal, even though you're a man? Do you know how I felt that day I lost Jason? Can you imagine if we lost little Rose like that – because you couldn't keep it in your fucking trousers! Put yourself in my place, Bal, think of what that did to me, knowing you were putting something in me that only hours earlier had been stuffed into someone else . . .'

Her words brought home to him the fact that his cock had been stuffed in Maggie's mouth not that long ago and he felt an urgent desire to go and wash himself again. Susan had only narrowly dissuaded him from pouring bleach on it, to get it really clean.

As she looked at her husband she felt an overwhelming hatred for him. She knew her words had meant nothing to him, could never mean anything to him. He was only ever interested in himself.

What he wanted, what he needed.

Never a thought for anyone else.

'Roselle will kill me, Susan.'

She didn't bother to answer him.

'Like I said before, you'll have to get a test. Nothing else you can do, is there?'

He didn't answer her.

'Look, are you sure Chopper got it off her? He might have got it elsewhere.'

'If he slapped her, then he'd traced back the source of his infection. I'll see him anyway, though. I have to, don't I?'

Susan nodded. 'I suppose this ain't the time to ask but I want to get a new three-piece, this one's had it.'

Barry nodded distractedly.

'Already? Okay, what you like, I'll pay. Do the place up if you want. But, Sue, promise you'll help me out. Come to the clinic with me, will you?'

She nodded sadly.

As much as he annoyed her, made her full of hatred and anger at times, she could never really resist the pull of him when he was like this. The real Barry as she thought of him.

'Don't worry, Bal, we'll sort it all out, mate. Now you'd better get to work or Roselle will be wondering where you've got to.'

Roselle was worried. Barry was acting so strangely. He had developed a swollen testicle, a boil according to him, so he couldn't have sex with her. But that had been over a week ago and she had sneaked a look at him in the bathroom mirror earlier on and he seemed to be in perfect working order to her. Then, when she had caressed him, he had almost pushed her from him.

'Is there something going on, Barry? Something I should know about?'

He looked down as he buttoned his shirt, so he didn't have to look her in the face. He raised his voice, as if he was annoyed, couldn't believe what she was asking him.

'For crying out loud, Roselle, I've been feeling really rough. It happens. I'll be okay in a day or two. Don't start hassling me, please. Just let me get meself sorted out.'

She stared at him.

'What's going on, Barry?' Her voice brooked no arguments and finally he looked her in the face.

'What do you mean?' He was still trying to fend her off.

'I'm telling you now, Barry, I need to know what the problem is. If you tell me, we can sort it out. If you don't tell me and try and keep up this charade of everything being hunky-dory, then I'm afraid I'm going to cause you untold aggravation until I get to the bottom of it. So let's talk now and see what we can do, eh?'

Barry stared into her beautiful strained face. She was everything to him, he knew that. But he also knew she would never understand his need for other women. Susan did. Because she was so grateful to have him, she would swallow anything. But Roselle was a different kettle of fish.

He also knew that she would haunt him until she knew the score. She wasn't stupid. She could nag for England when the fancy took her and he could see the fancy taking her even as they spoke.

He tried a different tack.

'Let me go and see babes, little Rosie. I promised Susan I'd run them up the clinic. When I get back we can have a proper talk, okay?'

She stared at him for a full twenty seconds before she answered.

'I want you back here by twelve and my questions answered. Otherwise, Barry, you are out. Out of here and out of my life. Right?'

He saw the sadness in her eyes and the determination and felt an overwhelming sensation of being trapped. He got his results today, he would know the score by then. He would have to play it by ear.

He smiled, a big sunny smile he could have sworn he did not have inside him.

'Let me go and see me babe and then we'll go from there, all right?'

Roselle nodded almost imperceptibly and Barry felt every muscle in his body relax. He had a few hours. If he wasn't infected he could sort himself out. Although it would not have bothered him if he gave it to anyone else, he was terrified of giving it to Roselle and even more terrified she had already caught it.

The thought brought him out in a sweat every time it entered his head. That the disease could already be moving through her veins, crawling through her body and waiting to give her the first attack, terrified him more than anything else.

He also didn't know if he could bring himself to touch her. Suppose she was infected and infected him with it again? It might make what he had even worse. Who knew? No one seemed to know very much about the illness.

At the Whitechapel VD clinic they'd seemed as ignorant about it as he was. But Barry had spoken to Chopper, and Chopper had told Barry that he had definitely got it from Maggie.

Like him, Chopper used women as and when the fancy took him.

Like him, Chopper was now shitting hot bricks and throwing them out of the window. He still had to explain the full implications of the disease to his wife.

Kissing Roselle briefly on the lips Barry left the flat, wondering if he was leaving it for the last time. Whether it would still be his home later on in the day. He used her car, just in case he never got the opportunity again. Because if he had the big H, as Chopper called it, he was well and truly fucked in more ways than one.

Susan made them both a cup of tea and placed Barry's on the table in front of him. She had sent all the kids to Doreen's so they could go to the clinic in peace. She had not retrieved them afterwards because of Barry's utter shock and disgust with himself.

He was positive.

The funny thing was, she still felt sorry for him. Because she knew him so well, she understood he never thought about anything until it was too late.

Well, it was too late now.

Roselle wouldn't touch him with a barge pole, and who could blame her?

'I'll kill Maggie Brittan. As God is my witness, I'll swing for that slut.'

He was angry, but Susan realised there was no conviction in his voice. He knew that what he had was never going away. Even killing Maggie couldn't make it go away. She'd given him the disease but he knew deep inside himself that he was the real cause. He had brought this on himself.

That was what he was finding so hard to accept.

'You'll have to tell her, Bal. She has a right to know.'

He pushed the tea away from him with a violent shove, sending it all over the table and the floor.

'How can I, Susan? You know what she's like. She won't swallow this, she'll go fucking mental.'

Susan picked up the mug from the floor and automatically started to clear up the tea stains with a cloth.

'Mental? She'll go ape shit. But she still has a right to know, Bal. This is too serious to brush under the carpet. Much too serious to forget about and hope it will go away. You heard what that man at the clinic said. Your first attack can be mild or severely damaging. It could kill her. You have to tell her.'

She was rinsing the cloth under the tap when Barry's fist hit her across the side of the head.

'Don't fucking tell me what I have to do, Susan. I'll deal with this in my own way.'

Her ears were ringing from the blow. She put her hand on the sink to steady herself.

'What you picking on me for, Bal? What have I done?'

There were tears in her voice.

'I'm your wife, mate. I've stood by you through everything and you do this to me? You hit *me* when all I'm trying to do is help?'

He stared at her, but she knew of old that he wasn't seeing her. He was thinking how he could get himself out of trouble as usual.

'Unlike when it happened with me, Bal, a few injections and a course of antibiotics won't be enough. She needs to get herself tested soon. As fast as possible.'

He was nodding.

'I could always say I got it from you, Sue.'

She widened her eyes and opened her mouth but no words would emerge from it.

He grabbed her arms and cried, 'It's the only thing I can say, ain't it, you silly bitch? She can't moan at me for giving *you* one, can she? You're me fucking wife.'

Susan shook her head in despair.

'You bastard. You'd let her think I had it so she'd swallow it a bit better? And who am I supposed to have contracted it from, Bal? The phantom herpes giver of East London? Who are you going to blame?'

He was biting his bottom lip. Wendy did it when she was worried about something. Any second now he would chew at the side of his thumbnail.

She knew him so well.

'I'm sorry, Bal, but there's no way Roselle will swallow that one. She knows me better than you do. She knows I wouldn't put it about. I wish we could say the same about you, mate.'

He was staring at her now, eyes fixed on hers.

'It's the only thing I can say. I can't come back here, Sue. I can't.' His voice was a whine. 'I'm used to better these days. I couldn't hack living here again. I'd lose me job then where would you be, eh? No more money coming in for you to spend on three-piece suites and the kids.'

Susan knew he was trying to talk her into taking the blame, make it easier for him with Roselle. Make her into the dirty individual who'd caused this epidemic of disease.

She shook her head sadly.

'I'm sorry, Bal, but there's no way I will carry the can for this lot. No way.'

She saw his fist clench and flinched instinctively, but he didn't raise it. Instead he stormed from the little house and slammed the door behind him.

Roselle's face was so white she looked terminally ill.

'Susan has given you what, Bal?'

He dropped his eyes to the carpet and answered her softly.

'Fucking herpes, the whore. Apparently she kipped with some geezer from the pub.'

He opened his arms as if he was trapped himself and unsure what else to tell her, which of course was true. Barry was playing it all by ear at the moment. Hoping against hope that Roselle swallowed everything and forgave him. Susan was her mate after all.

Roselle, though, was still trying to take in what he had said to her. Herpes? He had caught herpes? Off Susan. His wife.

She let the information seep into her brain for a full five minutes. The longest five minutes of Barry Dalston's life.

313

Then she started to laugh. It was a high-pitched wail of sound, nearer to tears. It had the underwater quality of laughter tinged with heartbreak and sadness.

'You rotten bastard! You'd blame poor Susan for something like this? Blame her for something *you've* done. Where did it really come from, Bal – Marianne? Was it that little whore you picked it up from or was there another one tucked away somewhere?'

That she had hit the nail so accurately on the head threw him. She knew him better than he'd thought. She wasn't about to swallow his story of getting it from Susan. His wife had too much respect for herself to sleep around. Deep inside he knew that much and so did Roselle.

She stood up, all righteous indignation and hurt pride.

'I want you to get your stuff and leave, please. I will not talk about it any more. I want you out. And, Barry, don't make me involve Ivan in all this. Because you give me any aggravation and I will involve him, I swear on my son's life.'

He watched as she pulled a jacket on, her face still set in that mask of incredulous shock.

'I'll be back in an hour and I'll expect every trace of you out of this place by then.'

He went to her, tried to pull her into his arms.

'Please, Roselle, I'll do anything . . .'

She interrupted him then, a half-smile on her face that was full of hatred and disgust.

'Don't you think you've already done enough? If I do have this herpes I'll hate you till the day I fucking die, you piece of shit!'

With that she pulled away from him and walked out of the flat, picking up her car keys from the hall table as she left.

'Shut them fucking kids up, Susan, I'm trying to sleep!'

Barry's voice was loud. Aggressive. He was angry inside and out. The kids' noise was driving him to distraction. All he wanted was to lie in bed and be depressed in peace. The kids' shouting and fighting, their laughing and screaming, were just about the last straw so far as he was concerned.

Susan came into the room and bellowed at him.

'I can't make four kids be quiet, Bal, it's a physical impossibility. Get up and sort yourself out. Come back into the world and be a man for once.'

She stormed into the bathroom next and slapped Rosie and little Barry across their fat bums, making them howl.

'Now keep it down, the pair of you, or I'll get you out and put you both to bed.'

The howling ceased immediately. They loved their bath. It was their favourite time of day. It also wore them out and got them settled for bed.

It was five-thirty on a Monday night in Bethnal Green. Barry was depressed because he had no life any more. Even though Ivan had told him of another job in Soho at a lesser club, and still on good money, he had lost the heart for it and was deciding what to do with himself next.

He was thinking of going back into the debts only this time doing it properly. Buying debts and then recalling the money himself. Making a bit over the top for his trouble.

He was convinced if he could prove himself to Rosclle everything would be fine. Yet she would have nothing whatsoever to do with him.

He had learned through Susan that her test had come back negative, and that had disappointed him. If she'd had herpes too then it would have made them even, given them something to bond them together even closer.

Barry was actually stupid enough to believe that.

Wendy put on a record in her room. It was Paul Young singing 'Wherever I Lay My Hat'. The lyrics were so poignant that he felt like crying. That was him before the herpes, before he had had his life ruined.

Wendy, enjoying the music, turned it up louder, and then Barry jumped from the bed and raced across the landing to the room that housed three little girls and his son.

'Turn that fucking crap off now, Wendy, just shut the fucking thing up!'

Wendy did as she was told but her face said a different thing altogether.

'Don't you look down your nose at me, girl. I'm your father!'

He was all self-righteous anger and red-faced temper.

'You load of little bastards. Why I bother with any of you I don't know.'

This included little Rose who since her father had come back home had gone off him overnight. He looked around the room, at the pop star posters on the walls and the hi-fi on the dressing table.

'Clear this fucking shit-hole up and all, you. Like your mother you are. A useless ponce!'

Susan shouted from the bathroom, 'Charming, I must say! But you'd know all about useless ponces, wouldn't you, Bal?'

She came out on to the landing and Barry, having had enough of everything, punched her until she dropped to the floor. The kids could all see him. Rosie screamed with fright, little Barry screamed too, and Alana hot footed it from the stairs back into the lounge. Wendy came out of her room and, feeling responsible for her mother's plight, grabbed at her father's hair and tried to pull him away.

It was pandemonium.

Barry slapped his eldest daughter in the mouth, splitting her lip.

It was only when Doreen came in that he finally calmed himself enough to leave the house.

She took Susan into the bedroom and laid her on the bed, her face a pulp. She got the little kids from the bath and with the help of Wendy dressed them and sent them to her house with Alana. She then sent Wendy for Kate, and told her to tell the older woman to bring the doctor on her way.

Doreen bathed her friend's face and sympathised with her.

'You have to get rid of him, Sue. Somehow, girl, you have to get shot, love.'

Susan didn't answer her.

She knew that herself.

But how?

How did you get rid of someone like Barry? Someone who wouldn't leave, wouldn't let anyone have any peace? Could see no wrong in what he did?

He had ruined so many lives, hers included. The kids', Roselle's, his mother's. Strangers' lives even with his violence. She had heard about what he'd done to Maggie Brittan, that had been another nine-day wonder.

Barry Dalston was a law unto himself and until he found alternative accommodation, as in another bird, she was in lumber and that was the strength of it. She just wished he would give the kids a break now and then. It was harder for them. After all, she was used to his outbursts.

The doctor didn't come but they knew Barry had broken her cheekbone and her ribs and did what they could for her as usual. Life was back to its old pattern and Susan had to sit it out and wait for new developments.

It was soul-destroying, but all she could do. Barry was in charge as he always had been.

The police finally arrived after he had long gone. Looking at Susan, they sighed, drank the cup of tea that Doreen brought them, made a few jokes about how they were just getting used to not coming round here any more when Barry came back on the scene and buggered up their night shift.

But they did not *do* anything. There was nothing they could do.

Barry came home at twelve-thirty, drunk and stoned. He had been out with his father-in-law and they'd tied one on like the old days. Susan was still in bed and Wendy had fallen asleep on the settee, watching TV. As he came into the room he saw her lying there, her lovely face vulnerable, abundant hair framing her head.

Her brand new breasts were straining against a too small nightie and dressing gown. Kneeling down by her, he looked into his daughter's face. She was going to be a knockout. At almost fourteen she was already an eyeful. Many people had said as much to him.

In his drunken state, he decided she was too lovely for the boys around here, too good for the shite she would eventually meet. He didn't listen to all the crap about university or college and a good education. That was all just bollocks.

What his daughter needed was a man, a real man who would show her what to do with her body. How to get what she wanted with it. That was what real women did in his book. They were sitting on a goldmine.

The expression made him laugh and this woke Wendy up. He saw the fear on her face and the instinctive way she covered her breasts from his gaze, wrapping her arms over her chest like a dead person. Like she was in a coffin.

He pulled them gently apart and sighed. Bending down he placed his cheek to her breasts and caressed her buttocks gently with his hand, holding her hands together over her head as he did so.

Wendy tried to force herself up from her prone position and he forced her down with his body. She could smell beer and whisky, fags and chips.

His lips were on hers now. She could taste his mouth and pushed him away in disgust, turning her head from him. Trying to make him leave her alone without disturbing her mother.

She knew that her mum would go mad if she learned of this.

But she was up in bed, her face swollen and bruised, her three youngest children still in Doreen's. Her mother could sleep in peace knowing they were all looked after, that Barry couldn't harm them.

Why had Wendy decided to come home? Why hadn't she stayed at Auntie Doreen's? She felt as if it was all her fault, that she was to blame for it all. Her records had started the fight, and her lying on the settee half dressed had caused all this.

'Please, Dad, stop it! Dad, please. Stop it!'

His beery breath was heavier now as he tried to force her legs apart. She could hear the animal grunts coming from him and taste the salt of her own silent tears. Finally she used all her strength and shoved him as hard as she could. In his drunken state Barry fell sideways and she ran from the room like the wind.

She fell halfway up the stairs and made a noise. She picked herself up and as she reached the top of the stairs heard her mother calling softly. Going into the room she allayed her mother's fears, told her that her dad had come in drunk and fallen over.

Barry came up the stairs, and when he was in her mother's room Wendy went to her own and pulled the chest of drawers against the door. Then she got into bed and for the first time in years wished her brother and sisters were there.

Barry fell into bed with his wife and went straight to sleep, his snoring loud and broken only by his mumblings.

Wendy lay in bed, terrified of the man she had always hated.

She could still feel his hands on her body, feel his foul breath and tongue trying to slip into her mouth. She heaved, feeling her whole belly rise up in protest at the thought of what he'd wanted to do to her.

His own daughter.

Chapter Twenty

Wendy brought her mother a cup of tea and some toast. Her father had gone out earlier and she had waited until he'd left the house before getting dressed and moving the furniture back into its usual place.

She had hardly slept all night. Every noise or movement woke her as she dozed. It was as if her whole body was on red alert. Waiting for something to happen.

As she looked into her mother's face Wendy sighed. If she confided in her there would be trouble, and looking at her bruised face and body she felt her mum had quite enough on her plate already.

'You all right, babe?' Susan's voice was concerned.

Wendy replied sadly, her big blue eyes brimming with pain.

'Mum, I'm fine. It's you we should all be asking about, for crying out loud! Look what he's done again. Can't we just make him go away?'

Susan looked at her beautiful daughter and felt the futility of her own life. She could cook for her kids, clean for them, protect them from the outside world. But where Barry was concerned she could do nothing.

She grasped her daughter's slim hand, its childish heart-shaped gold ring pointing up the woman emerging before her eyes.

'Listen to me, little heart, that man loves you all in his own way. I wish things were different, you know that, but I can't make him do anything he don't want to do. If wishes were kisses I'd drown you all in my love, darlin', you know that. All I can do is hope for the best. It's all any of us can do. He'll feel really bad later and everything will be all right for a while, you'll see.'

Susan knew her words were pointless, just words. But she so desperately wanted her daughter to feel better.

Every breath she took was a trial, her ribs were screaming with pain. But she had to pretend that nothing was too bad. That she was just a bit under the weather. That being beaten like this was nothing really, just another merry day in the life of Susan Dalston.

'Throw him out, Mum. Get rid of him, please.'

Wendy's voice was low, full of meaning and broken from her yearning to cry.

Susan grasped her hand tighter.

'I can't, darlin'. You know the score, love. Old Bill ain't interested, no one's interested in the likes of us. That's why I want you to educate yourself, get out of all this. Get a proper life for yourself where people are civilised and talk to one another and the use of their fists isn't the only option.'

Wendy felt such a rush of love for her mother then she threw herself into her embrace. Squeezed her mother to her as if she would never let go. Susan felt the love, and also the excruciating pain in her ribs from her daughter's embrace.

Pushing her away gently, she kissed her on the forehead tenderly.

'He will fuck off one day, I promise you that. We'll bore the arse off him soon enough. We always do. But until he deigns to leave, we're in lumber, mate.'

Wendy knew her mother's words were true but with the youthful exuberance of all girls believed that somehow there had to be a way of getting rid of him once and for all. There was always an answer to a problem, you just had to find it.

'Stay in bed and rest, Mum. I'll watch the kids, have a day off school. I need to revise anyway.'

Susan nodded, feeling better now that they had had a little talk. As Wendy stood up Susan saw the emerging body, the high breasts so like her own at that age, the beautiful face she couldn't believe belonged to a child of hers.

Wendy had a brain, a good one, and she would use it to better herself.

Susan was determined on that.

* * *

Roselle heard the banging and crashing on her door and sighed. She knew who it was and walking wearily out into the hallway, called, 'Go away, Barry, before I call Ivan and get you removed once and for all.'

'Let me in, Roselle, we have to talk.'

Leaning on the cool white-painted wall of the hallway, she felt an urge to cry. Barry was a piece of shit really, a wife-battering, violent thug, but not with her. Never with her. With her he had been the man he should have been all along if circumstances had been different.

Yet once out of her orbit he reverted to Mr Macho Man. It was laughable.

Picking up the phone she dialled quickly, knowing in her heart she had to make the final break.

Five minutes later two men arrived from Ivan's gambling den in Dean Street. She watched from the window as Barry was threatened with baseball bats and beaten severely on a busy London street in the early afternoon.

No one interfered, no one called the police, no one cared. Except her, and maybe Susan. Because she would take the flak. She would take the kickback of his anger and his rage. Roselle knew this and the thought disturbed her, but she had to get Barry Dalston out of her life.

He was her folly, her one crack at taking what she wanted whatever the consequences. How could a man's looks make you so unconcerned about everything else? She knew that if she looked into his eyes again she would be sorely tempted to forgive him. Something she knew she must never, ever do.

Unlike Susan she had back up, had people to 'sort it all out' for her in the only way people like Barry Dalston respected. With violence. With hard punches, with baseball bats, and if necessary maybe even a gun.

She phoned the ambulance, though, after he had lain on the ground for ten minutes. After all, she wasn't without her finer feelings.

* * *

June came in the house and without a word put on the kettle and looked through Susan's cupboards.

'You seem to be well stocked, love.'

Susan nodded. She was sitting at the kitchen table. Her face was still bruised but she was at least mobile five days after the latest hiding. Baby Rose was walking unsteadily around the room, opening cupboards and playing with the saucepan lids.

June smiled as she looked down at her.

'She's a little princess, ain't she? Look at them eyes! Who's nanny's little darlin', eh?'

Rose smiled, a big gummy smile that melted everyone's hearts.

'Me. Me.' Her little voice was like a corncrake when she got going and the words became a hoarse shout that made them both laugh out loud.

'Well, Susan, how's everything?'

June poured out the tea, her tight black skirt and high heels making her look much younger than she actually was.

'All right. The usual. He's been missing for nearly a week again so we've all had a bit of peace and quiet. Why?'

She knew her mother well enough to realise that June playing the caring grandmother could only mean one thing. She was on the ponce.

'If it's money you're after I am boracic lint, Mother. I ain't even got the money for an ice cream.'

June turned to her then.

'Why are you always such a fucking miserable mare, eh? I was going to offer you a few quid as it happens. Your father had a tickle at the weekend. He turned over the bookie's at Green Lanes in Ilford.'

She laughed then at Susan's shocked expression. 'He had a big winner. Anyway, I thought I'd spread it about a bit as Christmas is just around the corner like.'

She placed fifty pounds on the kitchen table.

'You can pay me back in the New Year, I'll be needing it by then.'

She laughed again and Susan nodded wearily.

'I'll see what Barry has to say before I spend it. To be honest he's out of work again. But I'm hoping he'll find something soon. I'm still claiming benefit. I have to, Mum, you know what he's like. I never know where we'll be from one day to the next.'

June nodded in understanding.

'Like your old man. I know what you're saying. Still, at least you've got him back now. That must be a touch.'

Susan rolled her eyes to the ceiling.

'Oh, it's wonderful, I was missing the hidings, the rows, the violent clashes of temperament. The kids were gutted when he left, couldn't get used to the peace and quiet. I was going to send them to the fucking Falklands so they could live with constant warfare.'

June grinned.

'You're a sarcastic mare, Susan.'

'Well, to be truthful, Mum, I wish him and me dad would drop down dead.'

June sipped her tea and took a puff on her Rothman's.

'Fucking tell me about it. I wish your father was brown bread meself. Old ponce!' She laughed then. 'I remember once, when you was a baby, he punched me lights out in Romford market. Said I was looking at a bloke. Which of course I was, me being me like.' She took a deep drag on her cigarette before she continued. 'He was handsome, though. Too fucking handsome really.'

Susan's voice was incredulous.

'Who, me dad?'

June laughed out loud then. 'No, the other geezer. He was a Turk or something, dark handsome fucker with great big eyes.' She looked off into the distance, to another time, another place. 'I had him, though. Your father never knew, but I went back and I had him. He was fucking blinding he was. All muscles and chocolate skin. I always liked the spades, me. Funny that, ain't it? They do something for me like, make me blood boil. Do you know what I mean, girl?' June was serious now and Susan felt the uneasy pity she always ended up feeling for her mother and her endless quest for men.

'They treat a woman how she should be treated, they're grateful like that you want them.'

'Maybe then, Mum, when it was all new to them, but not now. They treat you like all men do, I suppose. Not like Barry and me dad, but like regular people treat their wives.'

June nodded.

'I suppose so, but I did love it in them days. I loved the chase, you know? Loved the feeling of being someone, going somewhere, feeling like I had a life to lead. That I was important to someone.'

'You was important to me and Debbie, Mum.'

June shook her head and waved her cigarette in denial.

'Nah. You ain't wanted unless a man wants you, girl, remember that. It's hard you know, getting older. Men stop looking at you, just ignore you. See you as too old to bother with. It's hard when you was an attractive woman once. A head turner.'

Susan smiled softly.

'Well, Mum, you look better than I do, girl, always did and I'm still a young woman really. But I never turned heads. Never.'

June shrugged. 'You was always an ugly kid, love. Luck of the fucking draw really. If Debs had had your brains she could have gone places. She had the looks – no real body to speak of, but enough to get her what she wanted. Now look at her, stuck out there in Rainham with no kids, nothing. A right fucking miserable mare she turned out to be. Have you heard from her at all?'

Susan shook her head.

'Jamesie is at it, I heard through the grapevine. His bird had a baby as you know. Must have hurt Debs. In fairness, Mum, to be barren must be terrible.'

'Especially when you've lumbered yourself with a ponce like him! I never liked the Irish. Look what they've caused, them bleeding Catholics out there. Bombings and that . . . I don't know what the world is coming to.'

Susan felt an urge to laugh at her mother's ignorance but she didn't. June was June and that was all there was to it.

'Are you coming up the pub tonight?'

Susan shook her head. 'I doubt it, Mum. I can't afford it really and the kids need me here.'

'Leave them with Doreen's boy or get that fucking Wendy to have them. Do her good to give you a hand now and again.'

June had a downer on Wendy that made Susan angry.

'She's turning into a beauty, Mum. You want to see the body on it!'

June shrugged. 'No good to her if she don't use it, girl.'

Susan looked into her mother's eyes.

'Like you did, you mean, Mum? Or should that be, let her body be used? There's two ways to look at you and your life, you know.'

June shrugged.

'Have it your own way, but she'll end up looking down her nose at you lot, you mark my words.'

Susan laughed then, a loud vindictive sound.

'I fucking well hope she does. I want much better for her and the rest of them than anything we had.'

June suddenly looked crushed.

'I did the best I could for you and Debs.'

Susan laughed again.

'That's what I mean, Mum, that's exactly what I mean.'

It was Doreen who finally talked Susan into going down the pub that night. They were having a big party with a live band. Susan plastered her face with make up and dressed in her one good outfit, a dress and jacket from Marks and Spencer's. She and Doreen left Wendy in charge.

Susan's ribs were still giving her gyp, but she wanted to get out, see people, have a good time. And Doreen convinced her the best way to do that was go to the pub with all her family and friends.

Susan was glad she'd gone. Even Debbie had turned up. Overweight and sad, she had a miserable-looking Jamesie in tow and the remains of a black eye was clearly visible in her pudgy face. The two sisters sat together and Susan listened as Debbie systematically pulled everyone to pieces. Especially the ones she knew Jamesie had been after over the years.

The pub was alive with people of all ages, the music was good, loud and danceable. The drink fast-flowing.

All in all, a typical East End night out.

The women sat together, the men stood at the bar. Younger children sat outside on the wall and drank Coke and ate crisps, played kiss chase and had fights.

It hadn't changed much since Susan was a little girl.

It was where she felt safe.

After a few Bacardi and Cokes she felt herself relax. Felt the tension leave her body and the worry gradually lift from her mind. Doreen was acting the goat as usual and everyone was laughing. Even Debs relaxed and started to enjoy herself. As the band struck up yet another old Beatles number, Susan wished she was well enough to join in the dancing. But she clapped and sang along and made do with that. Then June and her father started to dance the twist and everyone watched them, geeing them up and egging them on.

Laughing like she had no care in the world, Susan joined in the clapping and the calling out. October the tenth, 1983 was a night she would remember for more reasons than one. For the first time since Barry's return home, she felt light-hearted, girlish almost.

Then she spied Peter White and waved at him across the bar. He waved back, and she watched him make his way through the throng to talk to her.

'He fancies you, Sue.'

She flapped her hand at her sister. 'Don't be silly. We go back years, to when we was all kids. He's just being polite.'

Debs laughed, a low dirty sound.

'He wants to be a bit more than polite, girl, you mark my words. He always asks about you.'

Sue raised her eyes to the ceiling.

'He's just being friendly, that's all, Debs. Now for fuck's sake give it a rest.'

Peter smiled at them both and nodded to the other women at the table. Susan loved the attention. Everyone was watching her talking to this very presentable, unmarried sailor who looked nice, was well dressed and seemed to have eyes only for her.

'Long time no see, Susan, how's life treating you then?' Peter's green eyes were twinkling and she laughed girlishly. 'The same as usual, mate, and you? Found yourself a nice girl yet?'

Peter, a few drinks under his belt, felt reckless enough to say to Barry Dalston's wife, 'All the best ones are taken, yourself included, girl.'

She blushed then. Her face went a bright shade of pink and her mother shouted across the pub, 'Oi, look, my Susan's doing a cherry! What's he asked you, girl, your bra size!'

Everyone started laughing, Peter included.

Susan shook her head and cried over the din, 'Take no notice, Peter, she's an animal.'

But the noise was too much now and they couldn't hear one another. Miming that he was going for a drink he walked away from her. Flushed and happy, Susan looked at her sister and grinned.

'My God, I think you're right. He *does* fancy me!'

Debbie sipped her Pernod and blackcurrant and said waspishly, 'Well, he must like your personality, that's all I can say.'

Susan felt her euphoria disappear and answered her sister in similar fashion. 'Well, there's no fear of anyone liking *you* for that reason, is there, you nasty little bitch?'

Debbie stood up unsteadily.

'You're right there, Susan, but I wouldn't want anyone to like me like that. 'Cos it means you're too ugly to get them any other way, don't it?'

She lurched off towards the bar and Susan saw her go up to Peter and put her arm around him. Give him a kiss and a cuddle. Watching it depressed her.

Doreen sat in the seat vacated by Debbie and said in Susan's ear, 'Look at her, the little fat bitch. Like anyone would fancy that without the help of hallucinogenic drugs!'

The two of them burst out laughing so loudly that everyone turned to stare at them. Debbie looked at them. Guessing the laughter was at her expense she sidled closer to Peter and poked her tongue out at her sister.

Susan gave her a wanker sign, and that made her and Doreen crack up again.

'I bet he does a lot of that on his ship – wanking, I mean.'

'Stop it, Dor, he's a really nice man.'

Doreen nodded.

'I know, mate, and why ain't he your man, eh? Think of the life you'd have had with him. Away at sea, only seeing him now and again. Regular money, your own life while he was away. Fuck me, I think I'll go after him meself!'

Susan grinned.

'He don't fancy me. He just likes me, that's all. As a friend.'

Her voice was wistful now and they stopped talking for a while, both engrossed in their own thoughts. Both wondering what it would be like to be with someone who actually liked you.

Then they saw him push Debbie from him at the bar and her laughter as she nearly fell over, her little fat legs like cricket stumps in her impossibly high heels.

'Do you know what? She looks just like me mother there, don't you think, Doreen?'

She nodded sagely. 'It *is* your mother, mate. Only a smaller, younger, more vindictive version. I wouldn't want to be them for all the tea in China. They ain't women, they're parasites.'

Susan nodded in agreement, but once again it depressed her.

'I want to go home now, she's really pissed me off.'

Doreen picked up her empty glass and chided Susan.

'Don't let her see she's bothering you, she's just jealous. You're a nice person, Susan, and they can't ever take that away from you. Remember that, mate. Always bear it in mind. Now shut up and sit there and wait while I get us a couple more doubles.'

Susan, as usual, did as she was told.

Barry was angry and he was stoned. He had been round a little bird's house in Manor Park. Christine Carvel was a thirty-year-old mother of five. She still had traces of her former beauty, a fat body but the best nature a woman had ever possessed.

Chrissy saw everything in terms of glowing enjoyment.

For six days since his attack on Susan, Barry had laid up there, being treated like visiting royalty, fed and watered until he felt back to his usual self.

Chrissy had then given him her supply of cocaine and amphetamines and rolled him a few joints to chill him out. Finally getting his head together, he had left her with promises to return soon and repay the compliment.

Chrissy was used to being used by men like Barry. She knew that at some point she would be given a few quid and a few drugs in return. People came to her when they needed a bed for a night or a week, if they were on the run from Old Bill or unhappy wives and girlfriends. She enjoyed the company and took it all for what it was. Thereby never getting any grief and never causing any.

Her children were all the colours of the rainbow and she adored them. But she could not resist a face, especially one as good-looking as Barry Dalston. She had taken him into her bed and had a good few days. Now he was jogging on, she let him go with a smile and a fiver.

That was the type of person she was.

Barry left her with a big smile and a bad case of herpes. But she wouldn't know that for a while.

As he let himself into his house he was already annoyed. The sulphate and Driminal had made him feel paranoid, and he was convinced Roselle and Susan had conspired against him. In Chrissy's flat he had lived in a make-believe world of closed curtains, good music and camaraderie. Outside in the real world he was feeling less of the good-natured woman's vibes. Barry Dalston was suffering from the Pete Paranoids as drug users called a bad come down.

Wendy, lying on the settee after settling the kids in bed, heard his key in the lock and froze. As he came into the lounge she was standing by the kitchen door.

Barry looked at her, saw the fear in her face and was appeased. At least his daughter understood who she was dealing with.

'Where's your mother?'

Wendy shrugged. 'She's gone out, but she'll be back soon.'

She knew better than to say Susan had gone down the pub

until she saw what kind of mood he was in.

Barry mimicked her voice and stance but she didn't answer him.

'What do you mean, gone out? I never said she could go out, did I?'

Wendy could see he was out of his head and tried to appease him. 'Shall I make you a cup of tea, Dad? Something to eat?'

Barry ignored her. Sitting on the sofa, he took out a small foil packet. Putting it on the table, he told Wendy to bring the mirror from the kitchen. She did as she was told and Barry started to cut the sulphate on the mirror. A razor blade was used to chop it expertly into a fine powder. When he was satisfied he made four fat lines, scraping them into shape, every sound amplified in the quietness of the room.

Then, rolling up a fiver, he snorted two lines one after the other. Holding his head back and hawking in his throat as he felt the first burn.

He looked at Wendy afterwards.

'Want to try some? Have your first buzz with your old dad, eh?' He looked almost friendly.

She shook her head violently.

'I don't touch drugs.' Her voice condemned and angered him.

'I don't touch drugs,' he mimicked her once more. 'You tight-arsed little bitch!'

Wendy wondered what she should do. She daren't leave the kids with him. In his present mood, if one of them woke up he was liable to give them a good hiding. Then her mother would kill her. She was caught between a rock and a hard place as usual.

'What were you watching on TV?'

'Nothing. I was just revising.'

Barry nodded slowly, as if he was too thick to understand what she was talking about. 'Oh, I see. She was revising. The clever little girl was revising.' He was talking as if there was another person in the room. He picked up the book she was reading. 'The Grapes of what?'

'Wrath. *The Grapes of Wrath*. It's a novel by John Steinbeck.'

'Who the fucking hell is he when he's at home?'

Barry threw the book down on the floor. 'Come and sit with your old dad, give him a cuddle.'

Wendy stayed by the door.

He stared at her for a few moments.

'I just told you to come here.' He pointed to the floor between his legs. 'So come here. Now!'

His voice was almost a roar, and thinking of her brother and sisters Wendy walked towards him. He pulled her between his knees and looked her over.

'There, that wasn't too hard, was it?'

He was holding her hands in his and she wanted to pull away from him, run out of the house, but knew she couldn't.

'You're growing up, girl, look at the tits on you already. Your mother was like that – ripe and ready for action. I bet all the boys want to go out with you, don't they?'

She nodded.

'I don't want to go out with them, though. I want to go to university first. Travel the world one day, I will.'

It was important to her that he should know what she was really like. That he understood her and her needs and wants.

Barry laughed. 'No fucking chance! You'll end up like all the rest of them. A belly full of arms and legs, married to a fucking waster. Your mother had all those delusions years ago. Well, I soon knocked them out of her and I'll knock them out of you.'

Wendy bit on her lip.

Barry looked into his daughter's face. She really was a good-looking girl. She was Susan if Susan had got the breaks. She had beautiful hair, thick and dark, like a chestnut halo around her head. Already she looked older than her years. Eighteen maybe. She had the body of a woman, though, with full breasts and long legs. She was like a young Joan Collins. All cheekbones and languid eyes.

He felt the pull of her then, the allure of her youthfulness.

He just knew she was going to be taken down by some young boy with rough dirty hands and nicotine breath. Some little shit would talk her round, give her the chat, and she would lie on her back for him. Barry knew exactly what would happen. Christ knows, he had done it enough times himself.

He pulled her on to his lap.

'Give your old dad a kiss.'

She tried to get up again and he laughed as she fought with him. He was joking with her at first.

But the feel of her gave his joking an added kick. He made a grab for her breasts, and then she really started to fight him. She could feel his hands all over, feel him laughing at her and her attempts to escape from his grasp. She elbowed him in his stomach, a violent shove that had the strength to knock him on to the floor.

As Barry landed heavily on his elbow he knocked the coffee table flying. Empty coffee cups and small cheap ornaments were crushed. Susan's pride and joy, a large glass bowl where she kept fruit and sweets at Christmas time, was shattered.

Wendy pulled herself to her feet and made to run, but she had to step across her father and as she did so he grabbed at her ankle, sending her sprawling on the floor. Landing heavily on the broken glass, she shrieked as she felt a sliver enter her knee.

Then her father was straddling her, sitting heavily on her stomach as he slapped her three times across the face.

'Fucking calm down, you silly little bitch.'

She bucked her hips in an attempt to throw him off her once more.

'Leave me alone, Dad, let me get up.' She was talking through gritted teeth and, looking down at his daughter, Barry realised she felt no actual fear of him. She was frightened of what she thought he was going to do, not frightened of him personally.

In his amphetamine-induced rage he felt this was wrong. That she should at least respect him.

'You're like your mother, Wendy, think you're better than me. You all think you're better than me. You, Roselle, your fucking mother. You all think you're something special just because you're women. Because you still have that fucking split-arse between your legs.'

He forced his face closer to hers.

'Well, you're not. Someone once said to me, "How can you

ever trust anything that bleeds once a month for a week and doesn't fucking die?" Well, they were right. You're all evil fucking bitches. Do you understand what I'm telling you? Well, do you?'

He was bawling at her and she started to cry at his words.

'Please, Dad, please . . . Let me get up. I'm hurting. You're hurting me.'

He stared down into her face, her beautiful face, strained and white. She was his daughter, his own flesh and blood. But was she, though? Was she maybe the product of Joey and his own daughter? In his paranoid state this thought was latched on to so he could justify to himself what he wanted to do to her. The sex act was Barry's way of punishing women. He could plant his seed, expend his lust, make the woman feel degraded. Make it good or bad for them, depending how he was feeling.

He thought back to her birth, to the trouble she had caused him with her crying and griping. Susan had no time for him or anyone except her fucking kids after that.

He was going to teach them all a lesson. Wendy, his mother, his wife, even Roselle. In his befuddled mind he believed he would also get one over on his lover by what he was about to do.

He put his hands on his daughter's breasts and kneaded them, a vicious action that made her squirm in front of his eyes.

'You're a cunt, just like your mother . . .'

Wendy was sobbing hysterically now and cried out in distress.

'Dad, please! Let me get up. I'm bleeding and hurting . . .'

Barry laughed. 'I ain't your dad, Joey's your dad, love, like he was dad to all of you. Your mother was shagging her own father for years. He ain't your granddad, he's your father. Not me. Rosie's mine, and only her. The rest of you disgust me.'

Wendy fell quiet as she listened to him. She was sure he believed what he was saying. Wendy knew of the tortuous relationship between her mother and her granddad. How June displayed jealousy at times if they were left alone together. Her granddad was a great one for wandering hands around on his little granddaughters too.

'You're all interbreeds, girl. Fucking duelling banjos, you lot.'

Alana and little Barry were standing at the door looking at him. He made eye contact with the two children framed in the doorway.

Barry was holding a teddy bear in his arms, a scruffy thing covered in Weetabix and rusk. Susan had to sneak it from him every now and then while he slept to give it a wash.

Barry, somewhere in his fuddled mind, knew he had gone too far this time. But the drugs gave him a feeling of omnipotence that took over.

His daughter's crushed expression made him sure that what he was doing was right.

'Get back to bed, you two, or you'll fucking know all about it.'

He pretended to rise and they ran back up the stairs where a crying Rosie was lying in her cot, wondering what all the noise was about and why she wasn't with the others in the thick of it all as usual.

Wendy saw her father's face coming towards hers and instinctively bit him. Her teeth sank into his cheekbone, the finely sculpted cheekbone she had inherited from him. She bit down as hard as she could, tasting his blood and her own fear as she did so.

Then Barry really hit her. Pain and anger mingled to make him demented. Wendy's terrified cries could be heard all over the house. Rosie was sitting on the bed with Barry and Alana as they all listened to the fracas down below.

As their sister's animal cries of pain and shock reached a crescendo, little Barry lay back on the bed and put his tattered bear over his face. They were all crying except Rosie who had spied a half-eaten biscuit on the floor and was pointing at it, trying to make Alana understand exactly what she wanted. For the first time in her short life she was ignored as Alana sat mute, silently crying as she guessed exactly what was happening downstairs in the front room.

'Did you see her? My God, I thought I'd die laughing.'

Susan and Doreen were walking home from the pub.

'I can't believe she did it, can you? I mean, imagine showing yourself up like that. And over a piece of shit like him and all.'

Doreen and Susan roared with laughter again.

'Still, he is her husband. You could see Debbie's point of view really. But the punch she gave that bird! Jesus, I felt it and I was at the other side of the bar.'

Susan nodded.

'Poor Debbie. That's the type of stunt Barry would pull, inviting his bird on a night out with his wife. I feel sorry for her really. I know she can be a mare but I mean, Dor, what a sod to do that to her.'

They were in the lane at the back of the houses.

'I'll see what my lot have been up to then I'll give you a knock if you fancy a cup of tea.'

'All right, Doreen. Give us ten minutes to get sorted and come on in.'

Susan let herself in at the back door and was surprised to see her four children sitting at the kitchen table. One look at Wendy's face told her all she needed to know.

'Where is he?' Her voice was low and taut.

Taking her daughter's face gently in her hands she looked at the marks and the bruising on it.

'What happened? Was he drunk?'

Wendy nodded then she spoke sadly, her voice husky as if she had not used it in years.

'And he was on drugs, Mum. He was like a maniac. He made me . . . He made me . . .'

She couldn't finish the sentence and Susan, looking at the blood on the girl's dressing gown, knew exactly what he had made her do.

'He said it was all right because he wasn't me dad. He said Granddad was my dad.' Wendy was sobbing now, her shoulders heaving with every word.

The other children were quiet, as if they knew something momentous had happened. Even little Rosie sat quietly on the floor eating a rusk, her face blank, eyes glued to her sister's face.

Susan felt the air leave her body as she realised exactly what had befallen her precious daughter.

She had been here herself, knew the self-disgust that her daughter was feeling inside, knew the pain of the knowledge that the man who should be protecting you was using you as no man should use a woman, not even a paid prostitute. Knew the anger and the sense of futility in her daughter's heart as she tried to come to terms with what had happened to her. Knew it would haunt her all her life, ruin every good day as she thought back on what had happened to her.

How it would make her feel dirty inside. How she would never again be the girl she had been because that girl had gone. Would never come back. Neither would trust. After all, who could you ever trust again if you couldn't trust your own flesh and blood?

Doreen came in then, a big smile on her face until she took in the scene before her. Her bleached blonde hair and heavy blue eye-shadow looked false in the bright kitchen; her tight top and high heels made her look like a pretend person. A Barbie doll look that suited her in a plastic, pretend way. Her bright red lips were parted in shock and horror as she looked at the girl in front of her.

'Oh, Sue, what's he done now?'

Susan felt the trembling begin. That utter shock that made her feel as if she was moving through water. She turned to her friend.

'Take them all in, will you, please? Take them into your place and settle them down. I have to sort him out now. Once and for all, I have to sort that bastard out.'

Her voice was low as if frightened he could hear her.

Doreen shook her head.

'Phone Old Bill, get him removed . . .'

Susan interrupted her.

'What, like they normally do, Dor? Keep him for the night and send him home in the morning? No, take the three youngest, I want to talk to Wendy on her own.' She stared at her friend and Doreen nodded absently.

'Whatever you say, Sue.' She picked up Rosie and the other two kids followed her without a word, as if they knew something was going to happen which they must not see.

When they had gone Susan took her daughter into her arms and loved her as best she could. She stroked the girl's hair and murmured endearments in her ear. Remembering her own mother's reaction to what had happened to her. The sheer uncaringness of June. The unspoken words that had clearly told her it was all her own fault. That she had made it happen.

'He's a pig, Wendy. A fucking dirty, stinking pig and you couldn't help what he did to you, darlin'. No matter what happens, you remember that, okay?'

Wendy nodded, face so sad that Susan felt rage so acute she could almost taste it.

'Is it true what he said, Mum? Is Granddad my dad?'

Susan pulled her closer but she didn't answer.

'Where is he?'

'Upstairs. He's upstairs. On the bed.'

Susan ran from the room and up the stairs. Barry was lying across the bed, out of it. She saw the bottle of cherry brandy he must have found in the cupboard in the front room lying beside him. It was empty.

Walking back down the stairs, she looked at her daughter. They stared into each other's eyes and then Wendy started to cry. Susan took her into her arms and comforted her again.

'It doesn't matter, remember that. None of it matters. I know, my love, I've been where you've been, darlin' and it doesn't matter. It can't change the real you. My Wendy, my little angel. It can only change you if you let it.'

Ten minutes later, after they had both stopped crying, Susan walked her into Doreen's. She told her friend to look after her cuts then take her to Granny Kate's and explain the situation. That Barry had beaten up his daughter badly and Susan wanted her out of the way for the night.

Doreen nodded, wondering what the upshot of all this was going to be. She wasn't stupid, she knew Barry had done far worse than beat the girl.

Then, back at her own home, Susan put on a coat and walked to the phone box on the corner. She called Roselle at the club and asked if Wendy could stay there for a few days because there had been some trouble with Barry. Roselle, hearing her tone of voice, agreed.

It was as if all the women in Barry's life had decided to conspire against him. Which of course they had.

Then, going back to her own home, Susan put the kettle on

and made herself a cup of coffee. As she waited for the kettle to boil she went out to the hallway. After looking carefully through the cupboard under the stairs she found a large claw hammer. Placing it on the table, she drank her coffee and smoked a cigarette.

She looked around her home, the place she'd loved so much when Barry wasn't in it.

She loved the doors scuffed from four kids' bikes, toys and scooters. She loved the wallpaper on the kitchen walls with its pictures of bowls of fruit and vegetables. She loved the old Formica table with its scratches from years of cutting bread on it for the kids' doorstep sandwiches. She loved the worn blue lino on the floor and the chipped mugs from the market.

It was her home, not his. The haven she had tried to create in the complete chaos that was her life with a man who saw nothing but what he wanted, what he needed.

Picking up the hammer, she walked slowly through the house, taking in all its sights and smells before finally she walked into the bedroom to find her husband. Her legal mate who was lying across the bed, his face bitten and scratched by his own daughter. The girl he had taken like an animal. Oh, she knew how it would have been for Wendy, she had experienced it herself on many occasions.

Looking down at her husband Susan felt a hatred so intense she felt she could murder the world if she had to just so she could protect her kids.

'What have you caused this time, Bal? You took her with your diseased body, like she was nothing – nothing at all. I hope it was worth it, wherever you are. I hope you felt it was worth it. I only wish you could really feel this, you drunken bastard. That you could look into my face and feel the fear your child felt.'

Susan raised the hammer above her head and brought it down with as much force as she could on his skull.

She repeated the act over one hundred times until there was nothing left of him. Nothing recognisable anyway.

Barry Dalston was gone for ever.

Susan was spattered with blood, bone and brain. She walked calmly from the room and made herself another coffee, afterwards smoking another cigarette. Then, pulling on her old coat, she walked to the phone box and dialled the police.

Doreen watched her from her bedroom window and felt a tear slide from her eye as she realised what her friend had done. But unlike the rest of the world she knew why her friend had done it.

No one would ever hear the real reason, not from her anyway. Susan had only been protecting her kids, as any decent mother would.

When the police arrived she had them all bedded down and asleep. Except Wendy, who was waiting patiently at her gran's for Roselle to pick her up and keep her until her bruises disappeared and she could face the world without revealing exactly what had been done to her.

Book Three

1985

No time like the present.

> – Mrs Manley, 1663–1724
> The Lost Lover, 1696

From marrying in haste, and repenting at leisure;
Not liking the person, yet liking his treasure.

> – Elizabeth Thomas, 1675–1731

What's done cannot be undone.

> – William Shakespeare, 1564–1616
> Macbeth, 1606

Chapter Twenty-One

Susan awoke to the noise of prison. It was a strange awakening, a banging on a door, a shout and then bedlam. As she opened her eyes she saw her new cellmate staring down at her.

Matty Enderby, hair immaculate, face cleansed and eyebrows severely plucked, smiled gently.

'Feeling better this morning?'

She had a husky voice, the kind of voice a porn queen should have. It was low, sexy, and held a hint of promise.

'Fuck off.' Susan's voice was gravelly from sleep and cigarettes. She coughed harshly, making Matty reel back in disgust.

'Shall I get you a cup of tea?'

Susan nodded. 'My mouth feels like a buzzard's crutch.'

Matty recoiled once more and Susan laughed.

'You're obviously a very genteel con so I'll moderate my language accordingly. In other words, piss off and get me tea.'

Matty left the cell and Susan sat up in her bunk.

She felt and looked dreadful.

Slipping from the bed, she picked up a towel and a bar of Camay. Then, staring in the small mirror attached to the wall above the sink, she poked out her tongue. She looked and felt ugly. Inside and out.

Her hair, which had never been her best feature, hung lifelessly around her shoulders. Its colour seemed to have faded from the lack of sunlight. Her skin was blotched from sleep, her chin looked like a haven for blackheads and her nose was flaky.

Only her eyes seemed alive and they were the eyes of a stranger. Alert, bright, full of wisdom and trouble.

Matty came back in with the teas and placed Susan's on the table by the door.

'It stinks in here.'

Susan nodded.

'I'm sorry, I was sweating like a pig in the night.'

'You were dreaming, mumbling and snorting.'

Susan grinned. 'And, knowing me, probably farting and all. Beans were never my favourite food.'

She knew she was making the other women feel uncomfortable and she didn't care. After her sojourn in Durham, all she needed was to be celled up with a finicky bitch like Matilda Enderby. What were they thinking of?

Instead of posters of naked men with dongers the size of baseball bats, she was in a cell with posters of bowls of fruit and women in old-fashioned clothes eating picnics on green grassy banks.

It was all too strange for her.

She was used to the rough and tumble of prison life. It had a sense of purpose to it. Beating the system. Being part of the sisterhood. Joking about men and their attributes, pretending they were all missing a leg over when in reality it was the last thing on their minds.

With this new cellmate she was stuck in some kind of alternative universe where people ate cucumber sandwiches and played by the rules.

It felt wrong.

Susan sipped her tea and stared once more at the posters.

'They're paintings by Monet.'

She shrugged, uninterested.

'Really? I thought they were posters.'

She drank the tea down fast, savouring the sweetness of it. Then, stripping off her night attire, she wrapped a towel around her and walked from the cell. As she made her way to the showers she encountered women of all shapes, colours and persuasions. Some smiled. Others looked at her warily, her reputation having preceded her.

She knew they were waiting to see what she was like before

they offered her anything, let alone friendship. But Susan understood this, could feel secure in the prison environment. With Matty she felt as if she was caught up in some kind of game.

In the showers she stood under the lukewarm water and shivered as she waited for her body to acclimatise. Then, soaping herself all over, she washed her hair and started to rinse.

A young black girl with tribal marks on her face offered her a tube of Head and Shoulders.

'That soap will ruin your hair, man. Use this.'

Susan nodded gratefully and did as she was bidden.

Savouring the creamy lather she enjoyed herself, taking pleasure in the simple act of washing her lank and greasy hair.

In the shower beside her two women were kissing but Susan ignored them, uncaring. Knowing that privacy was a thing of the past, she walked out of the showers without giving them a backward glance. The privacy she gave them was not to look, not to take notice. Leave them be. It was an unwritten prison rule.

As she walked back to her cell she dried herself on the rough towel. A PO with a severe countenance and shocking red hair waylaid her.

'Name?' The command was clipped and hard.

'Dalston, Susan, PX4414.'

The woman nodded. 'Visit at one-fifteen.'

Susan nodded and went on her way.

She hoped it was the kids but she didn't hold out too much hope. The social services were being tricky again. Trying to talk her into all sorts of things. She pushed it from her head, knowing it was futile in her present position to think about certain things. It was a knack you developed to stop yourself going mad.

Twenty minutes later she was reading her mail, the usual daily letter from the kids. Barry's scrawled 'I love yous', and Alana's little note talking about her new school and new friends. Susan held the two letters to her breast as if she could absorb the words into her body.

Then she opened Wendy's letter, her heart in her mouth. Her eldest girl was already a woman at fifteen. She'd had no choice. Her letters were adult, their content adult.

It was this that worried her mother the most.

Unlike Alana's talk of make up and pop groups, fashion and television, Wendy's letter discussed how the other kids were doing. How Rosie, the acknowledged perfect child, was faring at her foster home with the Simpsons. How nice they were but still not her real parents and never could be all the time her mother was alive.

These letters frightened Susan for more reasons than one.

Wendy blamed herself for everything, and she shouldn't, she had no reason to. Susan had to remind her of that constantly.

It had been hard in Durham, the journey so long and difficult. Susan didn't see the kids much, and when she did it was fraught. They were overexcited when they finally saw her and consequently played up, all vying for her attention. Then there was little Rosie who didn't really know her any more and cried when Susan picked her up.

She shook herself mentally. Things could change again now she was nearer to them. Rosie could start to see her more often and she could get up a relationship with her at last.

She brushed her hair with greater care in case the visit was from the kids. She wanted to look nice for them.

Matty came back into the cell and smiled at her, pleased she was washed and brushed up.

'I hear you've got a visit?'

'News travels fast in this place.'

'Shall I do your hair for you? Make you a bit more presentable?'

She was eager to please and Susan suddenly felt a wave of tiredness. She wouldn't cope for long with this woman, she knew she wouldn't. She'd end up on another murder charge.

But ten minutes later she had a neat chignon and had even been talked into wearing a bit of make up. When she looked in the mirror Susan was surprised at the difference. Matty laughed, pleased with herself.

'You look almost pretty. What you need now is a good skin care routine and a few nice clothes and you'll be a stunner.'

Susan snorted grumpily.

'Listen, darlin', if I won the fucking pools and went to a

plastic surgeon I still wouldn't be a stunner. Not with my body anyway. I reckon I might have a bit more luck with me boatrace, though.'

She admired the difference once more in the mirror and hoped it was the kids coming. She had one reception visit to use, and she wanted to use it wisely.

'You'd get that weight off if you tried. Stop eating stodge and keep to the veggies.'

'What is it with you, Enderby? Have you taken it on yourself to be my fucking personal assistant or something?'

Matty smiled annoyingly.

'That's one way of putting it. You have a good rep. Even Rhianna is wary of you and she isn't worried about anyone else.'

Susan didn't answer her.

Matty didn't push it. Instead she picked up some nail varnish and, smiling, informed Susan she was going out for some recreational nail painting.

Susan shook her head in disbelief at the woman's vacuous existence even in nick.

Matty stood at the cell door then and said seriously, 'Actually, I was a legal secretary – I hold a surgery here every day for the other girls. Giving advice and so on. You should look in, I might be able to help you. I might look like a bimbo but underneath all this is a brain like a computer.'

She blew Susan a kiss and walked from the cell. Susan poked her tongue out at the door and sighed. This bird was a head case, she was convinced of it.

She knew that her sojourn in Durham had made her reputation.

A lesbian had taken a shine to her, and Susan had explained that she liked her as a friend but that was as far as it went. The woman, a tall blonde amazon, had not been pleased.

Unused to being refused, she had taken serious umbrage, leaving Susan in a quandary. Julia Stone had made Susan's life unbearable. Everywhere she went, showers, toilet, exercise, Julia was there, looking angry, trying to intimidate her. Susan had heard through the grapevine that she was going to net her in the showers. She did not want to be raped, and she knew that Julia, being the type of personality she was, would not listen to reason. As far as Julia was concerned, Susan was going against her.

Placing a billiard ball in a sock, Susan had taken her walk to the showers and then she had hospitalised Julia Stone for two months. This act had achieved two things, Julia Stone had lost her status and Susan had acquired it. Which was the reason Rhianna was wary of her now, was the reason most people were wary of her.

Even the POs were impressed.

But Susan did not want to be like Rhianna any more than she had wanted to be like Julia.

It was survival, no more and no less.

The private visiting room was painted a dull green. It was supposed to make people calmer. Susan thought it looked like puke. Green bile-coloured. She sat at the table and bit her nails, the little bits of nail she had left anyway. When the door opened she sat up straight, her heart in her mouth as she waited for one or all of her children to walk in.

Instead it was a young man of about thirty, casually dressed. Too casually to be a brief but Susan didn't worry too much about that. He had brown hair that looked like it had been cut with a knife and fork, deep green eyes that were twinkling and merry, and a full mouth.

'Hi, Susan, pleased to meet you at last.'

She noticed he had nice teeth, even and straight. She could see him as a regular attender at a dental surgery. All caps, crowns and fillings. Pity he didn't worry so much about his hair.

'Colin?' He could hear the disappointment in her voice and smiled to cover his nervousness.

'Colin Jackson, we spoke on the phone.'

Susan nodded, taking in his scruffy jeans and well-washed jumper.

'So you're the hot shot lawyer who's going to handle my appeal then?'

Her tone of voice said everything and he had the grace to blush.

'I know I look very casual today but I have had quite a lot to do. I saw your children this morning.'

He saw her face light up and sighed inside himself.

'They're bringing them in on Friday. Friday afternoon.'

He saw her face drop.

'That's days away.'

Her voice was flat, dead-sounding.

He tried to jolly her along. Opening his briefcase, he took out a file. It was about five inches thick.

'I have all your papers here, everything pertaining to your case.'

'How thrilling. Well, you can argue what you like, I have nothing more to add. I took the hammer and I killed him. Simple as that.'

Colin smiled half-heartedly. 'It's not as simple as that though, is it, Susan? Something triggered that violent action. We know he beat you regularly, we know he was a violent criminal. I know he beat you badly a few days before you killed him. Why didn't you kill him then?'

She smiled nastily.

'I didn't feel like killing him then. I was sore, hurt, my ribs were broken and my face looked like someone had jumped on it. But the last trial proved that none of that matters. Mine was a premeditated act of murder, I'm surprised they're even allowing an appeal.'

'Well, things have moved on since then, haven't they? You only ever made one statement, on the night the incident occurred. In that statement you claimed you had had enough and that it was time for him to die. Those were your exact words. Now of course we can plead just cause. We'd have to prove he was going to harm you again, that you were terrified of him. If we can convince the court of that, I think we can get the sentence reduced to manslaughter then get you out on time served.'

He smiled, pleased with himself. Expecting her to be as pleased as he was.

'I have to pretend I was nutty at the time, is that it?'

Colin looked suitably chastened.

'I don't want you to think I'm asking you to lie . . .'

Susan shrugged.

'Listen, Colin, when I hit that ponce with the hammer it was the sanest I had ever been in my life. Now I know that might sound strange to you, but that's tough. I should have done it years before.'

Colin recognised the truthfulness of her statement. It was in her voice, in her eyes. Seeing her today, with her hair neatly put up, her face clean and scrubbed, she looked a different person from the one in the newspaper photographs of two years before.

Then she had looked fat and frightening. Her face so hard-looking. So bereft of anything remotely like remorse or even worry, certainly nothing like fear. She had sat stone-faced through her trial; her brief, realising what he was dealing with, did not put her in the witness box. Each and every psychiatrist had written the same report. Undecided on her mental state. Refuses to discuss the night in question. Refuses to acknowledge what she did was wrong. Same words each time. Just reiterates that it was time for her husband to die.

In the end the judge had given her a life sentence for murder, saying that he had no option as Mrs Dalston refused to tell anyone what had happened that night and still refused to acknowledge her part in it in any way other than as his killer. The police statement she signed had her admitting she would do it again if she 'had the chance'. The police had clapped themselves on the back, the tabloids had had a field day and Susan had disappeared into prison and away from everyone's attention and consequently their minds.

But her four children adored her and it was evident she loved them.

In short Susan had done everything possible to be put into prison. It was as if she'd wanted to be separated from her kids. Wanted to be classed a murderess. She refused to use intimidation or threats from her dead husband as an excuse. She came across as a woman determined to kill, and therefore the judge had to sentence her accordingly.

But Colin's boss was determined to get her out and had campaigned for an appeal. Now they had just a few months to put forward a new case. Everyone had thought she might finally tell the truth about that night. It seemed they were wrong.

'Listen, Susan, if you'd only see sense we could maybe get you out. Back home to your children, back to your life.'

She stared at him blankly.

'We know what he did to you, we've looked through your medical records, everything. It's no shame to have been badly hurt and to retaliate. We're all capable of it.'

She didn't answer him for a minute. Finally she spoke as if to a child.

'But I didn't retaliate, did I? You forget that. It was five days after he'd last hit me that I killed him. He was unconscious and drunk at the time. A sitting duck. But I tell you something, Colin, and you can write this in your little notebook – when I brought that hammer down on his skull it was the best feeling in the world. I just kept repeating the action. It was better than drink, drugs or sex. I'm locked up here but at least I released my kids from him and what he was. I ain't making excuses for what I did because I'm glad I did it and two years on I would do it again if I had the chance. Unlike Barry, I'll pay for my past deeds. Though he paid too in the end.' She grinned. 'Oh, he paid all right. I made fucking sure of that.'

Colin stared at her then. He was shocked by what she'd said though inside himself he knew she was in the right. Susan was an eye for an eye person. He understood that and after reading her medical files also understood how someone could reach the point where they would take no more.

If only she could see that they could get a case together for her, get her out on time served. But it was almost as if she relished being locked up, relished her punishment.

When the judge had passed sentence on her, Susan Dalston had laughed. It was the only time she had shown any emotion throughout the whole proceedings. She had refused her counsel's advice to introduce her previous medical history in evidence. She had refused to do anything, in fact, that would help her case.

In short, she had locked herself up and thrown away the key.

'What's happening with me kids?' she asked Colin.

He smiled.

'They're doing well. In fact they're coming in this week as you know. But all of them are doing fine. Rosie, is it, the youngest? She's settled well with her foster parents and they adore her. Is there no one you know who could take the others on, though? The eldest, I believe, lives part of the time with a friend of yours, Roselle Digby? Could she not maybe take the others too?'

Susan shook her head. 'Nah, she can't. I wish they'd let me mate Doreen take them. She was up for it.'

Colin nodded. 'I'm afraid social services wouldn't allow her to take them at any cost.'

Susan grinned.

'She might be a bleached blonde slapper with five kids by different fathers but I tell you something, mate, she's a wonderful mother and a wonderful person. It's all relative, ain't it?

'What will be the upshot with the kids anyway? No one seems to tell me anything really.'

Colin couldn't answer her as he didn't know himself. He had a meeting with the children's social workers later in the week.

'I'll know more after I've spoken to Miss Beacham, the social worker.'

Susan nodded again and lit another cigarette.

'So what are you going to do then?'

Colin shrugged.

'Doesn't look like there's a lot I can do, does there?'

'I'll just do me time quietly then. I'll be out in four, maybe a bit earlier. I don't know why you're still bothering with me anyway. I've nothing to add to what I said before.'

'I don't either to be honest. I'd like to ask you one thing, though, Sue. Think about your four children and what it must be like for them growing up without their mother. They love you very much and as a mother you received nothing but praise. Though where you ever learned to be one, I don't know.'

Susan did laugh now.

'You've met with me own mother then? Old bitch. She sold her story to the papers and made a pile.' She shrugged. 'Good luck to her really, I expected no less. But to answer your question, I did the opposite to her with mine, I made sure of that.'

'Well, I can't see any of your children murdering anyone.'

Susan's face blanched and she shook her head.

'No, Colin, neither can I.'

Standing up, she terminated the interview.

'Look at her, she really thinks she's something special.'

Susan didn't answer, but seeing Matty hold one of her surgeries was an eye opener. She watched as Rhianna took money or goods for Matty from each of the women who had come seeking the professional advice of a convicted murderess.

Susan saw the hope on the women's faces as they consulted her, saw their worries partially lifted after they had spoken to her, and decided that if Matty wasn't having anyone over then good luck to her.

Susan moved nearer the table so she could listen properly.

What Matty was saying to a young black prostitute was actually making sense and she went up in Susan's estimation then. As long as she wasn't trying to rip anyone off Susan was all for free enterprise, and the prison system and that seemed to go hand in hand. It was amazing what some people would do for a filter cigarette or a Mars bar.

Suddenly Lionel Richie was blaring out of the radio as one of the girls, hearing a favourite song, turned it up full volume. She was dancing around, singing was it her they were looking for, when the PO turned it down and one of the more rampant lesbians shouted out, 'No, it fucking ain't, you ugly whore!'

Everyone laughed and the girl carried on singing to herself.

Susan, still grinning, listened to Matty giving advice.

'You're in for affray and threatening behaviour, right?'

The girl nodded. 'And GBH.'

'Well, then, tell your brief to do a deal. Say you'll hold your hand up to the GBH but to drop the other charges and you'll plead guilty with mitigating circumstances. You was on drugs and not in complete control. Ergo you will have the twelve steps on the unit and be out in no time. I mean, you're up for a wedge on your previous anyway. This way you can get a reduced as well as a cushy time on the wrap programme.'

The girl smiled, full of hope now.

'Thanks, Matty. I'll do that.'

Susan watched her skip away happily. She knew that for many the worst part of prison was finding out what was going to happen to them so they could get their head around it. When they knew the score they could cope.

Susan was enjoying being on the remand wing while her so-called appeal was going on, though she had only agreed to it in the first place so as to get nearer the kids for a while. What she really wanted was to be placed nearer London if possible. It was hard only seeing them now and again, when the social services could find time to bring them up. It was such a journey for the kids as well, Durham not being the most accessible prison in the country. Nor the most comfortable either.

What she really wanted was Cookham Wood or somewhere with a secure unit and not too much travelling. Somewhere the kids could run about a bit, have a bit of a laugh.

She watched all afternoon as women came to Matty and she gave them advice. Susan listened and found most of it pretty sound. Then a young girl with long blonde hair and wide-set eyes approached and Rhianna stepped in front of her.

The girl held up two cigarettes. Matty shook her head and pulled a face.

'Fuck off, bitch, we ain't got nothing for you here.'

Rhianna's voice was hard. One of the women round the table stood up menacingly and the POs moved nearer, fearing a tear up as a fight was called in prison.

'Write to your boyfriend and ask his advice, you little bitch. He helped you kill the kid, didn't he?'

The girl dropped her head on to her chest.

'She still writes to him. He stabbed her little boy, burned him and tortured him, but you still write him love letters, don't you, darlin'?'

The women were getting annoyed, reminded of their own children in the care of relatives or the state. Children who were loved and wanted though their mothers were banged up in prison. In fact a lot of the time women were there because of their kids.

Prostitutes, shoplifters, fraudsters were often trying the only way they knew how to feed and clothe their kids, as everyone expected them to. They had men who did nothing other than impregnate them and then walk away, on to the next woman and the next kid, and the next.

When someone like Caroline Hart came along they hated her with a vengeance because she had let someone destroy what was to others the most precious thing in their lives. They might kick each other's heads in, fight and argue, but none of them would harm their kids. It was the unwritten law.

The PO escorted the girl from the rec room. They were trying to defuse the situation before it got out of hand. In fact she should be in isolation but it wasn't happening for some reason and so they had to be extra-vigilant in case one of the women decided to take the law into her own hands. Something that frequently happened in prison.

The tension left the room with Caroline and Matty started to pack up her stuff. Rhianna would give her the 'split' later in the day, and Matty, who didn't smoke anything except the occasional joint, would sell it on to the other women. Rhianna was also taking bets, and running a protection racket.

Susan watched it all. She knew Rhianna was watching her as hard as she was watching Rhianna; the other woman was probably worried Susan was going to try and take over from her. But she wasn't. She would have to talk to her about that at some point and put the record straight.

Until then she had to look hard, well able to take care of herself, and like she wasn't in the least bit bothered that a big black violent lunatic wanted to fight her at some point in the near future.

As she rolled another cigarette Susan wondered what her kids were up to and longed to see their little faces, bright with glee and happy because they were near her. She shook off the depressing thought that she could only see them at someone else's whim and made herself accept the fact once more.

One day, she promised herself, all this would be over. Really over. She would have done her bit, paid the price for being stupid enough to let Barry Dalston into her life.

* * *

Wendy poured coffee for herself and Roselle from the percolator. Roselle watched her, touched by the girl's obvious happiness at going to see her mother. In the last two years she had changed so much.

On the night Roselle had picked her up after the murder, the girl had been in a terrible state, shaking and stuttering with fear. Like a young gazelle caught in the hunter's trap. Roselle had introduced herself as a friend of her mother's and explained that Susan had asked her to take Wendy for a while until everything settled.

What was so shocking to Roselle, and so sad, was the fact that she knew without being told exactly why Susan had killed her husband. It was obvious what had happened to the girl. Roselle wondered then how she had ever seen anything in Barry. How she could have deluded herself that with her he was okay. Wendy was his own flesh and blood and he had taken her as if she was a nothing, lower than a paid whore. Roselle saw it in the way the girl walked, in the bruises all over her body and in the blood she was losing for a week after the event.

Hatred for Barry had entered her heart that night. She only wished she could have seen what Susan had done to him, been there with another hammer so she could have struck a few blows for righteousness herself.

She also understood Susan's reluctance to let on what had happened in her home that night and throughout her married life. She was protecting her daughter and herself. Why should people know that a man diagnosed with a venereal disease only a short while previously had taken his young daughter and raped her? The girl would have to live with everyone knowing that for the rest of her life. She did not deserve that, she was the innocent in it all.

Part of Roselle also felt responsible for what happened. If only she had not dumped him like she had . . . he must have suffered. But how could he bring himself to make his own child suffer so terribly?

She took her coffee from the girl and they smiled at one

another. They had never discussed exactly what had happened and Roselle would never force things. Her home had become a haven for the girl from everyone who knew what her mother had done. Who looked at her as the daughter of a woman who had slaughtered her husband in cold blood, without a thought for the four children she was leaving both fatherless and motherless. The woman made out in the tabloids to be a ruthless sort who happily lived off her husband's immoral earnings and embraced his way of life.

Barry had somehow been painted as a loveable cockney rogue who had become dependent on drink and drugs and therefore was not wholly responsible for his own actions.

As usual excuses were being made for him because he was a man. Men could be violent, it was in their nature, why wars came about. But not women. When a woman was violent it was deemed morally wrong. It was Susan who was the bad person because all she ever said at her trial was that she would kill him again if she had the chance.

The papers had jumped on that statement. Deprived of a Myra Hindley figure for so long, they'd turned her into a monster.

It was ludicrously unfair and something Roselle did not fully understand. Why didn't Susan let on what her life had really been like? That she wasn't some kind of gangster's moll who, after a night in the pub where her sister had had a fight with another woman and Susan herself had been drunk, had come home and decided to kill her husband.

By rights she should be out now and looking after her kids, the only thing in life she had ever wanted to do.

Wendy cut them both a small slice of cherry cake. Putting one carefully on a plate, she passed it to Roselle with a small linen napkin. Roselle took it, trying to hide her smile. She realised poor Wendy thought she was quite genteel. If only she knew!

'Are you going in to see Mum now she's nearer home?' the girl asked.

Roselle shook her head.

'I can't go. I can't bear her to be in there, to be honest.'

Wendy nodded in understanding and her face was so painfully

beautiful, and so like her mother's, that Roselle felt an overwhelming urge to cry.

Wendy had embraced the new eighties fashions wholeheartedly and Roselle had indulged her. Although she helped out financially with the other children, she didn't see that much of them. Only now and again when she did a check on Sue's behalf to see how they were really faring.

If people wondered at the close friendship between a night-club owner and a murderess, no one questioned it. Roselle knew her car, clothes and carefully modulated voice gave her all the creds she needed. She also kept in close contact with Doreen, and between them they did what they could.

Though Susan had once asked her to take on all her kids Roselle had refused, and Susan being Susan had understood and never asked her again. Roselle knew she was pleased Wendy had her to turn to when she needed her.

Wendy was Susan's biggest worry and privately Roselle knew why that was. But the girl seemed to have got over her trauma, one most people assumed was over her mother's violence. It had been a silent conspiracy. Everyone in the know had kept stumm and let nature and the courts take their course.

'I'm really looking forward to seeing her, though, Roselle. I do miss her. Sometimes of a night I think about the little things she used to do for me and the others. The times she went without food so we could eat. The times she sat up with us when we were ill. Made us laugh when we were down. I remember once, it was the summer holidays and she was skint as usual so we all had a picnic in the back garden. It was hilarious, all the neighbours thought we was mad. Like we were the Royal family or something. We had Marmite sandwiches and Mr Kipling cakes. It was a scream.'

Wendy smiled, her eyes misty as she remembered that day. The heat, the flies, the kids playing cricket in the alley.

'Then me dad came home and spoiled it all as usual.' She shook her head, remembering.

'He didn't half give her a hiding that day. We all ran into Doreen's when it started like we always did. But we could hear him shouting at her, and her hitting the furniture as he cracked her one.'

She was quiet again, full of her own thoughts.

'I hope she listens to me on Friday. If she doesn't, I don't know what we'll do.'

Roselle shrugged.

'Your mother has her own reasons for everything, and they're good ones. Don't you ever forget that.'

Wendy smiled but her face was so sad behind the smile that Roselle felt an urge to take her into her arms.

'I'll never forget that. I could never forget what me mum's done for me. Never. And one day I'll pay her back.'

Roselle sipped her coffee and nodded.

'Of course you will, darlin'. Of course you will.'

Susan was filling her mug with hot water on the bottom landing when she was approached by Rhianna. She had been expecting it since her arrival and was amazed that it had taken so long.

Three days, in fact, before Rhianna asked her just what the score was.

Now it was finally happening she felt sick with nervousness. For all Susan's reputation, she wasn't a hard case. She just pretended she was to save herself being used as a gofer.

From her first days in prison she had realised that what had happened to Barry frightened people. They did not want the same thing happening to them, so they afforded her respect. Gave her the kudos they thought she expected. All she really wanted was to get her head down and do her time in peace.

Hopefully once she'd explained this to the other woman she'd be left alone.

Rhianna had her hair in plaits, hundreds of them, tiny tight curly plaits that made her look younger and softer than she actually was. She had also filled a mug with scalding water and Susan watched her warily.

'So, what's the score, Dalston? What is it you want?'

Susan looked her in the eye, hoping her own rapidly beating heart and shaking hands would not betray how scared she really was.

She shrugged nonchalantly.

'All I want is to wait for me appeal in peace. I don't want anything you've got or that you've already worked for. I have no intention of taking over any rackets or causing you any difficulties whatsoever. But I won't take any shit either. I'll walk side by side with you, but I will not be put down or used by you or anyone. In short, I just want to do me time. Okay?'

Rhianna, who had been half expecting a fight of some kind, also relaxed. Susan's arms looked very meaty and big and more than capable of giving someone a good crack. Just thinking about what she had done made the other woman fearful.

'So what you saying?'

Susan sighed heavily, feeling her fear and relishing it even as she hated it.

'What I'm saying is, carry on as usual. Me and you could be mates or we could be enemies. What I don't want is to be a partner in any of your enterprises. In other words, leave me alone and I'll leave you alone. Simple as that.'

Rhianna still couldn't believe her luck.

'You don't want a bit of nothing?'

Susan shook her head.

'Just a bit of fucking peace, if that's possible in this dump.'

Rhianna laughed gently.

'You'll get peace, don't worry about that. And if I can be of any help, you let me know. Anything you want I'll get it for you if it can be got, okay?'

She held out a carefully manicured hand with long purple talons and Susan shook it.

'Fair enough, Rhianna, I do need some smokes.'

She smiled.

'You got them. Free for the first time as a sort of moving in present. After that it's the going rate.'

Susan laughed then and both women relaxed.

'Drop by my cell for a coffee, if you want?'

Susan was pleased to be offered the hand of friendship.

'Is it a normal cell with normal things in it?'

Rhianna laughed. 'Matty getting to you already, eh? Listen,

take my advice. She's a lot shrewder than she looks. Don't be deceived by the fluffy little woman act, she's a brainbox in high heels. You dig what I'm saying?'

Susan smiled.

'I had sussed that much out for meself, but she still drives me fucking nuts.'

'You want a bit of soft? I can arrange it for you. Take your mind off your worries.'

Susan shook her head.

'Listen, Rhianna, lesbianism has never done anything for me. In fact, I ain't even that enamoured of men.'

The black woman laughed, showing extraordinarily white teeth.

'Outside I don't touch soft either, but in here it's nice. A bit of company, a few laughs. Some soft sex. Takes the bite out of the days, you know?'

'Well, thanks for the offer but I'll pass it up if you don't mind.'

Rhianna and Susan looked at one another fully for the first time.

'You got a bad rep, you know. I never heard anything about you being likeable,' Rhianna observed.

Susan heard the surprise in the other woman's voice.

'Well, to be truthful, I could say the same about you. Maybe I will have that coffee after all.'

They walked to Rhianna's cell, which like Susan's was up on the fours. As they walked up the metal stairs from landing to landing their closeness was noticed and carefully monitored by all the others. People who had tried to bet on the outcome of a possible fight were saddened, but everyone was glad to see that the first confrontation was finally over and done with.

Inside the cell, Susan finally relaxed. As Rhianna made the coffee she looked at the pictures of Robert Redford and Spandau Ballet and sighed. This was more like it, this was real. The cell was full of contraband and mess, much as her own had always looked, and she felt she had finally found a kindred spirit.

A small radio played rocker's revenge and easy listening reggae music. Steel Pulse stared down from above the bunks, and make up and cheap moisturisers were strewn everywhere. It was like a young girl's bedroom, smelling of sweat, smoke and Lux soap.

It felt right to Susan. After three days of classical music and Monet paintings it was like she had finally come home.

But, most importantly, she'd had her biggest fear taken away and could finally relax properly and just get on with doing her time. Then she could go home, at last she could go home. She would have paid off everyone's debts by then.

Especially her own.

Chapter Twenty-Two

June answered the front door with a big smile on her face and a large drink in her hand.

'Can I help you, love?' Her voice was slurred with alcohol and full of camaraderie.

Colin smiled amiably.

'I'm here on behalf of your daughter Susan.'

June hitched up her ample breasts with her arm and smiled again.

'Are you from the papers?'

There was hope in her voice and Colin was saddened that a mother could exploit her own daughter so easily.

'Actually I'm her solicitor. I need to talk to you. Would it be possible for me to come inside?'

As he spoke a rasping male voice came from within the flat, shouting, 'Shut the fucking door, June, will ya!'

Colin took the opportunity to step across the threshold.

The flat was a real culture shock. The outside was pure council: dirty balcony, rubbish everywhere, the smell of urine. Inside was a different kettle of fish. It was all white walls, glass tables and white leather furniture. Dark brown shag-pile carpet and chocolate brown velvet curtains finished off the décor on which no expense had been spared but it looked as if it could all do with a good clean or at least a dusting.

In the lounge Joey sat in front of a large TV screen and video unit. Colin knew just where the money had come from to furnish the place like this.

June saw his expression and preened herself.

'Lovely, ain't it? I love seeing people's faces after they step in from out there. We bought the whole room ex-display. Just went in and bought the lot, even the pictures on the wall.'

Her voice was full of pride.

'I seen a room just like it on *Bergerac* once. Now, what's the little mare been up to this time?'

He heard the note of exasperation in her voice and wondered at a mother who could be so callous, so cold-blooded about her own child. He was getting an insight into Susan's upbringing that was as frightening as it was fascinating.

'You don't remember me, do you?'

June shook her head.

'I came to see you a while ago, about the children?'

Her face dropped.

'I remember you now – the scruffy git with the trainers.'

Colin smiled at her description.

'Is that what you're back for now? To hassle me again? I don't want any of them kids. She should have thought of them when she was hammering the fuck out of her old man.'

'I think, Mrs McNamara, that was exactly what was on her mind, don't you?'

Joey took his eyes from the TV long enough to bellow, 'Get that geek out of here before I give him a right hander. I'm sick and tired of that little mare and all the hag she's brought on this family. The shame and humiliation of being part of something like that cuts deep, mate. Fucking deep.'

Colin looked at the heavyset man with his designer tracksuit and badly permed hair.

'Your daughter was regularly beaten, Mr McNamara, she was used viciously and she retaliated. That's the long and the short of it. I think she had one too many *right handers*, don't you?'

Colin was frightened inside. He knew Joey McNamara was a violent thug like his son-in-law. He also knew that Joey had made a mint out of selling stories about his daughter's escapades. Had painted her as a violent woman intent on getting her own way. Where money was concerned this couple obviously had no morals, scruples or care. All they saw were the pound signs.

Joey got to his feet. Colin saw how big he was and his heart sank.

'I'd better warn you, Mr McNamara, that I am in the legal profession and I will have no option but to call in the police if you raise your hand to me.'

Joey looked at his wife and she pulled the young man from the room.

'Don't wind him up, he's got a short fuse, son. All this with Susan has taken its toll, I can tell you.'

He could hear the lies in June's voice and see them in her eyes. He knew they were frightened of the law as people like them always were. Not the police but the lawyers and the barristers. People in suits scared them. It was a class thing. People in suits owned houses and paid tax. People like the McNamaras couldn't understand them and would never try.

At the front door Colin tried to talk to June again.

'Listen to me, Susan is in danger of losing her children. Not so much the older ones but baby Rosie – her foster parents are going to try for adoption. They could be granted leave.'

June smiled.

'I hope they are, mate, give her a decent chance in life. More chance than that murdering bitch could ever do.'

Colin looked into her eyes.

'You really mean that, don't you? You can't see that a mother's love, a *real* mother's love, is probably the most important thing a child can have in its life. It means more than money, more than anything.

'I came here today to try and appeal to your decent side, your mothering side. But I was wasting my time, wasn't I? All that money you made off your daughter's back and you didn't buy your grandchildren so much as a packet of sweets. You disgust me, you really do. But whatever Susan did or didn't do, Mrs McNamara, her children adore her. Which I suspect is more than you can say about yours, isn't it?'

June opened the front door and literally turfed him out of her home. A woman was walking along the balcony and stopped to watch them. June started shouting at her.

'Had your fucking look, have you? Want a fucking photograph to keep the memory, eh?'

She slammed the door in Colin's face and as embarrassed as he felt he was glad that his final words had at least hit home. As he walked down to his car he heard a voice calling him.

'Oi, Mister!' He turned and saw Debbie walking towards him.

'I just seen me mum turf you out. Are you here about Susan?'

He nodded.

'I'm her sister Deborah. How is she?'

He sighed.

'Not very good to be honest. The photos in the papers didn't do you justice, you know.'

Debbie smiled. 'I never took a good photo, not even on me wedding day. I'm one of them people who look fatter as opposed to thinner, if you see what I mean?'

He smiled and found himself warming to her then.

'How are the kids?'

He shrugged.

'Not too good. They miss her dreadfully.'

Debbie sighed. 'Well, they would. I mean, in fairness she was a brilliant mother, old Sue. They was good kids, all of them.'

'They still *are* good kids. Why don't you go to see them, see for yourself how they are?'

She shook her head.

'My Jamesie wouldn't swallow that. He wants me to keep out of it. I just wondered, that's all. You know, curiosity like.'

He knew she was lying and wondered how a family became torn apart.

'Does this Jamesie have to know everything you do? I'm sure the children would be glad to see you. See someone they know. Especially the younger ones.'

He could see the confusion in her eyes and knew she would love to see them.

'Well, you know where they are, don't you? There's nothing to stop you from popping in if you're round that way, is there?'

He left it open, hoping she took the hint.

'What are you doing for Susan then?'

'Attempting to get her to agree to an appeal. She requested one but now it seems she's not bothering to try and help herself.'

Debbie smiled.

'She just wanted out of Durham, mate, if I know my sister. Used it to get nearer the kids for a while. It must be torture for her, they was her life.'

He could hear the underlying note of envy in her voice.

'Do you have children at all?'

Debbie shrugged nonchalantly.

'I don't, no, but me old man does.'

Colin heard the hurt in her voice and didn't know what to say to her.

'Well, these kids are motherless in their own way. I'm sure an auntie would be very welcome at this time. A familiar face, someone they know. Think about it.'

She didn't answer directly.

'Give Sue all the best for me, will you? Tell her I'll try and write or something, okay?'

He nodded, and watched her walk away on high heels that were obviously killing her, her unfashionable mini skirt displaying short fat legs and her backcombed hair bleached blonde. Colin wondered at this ill-assorted family where everyone seemed to be estranged or at loggerheads. But rivalry in families was common, especially in the East End he had been told. It had taken him all this time to see it first hand and it depressed him. No matter what happened within families, surely the children should still be a priority?

As he walked back to his car he cursed. At some time in the last twenty minutes someone had removed his side window and his radio.

'Shit!'

That set the seal on an already lousy day.

Susan was hyper. It was Friday and she was seeing the children, all four of them. She had woken at five after hardly any sleep. It was the second visit since she had been in Holloway and she was dying to see them again.

Matty laughed as she saw her making up her bunk. This was something Susan had recently started to do as it saved so much aggravation and stopped Matty's constant nagging about confined spaces and mess.

'See, if you do it as soon as you get up it's done, finished and over with.'

Susan laughed, her good mood embracing even Matty whom she still found wearing. Her constant tidying made Susan fit to scream most of the time. But she had to admit it did make life easier.

'I have a visit from my brief today – you'd like Geraldine actually. She's really on the ball but also a nice person. Which, with briefs, is rare, let me tell you. In my experience most of them look down on the rest of us,' Matty drawled.

Susan nodded.

'Well, you're the expert on briefs. Especially murdering them.'

She laughed at her own wit then apologised. 'I was only joking, Matty, you know I don't really mean it.'

Matty's eyes were full of tears as she said sadly, 'Unlike you, Susan, I regret what I did. But I had no option.'

Susan sighed and put one meaty arm around the other woman's slender shoulders.

'I know, love. We're in the same boat so if anyone understands what you did it's me.'

She felt bad about constantly taking the piss out of Matty though the woman asked for it really. She had the nous for nick, but that was about it. Everything else about her was screamingly middle-class. Although there were plenty of well-spoken cons, it was usually because they were fraudsters or thieves. Very rarely were they in on anything requiring a big lump, as a life sentence was termed.

Though by all intents and purposes, Matty would soon be out on appeal as she was now classed as a woman who was defending herself as opposed to a woman who had killed. She had killed, but it was self defence.

The same thing her brief wanted *her* to use.

But Susan, being Susan, did not want anyone looking too

closely at her case. She had her kids to protect. Especially Wendy. It was bad enough her own father had raped her but to have that out in public was something Susan Dalston would never allow. The girl would have to live with that stigma all her life and her mother would rather do time than have anything like that out in the open.

Some things in life were best left.

'Will you do me up today, Matty, make me a bit presentable for me kids?'

'Of course I will, Susan. I know you laugh at me but, be honest – don't you feel better when you know you look better?'

Susan ran her hands through her scruffy hair and grinned.

'Only if you make me look as gorgeous as you usually do. My little Barry told me I looked really pretty last time I saw him. Said I looked like a Queen – and judging by his social worker, he probably meant Queen as in a bit Stoke on Trent, if you see me point?'

Matty laughed.

'You're incorrigible.'

'Well, if you say so. It sounds nice, whatever it is.'

'Go and have a shower and I'll sort you out, though why I bother I don't know. You'll pull apart all my hard work once the visit's over.'

Susan batted her eyelashes. 'That's because that big lezzie screw keeps talking to me, no other reason.'

She walked from the cell, happily saying 'Good morning' and 'Hi' to everyone on her way down to the showers. Nothing and no one could bring her down from the cloud where she was floating. Her kids were coming and Susan Dalston was the happiest woman in England.

Little Barry ran straight into her arms. He had brought a picture of her, dressed in dungarees, the prison uniform, and with a big smiling face. All his sisters were around her and the sun was a big yellow ball in the sky. His dad was floating up to heaven as usual, and for once this didn't hurt Susan inside. Her son was nine and was obviously sorting it out in his mind as best he could.

She'd been a year on remand and a year away. It was a long time for a mother, and even longer for her children. But kids were resilient and Barry had adjusted better than any of them.

Rosie sat on the social worker's lap and watched her mother warily. The controlled environment made it difficult for any of them to act naturally. Wendy picked her up and, sitting beside her mother, chatted away to the little girl to put her at her ease.

Susan looked at Wendy's profile, so like her father's and yet like her own too, and wondered how in heaven they had produced four such beautiful children. Though Barry had been handsome on the outside, inside he had been rotten to the core. She just prayed that none of her children had inherited that from him.

'Granny Kate sends her love but she can't take the journey, Mum.'

Susan nodded and laughed as Alana chased little Barry around. It broke the ice somehow.

'Is she any better?'

Wendy shook her head. Her thick auburn hair waved across her face with the action.

'Her heart's not good, Mum. She can barely get about now, bless her.'

After Barry's death Kate had had a massive heart attack. Susan felt responsible for it, even though her mother-in-law had still tried for custody of the children and harboured no grudge.

She was the only one who had openly taken Susan's side, for all the good that did.

Susan worried about Kate, as she worried about Ivy.

For all her faults, Ivy had tried to stand by her granddaughter, but June and Joey had made any real contact impossible. It was as if Ivy, taking her part, would make them look bad in the eyes of the world. Make it seem that they'd been in the wrong.

Though people were disgusted with Joey and June, they knew better than to say so. Consequently, Ivy never discussed Susan, a very hard thing for her to do. She depended on Doreen instead, for information and message giving.

Doreen had lied to the police the night of the murder, telling them that Wendy had not been home. It was the story they had all told to keep the girl's experiences from the police. Susan was eternally grateful to her and to Kate for the lies they had told to protect her daughter.

Even the smaller children swore she was not there and now they actually believed it.

Doreen wrote weekly and always tried to keep Susan in a good frame of mind, though she never visited. She went to see Kate though, to make sure the older woman was well and being cared for. Kate was too ill even to go to court but they'd kept in contact by letter and this was a comfort to Susan. She'd often wondered how much her mother-in-law had sussed out for herself about the night in question but it was something they'd never discussed and she had a feeling they never would.

She stroked Rosie's fat little leg and the child gazed at her and smiled, making Susan's heart lift.

'Roselle sends her best, says she's written to you. That bloke Colin seems nice, Mum. I wish you'd listen to him. Get yourself out of here.'

Susan waved her hand in dismissal.

'We've been through all this, love, and there's no way I am going to do anything now. It's over, okay? Leave it like that. I'm all right and what happened that night is better forgotten. Are you listening to me?'

Wendy nodded sadly.

'I feel responsible for you being here, Mum. The kids need you . . .'

Susan cut her off.

'The kids are all right and they can't keep me here for ever. Now stop all this worrying. I'm the one who should be doing that and I look okay to you, don't I?'

Wendy didn't answer her. Instead she put Rosie on the floor and got up and looked around the room. Susan watched her. She worried about her more than any of them. Wendy looked very thin, even with her well-developed breasts. She also looked haunted at times.

Her face would go blank and Susan knew she must be thinking about what had happened, beating herself up over it all over again.

No matter how many times she told her daughter that nothing mattered, it was over, she knew Wendy would never believe it.

Not until it was really over and Susan was back home in the bosom of her family again.

Then Rosie put her arms up to Susan. Her rosy-cheeked face had a grin on it like the Cheshire Cat's. Picking her up and holding her tight against her chest, Susan convinced herself once more that everything was going to be okay. As she listened to Alana and little Barry telling them about the home they were living in in Essex, she felt some of the tightness around her heart relax.

They were good kids, they would cope.

She had to believe that.

But Wendy's face haunted her even after she had kissed them all goodbye. And even the fact that Rosie had cried when she'd had to go, which showed what a good time she had had, couldn't lift the feeling in Susan's breast that she was sacrificing all her kids for the sake of one.

But what else could she do?

'I hate the nights here more than anything, don't you, Sue?'

Susan lay on her bunk in the twilight and sighed her agreement.

'It can't last for ever, that's what I tell myself. That's what you have to tell yourself, too, Matty. Otherwise we'd all go mad. I mean, look at that Agnes, she's staring at a twelve stretch. Now that is a lump and a half by anyone's standards. She'll end up in Durham like I did and that'll be a culture shock for her, I can tell you.'

Her cell mate was quiet, which was unusual for her.

'Come on, Matty. Spill the beans, girl. What's rattled your cage then?'

'I just hate it in here, night after night. What a waste of a life! When you look around you at the Carolines, the child killers and abusers, and you think of yourself it makes you angry, doesn't it? I mean, we did something bad, I know, but it was a last resort.

'My husband *enjoyed* hurting me. He laughed as he hit or humiliated me. He pushed me as far as human endurance could go, and even though I got a good result in some respects, I still feel I got too long.'

Susan sat up and reached for her tobacco tin.

'You got four years, girl. That ain't bad for murder or manslaughter.'

Matty slipped from her top bunk and sat on the floor beside her.

'It was still too long for him. He wasn't worth four years, you see. He deserved what he got.'

Her voice was hard now.

'Christ, but I hated him!'

Susan rolled a match-thin cigarette and lit it in seconds.

'That's the funny thing, see, I never hated Barry. Not permanently like. I hated him at times if you can understand that.'

Matty opened up a small box stowed beneath the bottom bunk.

'Fancy a drink, Sue?' She held up an unopened bottle of vodka. 'I've got some lemonade as well. It always amazes me that everyone's so shocked by us getting drink in here. After all there's only one way it can come in and that's via a PO. Lucky they're so amenable really. Some of them, I mean.'

Susan was excited.

'I'll have some, mate. Thanks.'

They both had a large vodka in their mug with a touch of lemonade. Susan drank a draught of hers and smacked her lips appreciatively.

'Just what the doctor ordered, I'd say.'

Matty laughed.

'You're a nut, do you know that?'

'So I've been told on many occasions, especially by me dear dead husband.'

She held up her mug and laughed. 'To dead husbands – the only time they ever give you a bit of peace.'

Even Matty laughed at that.

'Do you know what I'd like now? I'd like me and you to be in my little house, with my kids and my records. Then we could have a few drinks, a few laughs, and afterwards you could go home to your place and in the morning my kids would all be waiting for me to cook them a bit of breakfast. Then I'd take them to school and have a laugh with me neighbours and come home and clear up. That's all I would want from life. I don't want to win the pools or marry a film star. Just that would do me.'

Matty heard the catch in her voice, felt the loneliness of this woman, and was sorry for her.

'It will happen one day.'

'But by then my kids will be a lot older and they won't need me as much, will they? By then they'll all be more or less self-sufficient. Even Rosie because she'll have been in care and in care means looking after yourself from an early age. You only have to listen to the girls in here. Most of them have been dragged through the system at some time.'

Matty refilled their mugs and they drank in silence for a while, both deep in their own thoughts.

'What exactly is happening with your appeal, Sue? You never discuss it like everyone else.'

She rolled herself another cigarette and snorted.

'Nothing to discuss really. I won't get it, but at least I'm nearer me kids for a while anyway.'

'But surely, if he was a wife beater and everything else, you can use that? This is 1985, Sue. Not the Dark Ages. Women are protected from violence now.'

'Are they really?' Susan's voice was sarcastic. 'Lot of help me and you got. Lot of protection there, eh? I had Old Bill round so many times I was on their Christmas party list. But they never actually *did* anything. Oh, they'd take him for the night, do me a favour like. Let him out the next day, good and sober, but then Barry didn't need a drink to be a bastard. He needed nothing but his own sick mind. I mean, if everything is so different, what are we doing in here? A man was let off last week for killing his nagging wife, right? The judge said her complaining must have driven him mad. Where's the difference? He got nagged and off on time served. We got the shit kicked out of us and still have to pay the price for the life we took. No matter how scummy that life was. My Barry was a piece of shit, but that didn't matter to the judge.'

Matty was quiet for a few moments.

'But you hardly helped yourself, did you? I mean, be fair. Your statement was like a confession by a serial killer. "I would do it again," you said. That's not what the court wants to hear. The laws of this country are made by men, for men. You have to play the system, be the little woman. Be the person needing protection. You came across as a Ma Baker figure who was up for a fight.'

Susan could hear the annoyance in Matty's voice and said seriously, 'Like you did, you mean?'

Matty, half drunk now, laughed.

'Exactly. You've hit the nail right on the head. That's why I appealed my sentence immediately. My brief Geraldine has all the women's groups behind her – everyone. I'll be out soon and then I'll be a feminist heroine.' She poked a finger in Susan's face. 'I'm writing a book about it, and I'm going to cash in on it. You see, I'm middle-class. I'm pretty, I'm educated. The courts hate to put educated people away. Because it's all class, really.

'But in my world, I committed a cardinal sin. I not only killed a man, I killed a man who was a barrister. Who was part of the system no matter what he did. But I'll fight them all and I'll win eventually.'

Susan was impressed by her acumen but unsure about the other woman's attitude.

'You're pissed.'

Matty laughed again, a loud raucous laugh that reverberated around the wing and caused a PO to bang on the door.

'Keep it down in there, you two.'

Susan was giggling along with her now, like two schoolgirls. Matty poured them more large drinks.

'I killed him, all right. But the funny thing was, you see, he wasn't expecting it.' She laughed again. 'You should have seen his face! Talk about shocked. He wasn't expecting it at all.'

'Well, I shouldn't think he was. In fairness no one expects to be stabbed through the heart, do they? I mean, it's just not done in polite society.'

They both started to laugh again. This time the banging on the cell door was louder as the night PO shrieked: 'Keep it down in there, I said.'

'I bet the lesbians get that shouted at them all the time, don't you, girl?'

Matty had to push the corner of Susan's blanket into her mouth to stop her laughter from bursting out again.

'Come on, pour the drink and let's get really sloshed.' Susan was having trouble talking already but the prospect of getting slaughtered looked good to her and she was determined to enjoy it.

'Well, no getting maudlin then, like Rhianna does.'

Susan shook her head. 'Don't worry, I won't.'

Matty moved her head nearer to explain what she was feeling.

'I tried it, you know. The lesbian thing. When I was on remand. But it wasn't for me. I like men. Well, actually, what I mean is, I prefer men if I'm going to do it at all.'

Susan grinned.

'I can fucking take it or leave it, girl. Barry never did it for me in all those years. Even when I really loved him, at first like, he still never did it for me. Now that bloke from Mad Max, the Australian . . . What's his name?'

'Mel Gibson.'

'That's it, Mel Gibson. Now him I could give a right seeing to. And I mean a seeing to and all. The full bifta. Whatever he wanted, he could have.' She looked down at herself and smiled wryly. 'Mind you, there ain't much here anyone would want, is there?'

'Have you never, ever enjoyed sex? Not even with yourself?'

Susan was shocked at the thought and told her so.

'Steady on, girl! I'm all for plain talking but that's taking it a bit far, to my mind.'

Matty was really enjoying herself now. She loved shocking other people and knew that talk of masturbation was as shocking as it could get for Susan Dalston.

'You mean, you've never had a wank? A frig?' She frowned then. 'And what's the other expression the girls in here use?'

Susan pulled herself upright against the bunk.

'I don't know, but one thing I do know is you're drunk. Drunk and disgusting at the same time.'

Matty laughed again.

'You make me die! Like all the others in here, all swearing and hard talk and yet something as normal as masturbation and you go all shy and retiring. One of the most natural things in the world. The best natural sedative there is. Yet you lot, who talk freely about periods and shagging, as you call it, find it embarrassing.'

Susan could hear the edge creeping into the other woman's voice and was quiet. She knew how people were after a drink. She should do after what she grew up with.

'All right, Matty, calm down. Keep your bleeding hair on. I don't talk about that or periods, I never have. It's how I was brought up, I suppose.'

She tried to make a joke of it. Matty wasn't having any of it.

'People like you aren't brought up or reared, you're dragged up. Dragged up to be just like your parents and theirs before them. It's how things are. It's called socialisation.'

Susan sipped at her drink and sighed.

'Well, whatever it's called, it's crap.'

Matty nodded in agreement.

'It's all crap, don't you see, Sue? That's what's so terribly funny.'

Susan laughed with her though she didn't really think it was funny. Indeed she had no idea what the joke was supposed to be. But she didn't let on. She believed everyone was entitled to let off steam now and again, and obviously Matty had a bit more steam than everyone else.

It always made Susan smile when the girls in for shoplifting or kiteing, using a stolen chequebook and banker's card, bemoaned their sentences. Six months and they acted like they were facing death row. They forgot that she and a few others were looking at 'real' time. In real prisons.

Most would leave here for an open nick, get a job on the farm or in the garden, and smoke and booze their few months away. Whereas she would be moved once more to a secure unit and have to acclimatise herself all over again.

'Go on, girl, have a good laugh, does you the world of good.'

Matty was laughing, belly laughing once more.

'All your little homilies . . . You really don't know, Susan, do you? *You really don't know.*'

She cracked up again but this time there was no humour in it. It was strained, forced laughter that was hollow-sounding and sad.

Susan filled their mugs again and they drank in silence for a while.

She knew Matty was away somewhere in her head, like she was, probably going over old ground that had been raked and sifted so many times it would be bald if it was real. That ground was always the same for Susan. She guessed it was for Matty too.

All ifs and buts. If only this had happened differently, if only that had happened before, ad infinitum.

Susan knew it all herself, she had been there so many times, but one thing she had learned: it changed nothing, absolutely nothing.

Barry would still be dead, the kids would still be without her, and nothing on the surface was changed no matter how much you *wished* it could be different.

'When I killed him, Susan, I knew I was going to do it all along. I'd known for ages what I was going to do.'

Matty stared into Susan's face. In the half light she looked grotesque.

'But *he* didn't know. Victor didn't know. I mean, how could he know? I couldn't *tell* him, could I? Spoil the surprise.'

She was laughing again. Quietly this time, like a child caught out with a box of matches.

'But I did it. I told myself I would and I did. That's called positive thinking. I remember reading about it in *Cosmopolitan*. Thositive pinking.'

Susan laughed with Matty as she tried desperately to say the two words.

'I am pissed, as you would say.'

Susan took the mug from her and helped her up on her own bunk. Then she covered her with a blanket.

'You have a little nap, mate. I'll put all this away. You get some sleep.'

She tidied away, leaving no evidence for the morning screws. As she opened the box under her bunk she saw a half bottle of Scotch and a lump of dope. Placing the vodka in with it, she slid it out of sight.

Then, pouring the two mugs of drink into one, she drained it down. Enjoying the feel of the alcohol. The warmth of it inside her belly.

'That hit the spot, girl, I can tell you.'

Matty turned her head and looked down at her.

'I like you, Sue, you're all right.'

Susan grabbed at her hand and squeezed it tightly.

'You're not too bad yourself, girl. Now get some Sooty and Sweep. You'll feel like a dog's turd in the morning.'

Matty laughed again, a girlish sound.

'Your kids are beautiful, Susan. Very beautiful. Even the screws admire their photos. I've seen them looking at them.'

She tried to nod to reinforce her words and Susan smiled to herself.

'I aborted two babies by Victor. I did, Susan. Isn't that terrible?'

Susan stood by the bunk and held Matty's hand again, pulling it into her chest as if she was one of the kids, sad and troubled by a little worry.

'My old man kicked a few out of me, girl. I know how you feel, love. Really I do.'

Matty was trying to focus in the darkness.

'Oh, it wasn't Victor, Susan, he wanted them. It was me. *I* didn't want any kids. Not by him anyway. I'm not the maternal type, I'm afraid. He cried after each abortion because I didn't tell him till after I'd had the op. Then it was too late, he couldn't do anything, could he? But Victor was never very good at doing anything really. That was the trouble, he irritated me. An educated, smart man yet he was as silly as a bag of marbles where women were concerned.'

Susan didn't know what to say. So she just held Matty's hand and tried to comfort her.

'Don't beat yourself up over it, mate. We all do things we regret.'

Now Matty's voice was serious.

'Oh, I don't regret it at all. Any of it, Sue. What is there to regret really? I rid the world of an ineffectual prick called Victor Enderby.'

'A violent ineffectual prick called Victor Enderby, you mean?'

Matty shook her head in the darkness.

'He wasn't violent, Sue. Give me a break! He was the quietest, kindest man in the world, was Victor. That was his downfall. I thought I could handle him and all he was but I couldn't, you see. In the end he drove me mad. Bored me rigid and made me hate him. I had to get rid of him. You do see that, don't you?'

Susan didn't answer her. Instead she pulled the blankets up around Matty's neck and tucked her in.

'Go to sleep, you'll have a head like a balloon in the morning.'

But Matty was gone, gone to another place entirely and this time Susan didn't envy her. In fact she decided that she wouldn't want to be Matty Enderby for all the money in the world. She was also wondering what the hell she was going to say to her the next day.

She could only hope that Matty would forget this conversation and never refer to it again. For herself, she was going to put out of her mind all that she had heard. Some things in life were best left inside a person's head. Susan had believed this for a long time and Matty had made her more aware than ever just how dangerous talking could be if you had something to hide.

And Matty certainly had something to hide.

Wendy awoke with the birds as usual. She lay in bed in the Charlton Home for Children, Great Wakering, Essex, and looked around her. The room was almost sterile. White walls and white Formica furniture.

Sitting up, she opened the window by her bed and lit a Benson and Hedges. Puffing on it deeply, she drew the tobacco into her lungs. If her mother knew she smoked she would freak out. But her mother wasn't here, was she?

Wendy scratched idly at her leg and sighed.

If Mr Potter was on night duty he would pop his head around

the door at any minute then stroll in and try to cop a feel. Well, she was ready for him this morning. She had a small blade hidden underneath her pillow.

She wouldn't hurt him with it, just threaten him.

As she heard the handle turn she threw the cigarette from the window and stared at the door, heart beating like a drum. Willing it to stay shut.

But Mr Alfred Potter was already on his way in.

He was old, as far as Wendy was concerned, being in his forties with blond wispy hair and bad teeth. A fact that obviously didn't bother him as he seemed to smile all the time.

Especially at the girls. The bigger girls.

'Up bright and early then, are we?'

Wendy didn't answer him as he walked slowly towards the bed.

'Been smoking, have we?' He was still smiling.

As his hand came out to touch her hair as usual she still didn't speak, but as it strayed towards her breast she brought the small blade out from under her pillow. Jumping from the bed, she held it in front of her.

'Come on then, Mr Potter, go for it!'

She hissed the words and was pleased to see his face blanch.

'You ever touch me again and I'll cut your throat! I'm more like me mother than people think, see. I'm as bad as her, you hear what I'm saying? I don't take any shit from anyone, right?'

Mr Potter was scared, really scared, and it showed on his face. Without a word he walked from the room and Wendy felt herself relax.

Forced herself to relax.

She had won! She could not believe he had rolled over so quickly. But he had walked out and left her there without a word.

She hugged herself with glee. She had taken the law into her own hands and she had won, as she'd known she must. No more waking at an unearthly hour, lying in bed wondering if he was going to come in, with his wandering hands and his bad breath.

She had taken control and fronted him up. She had won the battle and therefore the war.

She lit another cigarette to celebrate.

Then the door burst open and there stood Mrs Reading and Mr Potter and two other care assistants.

'She has a knife on her. She threatened me with it.'

Mr Potter, respected social worker and youth leader, knew exactly what he was doing. The blade was where he'd said and no one listened to the terrified girl's explanation as he'd known they wouldn't. He smiled sadly at Wendy as the police were called and smiled even more at her shock and horror.

Wendy realised she had won nothing. And Mrs Reading's next words stayed with her all her life.

'Blood will out, Mr Potter. I've seen it time and time again. Blood will out.'

Chapter Twenty-Three

Roselle could not believe what she was hearing about Wendy. It was against everything she knew about the girl, and she decided straight away that there had to be something more going on that no one knew about for the girl to threaten one of her social workers with a blade.

Roselle suppressed a smile. If they could see some of the weapons she had taken off young girls in her club before now. She had even confiscated a hand gun once from a little Brummie sort called Angelina. She had looked like an angel and talked like a navvy. And she had had every intention of using that gun.

But Angelina had been a hard-nosed little bitch who knew more about life than most scientists could ever guess at. Then, so did Wendy in many respects. Roselle wondered how poor Sue would react to the news. Locked up as she was, there was precious little she could do to make any real difference.

As she thought of her friend Roselle felt the familiar sickness in her belly. She was locked up for nothing really, it should have been Barry who had been taken away from his kids. Because he wouldn't have cared.

Ivan let himself into the flat then and Roselle smiled as he walked into the lounge.

'You're up early, Roselle. I was just coming in to drop off a few things for Joe. He's due home later today, isn't he?'

She smiled.

'Yes, he is, and you can come in and out of here any time, you know that.'

In days gone by he would find a locked door and know that

meant she had company. It had been many, many months since he had found a locked door now and that worried him.

'You're a young woman, you deserve a bit of fun. Don't let Barry's children take over your life. He was scum. By God, I wish I'd never clapped eyes on him. I knew he'd be trouble. But not as much trouble as he eventually was, I can tell you.'

'I'll get you a coffee. I could do with one myself.'

As she walked out into the kitchen, her pert bottom swaying as she walked, Ivan wished he could still find it in him to raise an erection. But those days were long gone and he had to accept that. He couldn't raise more than a smile these days and that hurt. Now he made money and waited for death, taking his enjoyment from eating, drinking and socialising.

For a while Roselle had given him back his youth. She had also given him a son, a fine handsome boy with good looks and a good brain. But he worried about her. She had taken on this girl as if she was family when of course she wasn't and never could be.

As Roselle walked back to him with the coffee he smiled at her. She saw the watery eyes of an old man and it saddened her. Ivan was really ageing lately and she wondered what the hell she would do without him.

As she leaned forward he saw a little flash of creamy flesh and dark brown nipple. He shrugged.

'These days, Roselle, I can look and that's all. A terrible thing for a man.'

She stroked his face tenderly.

'Only if the man never enjoyed anything in his life. You have your memories and you have me and Joseph. What more could you want from life?'

'Put like that, my dear, it sounds almost interesting. Now what's the latest on the girl?'

Part of Ivan's charm was the way he always hit the nail on the head. He knew she was worried and that it could only be for one reason.

'Apparently, Wendy threatened one of her social workers with a blade. They found it where he said it would be and brought in the police. But she must have had a reason. She must have. I know that girl and she's not like that, Ivan. If she had a blade it was to protect herself from someone or something.'

He nodded.

'Maybe someone there was giving her a hard time. In those environments it's not unheard of. Can you get to see her?'

Roselle nodded.

'The police were called in but the man, a Mr Alfred Potter, refused to bring charges against her. Which I think is good of him really. But then social workers are all bleeding hearts, aren't they?

'I mean, you read about these kids all the time in the papers. But it's only when you know one personally that your opinion changes.'

Ivan grinned.

'Those homes give us our best hostesses, don't forget that. They get a good education in those places. Not the education people think they're getting either!'

Roselle didn't laugh but she saw the truth of his statement. Many of the girls she had worked with over the years had been in care, a term she had found increasingly strange considering what happened to most of them while allegedly being cared for.

'I wonder if there's any way we could find out about this Mr Potter?'

Ivan shook his wizened old head and grinned again.

'I'll find out about him. You relax and get yourself ready for the day. I still have a few contacts here and there, especially in the police force. I'll see what I can dig up.'

'It's so strange that she threatened him, you know? Why would Wendy threaten anyone?'

Ivan didn't answer because he knew Roselle was already thinking along the same lines as he was.

Wendy was tired, tired and upset.

In the isolation room, as it was called, she was expected to reflect on what she had done. Remember that Mr Potter had been *good* to her, and ask herself why she had acted as she had.

She had toyed with the idea of telling them why but knew from the other girls that accusing anyone of sexual misconduct was a complete and utter waste of time.

The fact that they were young girls and boys in care meant they were already assumed to be sexually aware and active. Most of them were, which was sad but true. But most of them had learned what they knew from people like Mr Potter.

He was a predator. He tried to make them his confidantes and friends and then the real ugliness started. An arm around a shoulder that just brushed a breast. The game playing and pretend fighting which enabled him to grab and drag at their bodies, pretending it was all innocent fun.

Oh, she knew all these things, knew them off by heart. The girls talked about it among themselves, joked about it even. But it wasn't funny because when it went too far there was no one to listen and definitely no one to protect you.

Well, Wendy had protected herself and she was glad she had. It wasn't the first time and she had a feeling it wouldn't be the last.

The door opened and her heart jumped into her throat. She saw Miss Beacham with a tray of tea and sandwiches. The young woman smiled at her and Wendy smiled tremulously back. Never in her life had she been so glad to see anyone.

'I thought I'd bring you a little lunch. See how you were faring.'

Miss Beacham had an ugly face, a thin body and a beautiful speaking voice. Wendy could listen to her for hours.

'Thank you, miss.'

She took the proffered tray and set it on the windowsill, there being no furniture of any kind in the room except a small bunk.

'Can I get you anything?'

Wendy nodded.

'A cigarette wouldn't go amiss.'

Miss Beacham pulled one of her faces. She had facial expressions that said more than all the words in the English dictionary.

'I'll see what I can do, but no promises mind.'

As anti-smoking as she was, she knew the value of a familiar thing in this grim environment. Everyone had something they did to relieve stress. For most of the kids in her care it was a cigarette, even the youngest ones of seven and eight. It galled her, but she understood it.

That was her secret with the kids she cared for: she tried to understand them. And to help them. And the kids responded to this, because unlike her peers she didn't try to force her opinions on them. She simply expressed them and left them to make what they could of them.

'How's Mr Potter?'

Miss Beacham made one of her lightning changes of expression and shrugged.

'Well, by all accounts. Though obviously in shock.'

The words were said flippantly and without real feeling. She did not like Mr Potter and he did not like her. She knew it was because she was unattractive. He, like most men, only saw any value in women who were attractive.

'What will happen to me?'

She heard the loneliness and fear in Wendy's words and stifled an urge to take her in her arms and comfort her.

'A few days in here then pretend you've learned your lesson and go back to the usual. Oh, and Mr Potter has been changed on to days for some reason, so that's something to look forward to, eh?'

Wendy smiled then, a big smile. Miss Beacham was telling her she knew the score, understood. That meant more to the girl than anything. She had an ally at last, a real ally.

'Now eat that lot and keep your strength up. You'll need it, my dear.'

Wendy nodded, happier now she knew what was to happen to her.

'I'm on the sleepover tonight so I might be able to sneak in a couple of Benson's. I'll see, okay?'

Wendy nodded once more and when the woman left hugged herself in delight.

At least she had one worry out of the way. Potter was not doing any more sleepovers. She could relax at last.

* * *

Susan was tired but exhilarated. She had just had her first session in the gym and had been surprised to find she enjoyed it. In her pocket was a letter and it had made her so happy she had to keep touching it, just to remind herself it was really there.

Going back to her cell, she sat on the bunk and got out the two sheets of paper to read it again.

She was amazed that Peter White could find it in his heart to drop her a line. The letter had been posted two months previously. It had her name on the envelope and that was all. No prison number. He had just posted it to her care of HMP Holloway. It had been sent on to Durham and now it was back in her hand and making her very happy.

It was just a friendly note really, asking how she was, how the kids were, and telling her that he was off on the ACT 2 boat to Australia. He liked the meat boats, he said. Especially the new ones. He described it all to her then ended with his address at sea.

He wanted her to write back to him, he said. They both relied on letters to keep them abreast of things in the outside world so they should write to one another and catch up as often as they could.

Susan hugged the letter to her breast and sighed. It would be wonderful to write to him, hear his news, hear about the countries he visited. The people he met. She could maybe see the world through his eyes.

He had put a kiss underneath his name and that had pleased her too. She would write to him after lunch. Tell him the little bit about herself she could and then ask some good questions so he would have something to focus on in his reply.

PO Billings came in and smiled at her.

'Your brief's here, Dalston. Get yourself together, you're to see him now.'

Susan was startled.

'What's he want?'

The woman shrugged.

'You tell me, mate. Now get your arse in gear, he's already at visit.'

Susan tidied herself up as best she could and followed the

woman from the cell. She was scared now, frightened. She knew this wasn't a regular visit and she was afraid that something had happened to one of the kids. Her mind was racing as she thought of every bad scenario she could think. Rosie was ill to the point of death. Barry was lying somewhere with broken bones. The list was endless. Even though she knew she was torturing herself her mind would not stop working overtime.

Every door seemed to take ages to unlock, and everyone seemed to be hindering her progress. When she finally walked into the visiting room, Susan was sweating all over again. Colin was standing by the window, his slim frame outlined by the sunshine outside.

'What's the matter, is it one of the kids?'

He could hear the anxiety in her voice at once.

'It's Wendy. Now before you lose it, she's okay. Nothing physically wrong with her at all.'

Susan felt her whole body sag. Sitting in the chair by the table, she sighed heavily.

'What's happened then?' Her face was so white she looked like a corpse. Even her lips seemed drained of colour.

'She attacked her social worker with a small blade.' Colin held up his hand to keep her quiet. 'Before you start, hear me out, Susan. She's well, she's not being nicked, the social worker won't press charges. She is being punished at the home. It's no big deal. They cope with this sort of thing all the time there and they understand it. She's more worried about you finding out which is only natural.'

Susan was staring at him as if he had just sprouted a long red beard and pixie ears.

'She what! My Wendy did what?'

She sounded so incredulous, looked so shocked, that Colin felt an urge to laugh at her.

'Look, really, Susan, it sounds much worse than it is. Believe me.'

She was shaking her head in consternation.

'What did he do to her then? Why did she threaten him?'

Colin shrugged.

'I don't know.'

'What do you mean, you don't know? What, she just got a blade and decided to threaten one of the social workers, is that what you're asking me to believe? That my Wendy just flipped out, is that what you're saying?'

She was standing up now. She looked frightening. The PO on duty walked to her and lowered her back into her chair. Susan shrugged her off as if she was an annoying fly or mosquito.

'Calm down, Dalston.'

'Calm down! You're having a tin bath, you are. How can I calm down? My baby's in trouble and I can't even talk to her. Is she in a state? Is she okay? What?'

Colin closed his eyes in annoyance. This woman was causing him more trouble than anyone in his life before. She would not help herself at all. In fact it even seemed as if she didn't want to get out. Wanted to stay locked up. On top of all that, she expected him to take care of everything as if he was a blood relative, which thankfully he was not.

'Listen, Susan, will you just calm down?'

The PO hovered nearby. Susan could smell her deodorant, a thick cloying smell that made her stomach revolt.

'I can't take much more. I take oath, I can't take much more of this.'

Colin went to her and laid a hand gently on her shoulder.

'I understand, Susan, really I do. Why won't you help yourself now? You could be home with your children sooner than you expect.'

She pulled away from him, eyes downcast.

'You don't understand, Colin.'

He shrugged. 'I certainly don't, Susan. You're right there. I don't understand you at all.'

She was quiet for a few moments. She could hear the faint sound of talking and laughter coming from outside the window. A gentle breeze was lifting the curtains as it snaked through the outside bars. Susan stared at it and knew she was trapped. Completely trapped.

'So how's everything now? Is she really okay?'

He nodded. But he was angry at her reluctance to help herself and her children. It wasn't natural, not natural at all. It was obvious how much she loved those kids, so why wouldn't she help herself get out?

Matty was two rooms down from Susan, sipping coffee and talking of her appeal as if it was a foregone conclusion.

Which, so far as she was concerned, it was.

Her barrister, Geraldine O'Hara, QC, sat opposite her.

Geraldine was stunning. At thirty-nine years old she had the height and bone structure of a model. Her hair was a thick vibrant red, real auburn with golden highlights. She had mischievous green eyes and full lips. She dressed in power suits, black, tight-skirted and with large shoulder pads, and always had startlingly red lips and nails. She was every inch the eighties woman. Sexy, serious and achieving.

She was also a well-known feminist and media celebrity. Nicknamed 'The Man Hater' by colleagues, she was always chasing women's rights cases and fighting what seemed to her friends to be lost causes.

She had no husband, no boyfriend, no lover.

Not because no one wanted her. Geraldine was deluged with offers from men for whatever she desired, from dinner to bed.

She didn't want to know. She was only interested in work, work and more work. Men, she claimed, took your mind off the real things in life, the important things. No one was ever sure if she actually meant that or whether it was one of her jokes. She never bothered to explain.

Such was the personality of Geraldine O'Hara. But even with her feminist views and dogma she was finding it very hard to like the woman in front of her. Not that she would ever allow that to cloud her judgement.

From day one Matilda Enderby had given her a bad feeling. Even shaking hands with her seemed to make Geraldine's flesh creep. She avoided touching Matty as much as she could.

Matty was talking now and Geraldine forced her mind back to what she was saying.

'Victor was a pervert in many ways, you know. He was up for really kinky sex. Whips, blue films . . . He was really into pain.'

'Inflicting it or receiving it?' Geraldine's voice was clipped.

Matty stared at a point over her head and sighed. Her pretty face was even prettier in repose. Finally, after what seemed an age, she answered.

'Well, both really. But mainly inflicting it.'

Geraldine stared at the woman before her and half smiled.

'There was nothing found at the house or his office. Nothing pertaining to his sexual habits anyway. I intend to visit the prostitute he used.' She looked at her legal pad. 'A Mariah Brewster. See what she has to say this time round. I understand she wasn't very forthcoming at the last trial?'

Matty's face was the picture of an outraged wife's.

'I hated it when I found out about her, I really did. Can you imagine how that made me feel, knowing he was paying a stranger for sex?'

Geraldine shrugged.

'Awful as it must have been, if things were that bad surely you must also have been relieved?'

Matty nodded.

'Of course there was that.'

Geraldine sipped at her own coffee and lit a cigarette. Taking a deep pull on it, she smiled.

'You look well. You're bearing up okay?'

Matty smiled, one of her big sunny smiles that made her look very young and very vulnerable.

'I have to, don't I? I just keep telling myself it will soon be over and then I can get on with my life again.'

'Can you think of anywhere he might have kept his sex toys, whips, etc? Only your flat and his offices, even his garage, were squeaky clean. Unless we can come up with something we're not going to be able to use that one. There are no obvious marks on you, are there, that we can have looked at?'

Matty shook her head hard, her thick hair curling around her face.

'I'm afraid not. I am a good healer.'

'No scars at all?'

'You know there aren't. But surely the fact he used prostitutes says it all?'

Geraldine stood up and stretched. Her black wool suit was immaculate. Not even a stray hair ruined its appearance.

'Not necessarily. I mean, according to this Brewster woman he was a, quote, nice man.'

Before Matty could answer they heard an almighty crash coming from one of the other rooms. A woman's voice was screaming out obscenities at full blast, and Matty jumped from her seat.

'That sounds like my cellie, Susan Dalston.'

Geraldine was aghast. 'You're celled up with Susan Dalston, the hammer woman?'

Matty nodded as she walked to the door.

The duty PO popped her head around and smiled ruefully.

'I'll have to lock you in while I remove a prisoner. Sorry about this.'

'You rotten, rotten bastards! Rosie . . . I want my Rosie.'

Susan's voice was thick with tears. Inside the room they could hear her being restrained, her language telling them exactly what she thought of the officers concerned.

'I'll kill you, Colin, you fucking wanker!'

Geraldine instinctively put her hands up to her face.

'What on earth is going on?'

Matty shrugged and stared at the doorway as if she was going to be able to see through it at any moment.

'I don't know, Geraldine, I really don't know.'

Colin was in a state of pure shock. As he saw Susan being dragged bodily to the floor by three burly POs, he touched his neck and was surprised to find no blood. Although he could feel the raised welts of the scratches she had given him.

'Rosie!' It was a scream, a constant repetitive scream.

They were dragging her bodily from the room and out into the hallway. Someone had raised the alarm and Susan's anguished cries were drowned out by the screaming bells that told all the

POs there was a major incident. One was on her radio, calling for a doctor to sedate a prisoner.

Colin felt overwhelmed with guilt and remorse. He had had to talk to her and fast. What he hadn't banked on was how the news was going to affect her. He had expected her to be upset but not to try and throttle him with her bare hands. It had been a learning curve if nothing else.

Susan was disappearing under even more POs as they tried to restrain her. They dragged up the sweatshirt she was wearing and he could see her old bra and heavy breasts.

All the time she was shouting and screaming her daughter's name.

Finally, after what seemed an age, she was sedated by the doctor and even as she fought the effects of the Librium, was gradually calming down. Her one word was incoherent now as she battled to keep her eyes open.

Mercifully, someone had shut off the alarm. The quiet was as shocking as the noise had been.

The duty PO, Miss Dobbin, looked at Colin and said sarcastically, 'Done your good deed for the day, have you?'

She looked at the others.

'He only calmly told Dalston her youngest child was about to be put up for adoption by the foster parents.'

She shook her close-cropped head in disbelief.

'Have you any idea how she must have felt, mate?'

The other women all looked at him and he felt as if he was some kind of low-life slime. But it had not been like that, he had tried to break it to her gently! He opened his mouth to speak and was cut off immediately.

'Blow it out your arse! We'd better get this one to the Muppet wing quick smart. Chances are she'll be coming round soon and then we'll have it all over again.'

When Susan was gone, they unlocked the other doors and all the briefs on legal visits were allowed to leave. Colin knew they must have heard everything that had been said and fiddled with his briefcase as he tried to delay his departure.

Geraldine saw him. Intrigued, she hung back by the door

talking to Matty before she was taken to her cell. When he walked out of the adjacent room she was waiting for him. He recognised her at once. Geraldine O'Hara was not someone who needed to introduce herself.

'Are you okay?' she asked.

He nodded sadly.

'Your neck looks sore and she's ripped the neck of your jumper.'

'That's the least of my problems at the moment.'

Colin looked into a pair of green eyes that made him stop dead in his tracks. He hastily tried to tidy himself up, knowing how scruffy he looked even when he tried to be well turned out. It was a knack he had had since a little boy. It had driven his mother and every serious girlfriend since mad.

'Come on, I'll get you a cuppa, make you feel better, eh?'

In the mess, where Geraldine was well known, he received an education. She smiled and talked to everyone, and made a point of asking after children, husbands and families. He was impressed. Legals usually got a hard time in the prisons, especially when they were out to get murderers released. Geraldine seemed as at home in the mess as she would be in an up-market wine bar. She brought the tea to the table and smiled.

'So you're Susan Dalston's brief?'

'Colin Jackson. Her former brief probably. I think I might just have got the East End version of the bum's rush.'

'You can't blame her. She'd obviously had a shock and lashed out. It happens to us all. I've been dragged to the floor before now by a client in Wandsworth.'

Colin looked her over.

'I'm not surprised if you went in there looking like that.'

She grinned.

'An armed robber, a few years back. I had to tell him his wife had died of a brain tumour while he was on remand. Strange thing was he got a not guilty and five days after the trial he hung himself.'

'Tragedies one after another sometimes, isn't it?'

Geraldine sipped at her tea and lit a Rothman's.

'It's what we make our money from. Anyway, what's Susan Dalston really like?'

'What, when she's not trying to strangle her legal, you mean?'

She grinned, showing her perfect teeth.

Colin thought for a few seconds before answering and Geraldine heard the honesty in his words when he finally did.

'She's a good person. She shouldn't bc in hcrc. Shc should be with her children. Susan worships them and they worship her. You see, she was beaten mercilessly by her husband for years. He even kicked babies out of her belly and gave her VD. But at the trial they didn't use any of that because she refused to let them. All she ever said was: "I would do it again if I had the chance." Her legals certainly weren't going to put her on the stand for the prosecution to rip her apart so she got guilty and life. I think she only applied for appeal to get back to London, be nearer the kids. She was in Durham before. Today, I had to tell her that social services were going to give her youngest child's foster parents leave to adopt. She can't do anything about it. There's no one else to take the kids on, no family interested. So the powers that be have decided the child should go to the Simpsons.'

He laughed hollowly.

'That's when she tried to strangle me.'

'The way you do?'

Her voice was soft and he smiled at her again.

'Yes, Geraldine. The way you do.

'And on top of all that her eldest daughter threatened a social worker at her children's home with a blade last night. As you can imagine, that also went down like a ten-ton tart in the back of a Mini Cooper.'

Geraldine shook her head and sighed.

'What a tale. Some people's lives are unbearably sad, aren't they?'

'Unlike the delectable Matty, of course.'

Geraldine's eyes opened wide.

'You know her then?'

Colin grinned. 'Only by sight. I worked for Victor when I was doing my finals. A bit of pocket money. She was his secretary then, of course. They weren't married.'

Geraldine glanced at her watch and bit her lip.

'Look, I really am pushed now. Can we meet later on by any chance?'

Colin raised an eyebrow in a mock leer.

'I bet men fantasise about you saying those words to them normally.'

'Why aren't you then? Am I losing my touch?'

He grinned. He liked her and thought she liked him. He ran his hands through his untidy hair and laughed.

'I'm not doing anything. Name a place and a time and I'll meet you there.'

'How about Zilli's in Dean Street? I have to get to Soho soon. I have an appointment. About seven-thirtyish?'

He nodded.

'See you then.'

He grinned at her. 'You can take bets on that one.' He watched as she walked from the mess and felt as if his life had just taken a very big upturn. A male PO stopped by his table.

'Jammy bugger! How did a young pup like you get to have a cuppa with sex on legs then, eh?'

Colin looked at the man and said dead pan, 'I begged, of course.'

Rhianna walked into Matty's cell and cried, 'Is it true about poor Sue?'

'Yes, I'm afraid it is. Aren't they bastards to do that to her?'

Rhianna snorted. 'That's what they do, you stupid woman. I haven't seen my own daughter since she was three.'

Her voice was sad, remembering.

'Did they put her up for adoption?' Matty seemed genuinely interested for her.

Rhianna shook her head.

'Nah, not really. They gave her to my mum. She applied for custody. I signed the papers, as you do. Me mother moved away within days and I ain't seen either of them since.'

'That's awful.'

Rhianna mimicked her nastily.

'Yes, it was very awful, Miss Enderby. But it's life, ain't it? Me mum thought she was doing the right thing, I suppose.'

She lit a joint and dragged on it deeply.

'What are you doing?'

Matty opened her arms so Rhianna could see what was on her lap.

'I was just going through Sue's things, that's all. Here, look at this from little Barry.'

She held out the letter to Rhianna who snatched it from her, bellowing, 'What the fuck you think you're doing, girl? That is Susan Dalston's private and personal stuff. You got no right to look through it all.'

Matty stood up and shrugged.

'Where's the harm? She doesn't know, does she?'

Rhianna was fuming.

'It is the unwritten rule, Matty.' She poked one long purple talon in her face. 'You don't touch nothing you ain't invited to touch, you should know that.'

She started gathering stuff up.

Matty was annoyed.

'Oh, get a life, Rhianna, what harm will it do?'

The black woman faced her and Matty was surprised to see tears on her cheeks. She held the drawings and letters to her chest as if they were worth more than gold.

'You don't fucking touch nothing, you hear me, girl? You do and I'll rip your fucking face off. This is all Susan has left of her life outside. Her life, Matty, *hers*, not yours or anyone else's. Just hers. It's her private world she can go to when she wants. It's her memories, it's where she can hug her kids, talk to them in her mind. Where she can daydream about them and love them without anyone else interfering. And if you can't see that then you're more of a selfish bitch than I first thought.'

Matty was quiet. Her eyes were sad as she listened to the other woman.

'You know nothing about life, absolutely nothing about people or their needs,' Rhianna said furiously. 'You swan around here like you're somebody, like we're all beneath you and you know you're better than us. But you ain't, you ain't better than any of us. Because we all know the basics of living together and sharing with people what they want to share, not what we think we can have or just take. Now where did this stuff come from?'

Matty felt as if she had had her face slapped.

'All right, Rhianna, keep your hair on.'

She was so angry Matty was frightened for her own safety.

'You really don't know anything, do you, Matty? You really can't see what you've done, can you?'

Slamming the stuff into her hands, Rhianna said seriously, 'Put it all away and keep out of my fucking face tonight. I mean it, Matty. I ain't in the mood for you.'

Susan came round in a hospital bed, her arms restrained by straps. For a while she was not sure where she was. Her mouth was dry, sore. Her tongue felt as if it was ten times too big for her mouth, and her eyes were streaming. She realised she was crying, had been crying in her sleep. Then it all came back to her and she realised why she was strapped down.

They were giving her Rosie away as if she was a piece of cake or an old jumper. They had decided she was better off with the Simpsons, and she probably was. But that did not make it right. Rosie was Susan's baby, her last. Rosie was the little dote of the household. Even Barry had not been able to resist her.

Susan had carried her, nurtured and loved her since she had come into the world with her peachy face and high-pitched screams.

Out of the corner of her eye Susan saw the stuff from her pockets where they'd stripped her off. Peter's letter lay on the white Formica cabinet and she felt the sting of tears once more. It had been a lovely day. She should have known she wasn't allowed nice days or good things.

Her whole life she had blundered from one catastrophe to another. Yet she had always firmly believed that one day she would hit the jackpot. Get what she wanted. Just once. One time.

A face appeared by the bed. It was a little woman, in her sixties, with bad teeth and straggly hair held in place untidily by a head band.

'Want a bit of something to make you happy, love? Something to take away the blues?'

Susan shook her head. The drug that could cheer her up had yet to be manufactured. After today she did not believe she would ever know another happy moment. She wasn't sure if she even wanted happiness. It was always taken away again so fast she was beginning to be frightened of it.

Happiness was for other people, people in magazines or on telly. Not for the likes of her and her kids.

She cried again then, a lonely wailing sound, until finally they injected her and she could embrace oblivion.

Chapter Twenty-Four

Mariah Brewster lived just off Wardour Street. Geraldine was surprised when she saw her, having expected the usual prostitute. Instead she saw a middle-aged woman with nice hair, a good figure and a very modest C&A dress and cardigan. Mariah ushered her in as if she was visiting Royalty and once more Geraldine had a shock.

The flat was like a young girl's bedroom, all chintz and tables covered in ornaments and knick-knacks. On the coffee table she had laid out afternoon tea, including sandwiches and cake, a large pot of tea and some scones.

'Please sit down, Miss O'Hara. I'm so glad you're prompt. I hate to be kept waiting and I have a client in just over an hour so I didn't want to hurry you at all. That's so rude, don't you think?'

Geraldine was amazed but took an instant liking to the woman. Five minutes later she had a slice of Battenburg and a cup of tea balanced precariously on her knees.

'You have lovely hair, dear, but I expect you get told that all the time, don't you? My eldest daughter has lovely hair too. She's at university, studying law of all things.'

Geraldine smiled.

Mariah sipped her tea and daintily wiped her coral-painted mouth with a linen napkin.

'So what can I do for you? I really can't add to the last statement I made.'

Geraldine nodded.

'I understand that, but I have to pursue all avenues. I just want

403

you to tell me, in your own words, about Victor Enderby. What he was like? What he wanted from you?'

Mariah sat back in her chair and closed her eyes.

'He was a nice man, Victor, very polite and kind. I wish I had more like him.' She sat up and smiled. 'Would you like a scone?'

Geraldine shook her head.

'Did he ever want anything out of the ordinary? Sexually, I mean.'

Mariah Brewster laughed then, a tinkling sound that was pleasant to listen to.

'No! Victor?' She held up her hands. 'Straight sex and no kissing was old Victor. In fact, the sex wasn't very important to him really.'

She frowned, trying to explain herself.

'It was more like a date. He would bring me wine – good wine, too, not cheap crap. I learned a lot about wine from him, he was a bit of a buff. Wine buff that is.'

She laughed again.

'He'd open the wine and we'd talk. He first came to me over ten years ago. His mother was alive then, of course. Old witch she was. Led him a merry dance with her illnesses and constant carping. I think I was really a refuge for him, someone he could confide in, be with. Spend a pleasant afternoon or evening with and not worry about being Victor Enderby, barrister. Or, more importantly, Victor Enderby, son.' She smiled. 'We had some good times, me and Victor. The sex was a sort of added bonus for him. Over in no time. And with no complications.'

'He wasn't into bondage? S&M? No matter how mild – even just holding your arms above your head, that kind of thing?'

Mariah shook her head and laughed again.

'Victor wouldn't even do it with the light on! He couldn't talk about sex at all. I took the lead at all times. When his couple of hours were nearly up I'd take his hand and lead him to bed. Easy as that. He paid me in cash which he put in an envelope and laid by the bed. All in all it was a good arrangement. As I said earlier, I wish I had more like him.'

Geraldine could not imagine for the life of her how anyone

could wish for men like that, strangers, people off the street. They could be diseased or anything.

Mariah seemed to read her mind and in her good-natured way she said sadly, 'Look, love, I understand that my way of life may seem strange to you. But what you have to remember is, I am *not* you. I have brought up three kids, put them into good schools, taken care of their every need with this job. When my husband died I was absolutely penniless. He had gambled away everything we had. The house was mortgaged to the hilt, I was literally out on the street. This has given me back my independence in a way. I wouldn't have chosen it but it has fulfilled a need.

'My kids think I'm a civil servant, love, working on important things for the government. And why would they think otherwise? I'm their mother, their mentor, and go to work each day like everyone else. I'm there each night when they come home. I love them. Simple, isn't it? If I could have a few more Victors I'd be a happy woman, believe me. I'm knocking on and that's not good in my game. But I feathered me nest while I had the chance and one day I'll be a granny living in Eastbourne with a little bungalow and some credibility. We all have to live by our own lights, love, do what we can.'

Geraldine was embarrassed by the total honesty of the woman before her.

'I'm not judging you.'

Mariah smiled.

''Course you are. It's human nature to judge. Well, I never judge anyone, me. Like the Bible says: "Judge not, lest you be judged." Something like that anyway. I've been beaten up. I've been robbed. But I have survived thanks to the Victors of this world. The genuinely nice men, the ones who want succour not sex. When he met his wife he was so happy, you know. I was pleased for him.'

'He told you?'

Mariah nodded.

'Oh, he was over the moon. She was younger, very attractive, and he really believed she wanted him. Cared for him. He came here and told me he couldn't be with me any more as it wouldn't be fair on her. Matilda. He gave me a couple of ton severance pay, actually called it that. He was such a fair man. But he was back within six months of the wedding. I guessed he would be, it all sounded too good to be true.'

Geraldine couldn't believe her ears.

'You didn't mention this before, in your first statement?'

Mariah shrugged.

'Before, I didn't really want to be involved. As you can imagine it's the last thing I need. But after reading what was said about him I think someone should put the record straight. She tortured that man from day one. She ridiculed him: his sexual prowess and his life. The man became a shadow of his former self. He was a brilliant criminal lawyer, you know that. In the courtroom he was supposed to be fantastic. But with women he was like a lost boy. I can still see him, his poor face . . . he was devastated by what she was doing. Couldn't understand what had gone wrong.

'She aborted his babies as well. He told me that himself. If you're trying to get her out, tell her from me she's a lying little bitch. A child was the culmination of everything that man wanted in life. When she had them taken away he was broken. She set out to break him and she did. But if he hit her, I'm amazed. I refuse to believe he was capable of it.'

'You really mean what you're saying, don't you?'

Mariah pushed one well-manicured hand through her lustrous hair.

'I do. I knew him for many years. I *knew* him. I might be a tom but I am not the usual type of tom. I pick and choose and I've got myself a nice little clientele here. Mostly Victors. Professional men who want a bit of pampering, a bit of care. Nothing more. I used to say to him, "Get yourself a wife, a life, a family." That was all he needed. And shall I tell you something: I wish he'd wanted to marry me. I'd have jumped at it like a shot. He was a nice, educated, intelligent man. But where that little bitch was concerned, he was like all men. Fucked from the first touch of her tits.'

'Were you in love with him?'

The words were spoken slowly, in a quiet voice, and Mariah started to laugh again.

'After fifteen years of whoring you can't love anyone, darlin'. Not really. But you can like someone, respect them. I would have been grateful to have had him. Had me bills paid and just please him. Just him, not a succession of men, strangers mostly. I would have done whatever he wanted and spent every day of my life looking after him. Can you understand what I'm saying?'

The strange thing for Geraldine was she could understand. Probably better than most people.

'Thank you for your time, Mariah. I appreciate it.'

The woman shrugged sadly.

'I'm sorry I can't tell you what you want to hear, love. I wish I could.' She smiled then, a wistful smile.

'People look down on us prostitutes, but shall I tell you something? At least we don't pretend anything. We ask for money and we supply whatever is wanted. A service, if you like. Women like her, they take from a man all his life and don't give anything back. She's the real whore because I believe she went into that marriage for what she could get, and unlike me and my colleagues she couldn't get rid of him at the end of the day. I can go home, to me real home, and forget about all this. She couldn't. She had to look at his face morning, noon and night. That was her problem. I think she killed him to get rid of him. Because she'd made a mistake and he irritated her. She had the house, the money and the prestige, but nothing else. Because he loved her so much, he took a lot from her. I know that, and in your heart of hearts, so do you.'

Geraldine listened to the woman before her and knew instinctively that she was telling the truth. Her version of the truth admittedly, and from her point of view. But it had the ring of truth to it.

Worst of all, she was inclined to believe Mariah Brewster.

As she left, the woman shook her hand and smiled. 'Victor was a nice man, Miss O'Hara, he didn't have it in him to be any other way. And, if necessary, I'll stand up in court and tell them that. But as a prostitute I wouldn't be classed as a reliable witness. But I know the truth.' She punched her chest. 'In here, I know the truth.'

A tall, pensionable-aged man with iron grey hair and badly fitting teeth was climbing the stairs as Geraldine was leaving. He held an Oddbins carrier bag and had a shifty demeanour. She caught a smell of lavender aftershave and cigar smoke.

She turned and watched him walk into the little flat as though he was an honoured guest and heard Mariah's tinkling laughter before the door was closed.

Her stomach revolted, yet her heart understood her. She was more surprised about that than anything else. She liked Mariah Brewster, actually liked her. Which is more than she could say for her feelings towards Matilda Enderby.

'Can't you just for once be good, Barry Dalston?'

Mrs Eappen's words were clipped. She was irritated and it showed. Being the type of person she was this fact annoyed her too. She always liked to think of herself as a nice person, a caring person.

The fact she frequently felt an urge to strangle many of the children in her care made her feel slightly soiled.

She knew she was a good person deep down. It was just that Barry Dalston, nose running, trousers hanging off his thin frame and shirt buttoned up wrong, annoyed the life out of her.

'But, Miss, I don't like the Simpsons. I only like me mum. I want me mum.'

He was on the verge of tears again and this annoyed her even more.

'The Simpsons are very nice people who are going to look after your little sister. They've been kind enough to allow you and Alana to spend the afternoon with them and Rosie at an adventure playground.'

She attempted a smile but it came out as a grimace.

'So why can't you be grateful for that, Barry, eh?'

He looked at her then with his beautiful clear blue eyes and shrugged. His whole nine-year-old body seemed to bristle. He fixed her with a hard stare and said seriously, 'I want me mum. Why can't I go and see me mum instead?'

Mrs Eappen raised her eyes to the ceiling as if some miraculous event might occur to make Barry Dalston into a nice little boy.

'I think the Simpsons should fuck off and bring my sister back. They don't own her, me mum does.'

Mrs Eappen sighed and gritted her teeth. Kneeling down, she grabbed the little boy's arms.

'Bad language is what put your mother in prison, remember that, Barry. It will stand you in good stead all your life. Bad language is the beginning of badness in people. From bad language they become bad inside and do bad things. Like your mother did. Now you will go with the Simpsons and be a grateful boy. There are many children who would love a day out like this. They would know how to be grateful, I can assure you of that.'

He pulled himself free.

'Well, send them then. I'll go and see me mum.'

'You cannot go and see your mother unless it is a designated visit. I explain this to you fifty times a day, child. Your mother gave up the right to see you when she was naughty and the police took her away. Now do you understand that much?'

Her voice was rising though she was trying as hard as she could to control both it and her temper.

Barry still locked his gaze on her and this time he didn't answer.

'Do you understand, Barry?'

He sniffed. A loud, noisy, snotty sniff that made Mrs Eappen's stomach turn and caused her face to pucker up in disgust.

'Fuck off, you. I want me mum.'

It was said quietly and with conviction. His whole body seemed to be on red alert as he stared at her hard.

Alana came into the room then and laughed.

'Barry, stop swearing! Mum would give you a smack if she knew.'

She came over to him and tidied him up in seconds. Mrs Eappen watched with despair written all over her pinched face.

'He learned to swear here, Miss. We wasn't allowed to swear at home unless we was too small to know what we was saying and even then we got a good hiding if we kept it up.'

'Quite.' Mrs Eappen's whole body was stiff and unyielding and as she stood up to her full height she looked down at the two children as if they had just climbed out of a sewer before sitting down at her dinner table.

'Well, Alana, you look lovely. Look after Barry and see he's good for the Simpsons. They're very kind . . .'

Alana interrupted her then, half smiling.

'I know, Mrs Eappen. We should be very *grateful* and we are, okay? Very, very grateful.'

Mrs Eappen knew when she was beaten and made a hasty retreat. As she remarked to her husband that night, how could you take a child seriously when she was named after the wife of a bloody rock star!

But Barry and Alana went out for the day, played with their sister, and were completely unaware that soon Rose would be taken from their orbit. Would be a Simpson, and never again a Dalston.

Never again the dote of a house full of children and scuffed furniture, and a mother who had lived permanently on the edge of disaster. Where despite their father, lack of money and lack of luxuries, they had all been so very, very happy.

Geraldine walked into Zilli's and smiled a smile that took in everyone, from Colin sitting in the corner to every waiter, waitress and customer.

Colin was impressed. She knew the stir she created and gave everyone a little bit of her so she could relax then and enjoy herself. He had wondered all afternoon what it must be like to be that attractive. To be that wanted.

As he had showered and put on his only good shirt and trousers, he had wondered what people would think of him sitting down and eating with her. He hoped they would assume they were together, but knew that no one in their wildest imagining would really think that.

Geraldine smiled as she sat opposite him and he smiled back. Sod the world. She was here and he was here, that was all that mattered. Even if people did think he was a younger brother or a client.

'Sorry I'm late.'

'That's okay. I've been enjoying myself sitting here. I was early.'

Geraldine grinned. 'I thought you might be. You look the early type.'

He wasn't sure if she was laughing at him.

She ordered a good bottle of wine and they drank it together, chatting about nothing.

'I needed that. Shall we order our food now or have another drink first and relax?'

Colin just smiled and she took control again. Ordered for them both, had the waiter at the table in seconds and then they were together again without any intrusions whatsoever. He thought he had died and gone to heaven. She was exquisite, even more so than he had first thought.

'So, what's the goss on Matilda Enderby then?'

Geraldine's words were playful but he knew she was being serious and thought for a few moments before he answered her.

'Matty was only his secretary when I worked there, though there was talk about them even then. One of the women in the office returned late to finish an affidavit and caught them in a clinch.' He grinned. 'Actually it was more than a clinch. She caught him tied to the chair with Matilda's stockings and Matilda sitting on his lap. I leave the rest to your imagination. Funny thing was, Victor went up in everyone's estimation after that. Until then he had been seen as a brilliant lawyer but a bit of a damp squib.

'She certainly brought him out of himself, I can tell you.'

Geraldine didn't answer him for a while, lost in her own thoughts.

He waved at her and smiled.

'Remember me? We were having dinner together and chatting?'

She shook her head and laughed.

'Sorry, I was miles away there.' She gulped at her wine. 'What did you think of her? You met her, I presume, chatted to her?'

Colin ran his hands through his hair and sighed.

'I never liked her much. She was pretty, lovely really, and she dressed sexily in a sort of school marmish way.

'I think she went through most of the men in the firm before settling on poor old Victor. I mean, he was an accident waiting to happen. He had looked after his mother for years, he was shy and retiring. You know, if you saw him in court you'd never have believed he was the same bland man you knew at work. It was really strange.'

She nodded.

'I saw him once or twice, he was bloody good. Tore a witness to pieces in minutes. Yet he never raised his voice, not once. Brilliant.'

'You know what I mean then. But where she was concerned he was besotted. I mean, think about it. This young, very young, good-looking girl is all over him like a rash. It was laughable, really. A more experienced man would have had her and dumped her, like others in chambers did.

'But Victor wasn't really part of their enclave, if you like. He was respected but not a man who socialised with anyone or was part of the bigger picture. He was a great barrister but he went straight home afterwards. He didn't womanise, didn't have a joke with anyone, kept himself pretty much to himself.

'I think Matty knew that and fixed her sights on him. Of course, after the wedding, she wanted them both to be part of that world. Theatre, dinner, the works. I shouldn't imagine the marriage was a great success. She wasn't liked by anyone. Especially the wives. I think they saw through her and she knew it. Even Victor wasn't that thick-skinned, he must have guessed. But then, I suppose he loved her.'

Geraldine stared at the young man before her. He had put his finger on it, she was sure. It seemed with Matty you either loved her or loathed her.

Victor had loved her.

Was that his downfall?

The food arrived then and they were a few minutes getting settled again. 'I hate to say this,' Geraldine confided, 'but I feel there's more to Matty than meets the eye. All this poor little me and how she suffered, yet there's not one shred of evidence except a visit to the doctor a week before the killing. Matty apparently gave him a story about marital cruelty and how bad her nerves were. Even the doctor seemed sceptical.

'She never arrived at work marked. Was never seen marked by anyone. But even though it sounds implausible she said Victor liked a bit of bondage and you've borne that out by what you said earlier. So I'm back where I started, really. You see, I don't much like her either and that bothers me. As a professional I shouldn't like or dislike people though before Matty I've never actually disliked anyone I've defended. But she troubles me. Really troubles me.'

Colin nodded. 'I know what you mean. I feel the same about Susan. Only I like her too much. Even though she tried to strangle me today, I understood why she went berserk. I know how she feels for her kids and I certainly know how they feel for her. She kept that family going, no matter what happened to her.

'Barry Dalston was a piece of shit. He beat and degraded her. I have access to her medical records and listen to this. Her first child died because he gave her VD on her wedding night. Whether it was the fright of finding out that caused the stillbirth isn't known but it set the tone for the whole marriage. She gave and he took. Finally she hit him with a hammer over one hundred times. His face was gone, there was nothing left to say what he had looked like, what he had experienced before death, nothing. She walked in while he was unconscious and she killed him. Then she phoned the police and made herself a coffee. She was still covered in blood, brain and bone when they arrived. Now why did she kill him like that? Why did she take away his identity, if you like? It was as if she wanted to obliterate him completely so there was nothing left of him for anyone.'

He looked at Geraldine, who was staring down at her lovely chicken liver salad, and sighed.

'I'm sorry. I didn't think.'

Geraldine looked suspiciously green around the gills and he felt awful.

'It's just that it intrigues me, you know? Can a person take so much that when they finally flip, they flip for us all? For every slight, every punch, every hurt? Do they become so upset that rationality goes out of the window and they have to kill then? But it seems so premeditated. Did she walk into the room, see him lying there and decide to take him away from her world, her kids, her home? What made her do it then? He had hit her about five days before so she can't use that as an excuse. Why didn't she kill him the night he attacked her? Why wait? She had been on a night out and she was drunk. But according to her friend Doreen she'd had a great time and enjoyed herself. Susan admits that too. She says she came home and just decided to kill him.

'I don't believe her. I just don't. She took more than anyone else would take and she protected her kids. She would never have left them unless she had to. She worships those children, they are her life. So why did she all of a sudden decide she would do something that would take her from them? Leave them in care. She knew what her family were like. Lowlife scum, out for a few quid. She didn't want her own children in their care even if they offered. It just doesn't add up.'

'Perhaps it was the drink? It could have made her violent.'

Colin ran his fingers through his already untidy hair until it stood on end and made him look like a little boy.

'I don't think so. I don't think it was drink. I don't think it was anything we can rationalise.'

'What then? Why did she do it?'

He sighed.

'I don't know. I really don't. But one day, please God, I will find out.'

Geraldine studied him. She saw how tortured he was by Susan Dalston, could see how much he liked the woman, respected her even. She could feel his disapproval too, the feeling that somehow she had let her kids down by putting herself in a situation where she could no longer be there to protect them.

She thought he was very sweet and idealistic. If a little naïve.

'Maybe Susan Dalston just saw her chance – a chance to get him out of their lives once and for all?' Geraldine suggested. 'Perhaps the drink had done that to her. Spurred her on to take advantage of the opportunity before he awoke and the whole dreadful cycle started again. Maybe, seeing him like that, drunk, unconscious, she just saw *opportunity*. No other thought, nothing, just a chance to get rid of him.'

Colin heard the resonance in her words. She really knew what she was talking about. She understood the need that could come over someone, the need to make someone or something just disappear.

'Maybe she just wanted him to leave her alone.'

Colin saw the earnest expression on her face and felt as if he had been given a glimpse of the real Geraldine O'Hara. The Geraldine beneath the designer outfit and the well-styled hair. And what he saw he couldn't believe. He saw a frightened girl inside a very desirable woman.

She drank her wine in two gulps then, excusing herself, went to the toilet. Ten minutes later, just when Colin was terrified she had left without telling him, she came back.

She was once more the cool feminist barrister with good legs, a better brain, and that don't-you-*dare*-touch-me look about her.

He was relieved and saddened both at the same time.

Matty awoke to sunshine and a strange feeling of loneliness. It was odd, missing someone. Especially someone like Susan Dalston. But Susan intrigued her. She found it difficult to understand someone who could be so selfless. Think constantly about other people, little people who did nothing but make demands on her. Her time, her attention, her few pennies.

She talked about them constantly, as if they were real people with opinions and thoughts and needs. When in fact all they had was needs.

Children needed and parents, fools that they were, provided for those needs. Without a second thought, without anything except their own need to give.

It would never do for her. She didn't want anyone taking from her, least of all ungrateful people. People who couldn't even feed themselves for ages or make themselves understood. Matty shuddered at the thought.

She wandered from the cell, bored. She walked to the rec room and tried to play a game of solitaire but someone would always try and strike up a conversation so she got herself some coffee and made her way to Rhianna's cell.

Rhianna was inside with a young girl called Sarah. She was tall with great brown eyes and a heart-shaped face. She looked like she should be in a passionate Fellini film full of Italian men, all hairy and moustached.

Until she opened her mouth. Then she was broad cockney and romantic thoughts shot from people's minds. She was suddenly a slut with a bad mouth and her beauty seemed to fade away.

'Hello, mate, all right?' Sarah had a happy-go-lucky disposition that was the envy of the wing. 'You look like you just lost your virginity to the night screw.'

Her laughter was deep and infectious. Even Matty had to smile. Rhianna nodded to the girl and she sloped from the cell, all legs, hair and smiles.

'She's a funny one, that Sarah. No matter what she says, I never get the hump with her.'

Matty nodded.

'It's her disposition. Some people are like that. They never really see the shit they have made of their lives. It's to be envied.'

Rhianna was quiet. When Matty was like this it was best to humour her.

'Are you okay?'

Matty shook her head.

'I've got the prison skits, as Sarah would say. I'm fucked off, pissed off, and feel like a fight.'

Rhianna relaxed. This she knew, this she could cope with.

'I've felt like that for ages. You have to go with it, see if it disappears on its own. If not, have a puff. Have a trip. Get out of your head. The comedown normally sorts me out.'

'Do you think Susan is all right? I mean, she seemed so out of it. I've never heard anything like it in my life. There was such pain in her voice. Real heart-wrenching pain.'

Rhianna took a joint from her tobacco tin and lit it, blowing the smoke out noisily. She passed it to Matty who drew deeply on it.

'You know what I think? I think, Matilda Enderby, that for the first time in your life you have been affected by another person. You actually care about Susan Dalston and don't know what to do about it.'

She started to laugh and Matty sat on the bunk, not answering, letting her eyes roam over the cell. It was all male in here: males on the wall, males on magazine covers, male smells even. Dope, tobacco and stale sex.

Except the sex wasn't male though it should have been.

'I care nothing for Susan Dalston actually. It's just that I have to share a cell with her, and if she's going mad I think I have the right to know,' Matty said airily.

Rhianna nodded, still laughing.

'I've already asked about her so stop worrying. She's fine. Back on wing this afternoon. Susan loves them kids too much to be incapacitated for any length of time. She wouldn't give anyone the chance to say she wasn't fit. Stop worrying, Matty.'

The last bit was said slowly, as if Rhianna could see inside her head and knew she was worried whatever she said.

Sarah drifted back into the cell then. Her huge eyes were glistening from LSD and her body crumpled as she slid on to the other bunk.

'I fucking hate this place.'

No one answered her. There was nothing to add.

Susan listened to the psychiatrist. The man was elderly, with dyed brown hair and watery grey eyes. She liked his voice, though. It was a low Scottish burr and brought back dim memories of happier times.

'How do you feel now, Susan? How do you feel about your life?'

She thought long and hard. What did she feel?

'I feel like I did at home. When I was on top of everything. Then, just as I put in the last bit of washing, I would stand back, pleased with meself. And I'd see one sock. One dirty sock that had somehow escaped the machine. Then I would know that life was telling me there was always something or someone who got away from you. Or who ruined your routine, your life, your feeling of well-being.'

Doctor McFadden stared at the big woman before him and smiled. He decided he liked her, she was a philosopher in her own way. A dreamer who had never had the time to realise her dreams.

Like everyone else, though, she didn't know that.

'Do you ever think about what you did?'

She sighed then, a long, weary sigh.

'Think about it, doctor. If you was me, would you think about what you'd done?'

He bit his lip and thought for a few minutes. Then shrugged.

'It depends really, doesn't it? It depends on whether or not you feel that what you did was wrong?'

Susan smiled.

'You are a wily old fucker. I'll have to watch myself with you, won't I?'

'Coming from you, Susan Dalston, I'll take that as a compliment.'

Later in his notes, he wrote: 'Full of guilt, full of love for her children with whom she should be at home if there was any justice in the world.'

He knew the high ups hated him, thought him too liberal, too easy on the girls he dealt with. But that was what years of listening to sorrow and heartache did to you.

Wendy had woken with the familiar pain, a stinging sensation between her legs that made it impossible for her to wee without wanting to cry. She wished she was back in her room with her soothing cold calamine lotion.

This happened to her periodically, a legacy from her father and what he had done to her. He had given her a disease. Wendy sometimes wondered if it was a punishment from God. Her father had already had it when he took her, so God must have given it to him expressly so he could pass it on to Wendy.

She never could make sense of it.

She closed her eyes and dreamed her dreams. She imagined she was at home, with her mother and her sisters and brother. Her father had miraculously died in a car crash or a fire and they were all happy and fed and warm. They sat in the lounge and ate crisps, tomato sauce-flavoured, and drank cream soda to their heart's content. They watched *Bonanza* on TV and little Rosie took turns sitting on their laps and being fed tit-bits.

Sometimes it had been like that, when her father was away with his other woman, in his other life. Then they could all really relax and be happy as if his absence made their lives more real. They could all feel they existed for other reasons than being bawled at or pushed out of the way.

Their granny Kate would visit them with packets of Rolos and Wagon Wheels and a Jamboree bag for Barry who loved flying saucers that cracked his tongue with the sharpness of their sherbet. Granny would talk to them all with her lovely voice and her kind words.

She was dying now, couldn't even visit them. It had taken her hard, guessing what had happened that night. She knew in her heart what her son had done. Knew he was capable of it, which Wendy knew was much worse for her granny. 'Blood will out' careered around in her head and she forced it away. Forced herself to think of something else but now the pain was growing worse.

Wendy cried.

This was worse than any of the other times. She was so sore and could feel the blisters underneath her body as she moved. As if she had been burned there, by hot water or bleach.

She licked her lips with a dry tongue. What she really needed was some ice. Ice cooled it, made the hurt go away. Ice was good.

Mrs Eappen came blustering into the room, all hair spray and buttoned cardigan.

'Are you thinking of getting up, child?' Her voice was disapproving as usual, as if she automatically expected badness and therefore got it. Wendy hated to disappoint her and made a conscious effort to be bad if she could. She felt it cheered the woman up.

'I really don't feel well today.'

Mrs Eappen looked at her hard. She did look peaky, white and drained. She also seemed to be in pain.

'Are you okay? Do you need the doctor?'

There was concern in her voice now and Wendy was ill enough to appreciate that.

'It's okay. Just my period.'

Mrs Eappen looked at her suspiciously.

'You had your period not a week ago.' She stared down at the girl on the bed.

'I'll get the doctor. Better to be safe than sorry.'

It was Wendy's protest that made her phone in the end. The more the girl denied being in pain, the more convinced Mrs Eappen was that a doctor was needed. In her years in the service she had seen it all: home abortions with knitting needles and chop sticks, girls miscarrying in their nice clean beds with never a thought for the danger they put themselves in or the trouble they caused others.

The doctor duly arrived to find an hysterical girl who refused to allow him to examine her. Finally, Wendy was held by well-meaning arms and concerned faces stared down as the blankets were removed from her body and her terrible secret was exposed.

She heard the doctor whistle between his teeth and Mrs Eappen's low cry of: 'Dear God in heaven, what's wrong with the child?'

Wendy was found out on a bright morning when she was at her lowest ebb. Suddenly she was deluged with people all wanting explanations of when and with whom she had had sex.

When being what they really wanted to know.

Especially Mr Potter, who looked miffed as well as annoyed. There was relief on his face and it galled her.

Wendy kept silent. She had not learned much in life, but what she had learned she had learned at her Granny's knee. Granny Kate, who smelled of home baking and 4711.

'People only know what you tell them, child. Remember that all your life. Only tell your secrets to people you know will keep them just what they are. Who will keep them as they were meant to be. Kept. Secret.'

Wendy understood now what getting old was all about. It meant you knew things other people didn't know yet. It meant trying to warn them about the dangers of a life you were finished with. That was gradually winding down and emptying of everything but memories and secrets.

She lay in the bed and felt suddenly serene. She would tell them nothing. Let them guess the worst and they wouldn't even scratch the surface.

Her father was gone, and she was glad. Nothing could ever really hurt her like that again. Not even this thing she had been given by him could hurt her as much as he had hurt her in the giving of it.

She looked at them all with her big wide eyes. But she answered them not one word.

She knew Mrs Eappen thought she had been shagging under their very noses. This knowledge gave her a small rebellious sense of smugness.

Chapter Twenty-Five

Roselle was with a Soho hard man called Danny. No one knew his last name and no one had ever had the guts to ask.

He was big, black as coal and handsome in a bald-headed, muscle-bound way. The hostesses loved him and he loved them. Though only for a night here and there. He was harder to catch than syphilis off a vicar as the girls put it to each other.

He didn't talk much either, which suited them. They talked all night in the club, talked crap. Crap for men with dreams of perfect womanhood which were as far removed from real life as the moon was from the earth.

But they played the game and enjoyed Danny. His quiet strength, his lovely smile, and most of all his cock which was like a baseball bat or a cricket bat depending on who you talked to. He laughed at their jokes, understood their unhappiness and gave them a few hours of unpaid sex.

Roselle, however, knew him better than anyone. They went back years and when she needed a job done, he was the man she'd call. Now he sat in her car, all dark brooding looks and secret smiles, and she filled him in on the situation.

'When we see the man I want, you bring him bodily to the car but don't let passers by or anyone else guess anything's going on, right?'

He nodded. He did this all the time. He was the acknowledged master of the take.

'Then me and you are going to put the fear of Christ up him.'

Danny really grinned then, looking forward to it.

'If he's a nonce, surely I get to kick him in?'

423

Roselle laughed gently.

'Oh, he's a nonce, all right, and you do get to scare him. But let's see how he reacts before we start the pain. Sometimes the fear of a kicking is a much worse punishment. We'll see.'

Danny relaxed. He liked Roselle. Unlike most women she thought like a man. She was a loner like himself and understood the mechanics of fear.

Alfred Potter walked out of his flat at just after eight-thirty in the evening. He worked as a volunteer at a local youth club and was late tonight. He had just had a visitor, a girl called Leyla, eleven years old and well developed for her age. She was also educationally subnormal. His type of girl in fact. Her parents thought he was great the way he helped her with lessons and took her on days out. After all, he was a social worker and knew what he was doing. They could trust him.

Leyla, for her part, was a quiet, amicable girl. She understood the world only as feelings and thoughts. If she pleased people she experienced a feeling of well-being. If they were angry she cried. If she pleased Mr Potter she got shop-bought cake and Pepsi, things she never had at home.

Mr Potter and Leyla had had quite a long session that evening and he had forgotten the time. As they left he put her in a taxi cab and waved until she was out of sight.

Then, pleased with himself and feeling indestructible, he buttoned up his jacket and walked jauntily along the pavement, smoothing down his sparse hair.

The black man, he noticed, seemed to glide towards him. No expression on his face, nothing. It wasn't until he was in a vice-like grip and actually hearing the man talk that the danger he was obviously in occurred to Alfred Potter.

By then he was also in a rather dashing car.

His neighbour, Mrs Henderson, waved at him and he waved back. Because the black man informed him if he didn't act normally his gonads would be ripped off and put through his letter box.

He believed the huge man with the yellowing whites to his eyes and the impossibly white teeth. At least, he reasoned, he had no reason to disbelieve him.

Now the woman, very good-looking and well dressed, pulled away from the kerb and still waving to Mrs Henderson Alfred was driven away at a fair speed, though not so fast as to attract attention, and told to keep his mouth shut until he was spoken to.

He was terrified. Which was exactly what the two people with him wanted him to be. He did not disappoint them. He started crying before they left his road, and he was sobbing when they hit the motorway. If only they would say something, tell him what he had done.

But not a word was spoken by anyone and he wasn't going to risk incurring the black man's wrath for anyone.

Roselle found she was actually enjoying herself.

'Another night in nick, eh? What a thrilling prospect.'

Matty's voice was going right through Susan's head. It was as if she was determined to talk herself to death.

'Look, Matty, why don't you listen to me letter? See what you think.'

Matty nodded. She stopped her pacing and sat on Susan's bunk.

'Go on then.'

She cleared her throat and began to read.

'"Dear Peter" . . . that's his name.'

Matty sighed. 'Well, I hardly thought even you would get that wrong.'

Susan cleared her throat and started again.

'"Dear Peter, it was lovely to hear from you. I was pleased to hear from you. I hope you are well. I am as well as can be expected in the circumstances. The kids are all well. I think they miss me, but then I miss them as well.

'"What is happening with you? How is Australia and the ship? What is it like living on a big ship? What do you do on your days off on the ship? Are there any women on the ship – women sailors, I mean? Ha ha. Please write again soon, as it was so nice to hear from someone from my other life. From happier days.

'"Write soon. Love from Susan Dalston."'

Matty put her hands over her face and threw herself backwards on the bunk. Susan bridled in annoyance.

'It ain't that fucking bad, is it?'

Matty hauled herself up.

'Susan Dalston, that's the worst letter I have ever heard. You sound like a moron.'

Susan was getting really cross now and it showed.

'Not so much of the fucking moron, you. *You're* the moron. You don't understand anything about anything. I think it's a nice letter. It asks questions and answers queries.'

Matty wiped her eyes with her hand, a habit she had when annoyed. 'If you're interested in Peter, don't send that letter. I'll write you one to send.'

Susan shook her head vehemently.

'Oh, no, you won't. I don't fancy him and he don't fancy me. We're just mates. Old mates from school. He's stuck on a ship and I'm stuck in here. We just want to hear a word from another mate, that's all. Why does everything have to be about sex and fancying and blokes all the time?'

Matty shook her head and grinned.

'Because that's what makes the world go round. Women and men, men and women. It's what it's all about.'

Susan snorted and lit a cigarette.

'All the men I've ever known have caused me nothing but fucking hag. You can keep all that malarkey for people like yourself. For me a mate will do. Stuck in here, the last thing I need is a head full of nonsense. Romance is for prats, Matty. Prats like you and Sarah and the others who think that once they're out they'll be okay.

'Well, listen to me, I'm about to give you a wake up call. This will stay with you all your life. If you ever get another bloke, he'll always be wondering if you'll kill him and all. The sooner you realise what you've done, what you've caused, the better off you will be.'

Matty stared at her in that way she had. A hard stare without any kind of feeling in it whatsoever.

'You're wrong, Susan. We're victims and will be seen as victims by decent people.'

Susan shook her head in derision. Then in a temper she said something she should never have said.

'You ain't a victim, you admitted as much to me the other week with the vodka talking. None of us is really a victim. We marry these men and even when we see what they are we still stay with them. We're trapped but we trapped ourselves. Barry was me father, love. I married me father, the man I hated most in the world. I was a victim, all right. I was a victim of trying to get away from home, of trying to put some distance between me and my old man. That's all. There's no great plan, no big ideal. Fuck all but the truth – and that, as we all know, fucking hurts.'

Matty was staring hard now. She looked frightening. Susan realised she had gone too far, but Christ Matty annoyed her at times.

'What did I say then, on the vodka?'

Her voice was flat, eyes watchful, and Susan regretted mentioning it.

'Not a lot. I just sussed out the truth of it, that's all. But don't worry, I'm the last person to talk, ain't I?'

Matty stood up, and as small and petite as she was, she looked seriously menacing. Susan stood also and the disparity in their height and weight was obvious to them both.

'Listen, Matty, what you do is your trip, right? It's nothing to do with me. I have enough on me plate keeping body and soul together, looking out for me kids and trying to write letters. If I was going to use what you said I'd hardly have told you about it, would I?'

Matty saw the sense in what the other woman was saying and relaxed.

'I say a lot of silly things when I'm drunk, Sue. It doesn't mean they're true, does it?'

Susan shook her head. The tension had left the cell and Matty was smiling again.

'Well, I know what you're saying there, mate. I can't remember that much about it to be honest. Now give me a hand with me letter, eh? I bow down to your superior vocabulary.'

The storm had passed but Susan realised just how close to the wind she had sailed. She also realised that Matty Enderby was a dangerous person. It was far better to have someone like that as a friend than an enemy as her own husband had found out.

Alfred Potter was standing in a cold wood, far from home, and without his clothes. He had never felt so vulnerable in his life.

'Jesus, but that's a small prick! Wouldn't you agree, Dan?'

The black man nodded silently.

'It's much too small for a real woman, Mr Potter. Is that why you have a penchant for little girls?'

Roselle's voice was loud in the gloom and he realised exactly what was going down and was silent.

Danny grabbed him with one meaty fist and shook him.

'Answer the lady when she talks to you, man. Okay?'

Mr Potter really did not know what to answer so he shook his head vigorously.

Roselle laughed loudly.

'So you're calling me a liar, are you? You're not a beast, a predatory piece of shit who goes after the most vulnerable children in our society. Children in care, children taken from their homes for no other reason than their parents fucked up. You think it's quite all right to do that, do you?'

Mr Potter wanted to cry, he felt so vulnerable, so frightened and so powerless. Naked and cold, he was at the mercy of strangers, two people who obviously knew about him. About his quiet times with the children, as he called his little games.

'I wouldn't ever call you a liar, madam.'

He hated himself for the pleading tone in his voice. Get me out of this, God, he prayed, and I will never go near another child as long as I live.

Roselle grinned.

'How does it feel to be so exposed, to have strangers looking at you – strangers who could make you do anything they wanted? Because they are stronger, more evil, more vicious than you.'

He still couldn't answer. There was no answer.

'Is that what turns people like you on, eh? The fear, the defencelessness of the girls you abuse? Because it is abuse, you know. Abuse of the worst kind. You consciously work with children, pretending you are taking care of them. Like the little girl in Wales, now what was her name?'

She pretended to think hard, as if the name had escaped her.

'Was it Karen? Yes, Karen. The little girl with the pigtails. You still have photos of her in your flat. We've been in your flat, Mr Potter. Me and my friend here. We have been through all your things. Seen all your books, and your videos and your other crap. We know you better than anyone now.'

She was serious, hard-voiced and hard-faced.

'You left Wales, didn't you, Mr Potter? And the place in Newcastle, and the place in Leeds. You always leave before they throw you out, don't you? Before you can get caught. You keep it among yourselves, don't you? There are loads of people like you around.

'Well, I'm here to tell you we know what you're doing and we're watching you. The big mistake you made was going after my little friend, my good friend, Wendy Dalston. You see, unlike you, Wendy has us behind her.

'So where does that leave you now? I can't let you get away with it, can I? I have to make sure you understand exactly what you've done. Make sure you never want to do anything remotely like it again. So that means pain, I'm afraid, extreme pain.'

He dropped to his knees in the undergrowth. Could feel sticks digging into his knees and dirt collecting on his shins.

'Please, please, don't hurt me! I'm begging you. Please, I have a bad heart . . .' He was crying. Really crying.

Roselle was enjoying herself.

'Oh, the joy of hearing a man beg. Any man. Well, beg away, wanker. You've been found out.'

She walked slowly back to the car and left him with Danny. What Danny did next was up to him, that was always the deal. He gave out the punishment he felt befitted the crime.

She had a feeling he was going to mete out rather a harsh punishment and tonight could not find it in herself to be sorry for Alfred Potter.

* * *

Colin was nervous. As he sat in the visiting room with the children's social worker, Miss Beacham, he was sorely reminded of Susan's behaviour on his last visit and smiled sheepishly at the other woman who nodded to him, as if to reassure him everything was going to be fine.

He liked Miss Beacham. She had a nice way about her. She was a calming influence with the kids in her care and impressed him. It was a shame she was so ugly. With her personality she would have been much in demand if God had seen fit to give her a face to match her temperament.

He realised as the thought flashed through his mind that if he voiced it to Geraldine O'Hara she would demolish him in a second. But it was easy for the Geraldines of this world to be feminists. They were never judged on anything but their looks so they didn't have to go through the angst of mere mortals like himself and Miss Beacham.

The thought made him smile and Miss Beacham, assuming he was smiling at her, grinned back at him.

'I'm glad we both had visits booked at the same time, Colin. Maybe we could have a bite afterwards and I can fill you in on the latest developments with the children?'

He nodded.

Another thing he liked about her was that she ate like people should eat. In huge quantities, and always food that was classed as bad for you. He knew from Susan's children that she often took them for Wimpys, giving them large milkshakes and doughnuts as well as bender burgers and chips.

They all loved her, especially the eldest girl.

He had found Wendy an anomaly, though all the younger children had been there on the night in question and all argued that they'd seen and heard nothing.

It bothered him, because who exactly was supposed to be looking after them? He could not see Susan leaving them with Alana in charge, no matter what anyone said. Even Susan.

Rosie obviously could not have known anything, but even little Barry had only ever said, 'Daddy is gone and we are glad.'

Alana always said she knew nothing, saw nothing, heard nothing.

But, as he was beginning to realise, there was much more to all this than met the eye. People rarely listened to children or asked their opinion. It was as if adults automatically believed they had no thoughts on anything save what the adults wanted them to think. But these were shrewd, streetwise kids who missed nothing, no matter how trivial. The more he thought about it all, the more suspicious he was yet still he didn't really know what it was that was making him doubt Susan's story.

She came into the room then, all smiles and apologies. She looked at Colin sheepishly and put her hand up to her own neck instinctively.

'Hello, Colin, Miss Beacham.' Her niceness was back in place and he felt himself relax.

'How are the kids, and when can I see them?'

The raw longing in her voice was awful.

'Are they doing all right like?'

Miss Beacham held out her large bony hand and smiled.

'Hello, Susan, you look well, have you lost weight?'

She nodded, happy for it to be noticed.

'I have actually. It's the nosh. Fucking awful it is.' She rubbed her belly. 'Even me spare tyres – spare tyre – is panicking, I can tell you.'

The two women laughed together and Colin felt an outsider in this conversation.

'Maybe I should get myself a stint in here, I could do with losing a bit of weight,' Miss Beacham joked.

They both laughed again, and the atmosphere was relaxed once more. Colin, despite himself, was impressed. They all sat down. Susan lit a cigarette from a pack on the table which Miss Beacham had brought with her.

'Thanks, Miss Beacham, this is going down a treat. I'm sick of smoking roll ups.'

Colin was annoyed with himself. Why hadn't he thought of doing that? Miss Beacham cleared her throat and sighed.

'I have something to tell you, Susan, about Wendy. Now before you start, she's fine, really fine.'

Colin was watching from the window, smirking. That was exactly what he had said before the strangling episode. He decided to stay by the window for a while just in case Susan lost it again. Even the PO was on red alert now.

'It seems, Susan, that Wendy has picked up some kind of disease.' Miss Beacham looked straight into her eyes. 'I'm very much afraid it is a venereal disease. Now I know how powerless you must feel but as she is under sixteen we thought you should be informed, even though she is under the care of the courts.

'Can you shed any light on it for us? Have you any idea where she might have picked it up? Only, you see, she has not been in a position to get herself into any mischief at the home. If you understand me?'

The social worker sighed.

'Jesus, Sue, but this is the hardest thing I have ever had to tell a parent.'

She was nearly crying and Susan grabbed her hand across the table sympathetically.

'I know, mate. I understand, really I do.'

Colin was amazed. Amazed and astounded. If he had told Susan that, she would have been on a second murder charge. What the hell was it with women?

'So what has she got then?'

Susan's voice was dull and resigned.

'She has a thing called herpes. It's like a chicken pox virus, believe it or not. It came over from the States, I understand.'

Susan shrugged.

'Trust her to get something American. Good old British diseases not enough for kids these days, eh?'

Colin couldn't believe how well she was taking it and made a mental note to bring Miss Beacham with him on every visit in future.

'Can it be treated then? Is it dangerous?'

The social worker shook her head sadly,

'It seems no one really knows much about it yet. But they're doing all sorts of research into it. So hopefully something will happen soon, eh? But it can't kill so don't worry too much. She's fine now. Probably more worried about you finding out than anything.'

Susan nodded, her face blank.

'Can I see her soon?'

Miss Beacham nodded.

'Of course you can, they'll all be in on Friday as usual.'

'What's happening about this adoption malarkey then? Only I'm going to fight it, as Colin will tell you after I've talked with him today.'

Susan looked over at him and half smiled.

'I refuse to give up my kids to anyone, even the nice Simpsons. I'll get someone to have her, I swear that much. So you are forewarned. And I hope, Miss Beacham, that will not make you forearmed.'

'Oh, Susan, I wish you could be with them, they think the world of you, I know that. I also know you were a wonderful mother to those children.'

Susan sighed.

'You're a good woman, Miss Beacham. The kids all like you, and to me that says it all. If kids don't take to a person, I always feel they have inside knowledge that we don't have. They suss people out much easier.'

She smiled.

Miss Beacham stood up and shook hands with her again.

'I'll wait outside for you, Colin. I'll leave you two to talk in private now.'

She walked from the room after summoning a PO to escort her from the premises.

Susan and Colin looked into each other's eyes.

'If I had told you that, Susan, you'd have tried to murder me,' he reproached her. She laughed at his aggrieved tone.

'Ain't you sussed it out yet, Colin? You're a man. Of course you'd be killed. It's the law.'

She said it deadpan and with a half smile. Against his better judgement Colin laughed. So did Susan and the PO on duty. The smile barely reached her eyes and he guessed she was playing the part of hardened con once more.

But the news she had heard about her daughter must have been tearing her up inside. She chain smoked throughout the entire visit.

Mrs Eappen was not sure how to deal with the woman in front of her. Well dressed, well shod and oozing money, her voice didn't fit and it was this that threw the care assistant off track.

Roselle smiled at her as best she could and fought to be polite.

'I understand that Wendy is ill, but I'm sure she will see me.'

Mrs Eappen was nonplussed and it was not a feeling she enjoyed. In fact, this visitor was the last thing she needed today.

'Her mother and I are very close, have been for years. If Susan were here, she would have no hesitation in allowing me to see the child. Whatever was wrong with her.'

Mrs Eappen knew that this woman had Wendy overnight and sometimes for weekends. She also knew there was something fishy about her, though she could not put her finger on it exactly.

'Would you care to talk to my solicitors, Eversham and Hope in Great Russell Street? I'm sure they can find a precedent of some sort. I am, after all, here at the request of the mother. Now I'm aware the children are in care, but I wasn't aware they had become your sole responsibility just yet.'

Roselle was bullshitting, but she did it with such conviction Mrs Eappen saw no other course but to let her see Wendy Dalston.

Wendy's face lit up as Roselle was shown into her bedroom. They hugged then Roselle looked at the glowering woman in front of her and said cheerfully, 'Tea would be wonderful.'

As she left the room with a face like thunder Roselle sat on the girl's bed and laughed with her.

'Miserable old hag! Christ, but I should be up for an Oscar after that performance. Now then, how are you? The old trouble, is it?'

Wendy nodded. They never said the word unless they had to but skirted around it, both aware of the enormity of what had happened to her.

'The worst yet, Roselle. Honestly it's so painful.'

The pain showed in her words and in her face. Roselle hugged her again.

'I heard about Mr Potter, or whatever his name is, and the blade. You are a girl, you know. Pity your mother never had your spunk, eh?'

She laughed and Wendy answered her truthfully, 'I think she did once but me dad knocked it out of her. I was thinking about him today. I can't help it when I'm like this. It's as if he's in the room again and I can smell him . . .'

She looked out of the window to hide the tears and Roselle swallowed down the lump forming in her own throat.

'Well, I have some good news for you.'

Wendy stared at her hopefully.

'Mr Potter is no more. He has ceased to be, climbed up the curtain to meet his maker as John Cleese would say. He is an ex-social worker.'

Wendy's eyes were like saucers.

'You're joking?'

Roselle shook her head.

'Remember Danny, the big black man I introduced you to that time?'

Wendy nodded.

'Well, he had a word in Alfred's shell-like and talked him into resigning. It seems Mr Potter has had an accident, a bad accident, and can't work any more anyway. What a touch, eh?'

Wendy bit her lip and shook her head.

'Honestly?'

Roselle nodded. 'Honestly, I swear, cross me heart and hope to die!'

Wendy, grinning, finished off the playground rhyme.

'Stick a needle in me eye!'

The door burst open then and the other children bowled in. Alana had Rosie on her hip. She was laughing until they all saw Roselle.

'Oh, hello, Miss.'

Wendy laughed.

'This ain't a miss, this is Roselle, Alana, you know that.'

Barry grinned up at her and he looked so like his father that Roselle felt her heart lurch. She opened her bag for something to do and took out some sweets.

Plonking Rosie on the bed, they all dived in without a second's thought. Roselle picked up Rosie, who was clean and sweet-smelling, and watched them. Watched them just being children. Enjoying a few sweets, a treat. She felt so sad she wanted to cry for them and their wasted lives. Rosie, deciding she liked the visitor, gave her a wet kiss and they all laughed.

Then Mrs Jane Simpson came into the room and introduced herself. She was a pretty woman. As she took Rosie from her, Roselle saw the need for a child in the other woman's face and had to turn away.

'Rosie's going home now, children.' Jane's voice was loud and firm.

Barry, all innocence, looked at her and said, 'Is me mum back then?'

There was hope in his voice, longing even, and Roselle felt an urge to pick up her handbag and run. Run away from these children who were not her responsibility.

Jane Simpson sighed.

'No, Barry, your mother is not back home and won't be for a long time.'

Barry, ever the optimist, shrugged.

'She might break out and come and get us, like in the Westerns.' His voice said he was convinced she was capable of it. Whatever Mrs Simpson might think. 'She might get a gun, or a rifle . . .'

Alana interrupted his dreaming.

'All right, Barry, I think we get the picture.'

He wasn't to be shut up that quickly. He cried out loudly, 'Well, she might!' with all the conviction he could muster.

Mrs Simpson left the room with a crying Rosie and they were all quiet then.

'I miss Rosie, even though all she does is eat and shit.'

Alana smacked Barry this time, hard across his legs.

'Stop it, you. Like we ain't got enough trouble without you swearing all the time and causing more hag.'

Alana looked at Roselle and shrugged.

'I wish someone wanted to adopt him. I'd sign the bleeding papers meself.'

Wendy and Roselle laughed out loud.

'So would I.' Wendy's voice was high with pretend humour.

Barry looked shrewd. His eyes half closed, he said seriously, 'I wonder if Steve Austin needs a little boy? I'd love to go with him. I'd become bionic and eat nothing but Angel Delight and Twixes.'

He looked closely at Roselle.

'When you're bionic you don't need to eat proper food because you're not human any more.'

She nodded as if she understood what he was talking about. 'I see.'

Alana grinned. 'You're not human anyway, you're a boy!'

But Barry was above all the piss taking.

'Then, when me mum came home, so would I. And I'd bring her presents and stuff to make her feel happy.'

Roselle ruffled his hair.

'I'm sure you would as well. You're a nice little boy, Barry.'

He liked the attention but acted disgusted to make everyone laugh again. Warming to his theme, and with an attentive audience, he shouted, 'Then do you know what I'd do? I'd go and steal Rosie back so me mum had her when she came home. Like an extra surprise.'

Pleased with himself, he wandered from the room. He knew to leave an audience wanting more did Barry Dalston, it was part of his charm.

'He's a complete nut is our Barry,' Alana said with pride in her voice. She looked at Roselle.

'He has a reading age of eleven and he's just had his ninth birthday. That's where he gets his imagination from.'

Hearing the motherly tones Roselle hugged the girl to her. It was a spontaneous act but it made her a friend for life. Alana hugged her back, and the little bit of attention made her start to cry, and her crying made Wendy cry.

Alana was so upset she could barely talk.

'I miss me mum so much, and they're taking Rosie away, and

no one knows what she really likes. They give her what they want her to like. What they think she should like. But she likes Mars bars, not Milky bars, and she likes you to pretend to drop her on her head, and she likes to sleep with me and Barry. It's not fair, it's just not fair! We ain't done nothing. Rosie's three now and she loves us. How can they take her away?'

Roselle hugged the two girls to her tightly, the tears pouring from her own eyes. The three females hugged and cried together and it was like this that Mrs Eappen found them. She had finally decided to make her guest some tea. Satisfied that her first impressions had been correct she left the tray and with a self-satisfied smile walked from the room.

Let that terrible woman sort it out this time. She had caused it.

But the crying had done the two girls and Roselle the world of good. It had unleashed their emotions and brought them all relief.

Alana went off to find Barry and share her spoils with him: a five-pound note from Roselle. Alone again, Wendy looked into Roselle's face and shook her head.

'It's all so sad, ain't it? None of them have done anything. Yet they're the ones who are suffering. I wish that night had never happened.'

Roselle took the girl in her arms once more.

'Bad things happen to us all in life. I mean, I never dreamed I'd end up doing what I do. But you just have to get on with it, don't you, love? Like we all do.'

'What about Rosie, though? Me mum will go mad if they adopt her. She'll never sleep another night in peace as long as she lives. Rosie was the baby, everyone's baby, even me dad's. He adored her.

'We weren't jealous of how he was with her, we were all pleased for her. Even Alana, who was his favourite before Rosie came along. She stepped aside with pleasure, because Rosie is special. She should be with me mum and if it wasn't for me she would be. It's all my fault, Roselle. All this mess – I made it. Not me mum. Me.'

Roselle took the girl by her shoulders and shook her gently.

'Listen to me – what happened to you was not your fault. Your father was wrong, very wrong to do what he did. Your mother did what any other woman would. Any woman in the world if her child was hurt like that. So stop this stupidity. Your mother's proud to have done what she did, she was protecting you from him for the future. Making sure he never did anything like that again.

'And, believe me, knowing your father it would have happened, again and again and again. Once he got away with it the first time he would have seen it as sport. Your mother knew that and dealt with it, as she will deal with whatever happens in the future.'

Wendy stared into the severe face before her and sighed.

'You don't understand, Roselle, no one understands. If it wasn't for me, my mum wouldn't be in prison. The kids wouldn't be here in care. Nothing would have changed so drastically. She would never have killed him, never. She was too scared of him, you see. Do you understand what I'm telling you?

'Oh, she might have divorced him maybe. Or tried to get shot of him. But she wouldn't have killed him. Mum isn't capable of killing anyone.'

Roselle shook her head in consternation.

'We're all capable of killing, darling. That's what is meant by the mark of Cain in the Bible. We're all capable of killing. We can all be pushed too far.'

Wendy sighed sadly.

'That's what I am trying to tell you, Roselle. Me mum didn't kill me dad – I did.'

The words, once spoken, electrified the room and the two women in it.

'You what?'

Wendy licked her lips and said, slowly and clearly, 'I killed him. No matter what anyone says, I killed him. Me.'

Roselle held her tight.

'Stop taking the blame for it all. You couldn't help what happened so listen to me and listen good. Your mum is in that prison, away from you all, but what keeps her going is knowing that she did what she did to keep you safe. All of you. Because who's to say he wouldn't have been after Alana at some point in the future, eh?

'Now you get better and try and put all this nonsense out of your head. Your mum is up for appeal and I am going to make sure she gets it, whatever she says, okay? I am on board as from today. So stop worrying.'

Wendy leaned against her and her whole body felt slack.

'I love you, Roselle. And so does me mum.'

'And I love you too, sweetheart.'

They hugged once more and then Roselle stood up. Picking her bag up off the floor she took out a packet of Benson and Hedges.

'Open the window and me and you will have a field day, eh?'

Chapter Twenty-Six

Colin was surprised to see the woman he had just been admiring in the street standing in his office. He knew he was smiling inanely but she had flashed quite a bit of leg getting out of her car.

His shared secretary, Callie, looked at him. Sighing loudly she said in a thick Birmingham accent, 'You can put your eyes back now, Colin. She is real, aren't you, love?' She smiled at Roselle. 'Can I get you a cuppa?'

Roselle nodded. She liked the girl though she was aware that the young man could probably murder his secretary at that moment.

When the door shut Colin tried unsuccessfully to move a pile of papers and files from a chair opposite his laden desk. The papers fell to the floor with a hushing noise and Roselle bent down and picked them up for him, giving him a glimpse of creamy white flesh that made his face burn.

Standing again, she looked at him and grinned.

'You need a regular girlfriend, young man.'

Burning like a beacon now, he ushered her into the chair like an old-fashioned gentleman.

'So, Miss . . . What can I do for you?'

Roselle smiled and her slightly parted lips looked so luscious he felt faint.

'Mr Jackson, I'm a close friend of Susan Dalston's and I've decided I want to help her, whether she likes it or not.'

Colin was nonplussed for a few moments.

'How do you mean?'

Roselle smiled thinly. Her patience was being tried and it showed.

'I mean, Mr Jackson, I want to help Susan Dalston get out of prison. I have the money to provide her with the best legal representation. I'm willing to pay whatever it takes to bring her home to her kids where she belongs.'

Colin stared across the desk. He wasn't sure whether he was being sent up.

'Why now?'

Roselle shrugged.

'What difference does it make when, why or how? I just want you to find me the best counsel you can. I'll foot the bill and I'll also talk Susan into helping herself. Which, as I am sure you realise, is what stopped her getting out before now.'

Colin guessed this woman knew a lot more than he did. He also guessed she wasn't going to elaborate in any way. Like Susan, she only said what she considered relevant at the time she spoke.

They were both difficult women. He had had to accept that fact, but couldn't help pushing it.

'What do you know?'

Roselle laughed heartily.

'Enough. Now I'm going to arrange to visit Susan and talk to her myself. You find out who we can get on board and get working for her release.'

'Geraldine O'Hara is probably the best silk you could get but she's not cheap.'

Roselle nodded.

'Then that's who we'll have. Can you arrange for us to see her?'

Colin liked the 'us' part, it made him smile.

'I can try.'

Roselle leaned forward in the chair and said huskily, 'Has anyone ever told you about the power of positive thinking?'

Debbie watched as Jamesie got ready to go out. He looked lovely as usual, all brooding good looks and expensive clothes.

'No work today then?'

He ignored her as usual and carried on dressing.

She swallowed back an angry retort.

'Will you be home for dinner?'

He turned from the wardrobe mirror and looked her in the face.

'What's it to you then?'

Inside Debbie's head a voice was screaming at her, telling her not to let him treat her so badly. But she knew that if she retaliated he would go ballistic. It was Jamesie's answer to everything. If she questioned him about where he was going he would hit her, he always did. She was forever trying to keep the peace with him.

She knew he was going to Carol's. Carol who had given him a son. Carol the girlfriend with her blonde hair and blue eyes and trim little figure. Carol who looked her in the face, a half smile on her lips when they saw one another down the market. The girl's eyes told her she was a fool but Debbie knew that already. She didn't need a little tart in high heels to tell her so. She had to live with it every day of her life.

Five babies she had lost. The doctors said she couldn't carry them. She was heavy now from the pregnancies, from the comfort eating, from the drinking. She wiped a hand across her face. It was a tired gesture and Jamesie laughed.

'You are one useless ponce, Debs, do you know that?'

She looked him in the face.

'I should do, Jamesie, you tell me often enough.'

She saw his eyes narrow and his face harden.

'Getting a bit harry dash, are we, eh? Think you can say what you like, do you?'

She shook her head, the moment of retaliation over.

'I ain't flash, Jamesie. I ain't nothing.'

He poked a bony finger into her chest.

'You got that much right.'

He pushed past her and walked from the bedroom. She hated herself for following him and asking the inevitable questions but she couldn't help it.

'Will you be home tonight? Shall I do you a bit of dinner anyway, put it in the microwave?'

She could hear the pleading tone in her voice, hear the need inside her head, and hated herself for it. For letting it happen to her.

He turned at the bottom of the stairs.

'Do what you fucking want.'

He slipped on a leather jacket and Debbie tried to brush the shoulders for him. He slapped her hands away as if she was contaminated.

'Please, Jamesie, don't go today. We can go out or something.'

He sneered. His blue eyes and thick black hair made him too good-looking really. Even furious with her, he still had the power to make her want him.

'Where would I want to go with you, eh? Fucking bingo, where? I wouldn't be seen dead in the pea fields with you, Debbie. Surely you've sussed that much out for yourself.'

He was staring at her intently, amazed at her resilience, the way she could be treated so badly yet still come back for more.

'Bricks and mortar keep me here. I own this drum and I want you out. There, now I've said it.'

Debbie felt the familiar sickness in the pit of her stomach. The shaking inside herself as if she was facing a perilous journey.

She knew he was enjoying her discomfort, he always did.

'You rotten bastard.'

He grinned then.

'Got it in one.'

He walked out of the front door as if he didn't have a care in the world.

'You're not still writing letters, surely?'

Susan nodded, head bent over the table in the cell. In front of her was a pile of roll ups, a box of matches and a cup of tea.

'I am. I have to try and sort out something for Rosie. I'm even trying me sister Debbie though I don't hold out much hope. If only Barry's mum wasn't so ill, bless her, then I'd be sorted.'

Matty stroked her hair.

'Shall I talk to Geraldine for you, see what she has to say?'

Susan looked up at her.

'Would you? Really?'

Matty nodded, pleased.

'Of course I would. I think it's disgraceful what they're doing to you. Rhianna's been there too, you know. She told me about it. I can't imagine having kids. I think it's hard enough with just yourself to worry about.'

Susan lit another roll up and drew on it deeply.

'I hate these things. All me fingers are going yellow. That brief of yours is supposed to be the dog's gonads, ain't she? But don't she only work on cases like yours?'

Matty sighed.

'Your case *is* like mine, Sue. You were battered, weren't you? If you'd only help yourself more, you'd get out.'

Susan stared at her for long moments. 'Does everything that gets said in the court have to be made a matter of public record?'

Matty sat down on the bunk.

'Not necessarily, why?'

Susan shrugged.

'I just wondered, that's all. I mean, is there a chance it could be kept private?'

Matty looked into her eyes.

'Like I said, it depends. Sometimes if a murder is particularly gruesome the judge might say that certain aspects of it should not be made public. Perhaps child murders, things like that. It's deemed not to be in the public interest.'

Susan listened carefully.

'Why, what do you want kept secret then?' Matty probed.

Susan didn't answer her.

'Come on, Sue, you can tell me.'

Her voice was low, persuasive.

'Nothing. I just wondered, that's all.'

Her cell mate stood up, clearly annoyed.

'If you told me what was really going on, I could help you. Honestly, Sue, I could.'

Susan looked as if she was about to say something when the cell door opened wide and PO Blackstock stood before them.

'What's this, a mothers' meeting? Come on, Dalston, you have a real visit.'

'Who is it?'

The PO looked at her nastily.

'Well, who have you sent a VO to?'

Her voice brooked no argument and Susan followed her eagerly. She knew who it was and was amazed. After all this time she was both excited and nervous at the prospect.

She hoped she had done the right thing.

Geraldine and Roselle took one look at each other and a friendship was born. Two women, similar in some ways yet worlds apart in lifestyle, met in a plush office in Holborn and both knew instinctively they would be great friends.

'Sit down and I'll get us coffee. Unless you'd like something stronger, of course?'

Roselle smiled.

'A large brandy wouldn't go amiss. I'm about to blow my best friend's world wide open. I need something inside me for that.'

Intrigued, Geraldine made them both a drink and when settled looked at Roselle and raised her glass.

'Come on then, out with it. Before you change your mind and waste my time.' Roselle laughed gently. This woman had sussed her out already. 'I only saw you at short notice because of Colin Jackson. So don't disappoint me now.'

Geraldine watched as Roselle slammed back the brandy in one swallow.

'I needed that. All right, the truth. This is purely confidential, isn't it?'

Geraldine nodded.

'Of course.'

'Barry Dalston, believe it or not, was my lover. That's how Susan and I became friends as strange as it might sound. I know from Susan that he raped their eldest daughter Wendy. That was what drove Susan to murder him. The girl was given herpes by her own father, isn't that sick? Susan has never told anyone so Wendy can live without everyone knowing what happened to her at the hands of her own father.'

Geraldine was shocked to the core.

'You were his lover and his wife's friend, and she killed him because he raped their daughter – am I getting this right? I thought that Wendy wasn't even there that night.'

Roselle nodded.

'That's what everyone thinks. So what are you going to do about it?'

'Get us both another drink, I think.'

Roselle grinned.

'You do that and I'll start at the very beginning, shall I? You'll understand the situation much better then.'

Geraldine shook her head sadly.

'I hope so, but it sounds as if my understanding it will be the least of our problems.'

June sat in the visiting room looking every bit the unconcerned mother.

Susan smiled at her.

'Hello, Mum. How are you?'

She looked at her daughter and sighed, lighting a cigarette to hide her embarrassment.

'I thought I'd be the last person you'd want to see?'

Susan still smiled and that smile was making June more uncomfortable by the second.

'You are my mum.'

June shrugged dismissively.

'I hardly need reminding of that, do I?'

'Why did you come then?'

She shrugged again.

'I wish I fucking hadn't bothered to be honest. I suppose I just wanted to see how you were for meself like. As you said, I am your mum.'

Susan looked strange to her. She was much thinner and had a glow about her that June had never seen before.

'Well, you obviously like the life inside. It suits you, if you don't mind me saying. You look really well.'

It was the closest June would get to being motherly and Susan was grateful for it.

'You look great, I like your coat.'

The full-length leather was June's pride and joy.

'Well, you've got to make the effort, ain't you?'

She lit another cigarette from the butt of the previous one.

'Must have cost a few quid?'

June looked at her spitefully.

'It did. I bought it from the money I got from the papers, Sue. So now you know.'

Susan closed her eyes in distress.

'I don't want to argue, Mum, what's done is done. I wanted to ask you a favour.'

June blew the smoke out of her lips in a belligerent fashion.

'I thought it would be something like that. Well, if you want me to take on your four fucking kids, you can think again. I don't want them.'

Susan closed her eyes and willed herself to be calm.

'I don't want that, Mum. I wouldn't want my father near those children and you know why, don't you? I want to ask you if you'll try and talk our Debbie into having them for a while.'

June did laugh now.

'You are joking? With that Irish ponce of an old man of hers? He sees you as letting down the family, girl. Thinks you're scum. Poor Debbie has had to put up with all sorts over you.'

'No, she hasn't, Mum. Stop exaggerating all the time. She had hag with him from day one. He even had a baby by someone else.'

June sniffed.

'That Carol's a slag. Apparently her own mother and father are disowning her. Should have brought her up better, shouldn't they?'

Susan shook her head in disbelief.

'You know what? You really amaze me, Mother. You've had more men than a fucking dock dolly and yet you have the neck to sit there and slag that girl off. Your husband was after his own child and you never did a thing about it, did you? I'm in here because of you and him. You talk about bringing up kids after what you did to me and Debs . . .'

As June made to rise Susan grabbed her wrist tightly.

'You walk away and I'll rip your fucking head off. Do you hear me, Mother?'

June sat down opposite her daughter and felt fear rush over her.

'When I think what our lives were like with you and him, I could fucking strangle you! Barry was just like you and me father, a selfish ponce always out for himself. Like you still are.

'Do you know what it did to my kids, you selling that load of old crap to the papers about me and him? Blaming me for it all. Implying I was an unfit mother. Though you could never actually come out and say that, could you, because it ain't true. If you'd loved us like I love my kids we'd have been all right, me and Debs. I vowed I'd do it differently and I did. My kids had everything a kid should have. They had clothes, they were fed and they were *loved* – really loved. They still are.

'I wanted to see you to try and put the past behind us, try and make some sense of it all, but I should have realised I was wasting my time. Go on, fuck off. You can tell all the neighbours you've seen your daughter the murderess. Get you a few drinks down the pub that will. You two-faced old witch!'

June was white with shock. She looked into Susan's face and for the first time in years felt a spark of affection for her daughter. Respect even.

'Well, if you want me to do you a favour you have a funny way of getting round me. I'll get us a cup of tea, eh?'

She pushed the fag packet across the table.

'Have a tailor made while you're waiting.'

Susan watched her as she sashayed across the visiting room, hair immaculate, clothes too young and too tight.

She wished she had told her what she thought of her long ago. If nothing else it had made her feel better inside.

Much better.

Whatever happened today, at least she had seen her mother. For some reason Susan still needed her. Though why that was, she had no idea.

* * *

The Simpsons were due to pick up Rosie after her visit to the other children. Mrs Eappen was giving them sandwiches and cups of tea. She was worried about Wendy, the girl looked really ill.

'Come on, Wendy, eat something, dear.'

She shook her head.

'Honestly, I couldn't eat a thing.'

Barry took the sandwich from her plate.

'I can. I can eat anything, me. I have a cast iron stomach.'

It was said with pride and they all laughed.

Wendy lay back on the chair and closed her eyes. Little Rosie was falling asleep on her lap and she could smell the little girl's freshly washed hair and her baby sweat. Little fat starfish hands held on tightly to her bra straps through her jumper. Instinctively she hugged the little girl closer to her, kissing the top of her head.

'They won't really let her be adopted, will they?'

Mrs Eappen shrugged.

'I can't say. Your mother has every right to fight it but unless one of her family comes forward soon, I'm afraid it looks inevitable.'

Wendy nodded absently.

'It's not fair. It's just isn't fair.'

Mrs Eappen held her arm gently.

'I know, dear.'

Colin walked into the day room then, his face all smiles.

'Hello, you lot.'

The children smiled at him, even Wendy.

'Colin, if I was sixteen could I have custody of this lot?'

'Maybe, it depends. You'd need a lot of help.'

Wendy shrugged.

'Anyone would need help with Barry on board. But I'm being serious, is there any chance at all?'

Colin shrugged.

'I could look into it for these two but Rosie would be a different kettle of fish.'

Wendy's face fell. It was as if someone had turned off a light from within.

'It's Rosie I really want to see sorted out, though. I know the Simpsons are nice people but they can't keep me mum locked away for ever and she'll want us all when she comes home. That means Rosie as well. Surely there must be someone who can help us?'

She looked at Colin and Mrs Eappen. Neither of them could give her an answer.

'I wanted to talk to you actually, Wendy. At some point. When you're up to it, of course.'

Colin smiled encouragingly at the girl but she didn't smile back.

'What about?' The blank look was back on her face.

'There's a few things I need to ask you, just things I want to get straight in my own mind.'

He looked at her earnestly and she dropped her eyes. Mrs Eappen noticed the girl's frightened expression and wondered just what went on inside that pretty little head at times.

After that Wendy was quiet and the day seemed strained. Mrs Eappen watched her closely. The girl was constantly on edge. But that was only natural after such a tragedy in the family.

June walked up Debbie's path and threw her cigarette butt into the planter hanging by the front door. She smiled. Debbie really thought she was up market these days even with an old man who was out shagging anything with a pulse under the age of sixty-five. Little Carol couldn't keep him to herself though she tried from what June had heard through the grapevine. She certainly seemed to do a better job than June's daughter anyway. At least she saw him regularly by all accounts which was more than Debbie could say.

The door was opened by Debbie herself, her face blotchy and red. Her mouth turned down at the corners, giving her a childish expression that seemed out of place on her adult features.

'Oh, for fuck's sake, you miserable mare! No wonder your old man's out and about all the time with a boatrace like that waiting for him every night!'

Debbie burst into tears once more and June, pushing past her, walked up the hallway and into the kitchen. She put the kettle on before she talked again, eyes taking in every detail of the house.

'This place is too clean, Debs. It's more like a fucking show house than a home.'

She opened the cupboard and took out two white mugs.

'Is it right that little whore is pregnant again by Jamesie?' She was spooning sugar and coffee into the mugs as she spoke. 'If she is, you need to aim him right out this time. The shame is terrible for me and your father. It's bad enough we have *one* daughter up for murder, now the other one has her name up as a right fucking prat. Give me Susan's solution to the problem every time.'

Debbie sat at the little breakfast bar that had once been her pride and joy, and shut her brain off. It was the only way she could cope with her mother.

'Stuck out here in Rainham, in the fucking sticks with loads of weirdos for neighbours. Never say a word to one another this lot.'

'It's only us they don't talk to, Mum. Not since you informed Mrs Black next door that you'd give her husband one, if you had the chance.'

June shrugged.

'Well I would. He's a bit of all right. But her! She looks like a well-slapped arse. You should never have left the East End, either of you. At least round there you could have kept the beady on Jamesie. Ponce that he is.' She poured water into the mugs and stirred vigorously.

'I saw Susan today.'

June was pleased by the expression on her daughter's face.

'You what!'

June poured milk into the coffee and slopped it all over the worktop. For once Debbie didn't go mad.

'You really went to see Susan? How is she? I can't believe she's still talking to any of us after the last turn out with the papers.'

June ignored her.

'She understands does Susan, always had a bit of nous, her. Anyway she wants to see you.'

She lit a fag and Debbie automatically got up and opened the back door. Jamesie hated people smoking in the house.

'Why does she want to see me?'

June grinned, showing big yellowing teeth.

'She wants you to have little Rosie for her until she gets out.'

'She's got to be joking!'

Her mother shook her head, deadly serious.

'She ain't. They're going to adopt her out to this couple, the Simpsons, and Susan naturally thinks this is a bit of a piss take. So she has turned to her family for help and support.'

Debbie listened to her mother's self-righteous tone of voice and realised June was even more unbalanced than she had previously thought.

'It's the least we can do for her, isn't it? I mean, stuck in there, all on her Jack Jones. And in fairness to Susan, she was a good mother.'

The latter was said grudgingly. June looked at her daughter's sceptical expression.

'Even in the papers, whatever else I might have said, I always said our Susan was a good mother.'

Debbie stood up, slowly and deliberately. Her voice when she spoke was a deep growl. Her mother had finally pushed her over the edge. Every nasty remark, every vicious word, was conjured up in Debbie's head and her depth of feeling came out in three small words.

'Get out, Mum.'

June's face paled.

'You what?'

Debbie pushed her none too gently towards the door.

'You heard. Get the fuck out of here. Piss off.'

June felt herself being propelled down the narrow hallway. Thrusting her daughter from her, she turned on her like a vixen.

'Don't you dare tell me to piss off, you useless wanker!'

Debbie was laughing at her now and June wasn't sure what to do.

'What are you laughing at, you bloody div?'

Debbie laughed until the tears were running down her face.

'You are a piece of shit, Mother, do you know that? Poor Susan has had the pain of knowing her kids were with strangers all that time and you didn't give a shit. What did she offer you, eh? What did she offer her *own mother* to get her to do her a favour? Another lucrative story for the press? Come on, Mum, I'm interested. Tell me.'

June was seething with anger and resentment.

'You little mare! You really think you're better than me, don't you? You, with your fucking terraced house and your mown fucking lawn. Your velvet curtains and Dralon three-piece. Oh, you really think you're the dog's bollocks, you do.

'Well, listen to me, lady. You have nothing, neither chick nor child, no old man and no life. My Susan had a bit of go in her, at least she had that. At least she had the guts to top that bastard for battering her.

'What guts have you got, eh? He's got another bird, a family with her, and you haven't even had the guts to give him his marching orders. Susan understands why I did what I did. She knows the value of a penny she does. Unlike you she's had to scrimp for everything she's got. You and him stick at it because of this house, that's all. Well, let me tell you, a house is just a fucking house. If you ain't happy in it then it means nothing.'

She waved her arms around.

'You think that by cleaning and washing all day you'll be happy? Well, you won't. I know I'm an arsehole, I've been perfecting it for years. What excuse have you got, eh? You are a vindictive, bitter, miserable little mare. Susan has had the guts to tell me what she thinks of me, yet she still knows that whatever I might have done I'm her mother. Even I realise that much now. Well, you're her sister and you could easily take that baby. Christ knows, you ain't ever going to have one of your own . . .'

Both women fell silent then as if each realised they had gone too far.

'Christ, Debs, I never meant it like that.'

'Get out, Mother. And this time, don't come back.'

June pulled her long leather coat around herself protectively and said quietly, 'I won't come back, Debs. But before I go, listen to me. Susan and you are sisters and I'm your mother, whether you like it or not. Go and see her. Try and help her. Christ knows she would have done it for you and even you know that's true. If the boot was on the other foot you wouldn't even have had to ask her, would you?

'I hate to say this but she's better than us all put together is Susan. Even made me feel ashamed.'

June let herself out of the house. Debbie silently watched her walk down the path to the gate. Closing the door, she went through to the kitchen and began to tidy up the mess her mother had made.

As she got the bleach out from under the sink and poured it on to the worktop the overpowering smell made her eyes water. Looking down at her hands she saw their redness from all the hot water and detergents. Her gaze went around the kitchen, looking at the perfectly arranged cupboards and the pristine tiled floor, and she wondered what the hell she was doing here.

Jamesie would rather spend his time with a little tart in a one-bedroom council flat with a damp patch and mould as part of the décor. Though she had a feeling that what he really wanted was Carol, his boy and this house.

He wanted Debbie out.

He had not been home properly since his little boy was born.

Who was she trying to kid that she still had a marriage?

Carol made Jamesie a sandwich and a cup of tea. Her kitchen was small but well fitted with cupboards. She, though, never bothered to put anything away. The bedroom was full of ironing and the lounge full of toys and games. The kitchen looked like a bomb site. She just swept everything into a pile and made room for herself.

Cleanliness to Carol was more a case of what you could get away with. She never saw the sense in wasting your life cleaning when you could be having a good time.

Jamesie bit into his ham sandwich and laughed at little Jamie's efforts at building a tower with bricks. As Carol made her own sandwich he called out to her constantly.

'Come and see him, Cal. Look how he built that. He's a bright lad him. Look at the size of his shoulders. He'll be a big one.'

The complimentary remarks were constant and Carol basked in

the knowledge that Jamesie was hers. From the moment he had seen the red scrunched up face of his son, he had been hers. She caressed her belly. Now she had another one inside her and knew without a shadow of a doubt that he would give his old woman the big E. Fat Debbie was about to be turfed out of that little palace she loved so much. Carol wasn't bothered by that. In fact, she thought Debbie had asked for it. Any woman who put anything before their man was a fool.

As Carol sat on the sofa and watched her two men playing together she smiled, a long slow smile like a cat who had caught a particularly big and juicy rat.

Which was, although she didn't realise it, exactly what she had done.

Wendy sat in her room and watched the evening sun disappear behind a row of detached houses nearby. She could see into the gardens and often observed the families there as they relaxed. She saw them doing their gardening, reading books in deckchairs. Saw children playing in paddling pools. She heard the laughter and sometimes the cross words and bickering brought to her courtesy of the evening wind.

She envied the children their safe houses, their nice clothes and their parents. Mostly she envied them their parents.

What she wouldn't give to have her mother's arms around her now, her mother's voice telling her everything would be all right.

She put her head on her arms and closed her eyes.

She was still, perfectly still for a moment. Then she went to the bureau and opened a drawer. Inside was a bottle of paracetamol tablets. She caressed the glass gently.

She had a desperate urge to take them, one by one. Swallow them all. If she was gone, everything might get better.

She was the cause of everything. If she had not been home that night . . . If she had gone in with one of the younger kids . . . If she had only kept out of his way, none of this would have happened. Rosie would not be with the Simpsons and the other two would be asleep in their own beds.

She had caused so much trouble with her actions, upset so

many people's lives, it really would be better if she was gone. It would be right and just for her to take her life after ruining so many other people's.

She thought of what Colin had said to her earlier in the day. He knew something wasn't right and had tried to pry out of her why she was at her gran's and the kids left in Alana's charge. A child's charge.

Wendy had not answered him.

Her mother would sit it out for ever before she let anyone know what had happened to her daughter.

What her daughter had done.

Wendy knew she could never tell even if she wanted to because it would break her mother's heart.

Opening the bottle she took out the tablets. Then, sitting on the bed, she poured herself a large glass of orange from the jug on her night table. She gripped the bottle hard, feeling the sweat as it poured from her palms and seeped through her fingers.

All she had to do was take these tablets and everything would be better.

Chapter Twenty-Seven

'She's what? And you haven't mentioned it till now!'

Susan's voice was incredulous. As she was told about her daughter's attempted suicide she felt her world collapse around her ears.

The Head PO felt such overwhelming pity for the woman before her she worried she might cry herself.

'Listen to me, Susan, she's okay. Honestly. We didn't get you up in the night because we didn't see the point in worrying you. I made that decision because I felt it was the right one at the time.'

Susan didn't answer her; she was looking around the office as if some miraculous escape route would materialise in front of her eyes.

'My baby, my little girl, was in intensive care and *you didn't want to worry me?*'

Mrs Carlin shook her head sadly.

'There was nothing you could have done, Susan. I felt it would be wicked to give you that worry in the night when there was nothing you could do.'

Susan looked into the kindly woman's face and whispered, 'I could have prayed, Miss, I could have done that at least.'

Mrs Carlin walked around the desk. Picking up the cup of hot sweet tea she placed it gently in Susan's hands.

'Drink up. I'm going to the governor to see if we can get you a visit.'

Sue grasped at the heavy white mug in despair.

'They ain't going to let me out, are they?'

Mrs Carlin's heavily lined face softened as she spoke.

'Well, Susan, we can but try. We can but try.'

* * *

Wendy was tired, so very tired.

As she lay in the hospital bed, hearing the noisy movements on the ward, she felt a feeling of utter desperation roll over her.

She couldn't even kill herself properly.

A nurse, a pretty Irish girl with big blue eyes and shocking red hair, popped her head around the door.

'A cup of tea, my little love? Or a drink of water perhaps?'

Wendy smiled wanly, her face so sad the nurse felt depressed just looking at her. She came into the room and sat on the bed. She smiled widely and professionally.

'Come on, give me a bit of chat, I'm mad to talk to someone nearer me own age. Jesus knows but the English are reticent and the ward sister's a bitch in a dress.'

Wendy did smile now, a sad smile.

'Will they send me back to the home soon?'

The nurse shrugged.

'Sure, how would I know? They tell me nothing while I'm training.'

She pushed Wendy's long thick dark hair from her brow.

'Would you look at that hair? Jesus, I'd give all me wages for hair like that. It's gorgeous. I bet it attracts the fellas, eh?'

She realised she'd said the wrong thing by the look of utter contempt on the young girl's face. Wendy pulled away from her and said heavily, 'I don't want to attract fellas, thank you. I just want to be left in peace.'

'Come away out of that, would you? That's why we're all here. You'll feel differently soon, believe me. Is that what made you . . . you know?'

She was genuinely interested and Wendy saw a young girl like herself, trying to fit into the grown-up world and at a loss as to how to do it. She didn't answer her and they sat in silence together.

'We all get experience one day, I suppose. You have to. Have to learn it all.'

The girl's voice was low, she was trying so hard to be friendly.

'I know too much already and I don't want to fit in. Not any more.'

Wendy's voice was so desolate the young nurse felt saddened to the core.

'Ah, don't be letting yourself get depressed again. Life's a big present from God but what you do with it is up to you. You get one crack at it, it's not a dress rehearsal as me mother used to say. Six months from now you'll be wondering what the feck you were so worried about.'

Wendy smiled at her jovial voice. If only she could be like this little person with her starched uniform and sensible shoes.

'Six months from now all my problems will still be there, and they'll be worse not better. Believe me, I know.'

Rosie would be gone for ever by then.

Little Rosie, everyone's pride and joy.

'You can't say that for definite. Everything changes. Everything has to change. Sure, that's what life is all about, isn't it? Making things happen, making things change.'

Wendy looked into the girl's pretty freckled face and sighed heavily.

'I think I will have a cup of tea now.'

The nurse jumped from the bed and grinned.

'I'm Orla by the way. Orla O'Halloran.'

Wendy smiled. 'I'm Wendy Dalston.'

Orla laughed loudly.

'Sure, don't I already know your name, child? It's above the bed.'

She skipped merrily from the room and Wendy lay back against the cool pillows and was half sorry and half pleased the exuberant girl had gone.

Happy people, she decided, wore you out.

And she felt worn out inside and out, as if she had lived a hundred years already.

Geraldine was in her office going through Susan Dalston's case file and the reading was heavy. As she looked through the witness statements and police reports she was growing angry. She could see all too clearly that the police had accepted Susan's story without once questioning it. It was full of contradictions, had enough holes in it to make it practically inadmissible. But she also knew that these men who had visited the woman's house on numerous occasions, who knew the treatment she had suffered at the victim's hands, were just out for an easy conviction. Short and sweet. Barry had battered Susan five days before and she had decided to kill him after a night out in a local pub where she had, quote, 'had a great night'. If she was in such a good mood, why did she decide that night of all nights to hammer her husband's head until it was gone? Until there was nothing left but bone and brain.

The coroner's report stated he had been hit viciously and repeatedly. The first few blows had killed him, it decreed in its wisdom. So why did she carry on with the attack which they estimated must have taken at least fifteen minutes?

Now Geraldine knew about the daughter she understood a lot more than they had, obviously. But at the same time it still seemed so extreme. Even knowing what he had done to Wendy, it seemed extreme. It was as if Susan Dalston had wanted to obliterate every trace of Barry Dalston. Wanted to take his face away.

She pulled out the psychiatrists' reports. Each one stated that Susan was sane and of sound mind *during* the event.

Susan herself claimed she was sane and of sound mind when she did it. In fact, she went on to say, 'I would do it again if I had the chance.'

Why had she never tried to defend her actions?

The girl was raped by her own father. In fact he had given her herpes which could easily be established before a court. Susan's not wanting people to know about the rape was understandable. No woman would want their child to have to live with the stigma of that. But the girl should have had treatment, surely Susan should have seen that much? That Wendy needed counselling. Help to cope with a rape and her mother's actions after that rape. Surely Susan Dalston didn't think the girl was going to get better by herself? On top of all that the father had given the girl a disease she would keep all her life. Susan Dalston, as the girl's mother, should have realised that at some point all that trauma would eventually tell on Wendy in some way.

Did she really believe it was better for the girl to pretend it had never happened? That she would cope without her mother. That her other children would cope without her. A woman who was, by all accounts, a good and caring mother who worshipped her children and had brought them up as fine individuals even though she'd lived with a man who treated her like a dog.

None of it added up.

There had to be something else going on, a deeper reason, and until Geraldine found out what that reason was she knew Susan Dalston would rot in jail.

In court it had been made to sound as if Barry Dalston, albeit a wife beater and one-time thug, had got drunk and while lying innocently in bed had been murdered in cold blood by his own wife.

A woman who was overweight, unattractive, and looked like a murderess. Looked the sort who would kill her husband on a whim.

And Susan Dalston had done all in her power to perpetuate that myth. The newspaper photos showed a hard-faced woman sneering at the camera. In court she had laughed out loud as they'd talked about her husband's life. How he was a likeable rogue. A basically decent man who was dragged down by his lifestyle. His lack of education. Who came home to his family and was murdered viciously by a monster.

Susan had never once tried in her own defence to argue that he was any different. That he had systematically abused her, beaten babies from her belly and tortured her with his fists and words. A man who'd left her short of everything from affection to money. A man who slept around and even had a long-running affair with an ex-prostitute who miraculously became his wife's friend and mentor.

Roselle had told Geraldine this yet she could have guessed as much from the police reports and the witness statements.

Even Susan's family had betrayed her for money offered by the gutter press. What kind of people were they to turn her distress into pounds, shillings and pence? That said it all about Susan's lifestyle and upbringing really. Her own parents would sell their daughter's soul for money.

Now Geraldine had the unenviable task of trying to talk Susan Dalston into coming clean. And that, she decided, was going to be a very hard task indeed. But she was determined to get Susan out.

This was personal now.

This was Geraldine O'Hara's crusade.

Barry, Alana and Rosie were all together in the bright room reserved at the home for quiet times. This room was used when children had to be told bad news or to be calmed in some way. Miss Beacham, who had forfeited her day off to be with them, looked at the Dalstons with pity tinged with anger.

So far as she was concerned Susan Dalston should be at home with her kids and that was that. She frequently saw children abused by their fathers who were sent here then sent back home to face exactly the same treatment. But these children no longer faced danger at home, not with their mother alone. Only Susan was locked up, unable to care for them, and it was wrong. The whole system was wrong.

Sometimes the power she wielded frightened Miss Beacham. The power of social services frightened her. They were expected to make decisions on a daily basis about real people living real lives.

Barry and Alana were holding hands. Even little Rosie sensed something was wrong and was quiet, playing with a few building bricks and half-heartedly making a tower. Miss Beacham knew the Simpsons had not wanted to bring her in today but had guessed that her presence would comfort the other two children. She had been right. These children had bonded and that was thanks to their mother.

There was no rivalry between them which was often the case with children in care. So many parents made one child a god and the other children had to strive all their lives to get the same attention. To be accepted. She saw it every day of her working life. These four kids adored one another, applauded each other's achievements and looked out for one another. If one child did well the others were happy for them. There was none of the usual putting down or trivialising of achievement that was common with other kids in care.

She opened her bag and took out two Twixes, Barry's favourite. He smiled his thanks and put them on the table in front of him.

'I'll save mine for Wendy, for when she comes back.'

Alana opened hers and gave him half.

Miss Beacham watched the generosity with tears in her eyes. She saw Barry break a small piece off and pop it into Rosie's open mouth without a second's thought. It was natural to him. Rosie was like the Dalston family mascot. It was as if so long as she was safe and with them they would be all right.

Miss Beacham stood up and clapped her hands, making the three kids jump.

'Come on, I think it's time we all went to the hospital, don't you?'

Alana and Barry grinned.

'Really? Mrs Eappen said we couldn't go.'

'I know what she said, but I think you lot would be better off seeing your sister for yourselves. And I have a feeling Wendy will be all the better for seeing you too.'

Alana picked up Rosie and they walked quickly from the room. Mrs Eappen saw them all getting into Miss Beacham's car and hurried out on to the gravel driveway of the home.

'Where are you going?'

Miss Beacham shut the door and walked the irate woman away from the car and the children's earshot.

'I'm taking them to the hospital, this is doing them no good at all.'

Mrs Eappen sighed.

'I've strictly forbidden you to take them to the hospital, Miss Beacham, and you know that.'

Miss Beacham smiled. It was a lazy, tired smile.

'You like forbidding people, don't you, Mrs Eappen? Well, today I don't give a toss. I am taking these children to see their sister and if you don't like that, then tough shit.'

Mrs Eappen's face was a picture of shock and anger. She could not speak. Miss Beacham walked back to the car. Opening the driver's door, she smiled over her shoulder.

'By the way, it's my day off. I don't have to pretend anything then. Remember that in future.'

Mrs Eappen watched as the best social worker she had ever come across wheel-spun off the gravel drive and headed for the local hospital. She glanced around to see if their exchange had been overheard. Satisfied it had not, she walked sedately back through the large double doors of the pristine and depressing children's home.

Susan was handcuffed to Miss Henning, a loud and good-natured PO from A wing who always did the escorts. As she walked into Southend General Hospital she saw people staring at her openly and made a conscious effort to ignore them. She herself would stare at anyone handcuffed. It was human nature, nothing personal.

As they took the lift up to the ward her daughter was on she felt the hammering of her heart.

They walked from the lift and a pretty young Irish nurse was waiting for them.

'Ah, you must be Wendy's mother. She doesn't know you're coming, we thought it would be a grand surprise for her. She's a gorgeous girl.'

Susan smiled and followed her eagerly through the doorway and down a long ward into a side room. The curtains at the bed had been closed to keep out prying eyes. Her daughter's joyful face as she finally saw Susan was worth more than all the gold bullion in the world.

'Mum?' She said the word over and over. It grew louder and louder until it was a scream of delight.

The PO handcuffed to Susan was also dragged on to the bed with the force of the girl's embrace.

'Oh, Mum, what happened? How come they let you see me?'

She was grasping her mother's hand tightly, afraid to let it go.

'I got a compassionate because of you. Oh, Wendy, promise me you'll never do anything like that again. I nearly went out of me mind with worry when they told me. Promise me, Wend? *Promise me!*'

Susan looked down at her beautiful daughter, so young and with all her life ahead of her, and felt the tears come again.

'If anything happened to you I would die, love. I'd die inside. I'm always thinking of you. I like to think you're outside, making a life for yourself. Please don't ever think anything's so bad to have to kill yourself. Nothing is that bad. Nothing.'

The PO stood up awkwardly and unlocked the handcuffs.

'I'll give you ten minutes, Dalston. I'll be outside the door watching you.'

Susan smiled at her gratefully.

'I ain't going nowhere. I hardly see me kids as it is. I wouldn't jeopardise anything by going on the trot, I swear.'

The woman believed her.

'You have a few minutes in private, okay?'

Her voice was gruff with emotion. She liked Susan Dalston, knew she was all right.

Alone, mother and daughter clasped one another once more, their tight embrace a testimonial to the love they bore one another.

'Why did you do it, my love?'

Wendy sighed and rested her head on her mother's shoulder.

'You have to tell the truth, Mum. I can't keep it inside any more. I just can't.'

Susan heard the defeat in the girl's voice. The deep grief she was feeling seemed to seep into Susan's bones and become part of her.

'You're wrong, love. You *have* to keep it quiet. Otherwise all this was for nothing. You didn't cause any of it, remember that. I chose to do what I did. I *chose* to. So if you tell everyone what happened, it'll just be a waste. Anyway, no one would believe you now. It's too late.'

'But what about Rosie and the Simpsons? We can't let that happen. I even thought of running away with her. I thought of everything I could do and nothing would work. Not for any length of time anyway. If they take Rosie then the family will break up, I know it will.'

467

Susan grabbed the distressed girl and held her tightly.

'Let me worry about it. I'm still working on it all. Believe me when I say I will sort it out. I promise, I'll sort it all out.'

'But if you'd just tell them, Mum . . . I can't keep it inside much longer. It's eating at me because it's all my fault. I caused it all and you know that. You should never have got involved, Mum. I should never have let you do what you did. I was so frightened, I did what you told me without thinking. Now I know what I did was wrong. I should have stayed that night and faced the music.'

Susan looked into her daughter's face, a beautiful, young face that looked as if it had the cares of the world already etched on to it.

'Listen to me, Wend, and listen good. I'll sort out Rosie, I swear. I'll get an appeal somehow. I'm seeing a new brief soon that Roselle got me. I'll do everything I can to get sorted. You just keep it all to yourself. Forget about it. I know that's hard but it's for the best.'

She kissed her daughter's face gently, little heartfelt kisses.

'Let me do this one thing for you, heartcake. Please, let me take care of you the only way I can.'

Wendy was crying softly now. Susan held her to her bosom and stroked the girl's hair and murmured endearments into her ears.

'Let Mummy do this for you, love. If you don't then my whole life will have been a sham. A meaningless existence. Because you lot were the best thing to happen to me. And you were my first girl, my little heartcake, remember?'

Wendy nodded, too choked to speak.

'I still think you should tell the truth. It will come out one day, Mum.'

Susan stroked her face and grinned.

'Who says it will? Only you and I know what really happened that night and I'll deny everything, I mean it. So if you ever think of telling the truth, remember that. And remember that I love you so much I'd give my life for yours. So that you can have a chance. One little chance. You'd do the same for your own daughter, Wend, I know you would. Let me do this one thing for you, eh? It's what mums are for.'

The door opened then and Susan turned to see her other children bowling into the room with Miss Beacham. She grabbed them all into her arms.

She knew she had just blackmailed her eldest daughter into keeping quiet about that night, but it was all she could do. As little Rosie planted a big kiss on her cheek she felt the rightness of what she had done for Wendy.

Your children were given to you and you had to protect them as best you could. It was as simple as that.

Matty walked into the visiting room with her usual grace. Yet anyone looking closely would have seen the fine lines around her eyes and tightly pursed mouth. She glanced quickly around the room and her gaze settled on a dark-haired heavyset woman sitting alone by the officer desk.

Matty walked over to her, a wide smile on her face.

'Hello, Angela.'

The woman smirked and lit another cigarette, staring at her.

'You always had the poise, didn't you? Always that nonchalant way with you. Nothing fazes you, does it?'

Matty grinned then.

'Why should it? Now since you're here, I'll have a black coffee and a bar of chocolate from the snack bar over there. I've a feeling this isn't exactly a sisterly visit.'

Angela stood up and took a purse out of her pocket.

'You've got that right anyway. Still as shrewd as ever, I see.'

Matty watched as she walked over to the snack bar. Angela's clothes were cheap, her shoes worn through. She smiled as her sister obediently fetched what she'd asked for. This might be easier than she'd feared.

As they settled at the table Matty spoke.

'Don't tell me, Angela, the money's run out.'

The other woman grinned.

'Got it in one.'

Matty shrugged.

'Well, I haven't got any so this was a wasted journey. All mine went on legal fees.'

Her sister shook her head sadly.

'Shame. But then I do have an appointment with your brief later on. I'm sure she'll be very interested in what I have to tell her. And then there's the newspapers – they pay very well, I hear.'

Matty fronted it out.

'What is there to tell, Angela?'

She looked into her elder sister's deep green eyes and felt a prickle of apprehension.

'Our family history for a start. I admit no one ever suspected you even when it was splashed all over the papers. Even Mother didn't put two and two together. But then, she wouldn't, would she? You left her brain damaged, didn't you?'

Matty closed her eyes briefly. Even intimidated, she didn't show any emotion.

'That was an accident, you know that, Angela.'

She grinned.

'Almost fatal, wasn't it? Poor Mother. She fell two floors on to a concrete driveway while cleaning the windows. Of course, you and I know she never cleaned a window in her life. But that's neither here nor there, is it? We put her in a home and divided up the spoils. Such good daughters we were. Only now I've gone through my money and I think I might want a bit of yours. You see, I understand you'll be home soon and I'd hate to think of anything interfering with that, wouldn't you?'

Matty sipped her cold coffee and sighed.

'It was an accident, everyone knows that.'

'No, everyone *thought* that, which is a different thing altogether.'

Matty for the first time looked worried and Angela glowed inside as she watched her sister squirm.

'Matty you call yourself now. Very different from Tilda. But then, you changed your surname too, didn't you? In fact you changed everything about yourself. Don't you think people might wonder why that was if I brought it to their attention?'

Matty stood up and ended this torture.

'I'll send you another VO soon. Let me think and then I'll tell you what I'm going to do.'

Angela smiled. She knew she was home and dry and she also

knew not to push it. Especially not with her sister.

'Don't you want to know how Mummy is?'

Matty stared at her seriously.

'Why on earth would I want to know about that?'

She walked away quickly but calmly. Angela watched her go with a smile on her face.

Susan came back on to the wing like a pop star. Everyone crowded around and started shouting questions. Even the POs were pleased that she had been let out to see her daughter.

Rhianna brought her through the throng and led her into her cell. Shutting the door, she took out a bottle of brandy and waved it high above her head.

'A bit of a celebration, eh? How's the girl?'

Susan sighed.

'She's okay. It was a half-hearted attempt really. Bless her heart, she don't know nothing about killing herself. I think seeing me helped more than anything.'

Rhianna hugged her.

'You're all right, Susan Dalston, do you know that? The whole wing was rooting for you today. It was like it had happened to us all, you know?'

Susan took the proffered brandy. After a stiff drink she said gently, 'I know. I'm lucky with me mates. Even luckier with me kids.'

Rhianna smiled widely.

'We all know that, Susan. Even the POs were worried today. It was a real downer for everyone.'

'Where's Matty?' Susan realised she hadn't seen her.

Rhianna shook her head looking worried.

'Came back from a visit like a bear with a sore arse. Fuck knows what happened to her, but you know Matty. Best not to ask. I'm glad I ain't celled up with her, I can tell you.'

Susan shrugged.

'You get used to her after a while.'

Rhianna poured them both another large drink.

'You can get used to anything, or so they say. Fuck knows, I'm used to being inside. But then, I've been here so many times they send me Christmas cards!'

Susan roared with her. They laughed until they were spent then Rhianna said seriously, 'You deserve to be home with them children, Susan, you got to try and get this appeal. You do realise that, don't you?'

Susan looked into the other woman's eyes, deep brown, full of affection and concern for her.

'You're a diamond, mate. You know that, don't you? And you're right. I have to get out. But it's how I can do it, you know? I have a lot of things to sort out first. I have a hell of a lot of thinking to do.'

Rhianna looked at her oddly.

'What's to think about? They need you so you have to get out.'

Susan finished her drink in one large noisy gulp.

'If only it was as easy as that, mate. But it's not and I can't tell you or anyone why it's all so difficult.'

Rhianna filled her glass.

'Keep your own counsel, Susan, it's all we have left in this place. The privacy of our thoughts.'

Matty popped her head around the cell door then, a strained smile on her face.

'I hear everything's okay now, Sue?'

She nodded, pleased to see her cell mate.

'Any of that brandy going spare?' Matty enquired.

Rhianna poured her a glass.

'You okay, Matty? Only you look like you've had bad news. How was the visit?'

She shrugged her slender shoulders and laughed lightly.

'I just have the prison blues, that's all.'

Rhianna lifted her own glass high in the air.

'I'll drink to that, girl. The prison blues – and getting a good man one day.'

Matty put her hand into her overall pocket and passed Susan an air mail envelope.

'Talking of a good man, this came for you today.'

Seeing Peter's scrawly handwriting she felt her heart lurch.

'He's keen, girl. He must have written return post.'

Susan popped the letter into her pocket, the joy she got from seeing his writing all over her face.

Neither Matty nor Rhianna mentioned the letter again. It was as if they both knew that Susan wanted to hold it inside herself. She was frightened to be happy and they understood that.

It was what prison did to you.

Chapter Twenty-Eight

Peter's letter made her laugh. Susan read it and escaped into the world of meat boats, sunshine and camaraderie. He told her all about the chef on the ship, a homosexual called Bobby, describing his attempts at being macho though everyone knew he was gay. He told her all about his billet, a tiny room that sounded to Susan like an up market cell. He said how pleased he had been to hear from her and reminisced about them both as children, making her remember classes at school. The snow-covered winters and long hot summers seemed within her reach as he described events that had taken place twenty years and more ago.

It was just what she needed, light-hearted and without any pressure. They were mates, friends, people who had known each other for a long time and had a lot of catching up to do. There was no hint of romance and Susan was pleased. The other women had been ribbing her about Peter relentlessly but she knew he wouldn't want her in any other way than as a good friend. He was handsome and he was nice. Far too good for the likes of her.

But she loved having a friend, a pen pal. Someone who'd known her before all the trouble. Before the upset. When she had been plain old Susan McNamara.

She put the letter in her cupboard and her thoughts strayed to Barry. Peter's reminiscing had brought back her school days and now she recalled the way she had seen Barry as the answer to all her prayers. When his touch had set her alight and his voice had been like music to her ears.

A vision of him, faceless, rose before her eyes and her belly revolted. She felt her breakfast rise inside her.

Pushing the picture from her mind she forced herself to think about her daughter. To think about Wendy.

She felt a film of sweat all over her body, the sickly sour-smelling sweat of fear. If Wendy talked, then everything would be turned on its head and her daughter would have to face the consequences.

Susan could never let that happen.

Geraldine looked around her flat. As the doorbell rang she automatically straightened a white cushion on the sofa and tidied her hair. At the front door she glanced in an antique mirror and gave herself a quick once over. Then she opened the door.

Colin Jackson looked as usual as if he had just emerged from under the blankets of a bed he had slept in, clothes and all. His hair stood up in all directions and his jeans looked as if they were intended for someone twice his size. He needed a belt to keep them up. He wore a Ramones T-shirt and old brown desert boots.

As he looked at the white carpet he wondered if he should remove them. One glance at Geraldine's face and he had the answer. He slipped them off outside the door and reddened as he remembered he had a hole in the toe of his right sock.

She smiled good-naturedly.

'You do me good, Colin. You remind me what it's like to be young.'

He grinned, showing even white teeth.

'Not so young these days. I'm nearly thirty.'

He followed her through to the lounge, amazed at the luxuriousness of the surroundings. This place was like a magazine layout.

She smiled, pleased at his reaction. On the oak table stood a bottle of wine and two large goblets. There were also sandwiches and small cakes. He settled himself on the dark blue damask sofa with contrasting white cushions and immediately felt out of place.

Geraldine gave no hint that he looked like an overgrown college boy who had hit the jackpot in the female stakes. Instead she poured him a glass of chilled wine and sat down next to him.

'You can put your eyes back in your head now. We're supposed to be working, remember?'

She was wearing white silk trousers and a matching shirt. He could make out the dark shadow of her nipples through the fabric and wondered how the hell he was ever going to get a coherent sentence out without mentioning them.

'Drink up and relax, this is going to be a long one.'

He smiled lewdly. She could say that again!

'If Susan will see me next week then we must have something concrete to put before her. I have some new information from Roselle that sheds further light on the case but also makes it more difficult. It seems Barry Dalston had raped the eldest daughter.'

Colin nodded, his mind working overtime now, Geraldine's appearance of secondary importance.

'I knew it. I had a feeling there was something not being said. Susan adores her kids and would never have let herself be taken away lightly.'

He gulped at his wine.

'The dirty bastard. The herpes is from him, I take it?'

Geraldine nodded.

'It was in the coroner's report in black and white. It wasn't used because no one saw the relevance. Or at least that's what I've been told. No one seemed to think it would make him out to be a womaniser, a man who was promiscuous and obviously knew he was diseased when he took his own daughter. Roselle had been his long-time girlfriend. Don't ask me what she saw in him. I can only surmise he was different with her. Maybe she thought she could change him, there are women that stupid walking the earth. But Roselle's not stupid or doesn't seem it to me. Though where men are concerned she may not be as intelligent as the rest of us.'

Colin grinned.

'By the rest of us, you mean women like you, right?'

Geraldine was annoyed and it showed.

'I have never yet met a man worthy of spending my time on. Believe me when I say many men have tried to get me to see them from their point of view but I always suss them out. It's a knack I developed at a very early age.'

Colin was sorry to hear it. She was a sexy vibrant woman, kicking forty admittedly but all the better for that fact as far as he was concerned. Her words made him think of his spinster aunt, a real man hater if ever there was one.

'Hey, we're not all bad, you know.'

Geraldine looked him in the eye.

'Aren't you? I'm glad to hear it. Anyway back to Susan Dalston.'

She picked up her own wine and the gesture ended their previous conversation. He watched as her perfectly painted lips caressed the side of the glass and sighed inwardly. Why did she get herself so dolled up if she wasn't into attracting men, for Christ's sake?

'Susan came home from a night out. Wendy had been looking after the children. Barry had been missing for five days – Roselle even knows the woman he stayed with if we need her. She's really done her homework. Anyway, he took Wendy on the front room floor. Susan came home, the kids were all there and she sent Wendy to her mother-in-law's. A very nice but very ill woman who I'm sure would do anything to help get Susan out. No one in authority realised Wendy had even been there. Even Susan's neighbour Doreen kept up the charade.

'It seems everyone saw Susan's point of view about what had happened. She did what she did so her daughter would never have the stigma of rape by her own father hanging over her head.'

Colin was quiet. Standing up he walked to the window and looked out across the Thames.

'This is some view, isn't it?'

Geraldine didn't answer him, she knew he wasn't expecting an answer. He was trying to sort it all out in his own head. He was quiet for some minutes.

'If Susan has kept it to herself this long, sat in prison knowing all this, she's never going to admit it publicly. You realise that, Geraldine, don't you?'

She sipped her wine and let what he had said sink in. Still she didn't answer him. He turned from the window and stared at her.

'Why didn't Roselle tell me any of this? Why did she decide to tell you and not me?'

Geraldine shrugged. It was a very feminine, very graceful action. But it was lost on Colin. He was angry, hurt and humiliated.

'Couldn't trust a mere man, is that it? We're all the same, are we? To the Geraldines and the Roselles of this world. Shitbags the lot of us. Is that it?'

He was looking at her now and she stared calmly back at him.

'You'd really have to ask her that. I don't know why she decided to tell me and not you. Maybe because it was easier to tell another woman about a friend's private and personal business. Maybe because I had a better, plusher, more expensive office. I really don't know. All I do know is we have to help Susan Dalston in any way we can. Even if that means getting her out some other way.'

Colin was nonplussed, not sure he had heard her correctly.

'What are you talking about?'

Geraldine sighed and refilled their glasses.

'What I mean, young man, is maybe we have to keep Susan's secret and work on another way of getting her home with her kids where she belongs.'

He stared at her in amazement.

'You cannot be serious!'

Geraldine laughed.

'You sound just like that mad American tennis player. Listen to me, Colin. If that woman has sat it out for over two years to try and protect her child then she deserves to be helped in any way we can. I have Matilda Enderby on my client list, I have all the feminist organisations behind her, she's as good as out. Yet I know in here,' she punched her chest forcefully, 'that she killed her husband and probably enjoyed doing it.

'You know we tread a fine line daily. Even if people are guilty it's our job to give them the best representation we can. No matter what a client has done. Even paedophiles are granted the best legal representation. Surely someone like Susan Dalston is as entitled as Matty Enderby or a child molester to be helped? I am commonly supposed to have one of the best legal minds in the profession. My name alone will ensure she gets a fair hearing. You know that's true.

'I am my father's daughter – Terence O'Hara, the legal eagle of his day. I want to help Susan Dalston and I'd do it for nothing if I had to. Just once I want someone I know is a good person, whom I know does not deserve to be locked up, to walk free. It would make me feel that for once in my whole miserable, worthless life I really did make a difference.'

Colin stared at her as if he had never seen her before. The force of her words alone was enough to persuade him she was right. He sat beside her and smiled gently.

'I never knew you had a miserable life.'

He looked around the expensive apartment. His eyes took in the bareness of the walls and surfaces. Not a photo, not a knickknack, nothing. It was completely devoid of anything that said Geraldine lived there. It was almost clinical.

In her eyes he saw loneliness and hurt. It grieved him.

'So we're in this together then?'

Her voice was small.

He smiled sadly, a lop-sided grin that made him look very handsome and very young.

'It looks like it, doesn't it?'

Debbie walked into the hospital room. Holding before her a carrier bag full of sweets and drinks, she smiled nervously at her niece.

'Hello, love, how are you feeling?'

Wendy was so astounded to see her Aunt Debbie that she started to cry and laugh at the same time.

'I thought it was me mum for a second. Come and sit down, it's lovely to see you, really it is.'

They were the right words. Debbie walked in and sat on a chair by the bed. She hadn't seen Wendy for two years and the change in her was remarkable. The girl looked almost a woman now with that thick hair inherited from her father and the big chest that was Susan all over again.

'You've grown, I can see that.'

Wendy nodded. Her aunt looked terrible. Aunt Debbie who had always been the arbiter of fashion looked old and tired. She wore no make up and her hair was lank. Her clothes were too tight but nondescript. Her appearance made Wendy sad. She didn't know why.

Debbie saw the appraisal and smiled.

'I had a long journey, love. So, how are the kids then?'

'They'll be here in a minute. Miss Beacham, the social worker, is bringing them. She's ever so nice, Debbie. We're seeing as much as we can of Rosie before she goes, I suppose.'

The desolation in the girl's voice brought a lump to Debbie's throat.

'I had a lovely letter from your mum, love. She asked me to keep an eye out for you like.'

Wendy sat up properly in bed.

'I have to see a psychiatrist apparently. Tell them why I tried to top meself. Like this situation doesn't say it all! Still, at least I can go back to the home soon. I wish I hadn't done it, Debbie, I really do. I caused me mum so much grief and stuck in nick there was nothing she could do, was there? I just worried the life out of her.'

Debbie saw a girl who was half child and half woman and it hurt to know that she herself had not tried to help the children at all since Susan had gone.

'How's Uncle Jamesie?'

The question was asked merely out of politeness and it showed. Debbie smiled.

'The same as usual, love. He'll never change all the time he's got a hole in his arse.'

The way she said it made them both laugh, though neither of them knew why they were laughing so hard.

'How's me nan and granddad?'

'The same. They're still a *pair* of arseholes.'

They laughed uproariously again and Miss Beacham heard the laughter and was pleased as she walked the children down the ward.

If Wendy could laugh like that she had to be over the worst.

Barry and Alana walked in with Rosie between them. She looked lovely in a little yellow dress and shoes with a large hat to match, courtesy of the kindly Simpsons. She ran to the bed. Putting up her chubby arms, she immediately wanted to sit on Debbie's lap.

Debbie lifted up the beautiful child and smiled at her. Rosie smiled back happily and, pointing to the window, said loudly, 'Garden. Doggie.'

They could hear a dog barking in the distance and all laughed with her. At three she was slow speaking but had picked up more words over the last few weeks.

Barry, spying the sweets, said jauntily, 'Shall I put all this away in your dresser for you?'

He had already opened the carrier bag and was sorting through the booty.

Alana smiled at her aunt nervously. Debbie smiled back. Miss Beacham stood and watched until Wendy, remembering her manners, introduced them.

'This is me mum's sister, me Aunt Debbie. This is Miss Beacham, our social worker.'

The two women nodded at one another.

Debbie felt so out of place she went quiet. It was guilt, the guilt of knowing that while she had been wasting time trying to hold on to a man who was no good and never would be, these four children, her own flesh and blood, had been trying to come to terms not just with the loss of their father but also their mother.

'Ain't it lovely down here, Auntie Debbie? We're going to the sea front later. Miss Beacham promised.'

Barry's voice told everyone, especially Miss Beacham, that he was going whatever anyone else thought.

'Why don't you join us, Debbie? I'm sure the kids would like that.'

Alana didn't look too sure but little Rosie had taken a shine to her auntie and was grinning all over her face as if she understood what they were saying.

Debbie didn't answer, but she smiled and that was an acceptance.

Later, as she watched the kids playing around together, enjoying each other's company, as she saw the deep affection they held for one another, Debbie envied Susan what she had achieved against all the odds.

She had produced four beautiful loving kids who still worshipped the ground she walked on. Even though she was away from them, had been away from them for so long. If nothing else the visit had certainly put her own life into perspective.

'You all right, Matty?'

'If you ask me that once more I'll go mad,' she snapped.

Susan shrugged. 'Well, you look ill, girl. Depressed. I'm just worried about you, that's all.'

Matty stood up. Pushing Susan down into a chair she took over tidying her hair. As she expertly fashioned it into a neat French pleat, she said sadly, 'Sometimes, Susan, the past catches up with you and you can't be bothered to fight it any more. No, I'll rephrase that. You're not in a position to fight it any more.'

'What you on about, Matty?'

'What I said. I've come to what's called a watershed in my life.'

Susan laughed.

'You don't half come out with some things, Matty. I thought a watershed was where you went before they invented indoor toilets.'

Matty grabbed her hair playfully and made her sit still.

'A watershed is when something happens and you have to make a decision. A decision that will affect the rest of your life. Sometimes I wonder what I'm doing, don't you? We breeze around this place yet we're captives. Whatever else we do, whatever we think inside, we're captives here and basically we know it. All our thoughts are on getting out, being back in the world. In your case, being back with your family is your priority. I mean, I'm basically a very selfish person. I always was and prison hasn't changed that. If anything I'm even more selfish than ever.

'*You* are learning that you should have been more selfish. If you had been, you wouldn't even be here. You did the same as me ultimately, you protected yourself. But, unlike me, everyone here believes you.'

'Stop it, Matty. You have got the prison blues, like you've had for ages. Christ, your appeal is a foregone conclusion. You've even got celebrities saying you should never have been locked up. What have I got, eh? I can just see Wham! signing a petition for getting me out, can't you?'

Susan laughed.

'Cheer up. If you let yourself get down in here, you're lost. Every day I have to make myself cheerful. Make myself face the day. My kids' letters get me over the blues. You need to do something else with your life. If ever anyone needed someone else to think about, that person is you. Do you the world of good.'

Matty walked around and stood in front of her. Placing her hands on her shoulders, she said seriously, 'Susan, you're the only person I've ever really cared about. I told you I would talk to my brief and I didn't. I didn't because at the end of the day I wanted her to work for me and only me. That's how big a person I am. I didn't even want to help you when it came to it. I'm not noble or nice or any of the things you make me out to be.

'I'm a sociopath, Susan. I know that and you should be warned about that. Be on your guard against me and people like me. We're destroyers. We destroy everything we touch because we want to. We can't help ourselves. I'm Barry in a dress with a pretty face and a trim little figure. Please stop pretending I'm anything else.'

Susan looked into that earnest face and sighed sadly.

'You're not. You're unhappy and lost deep inside, just like I am. You need to talk to someone, get all that rottenness out of you. I ain't a shrink but I sussed out you wasn't all the ticket, mate. But people get like you are for a reason. Parents shape their kids. Husbands and wives shape each other's lives.

'Now I don't pretend to have your brain capacity, Matty. You're clever, really bright. Turn that brain on yourself, help yourself, because at the end of the day that's what we all have to do. Look at ourselves in the mirror and see ourselves for what we really are.'

The two women were quiet for a few moments then Matty said seriously, 'But that's just it, Susan, I have turned my brain on myself and I know what I am. That's what I'm trying to tell you. I *already* know myself inside out. It's knowing myself so well that's depressed me. The past catches up with you, no matter how clever you think you've been. The past is the future but you don't realise that until it rears its ugly head again.'

Susan shook her head and said vehemently, 'You're wrong, Matty, so wrong.'

She grinned, the same little grin she always put on when she wanted people to like her.

'Am I? Are you so sure about that, Susan?'

Geraldine stretched. She was tired but feeling much better than she had before talking to Colin the whole afternoon. She had opened another bottle of wine and now felt the tightness around her eyes that white wine always gave her. She was not a drinker.

Colin, though, could gulp wine at an astonishing rate. As she saw him refilling the glasses she accepted the hangover she would have the next morning.

She liked him. He was easy, uncomplicated and kind. Very kind.

'Do you think Susan will work with us? I mean, Geraldine, I know it all sounds great in here but this is a false environment. At the end of the day it's what she wants, not what we want.'

Geraldine took the glass of wine and shrugged.

'I think after what happened with Wendy she'll be willing to do anything to get out.'

Colin still wasn't convinced.

'If we can get a closed courtroom we could tell the truth, and that's more powerful than anything we could dream up. Plus the truth is much harder to disprove, isn't it?'

'We can only wait and see what Susan thinks of our plan. That's all we can do at the moment. Leave it for now.'

He sat beside her.

'You look tired.'

'I'm half drunk! I never was much of a drinker.'

He grinned.

'You don't take after your father then? His reputation for putting Scotch away is legendary. Almost as legendary as the cases he fought and won.'

Geraldine didn't answer him.

'Do you miss him?'

She stared into her wine glass for a few moments.

'No, actually, I don't. I never really liked him.'

Colin was amazed at her words and it showed on his face.

'Other people loved him. He was the typical Irishman made good. A brain like a computer coupled with a natural charm that made him everyone's favourite paddy. But you see, Colin, at home with his wife and daughters he was a bully. A big, brash, drunken bully. So, no, I don't miss him at all.'

'I never realised . . .'

His words were faint and inadequate.

'No one knew. We could hardly broadcast it to the nation. Even after his death we kept up the charade. It's what people do, isn't it? When he died he was actually with a seventeen-year-old prostitute. He had her in his chambers at Holborn. But friends rallied around, you know what the legal profession is like. That's why Matty was put away, because her husband was one of us. A legal. Though I also have a sneaking feeling she killed Victor Enderby in cold blood.

'Nothing in life is ever quite what it seems, is it? You thought my father was a saint like everyone else, champion of the underdog, the little man's protector. Well, he didn't give a toss about any of his clients. He cared about winning, though. That was everything to him.'

Colin was quiet. There was nothing to say and suddenly Geraldine felt sorry for him and for all she had laid at his feet.

She was drunk. She should never get drunk. It was dangerous, and she should know that better than anyone.

She placed a hand on his arm and smiled.

'I'm sorry, Colin, I shouldn't have said any of that.'

He smiled at her, a friendly smile. She knew her secrets were safe with him.

'I think you had to say it one day. Everyone has to say these things at least once in their life.'

She nodded and sipped once more at her wine. Lying back, she relaxed into the soft cushions and sighed.

'My family were boringly normal,' he told her. 'Nice mum, nice dad, nice sister. I still lived at home until two years ago.'

The last was said sheepishly.

She put a hand on his arm and said gently, 'Then you were very, very lucky.'

He grinned again.

'So it seems. I haven't any hidden secrets like most people. My life was textbook really. Nice semi, nice holidays, nice everything. But crushingly boring.'

Geraldine finished her wine at a gulp.

'Don't knock boring, Colin. Some people would give everything they have for a nice, safe, boring life. Believe me.'

He looked into her eyes and said seriously, 'I do, Geraldine. I believe you.'

Jamesie walked into the house with the usual scowl on his face. On the table in the kitchen was a large roast dinner and a trifle. He was hungry after a day's work and looked at the food appreciatively.

Debbie piled his plate with roast beef and Yorkshire pudding, carrots and cabbage, roast potatoes and mash. She had even made him his favourite swede. He always came home on a Sunday. It was the only day she could ever really expect to see him, a ritual now. He worked overtime on Sundays. Getting himself a stake, was how he termed it. Debbie knew the money went to Carol and the boy. Now it would go to the new baby Carol was flaunting so proudly.

Debbie smiled at him as she tucked into her own food.

'You look pleased with yourself?' he grunted.

She smiled again.

'I am, actually. I went to see Susan's kids yesterday.'

'Really? Well, make the most of it. You won't be going again.'

He bit into a piece of beef and she saw his uneven teeth and wondered why she had never noticed them before. He ate with his mouth open as usual.

'Is that right?'

Debbie sounded nonchalant.

Jamesie placed his knife and fork on his plate and looked directly at her.

'Yeah, that's right.'

She carried on eating as though he had never spoken.

'Are you listening to me, Debbie? Taking on board what I'm saying, are you?'

'They're nice kids, Jamesie. She was a good mother, Sue. I never gave her credit for that before. Always felt it was unfair, her having kids like nobody's business and me and you left without any. I hated her at times.'

Jamesie was staring at his wife as if she was about to be transported from the room by aliens.

'She was a murdering cunt! That's what she was. Going soft in the bleeding head, you are. You keep away from them kids. You can't have any and that's that.'

'No, but you can, can't you? I hear Carol's expecting again. Sure it's yours, are you? Only she's been round the turf more times than Red Rum. Even me mum looks down on Carol and that's saying something.'

He looked into his wife's face and was not at all sure what to do before the change in her. Gone was Debbie, the little wife, grateful to see him. Trying her best to please him. In her place was a woman with stone hard eyes and a smile that did not quite reach them.

'You're asking for a fucking slap, Debbie. I'm warning you.'

She laughed then and carried on eating.

'You ever slap me again and you'll know all about it, Jamesie, believe that, mate.'

He pushed back his chair, the scraping noise loud in the small kitchen. Debbie was up before him. She had the meat knife in her hand.

'Go on, you big fat bastard! I dare you. Then you'll get some of what Barry Dalston got. I know me rights, mate. I can have this house all to meself and you can whistle for it. You ain't got no claim on it. I have had advice, boy. I know me rights now. Tell Carol the cunt she ain't ever getting across this doorstep, her or her fucking kids.

'I have had enough of you and your whoring. I've had enough of you and what you want. What about me, eh? What about me, your wife? What about what I want for a change?'

She still held the knife above her head as if ready to plunge it into him at any second.

'Put the knife down, Debbie, I'm warning you.'

She shook her head.

'Get out, you prat, and go back to that thing you spend all your time with. I have had enough. At last I have had enough. I wouldn't have you now if your dick was dripping in diamonds and you farted perfume. So piss off.'

Everything he had ever done to her was written on her face, there in the words she used.

He looked down at his dinner. He was starving and knowing Carol all he would get there was a sandwich. Suddenly his home comforts seemed rather attractive.

Debbie walked slowly round the table.

'Get out, Jamesie. Piss off back to her. I don't want you any more. I will not have you and all you stand for in my kitchen. This is my house. I cleaned it, decorated it, and kept it for you. Now it's mine.'

As she took another step towards him he backed away from her. Finally he walked from the house.

Debbie bolted the door behind him and sighed heavily.

She had done it, really done it.

He was gone.

Chapter Twenty-Nine

Rhianna watched as Matty sat by herself, face drawn and white, eyes listless. She looked terrible. Even her hair was lifeless.

Rhianna crossed the large rec room to talk to her. As she approached Matty said loudly, 'Not today, Rhianna. I'm not in the mood.'

Rhianna sat down beside her anyway.

The rec room was noisy. A TV blared out and a radio tried to compete. A nature programme was on, *Survival*. Polar bears chased one another around a frozen ice cap trying to mate. The women shouted out lewd and obscene remarks. The radio played pop music. It was bedlam.

At the far side of the room other women played cards, drank coffee and smoked. A hazy fug hung in the air giving the place a look of squalor.

Still Matty ignored her, and still Rhianna sat there waiting for the other woman to talk.

Sarah cruised over to them, her pupils dilated, mouth moving in time to a song no one could distinguish.

'Any chance of a drink, Rhianna? On tick so to speak. Until I get me next share out?'

Rhianna shook her head.

'No chance. You're too out of it, Sarah. If you're not careful you'll fall asleep and that will be it. You'll be finished.'

Sarah sighed.

'Sounds pretty good to me.'

Matty wiped one hand across her face. It showed her anger.

'Everything sounds good to you, you stupid little bitch.'

Matty's voice was heavy with menace.

'What are you complaining for? You're on remand for a piddling offence. You'll walk from court on time served so why don't you leave us alone and keep your stupid druggy ramblings to yourself?'

She stood up and pushed the girl none too gently from her.

'Go on, piss off before I lose my temper. You're a spoiled little overgrown schoolgirl. Stop whining and keep away from me. If you know what's good for your fucking face.'

The punch was as hard as it was unexpected. No one would have credited Sarah with the nous to have done it.

Women went quiet.

Sarah stood there unsteadily, her fists clenched.

On the TV David Attenborough's voice extolled the merits of the polar ice cap and on the radio the Sister Sledge sang 'We Are Family'.

'Come on then, hard nut! Hit me back.'

Sarah was up for a fight. Matty stared into her unfocussed eyes and pushed her away once more.

'You're too out of it to hit. Can't you see that, you silly bitch?'

Sarah slapped her this time, a ringing slap.

Matty's cheek was stinging from it.

Picking up her thick white coffee mug she hit the girl with as much force as she could across her cheekbone. It collapsed beneath the blow and the girl, watched by everyone including the POs, dropped first to her knees and then to the hard floor. Then it was bedlam.

POs were everywhere. Rhianna was kneeling by the girl, trying to see the damage, and Matty was hustled from the room to the block.

There was pandemonium. Matty merely smiled demurely as she walked out. The PO in charge would have bet a month's wages that Enderby would never get physical. It just proved how wrong you could be.

Rhianna stayed with the unconscious girl until the doctor arrived then went back to her cell. Sitting on the bed with her head in her hands, she wondered at a system that put the Mattys of this world inside with Sarah and the other young girls.

Susan burst in.

'Is that right, Matty done poor little Sarah?'

Rhianna nodded.

'She's not right – something happened to her last week. On her visit,' Susan explained.

Rhianna shook her head.

'Don't make excuses for her, Susan. She'd have hurt someone some time. It's the way things are in here.'

She looked into her friend's face.

'If you ain't like it when you arrive, you're like it when you leave. Remember that.'

Susan left and went back to her own cell.

She looked at the enclosed space, at Matty's hair products and make up. Saw her hairbrushes and conditioners and felt a terrible sadness sweep over her. Was this going to be the next phase of her own life? Violent episodes and unbalanced people? Different cell mates, different faces?

She felt the walls close in on her and willed herself to swallow down the panic inside her.

Matty had just fucked her appeal.

If she was nicked she was finished.

But Susan wondered deep inside if that was what the other woman wanted.

Roselle liked the club during the week. It was quieter, soothing. Even the strippers didn't bother much week nights. Just went through the motions, sure in the knowledge the men watching didn't want too much from them. It was all very relaxed.

She walked through to the main dance floor and saw Denise going through her act. She liked Denise, a large girl with tits that hit her waist and thighs that could crack walnuts. The men always liked her too; she was attainable for some of them, which was basically what they were after. Men paid for women they could not get unless they were prostitutes. They knew a woman like her would blank them if they asked for a date.

The thought made Roselle smile and Mad Mary, one of the older girls, cackled with her. Mad Mary worked week nights because she knew that at her age and with her looks she wouldn't stand a cat in hell's chance come the weekend.

Mary actually drank the club champagne. She drank anything.

Roselle looked at her then, as if for the first time. The lines around the eyes and mouth, the hard glint in her eye. The professional smile.

'Any chance of a sub, Roselle?'

She shook her head.

'Not a hope in fuck, Mary. If I give you a sub you'll piss off and go somewhere else until you owe them money then you'll come back. I've sussed you out.'

Mary wasn't at all put out by this bit of logic. In fact it made her laugh harder.

'True, but I'm gasping for a drink.'

Roselle walked past her without talking but at the bar she told the barman to take Mad Mary a large vodka and Coke.

She wasn't as hard as she made out.

In the foyer she glanced around her professionally. All was in order. Linette, a tall Spanish-looking girl with masses of curly hair and large doe eyes, was on reception. She had hips like a battleship and small hard tits. Staying put behind a counter was her best hope. She was used when it got packed and all the other girls were gone case. Linette also had a rather noticeable speech impediment.

Mandrax made her slur her words.

Roselle ignored her and walked out into the cold night air.

The doorman, Harry Allbright, smiled at her.

'Nice night.'

She nodded but didn't answer him.

Harry was a godsend. He didn't drink or smoke and would not touch a tom with a barge pole. He hated them. He had a nice wife, nice kids and a nice house in Becontree.

'You look upset, girl. Everything okay?'

His voice was gruff yet concerned.

She smiled.

'Just feeling a bit down, that's all.'

He shook his leonine head in despair.

'It's the clubs do it to you. All that fucking pretence, I hate it. But at least it pays the bills.'

She stood in silence listening to him.

'They're all slags, the lot of them. Depress anyone they would with the lives they lead. No respect, see. No respect for themselves, no respect for no one.'

She walked back into the warmth of the club. Without realising it, Harry had depressed her more than ever.

Joseph was skiing with his school. The thought made her happy. He would have it all, all she was capable of giving him. Love and money. The things she'd never had.

She thought of Wendy then, and the others. But Wendy in particular.

In her office she looked at a photo she kept in a drawer. It was of her and Barry. He looked beautiful, like a male model. His eyes were smiling, and he was happy, really happy.

Then she opened her bag and took out a photo of her and Wendy, taken at her flat. The girl was so like him, almost identical.

Yet the child she was beginning to love like her own had been taken viciously by the man she had once loved. How could she not have seen him for what he was?

But she had known, deep inside. That night Susan had turned up, in her old blanket coat, smelling of babies and pregnancy and no money. Roselle had known then just who she was mixed up with. She had known Barry Dalstons all her life until Ivan. She had gone back into the gutter with Barry and that frightened her more than anything. It must not be allowed to happen again. For the sake of Wendy and maybe others like her.

This whole experience with Barry and his family had changed Roselle. Had made her look at herself and her life and decide she had to make major changes.

Starting with the club.

She would sell it one day, when poor Ivan had breathed his last and she had settled him in a nice Jewish cemetery somewhere. She would unload it then and make another life for herself, a respectable life, maybe a nice wine bar or a restaurant.

Somewhere she could relax and look at the clientele without a feeling of disgust and hopelessness. Where the waitresses were clean inside and out. Where money was earned legitimately and spent on honest enjoyment.

It had taken Susan Dalston to make her see what an attractive prospect that was. Susan and her constant struggle to keep her head above water, her kids on the straight and narrow and her hips within acceptable limits.

Laying her head on her desk Roselle cried as she had never cried before. God, she hoped her friend would understand why she had broken her confidence and told Geraldine the truth. She just prayed that in her desperation to help she had not betrayed the only real friendship she had known in her life.

June and Joey sat in front of their big new TV and watched *The Professionals*. June was drinking more heavily than usual. As Joey saw her pour another large Scotch into a cut glass tumbler he commented, 'You're putting it away, ain't you?'

She looked at him, eyes bright with the alcohol.

'I need it. I had another letter from our Susan today.'

Joey rolled his eyes to the ceiling.

'Here we go again. What's she done now?'

June shrugged.

'She ain't done nothing. Susan never did nothing, did she? Not like us. Not like we did.'

He closed his eyes in annoyance.

'You ain't starting that again, are you? She killed Barry and whatever he was he never deserved that.'

June shook her head.

'But he did deserve it, Joey, and she should have done it years ago. He treated her like shit. Why are we still pretending something we know is a lie? We made money off her and we made money off them kids and we've never given them a penny. Not so much as a single fucking sweet.'

Joey turned up the TV and said in a bored voice, 'Piss off, June. Piss off round Debbie's. Another one her. Where did we get them two from? Pair of moaning fucking Minnies.'

June drained her drink in one gulp.

'Susan was right not to want them girls here with you. She was right about that too. Even you can't deny that. I saw the way you looked at Wendy. So did Susan. You was after her for half her fucking life. Remember that time I caught you in the kitchen? I knew you was after her and I was jealous.'

He stared at the screen.

June shook her head drunkenly.

'All those years I hated her over you. Yet what were you really? A ponce, Joey. A ponce and nothing more.

'Debbie's been to see the kids and she's over the moon with them. Told me to fuck off and she was right and all. When you get to our age all that's left is your kids and your grandkids.

'I hear the women on the estate talking. "Taking me daughter's little ones out to the zoo or the museum." They give their grandchildren a lot more time than they gave their kids. Stands to reason, don't it? They're the future, the next generation. And what have me and you got, eh? A big fucking telly and a nice drum bought with Susan's blood money.'

Joey stared at the screen; it was as if he was deaf, as if her words didn't reach him.

'Every day this week our Debbie's been to that home. Every bastard day. It's like they've given her a new lease of life. I might go meself. She reckons Rosie's a right case and Barry Junior is a diamond. Alana and Wendy are beauties and all. Wendy tried to kill herself, Joey. A little girl like that tried to top herself.'

'I thought she told you to fuck off. How do you know all this?'

June laughed then.

'Of course she told me to fuck off but she don't mean it, does she? It's just a row. They're normal in families. I went back round there like nothing had happened and she was all right. She's shown Jamesie the door.'

Joey turned in his chair and bellowed, 'I ain't interested, June. You want to go all maternal, that's up to you, girl. I do not want to know.'

She refilled her glass and gulped at the burning liquid.

''Course you don't. That's the trouble, you never did.'

He looked at her and sneered.

'Well, mate, you've left it all a bit late, don't you think? To be coming over mumsy and nice.'

June stared into her glass.

'Far too late, Joey. That's what's wrong.'

He looked at his wife then, really looked at her, and sighed. She looked old. Underneath the make up and the hairdo she was old. They both were.

'You've still got me, June.'

She looked into his face, saw the lines of hatred around his piggy eyes, the viciousness of his mouth, and sighed heavily.

'That's right, Joey. Cheer me up, why don't you?'

He went back to *The Professionals* and hoped his Junie was going to get back to her normal awkward self, and soon.

This one was getting on his tits.

Susan smiled a welcome at Colin. She glanced at the woman with him and nodded politely. Geraldine was not ready for Susan's appearance. She looked a different woman from the photographs of her on file. Gone was that lardlike heaviness. Though the woman before her would never be thin she looked fit and healthy and actually had a waist. Her hair was up in a French pleat and she wore discreet make up which took years off her.

Geraldine held out one well-manicured hand and smiled.

'Geraldine O'Hara. Pleased to meet you.'

Susan smiled widely.

'So Matty talked to you in the end?'

She was inordinately pleased. Her friend had been on the block for over a week. No one knew what was happening with her or how she was.

'Is she okay?' Susan asked anxiously.

Geraldine shrugged.

'She won't see anyone, I'm afraid, not even me.'

Susan frowned. She stared at Colin and the PO who shrugged as if to say, What are you looking at me for?

'I see. So how did you get in here then?'

Susan had a bad feeling on her, a feeling she was being brought into something big. This was not a small-time lawyer like Colin, this was a big name, someone people listened to.

'Roselle came to see me . . .'

Susan felt as if the room was filling with damp air. She held up her hands.

'I ain't got the money for you, lady, so let's stop this right now, shall we?'

'Susan, we know what happened. We know everything.'

Her face went white.

Geraldine's voice was low.

'We just want to help you, that's all.'

'I don't need your help, love. Thanks all the same. I'm OK with Colin.'

He shook his scruffy head in distress.

'Will you at least hear us out?'

Susan shook her head vehemently.

'There's nothing to say. Now go, please, and leave me alone.'

'We know what Barry did to Wendy. We know *everything*, Susan.'

'You know nothing, lady. And anything you do know I'll deny. Can't you see what Wendy is doing? What Roselle is doing? They're saying anything to get me out. Even if none of it is true.'

'None of what is true, Susan?'

'Whatever the fuck they said.' She was panicking.

'I could probably get a closed courtroom. No one else need know anything,' Geraldine said quickly.

'Piss off, the pair of you.'

Susan looked over at the PO.

'Get me back on me wing, I'm finished here.'

'Maybe you should listen to them, Dalston.'

'Yeah? And maybe you should shut your fucking trap and do your job!'

'They're going to offer Rosie for adoption and split the other kids up in different homes. Do you really want that, Susan? Haven't they had enough to cope with? Wendy tried to commit suicide over what's happened. She needs professional help, woman. I thought you wanted what was best for them. How can you not want this?'

Geraldine's voice was loud in the little room. It seemed to bounce off the walls and back at her. Susan hesitated for a split second and Geraldine seized her chance.

'I could get you home in no time. Back to them. I'm a force to be reckoned with in my profession and I'm willing to help you for nix. Nothing. Not a penny. Don't throw this back in my face, *lady*, because I won't offer twice.'

Her voice was so strong, so sure, that Susan realised she'd be giving up her only chance of freedom if she refused.

Geraldine looked at the PO and said meaningfully, 'I want to see *my client* alone, please?'

The PO walked from the room without a backward glance.

'If you don't want it to come out we'll find another way round it, I promise you.'

Susan looked at the immaculately dressed woman before her.

'Why do you want to do this so much? Why do I matter to you?'

'Susan, if only you'd realise it you matter to a lot of people, not least your own kids. We know what Barry did to your daughter. His daughter. We know you had to eliminate him for what he'd done. We're on your side, if you could only see it.'

She looked to Colin for confirmation and he smiled.

'Straight up. Don't let this go because it's pretty much the only chance you'll get.'

'What else could we do then?'

Geraldine relaxed, unsure why this woman allowing her to help made her feel so good inside herself. So right.

'Hospital reports state he gave you a venereal disease and you lost a child. He kicked other children out of your belly. He attacked you constantly. If I use that I can get you out and no one need ever know the truth. Even his own mother is willing to testify about Barry and what he really was. I promise you, I can get you out on time served if I really let rip with details of his past life.'

Susan smiled.

'Kate hated him, bless her.'

She sat down at the table and stared at Geraldine.

'Will they look at the forensic evidence closely, do you think? The prosecution, I mean.'

Geraldine was thrown by the question.

'They'll bring into play the fact you hit him repeatedly with a hammer, yes. That's all they had, really, the way the attack was carried out. But I can get a psychiatrist to say that it was a one off act of retaliation brought on by years of abuse. Which is what it was, wasn't it?'

Susan nodded absently.

'But the forensic evidence . . . will they have kept things? You know, samples and that?'

'What is it with the forensics? All the reports state is that Barry was hit repeatedly with a hammer. We know that already. What we need now is some serious damage limitation to make that fact irrelevant. You must come across as a woman still in shock at her own trial. One who felt she deserved to go away for taking a life. Even though that life was hardly worth getting in a bloody lather about in the first place.'

Susan looked at her and grinned.

'I like you, you're all right.'

Geraldine laughed back.

'I like you too actually. I had a feeling I would.'

Colin watched them and once more marvelled at women's instinctive empathy with one another.

'So what you're telling me is, we tell them the truth but not the whole truth. Is that it?'

'In a nutshell, yes.'

'But the forensics – will they look at them and try and find something else?'

'Such as?' Colin's voice was exasperated.

Susan shrugged.

'I don't know, do I? You're the experts.'

Geraldine looked into her face.

'Is there something else they could find?'

Susan didn't answer her directly. 'Are you really doing this for nothing?'

Geraldine shrugged.

'Roselle says she'll pay. But we'll see. If I lose, I won't charge a halfpenny. How's that?'

Susan looked her over, from her hand-made shoes to her expensive haircut, and sighed inside.

'Go on then, you've convinced me.'

Which was something Geraldine O'Hara had never had to do in her life before. People usually begged her to take their cases; that was how things were done in her world. You had the experience so you charged for it. Yet here was a convicted murderess doing her a favour by taking on her expertise, her knowledge, her time.

Geraldine laughed inside and out.

'You're on.'

Susan put her head in her hands and thought of Wendy and Rosie and Barry and Alana. Her four children, so different and yet so alike. She had to get back to them and this good-looking woman with the nice smile sounded like she could arrange that.

Wendy needed help. Those words were filling her brain. What Wendy needed, what they all needed, was their mother. It was time Susan Dalston allowed herself to go home.

Matty sat in the punishment cell on the block. She had no access to writing materials, books or radios. It didn't bother her. She sat on the bunk, day in and day out, without moving.

The night screw opened the cell door. She was a thin woman with angular features and a weakness for Danielle Steel novels. Matilda Enderby was worrying her.

'Can I get you a cup of coffee or anything?'

Matty stared at her as if she didn't know who she was.

'Sorry?'

'You heard. Do you want a coffee or not?'

'No, thank you. I'm fine.'

The other woman walked from the cell and locked it. At least she had tried. She could get back to her other world now, full of sexy women and intrigue.

Matty stared at the graffiti on the walls and smiled. Some of it was quite amusing in an ignorant and filthy way.

She tried to concentrate on it, but all she saw was Victor, poor Victor standing in front of her, begging her to tell him why she was so unhappy. Why she was so awkward. So nasty to him. Asking her to explain what was making her so miserable. The bewildered look in his eyes as he ran his hands through his hair in agitation.

She had felt the knife underneath the tea towel. Knowing it was there, waiting for her, had given her such a good feeling. As he had followed her she had caressed it, knowing she had the power of life or death. It was such a heady feeling. Oh, she had done her homework all right. Once through the heart. One thrust, the act of a desperate woman. She had seen the doctor, shown him her bruising. Told him of her husband's cruelty. His tempers.

Victor had looked so shocked when she stabbed him. Kneeling on the floor in front of her, his face so pained, so white. She had thought he would never die. Even when he was lying on the white-tiled floor, the blood pooling around him, she had thought he would survive. She had stood over him for ten minutes, making sure he was dead.

She wasn't taking any chances.

Then that last horrible gurgling noise. That had been terrible.

She had made herself a drink, a stiff G&T, drunk it down then picked up the phone and screamed and hollered into it.

The performance of a lifetime.

She had told her story to dozens of journalists, made herself a figurehead for battered women. And now Angela had turned up. That fat bitch was out to get her. Make her lose control, make her attack Sarah.

Matty would have to think up something good for Angela, something she would not be expecting. Give her something special, like she had her mother.

The thought made her smile.

Maybe a fire . . . fire was cleansing. And Angela needed cleansing. She had always had a dirty mind, a dirty mouth.

Matty got up off the bunk and banged on the cell door. The screw hurried down. This prisoner was on suicide watch.

'I will have that coffee now, please. I'm suddenly feeling much better.'

The screw smiled at her in friendly fashion.

'Could you eat something, do you think?'

She had not eaten for days and was suddenly ravenous.

'I think I might just manage a few mouthfuls.'

'A sandwich, perhaps?'

Matty laughed happily.

'Barbecue chicken springs to mind but a sandwich would be wonderful.'

Chapter Thirty

Roselle picked up Wendy from the home. As she walked through the double doors she felt the usual sadness as she saw the kids milling around. All colours, all creeds, all unwanted. It was heartbreaking. These young minds were well aware they were not valued. You could see it on their faces, in their walk, in their actions. Sullen teenagers smoking cigarettes; younger children sitting around the house and grounds just watching the world go by. Knowing it was something they would never be able to join. Not really, not fully.

They had already been tainted, were already used to being overlooked unless they did something to get themselves attention. Something senseless and violent or self-destructive.

This could so easily have been the fate of Sue's children except that whatever else happened to them they knew their mother adored them.

Roselle walked to the office and knocked gently on the door.

Mrs Eappen's voice called disdainfully, 'Wait there.'

Roselle knew she could see through the glass who it was. She also knew Mrs Eappen was not at all sure about her. About her car, her clothes, her expensive watch. She knew she upset Mrs Eappen's ideas about right and wrong. Roselle wondered how the woman always managed to put her on the defensive, made her accent much stronger. She found herself saying 'geezer' and 'mate', words she'd never use at any other time. It wasn't even her own accent, for Christ's sake.

She was kept waiting nearly five minutes until she was summoned with a one-word command.

'Enter.'

Walking into the room she was transported back to her school days once more. She felt she was in trouble though she knew that was absurd. She was a grown woman, not a kid. But the Mrs Eappens of this world made a point of treating everyone as if they were twelve years old.

The woman looked her over in that cold, critical way she had.

'Ah, Miss Digby.'

The 'Miss' was emphasised as if any woman of her age without a 'Mrs' to her name was an out and out failure.

'What can I do for you?'

'Drop dead' sprang to Roselle's mind but she knew how to play this game.

'I'm here to pick up Wendy Dalston as usual. I thought today I'd take her for tea at Claridge's then maybe on to Regent Street for a bit of shopping. I know she's really looking forward to that.'

Her accent was atrocious. She knew it and it pleased her, especially when Mrs Eappen closed her eyes in obvious distress.

'Quite. You do realise that after her ordeal she's still tired and somewhat depressed?'

'Not after today she won't be, I can assure you of that. I also have a VO with my name on it and hers. So she'll see her mother and all.'

Roselle had saved the best till last and had the satisfaction of seeing the other woman pale. As Mrs Eappen opened her mouth to speak again Roselle walked from the tiny cluttered office, with its pictures of Pooh Bear on the walls and its charts on the kids' progress in red and black marker pen.

Mrs Eappen treated the children in her care as objects as opposed to young people and that was always going to be her mistake.

Wendy was sitting forlornly in the reception area. Roselle watched her for a second. She looked like a grown woman sitting there in her jeans and black T shirt, even with no make up and her glorious hair tied back in a sleek ponytail. Seeing Roselle, her face lit up in a smile.

As they walked out to the car Debbie got out of a cab. She looked better than she had for months. The strained look had gone from her face and the fine lines around her eyes looked more like laughter lines now. Her face had a jolly appearance to it.

'All right, love. Off out, are you?'

Wendy nodded and introduced the two women. Roselle was aware of being looked over by a pair of shrewd blue eyes.

'Heard a lot about you, Roselle. I'm Susan's sister, as if you didn't know.'

Debbie's words told Roselle she'd guessed more than she had heard and wasn't in the least bothered.

'It took me a while to get around to seeing the kids but at least I'm here now . . .'

It was the nearest Debbie would ever come to an apology for leaving them alone for so long.

Roselle smiled.

'Where are you taking them?'

'Round my house. I thought I'd give them a day in the garden. The summer's nearly over. I thought I'd do them a bit of grub, let them have a laze about. It's nice where I live. Quiet like.'

Roselle nodded.

'I have a VO. Me and this one here are going to see her mother to talk her into letting a new brief help her. That's if she hasn't already been convinced, of course.'

Debbie nodded.

'Susan told me about her. I got a letter yesterday. She seems right on it if that's any consolation. Seeing a light at the end of the tunnel was how she put it.'

Wendy was quiet throughout the exchange but neither of the women realised that. They were too busy sizing each other up.

'Well, have a good day.'

Debbie grinned.

'I will. I missed a lot of time with them kids and I intend to make up for it.'

Roselle smiled sadly.

'They're a nice bunch, if I say it myself.'

They parted happily. Roselle watched the dumpy little woman

with the fat legs practically racing up the drive to get to her nieces and nephew.

Wendy was settled in the car before she spoke.

'Me mum won't let the truth come out. Not for anyone.'

Roselle looked at her, eyes suddenly tired.

'Your mum will do what she's told for once. Now let's get going and have a nice day, eh?'

She drove out of the home but the shine had somehow been taken off the day. Wendy looked haunted again, depressed.

Roselle made a big concession and put on Radio One. She knew the girl liked the latest pop songs. Hopefully they would cheer her up.

Matty came off the block to a sea of faces. She looked around her at the girls and women she had helped, given advice to, and wondered at their resilience. That they were still concerned for her even after what she had done.

Sarah watched her warily, her eyes bleak but unclouded by drugs.

Matty smiled and waved at the girl and saw her visibly relax.

Grudges could be nurtured in a prison environment, could escalate into violent episodes at the drop of a hat. With nothing else to think about, especially on the block, feuds were commonplace. The Mattys of this world made life difficult. Everyone was wary of her and others like her. They sensed people like that didn't really need a reason to be violent. Anything could trigger them off.

Susan had the cell in pristine condition and this made Matty smile.

'I've been cleaning all bleeding morning.'

Susan's voice was high. She was nervous and for some reason this depressed Matty even more. She looked around her, as she knew she was expected to, and smiled in charming fashion.

'It's as if I was never away.'

Susan snorted.

'You wouldn't have thought that earlier! It looked like a bomb had hit the place. But you know me, mate, what you see is what you get!'

Rhianna came in then and filled the small space even further.

'I was in the gym, I just heard you was back.'

Her thin face looked eagerly at Matty who saw true friendship there.

'How's Sarah?' she asked.

Rhianna shrugged.

'Took the can for it, as expected. Said she wound you up, was out of it and caused a fight. The usual.'

Matty nodded slowly.

'I guessed as much. They don't tell you anything, do they? I still don't know whether they're going to charge me or not.'

Rhianna smiled.

'No chance. The girl's not stupid. She's done her stuff. There'll be no comebacks.'

Matty was quiet for a moment.

'Maybe. We'll see.'

Rhianna and Susan looked at one another. This was not what they'd expected.

'You okay, Matty? You need anything?'

'Believe it or not, I just need a bit of peace and quiet. I want to write a letter.'

The other two grinned.

'Who to?'

Matty looked at them seriously.

'My sister.'

'I never knew you had a sister?' Rhianna's voice was high with disbelief.

'There's a lot you don't know about me, ladies. But I expect you'll find out one day, if I'm not careful.'

Matty laughed then and the two women laughed with her. But both of them knew that whatever they were laughing at it wasn't in the least bit funny. Not really. Rhianna pulled Susan gently from the cell, leaving Matty to her letter writing. They sat in Rhianna's cell and stared at one another.

'She's different again, ain't she?' Susan commented.

Rhianna nodded.

'She, if you don't mind me saying, is madder than the maddest person who was ever mad. You can practically feel the animosity coming out of her pores. Aren't you nervous, Sue? I would be.'

'Not a lot I can do, is there? But that sister has rattled her cage by the sound of it. Let's hope her letter writing eases her mind. I've enough on me plate without worrying about Matty.'

Rhianna shook her head.

'The sooner you get an appeal date, the better.'

Susan hugged herself with delight.

'I think I really may be in with a chance with this Geraldine bird. I wonder how Matty will react to me having her on my case as well?'

Rhianna didn't answer. But she had a feeling that the mood Matty was in, she wasn't going to be too pleased.

'You be careful, Susan. Keep an eye out. When Matty's like this she's capable of anything.'

Susan shrugged good-naturedly.

'She'll be all right once she gets back in the swing of things. And Sarah's saved a lot of hag, hasn't she? Holding her hand up like that. Matty will get over it in time. Like we all do.'

Rhianna didn't answer.

Susan's head was full of thoughts of Wendy and Roselle. She was about to see the friend she hadn't clapped eyes on for over two years. She couldn't wait for this visit. It was going to be brilliant.

'Anyway, I've got me girl in today and me best mate, Roselle. I ain't seen her in the flesh for so long I feel all excited at the prospect. I want to take a good gander at her, see how the last few years have treated her.'

Rhianna was caught up in Susan's enthusiasm.

'Roselle who? You're always talking about her, I know the name.'

'Roselle Digby. She lives in Soho.'

Rhianna looked impressed.

'Not *the* Roselle Digby, runs that club in Dean Street?'

The tone of her voice said it all and Susan laughed.

'The very same. Me and her go back quite a few years now. She's a fucking good mate. It's her offered to pay for this Geraldine bird, though she says she'll do the case for nix if necessary.'

'I'll bet. You'll get her press coverage and kudos, remember that.' Rhianna was impressed, though, and it showed. 'You should have let your secret out long ago. You'd have been treated like visiting Royalty in here with her on your case.'

Susan sighed happily.

'Maybe, maybe not. Still, it's all coming together now, ain't it?'

Rhianna smiled.

'You'll get out, Susan. I have a good feeling about it.'

'So do I actually. I finally feel able to look forward, you know?'

Rhianna knew exactly what she meant and felt a fleeting moment of jealousy.

'I know exactly how you feel. Believe me, *I know*.'

Geraldine was surprised at the change in Matty. She looked thinner, if that were possible, and red-faced, as if she had been running, which was definitely impossible in this place.

'Hello, Matty. I take it they've explained everything?'

She nodded.

'The girl picked a fight. It happens in these places, Geraldine. I had to defend myself.'

Geraldine wasn't sure about that.

'Well, anyway, we have an appeal date. Four weeks' time, the third of November. How's that?'

Matty smiled, her face disarmingly pretty in the early-afternoon sunlight.

'Great. I can't wait to be out.'

Her voice was like a little girl's. Geraldine swallowed down the feeling of revulsion that swept over her every time she talked to this particular client.

'You should be fine, going by the advance press coverage. I think the climate's right now. People are interested in battered wives. It's political. Laws are being brought in and enforced. I think you have a good chance of coming home.'

Matty smiled again.

'Good. Because this place is starting to get me down. I want to put Victor and everything that happened behind me. Start a new life.'

'It'll be hard to put it behind you when your book is published, won't it?'

Geraldine couldn't resist the jibe and Matty shrugged again. Even more nonchalantly than usual.

'If people want to hear my story, why shouldn't I tell it? Other women may be inspired to leave similar domestic arrangements before it's too late. I left it too late and look what happened to me. A cautionary tale is just what's needed, don't you think?'

She could justify anything, Geraldine knew, and let the matter drop. But it hung in the air between them and made the atmosphere heavy.

'I'm representing Susan Dalston as well,' Geraldine said to change the subject. 'Did you know?'

Matty's face paled and she pushed her hair back from her forehead in an action Geraldine now knew meant she was angry.

'No. No one bothered to enlighten me on that fact. Least of all my own counsel.'

'Come on, Matty, calm down. I have many clients, you know that. I always deal with women in trouble. Which is exactly what Susan Dalston is. Her children need her. She needs them. If ever a woman shouldn't have been locked up in the first place it's Susan Dalston. I mean, this was serial abuse of the worst kind. I know, I can prove it. Get her out and back home again. I'm looking forward to it. I liked her from the word go.'

Matty didn't answer. She was listening to the noise outside. It was visiting time and she could hear the chatter of husbands and boyfriends, kids and mums. She had had one visit since she had been in prison that wasn't a legal consultation and that was a visit she could have done without.

'Before I forget – a woman rang asking to see me about you. Angela something or other. But she didn't turn up. Do you know what it might be about?'

Matty's expression didn't change. She knew Geraldine had deliberately slipped this in to gauge her reaction.

'Could be a journalist. I don't know any Angelas off hand. Why, did it seem important?'

That innocent look was back. Geraldine shrugged.

'No. It just seemed strange, that's all. I thought it might be someone who could help you.'

'The only person who can help me is you, Geraldine. You're all I've got.'

'Plus the women's groups and the feminists. Let's not forget them.'

Matty looked at a point above her head.

'Oh, what do they know really? You're the important one, aren't you? Without you I'd have been left to rot in here. No, this is all down to you, Geraldine. I can't tell you how I feel.'

She had the distinct impression that Matty was laughing at her and knew she could do absolutely nothing about it. Everyone was entitled to a fair trial, whatever the personal feelings of their counsel. Geraldine knew inside herself that Matty's release could be the forerunner to a lot of women receiving true justice for crimes they'd been forced to commit. The Susan Dalstons and so many others like her. So why did she feel no sympathy with this woman? Why did she feel she was making a big mistake in representing her? Everyone else thought Matty was wonderful, the dream client, intelligent, witty, articulate, very attractive.

Yet privately she felt sure that Matilda Enderby was a cold-blooded, murdering bitch. Geraldine was depressed again.

Matty always did that to her.

Susan saw her daughter and her friend sitting waiting in the drab visiting room and grinned like a Cheshire cat. Roselle hugged her until a PO forced them apart. They sat at the rickety table and Wendy went to get coffees and a Coke so they had a few minutes alone together.

'You look bleeding fantastic, Roselle. Really great. And not a day older.'

Susan's voice was full of admiration.

'You don't look too bad yourself, girl. You ain't half done some weight.'

Susan sighed.

'Better than a health farm in here. I wish I'd been banged up years ago, I'd never have got so bleeding fat.'

But she was pleased with the compliment and it showed.

'I'm only ten stone now. Christ, I feel like Twiggy.'

Susan's fine features were once more in evidence and although she would never be beautiful she was certainly attractive and this pleased Roselle no end.

'How's Wendy seem?' she asked her friend anxiously.

'Much better. I think knowing you might be coming home is a real help. Oh, and I heard through the grapevine the adoption's being rushed through.' Roselle raised her hand to shut Susan up before she started. 'Geraldine will deal with that, it's all part of the process of getting you out – the fact you was such a brilliant mother. So stop worrying. I have the dosh to hold them up in court until the year two thousand if necessary.'

Susan felt herself relax.

'You're a good mate, Roselle. I don't know what I'd have done without you. If nothing else at least Barry gave me the kids, and in a funny way he gave me you and all, didn't he?'

Roselle grasped her hand tightly.

'And he gave me you, and through you Wendy. I'm so fond of you both now, you're more to me than family. Except for my Joe, of course.'

'Of course. How is he?'

Roselle went into overdrive about her son and his merits and Susan listened gleefully. Her cup was running over. Seeing Roselle in the flesh made up for everything, such was the power of their friendship.

A few of the women in the visiting room stared in disbelief at Susan Dalston and Roselle Digby. Susan had not realised how well known Roselle was and saw now why her friend didn't want to visit her before. She was a curiosity to them all. A well-known face who had never had so much as a parking ticket. Ivan's woman she was often called, even though anything between them had been over years ago.

Susan quite enjoyed the stir they created.

'Cor, if I'd realised, I'd have made you visit me before. I can do with all the help I can get in this place.'

A female prisoner stopped by the table and nodded hello to

Susan and Roselle. Wendy brought the coffee back and said delightedly, 'They're all talking about you up by the coffee bar. Nice things of course.'

Roselle sipped the coffee and grinned.

'Would they dare say anything else?' Then, changing the subject abruptly, she asked Susan the burning question. 'What do you think of Geraldine O'Hara then?'

'I think she's great, Roselle. She's also looking after Matty, me cell mate.'

'Give you more in common that will. Geraldine seems to think you getting out is a foregone conclusion.'

'Yeah, well, I'll wait and see. But even I have a good feeling. I daren't get too excited, though. That's fatal in this place. You have to think of the worst that can happen. Anything over and above that is a bonus.'

Wendy listened to them both intently.

'Tell them the truth, Mum. Let's get it out once and for all.'

Susan looked at her daughter and said stiffly, 'They'll get enough of the truth, love, to last them a lifetime. We don't need to involve you in any of this.'

Wendy looked into her face.

'You still can't see it, can you, Mum? Maybe I need the truth to be told so people can understand me a bit better. So I can understand meself. Try and make a bit of sense of my life.'

Susan looked into the lovely troubled face and said seriously, 'There's nothing to make sense of, love. You were caught up in something that wasn't within your control. I know, I was there meself for years. Your dad was a user, of people and of things. I can see that now. I lie in that bunk at night and wonder at how much power I let him have over us all. I was a bloody fool. I should have gone on the trot years before. Let him stew in his own juice. But I never. I sat it out. And for what, eh? For this. Now, if you open your mouth, you kick it all back in my face. Bear that in mind, love.'

Wendy stared at her for long moments.

'This ain't about you now, Mum. Even I can see that much. This is about blame, about who did this and who did that. Well, I should take my part of that blame. I should start to accept responsibility for what I did.'

Roselle watched the mother and her nearly grown daughter and was amazed how they were reacting to each other. It was as if they were going to fight.

'Calm down, you two.'

Her voice broke into their study of one another.

Susan leaned forward in her chair and hissed, 'You tell no one, you hear me? You do and I'll call you a liar. Say it's all so you could get me home and they'll believe that, mate. They will.'

Something was going on and Roselle was not sure what it was.

'Ain't I got enough on me plate with Rosie and the fucking Simpsons, Barry's school work and Alana's unhappiness, without you starting now and all? I don't need this, Wend. I really don't need this on top of everything else.'

Susan's voice was shaking with emotion.

'It would mean a retrial, all sorts of trouble, so let it go. Please, just let it go and then when I get home I'll make it all all right. I promise you, darlin'.'

Wendy got up from the table and walked out to the reception area where the public toilets were.

Susan took one look at Roselle's expression and said, 'This is between me and her.'

Roselle nodded gently.

'So it would seem. But like Geraldine said, a closed courtroom might do the trick if you'd only see as much. What he did to her would get you a walking sentence straight off and, whether you want to hear this or not, Wendy *needs* to help, to make her feel better inside. Can't you see that, Susan? That child is full of guilt and remorse over what happened. She needs to make things right inside herself. To make herself feel better.'

Susan didn't answer her. She was miles away. Back in her little house looking once more at the dead body of her husband.

'She ain't a child any more, Sue. She's a woman. Barry saw to that. Now it's up to you to let her know that you respect her as an adult. As someone who can make her own decisions. It happened to *her*, Sue. It happened to *her*, not *you*. She has to be able to sort it out herself or Barry's won again, hasn't he? He's still controlling you all.'

Susan didn't answer her.

There was nothing she felt she could say.

Wendy came back. She smiled gently at her mother.

'I miss you, Mum, and I have to get myself better inside. I won't if you keep protecting me. I need the truth to come out. Need people to know what happened.'

'No one needs to know all about that, darlin'.'

Wendy looked her mother full in the face.

'That night he told me I wasn't his. He said me granddad was me father. I asked you about that once and you never answered me. I need to know, Mum. I need to know what I am and where I come from. No matter how bad it is. Nothing could be worse than what I feel now. Every day when I get up, every morning when I lie there trying to get meself together to face another fucking day full of guilt and hatred.'

Susan shook her head. Her voice was dragged from the depths of her being as she answered her daughter.

'Barry was your father all right. I wish I could tell you differently, believe me.'

Wendy nodded.

'I thought so. But I had to be sure. You can see why, can't you?'

Susan nodded sadly.

'Of course I can, love. This is why I want it all over. So you don't have to think about it ever again. Won't have to face any consequences except the knowledge of what happened. And even that will fade in time, I promise you. I'll make it right, I promise, heartcake.'

Wendy sighed heavily.

'You can try but nothing can change the truth, Mum. You can dress it up, rearrange it, but the truth is still the truth whatever you say.'

She looked steadily at Roselle.

'I killed me dad. Not her. It was me. I killed him with the

brandy bottle. He was already dead before she got home. Weren't he, Mum?'

Susan stared at her cold cup of coffee and didn't answer.

There was nothing else to say.

Chapter Thirty-One

Roselle sat in her flat and sipped a large brandy. She was still in a state of extreme shock. Why had she never sussed it out? Why had she never guessed it was Wendy who'd killed Barry?

But then, why would she think that? Why would anyone think that? Wendy was a child, a victim.

Now it left them with a dilemma of Olympian proportions.

If Wendy let the truth out, and it seemed that was what she wanted, the girl could be left in a much worse position than she seemed to realise. She would be put away, as her mother was, but in her case detained at Her Majesty's pleasure. She was too young for a trial and too young for prison so it would be a secure unit somewhere.

Detained indefinitely.

Roselle walked through to the bedroom and stared down at the sleeping girl. It was as if admitting what had happened had taken the weight of the world off Wendy's shoulders. She was visibly more relaxed now.

Even Mrs Eappen had sensed something and allowed her to spend the night at the flat without too much aggravation. For the first time in what seemed like years Mrs Eappen had no Dalstons on her premises. The other three were spending the night with their aunt. Roselle had heard the relief in her voice at that and had smiled knowingly.

The old bitch would be talking about them all now, it seemed they gave her the only topic of conversation she had these days.

The murderer's children.

What if she found out that the daughter was the real perpetrator of the crime? She'd love that.

Roselle sipped at her brandy again.

Poor Susan, innocent all that time. Sitting in prison, listening to all that shit and knowing she shouldn't even be there.

Did Wendy really know what her mother had done for her? What she had prevented from happening to her child? Roselle would have done the same for her son, she knew that. But she couldn't believe Susan had never once hinted at it to her.

Then, Susan was shrewd. She knew that a secret once divulged lost its mystery, making it easier to reveal again and again and again.

Which was what they feared now from Wendy. Now the truth was finally out, would the girl feel the urge to shout it from the rooftops?

Roselle went back to the lounge and phoned Ivan.

'I need a number, as soon as possible.'

She smiled into the phone and said politely, 'Of course I know what time it is, Ivan. But fuck it, this is an emergency!'

When she replaced the receiver she settled herself on the sofa and lit a cigarette. This was going to be a hell of a long night.

Susan lay on her bunk. She was in turmoil. Wendy had blown everything wide open. Even though she trusted Roselle the fact was the story was out now. The truth once told could be a terrifying thing. At times it could do far more damage than lies.

She'd known that all her life. Her mother and father had taught her well. She rested an arm across her eyes and sighed.

Matty slipped from her bunk and knelt beside her.

'I thought you wasn't talking to me, Matty. You've hardly said a word, have you, since I came back from me visit?'

Matty didn't answer her at once and in the half light Susan could see her eyes, bright and luminescent.

'So, not content with taking my friends from me, you also want my barrister? That's what I get for being nice to you, for being your friend.'

Matty's voice was so low and sweet, Susan wondered if she had heard her correctly.

'When I think of what I have to put up with in here, sharing a cell with someone I wouldn't even employ to clean my house. Yet I'm expected to help you, be nice to you. So I take you under my wing. I try to help you and you're just like all the others – a user, an ignorant user.'

'You what? What you on about?'

This was the last thing Susan Dalston needed tonight.

Matty grinned.

'Oh, I know your game all right. I know people like you, Susan. You're the takers of this world. I give you my friendship and then, like everyone else, you abuse it. Use it for your own ends. But you won't get away with it this time. This time I'm going to nip it in the bud. I'll kill you before I let you take everything from me.'

Susan didn't answer her. She could feel something cold against her throat and guessed it was some kind of weapon.

Matty seemed to be talking to herself now.

'All the time . . . I have to do everything. Otherwise nothing ever gets done, does it? You're like Angela, like my mother, like Victor. Without me you're all *nothing*.'

Susan listened. In the distance she could hear footsteps as a PO did the night round. Soon the peephole would be opened and an eye would look in, making sure all was as it should be.

Only it wasn't but Susan wasn't going to be able to tell her that, was she?

'Victor made the same mistake . . . Talking about me to people. Telling them how I'd changed. But I hadn't changed, not a bit . . . just stopped pretending. Pretending everything was so great, that I loved him. I cared about him.

'Can you imagine how hard that was, Sue? Pretending to care about a tall, ugly boring man? A man whose conversation was so dull I had trouble keeping awake. I'd yawn in his face sometimes. Yawn, right in his face, and he'd pretend not to notice.

'Now I have you to deal with. The woman I made my friend or the nearest to one I ever had. I was going to speak to Geraldine for you but you went behind my back, didn't you? You went behind my back and took her away from me. She doesn't like me any more because of you. I could tell today, could feel it off her. I make her uncomfortable, you see, because she sees herself in me. Like you all do.'

The peephole slid open and a voice called softly, 'All right in there?'

Matty smiled brilliantly.

'Just chatting. Can't sleep.'

The peephole was closed and the heavy tread moved on.

Susan couldn't breathe. She was frightened to make a sound in case she set Matty off again.

The other woman was still, still and quiet. After long moments she spoke again in the same quiet sing-song voice.

'Now Angela's come back and stuck in here I can do nothing. She wants everything from me as usual. Everything I have. She always wanted it all. People see me as their means of getting on in the world. Even as a child people saw me as someone to be reckoned with. So I'll deal with Angela, I've already planned how to deal with her. Which just leaves you, doesn't it?'

Susan was terrified. She knew Matty was capable of anything.

'What are you going to do?'

Matty smiled, a wide friendly smile that even in the dimness lit up her pretty face.

'I'm going to kill you, of course. Isn't that what I always do?'

Geraldine was roused from sleep by the persistent ringing of her phone. Picking up the receiver, she breathed a tired hello into it. Hearing Roselle's voice, wide awake and excited, she sat up in bed.

'How the hell did you get my home number?'

Roselle laughed gently.

'You'd be surprised what I can get if I want it. Now I'll give you my address – you'd better come to my flat straight away. And before you start, this can't wait till morning and when you find out what it is, you'll be glad I rang when I did. Believe me.'

Ten minutes later Geraldine was making her way across London. She was intrigued, she was tired, and more than anything she was annoyed.

Wendy stepped out of the bedroom. She looked so adult standing in the light of the hallway, and so like her father, that Roselle was stunned into silence.

'Was that the brief? Me mum's brief?'

She nodded.

'Good. Can I make meself a cup of coffee, please?'

Roselle nodded again.

The girl was a woman now, in every sense of the word. Could any of them control her? Could they stop her from doing whatever she wanted?

Somehow Roselle doubted that.

Jamesie came into the house via the cat flap. If he forced his arm through and up he could unlock the back door. It was something he had never told Debbie because he'd always had a feeling it was something he might one day have to use. He was right as usual.

As he shut the door quietly he smiled to himself. This should give her something to shout about. Turning, he saw a boy standing by the kitchen door.

Jamesie shook his head in consternation. She wouldn't dare . . .

Striding across the kitchen, too angry to care about the noise, he snapped on the light.

'Hello, do you live here?'

Barry had forgotten him, forgotten who he was.

'Where's your Aunt Debbie?'

A deep voice answered him and the sound of it made him wince.

'She is in here with me, mate. We heard you coming round the back. Got up a welcome party to greet you.'

June's voice was as strident as ever.

Jamesie closed his eyes in distress.

As he walked into the lounge he thought he had walked into the wrong house. The place looked like a tip. Or the nearest to a tip Debbie would allow it to be. It actually looked lived in. The three kids were in there, little Barry now ensconced on his aunt's lap.

'So what brings you back here then? Carol dinged you out, has she?' June enquired.

He didn't answer and Debbie laughed out loud.

'You hit the nail on the head there, Mother. Well, Jamesie, I'm afraid you lucked out, mate. This place is full up and will be for quite a while.'

'This is my house, Debbie. I say who comes in and who goes out.'

June's voice was low.

'Well, my husband, her father, might have a different opinion on that. I'd better warn you about that straight off. Well upset Joey is at the treatment you've meted out to his baby. Always his favourite was my Debbie. She kept a lot from him, but not any more.'

Jamesie felt the icy fingers of fear at his throat. He looked at his wife and she stared back all innocence.

'I haven't told him everything, stop worrying. You'd have heard from him by now if I had, don't you think?'

Jamesie turned on his heel and walked from the house. Everyone knew he would never come back.

June looked at her daughter and laughed.

'About time your father came in handy, ain't it? Even if it is only for frightening cowards, old people and small children.'

They all laughed.

Even Rosie.

Alana, always with an eye to the main chance, said loudly, 'Any chance of hot chocolate to make us all tired again?'

'Just like you were, that one. Doesn't miss a trick,' said June fondly.

Debbie grinned.

'I hope she has more sense, Mother. I really, really do.'

June looked at her granddaughter and felt a spark of affection.

'She will. She's her mother's daughter that one. Susan was a lot of things but she wasn't stupid.'

Debbie looked at her seriously.

'Oh, but she was, Mum, that's the trouble. We both were. But not these kids. I'll tell them what to look out for in life so they never make the same mistakes.'

June didn't answer for a while. Then she said softly, 'Yes, love. That's a good idea.'

Susan was aching. She had been in the same position for over an hour and was too frightened to move. Matty held the blade to her throat and kept talking.

Susan felt she would go mad if she didn't stretch herself soon.

'Geraldine came to me through Roselle, Matty. I swear that to you.'

She shook her head.

'Don't lie to me. You went through my things, I checked. You've been reading my letters. You two-faced bastard.'

Susan shook her head gently.

'I wouldn't do that, Matty, you know I wouldn't.'

She felt a trickle of sweat as it dripped from her forehead on to the hard pillow.

Matty laughed again.

'But you would, Susan, you wouldn't be able to resist it. Who could? I've been through your stuff loads of times. Even after Rhianna told me off. But then, Rhianna prefers you now, doesn't she? All the women prefer you to me. I wonder why that is?'

She sounded forlorn.

Susan hastened to reassure her.

'No, they don't. They all take the piss out of me, you know they do.'

She felt the blade slide into her skin and swallowed hard.

'You're cutting me, Matty. I can feel it, feel the blood.'

And she could. It was dribbling down her neck mixing with the sweat. Surely her life wasn't going to end in a cell in Holloway prison, another victim of Matty Enderby and her psychotic fantasies?

Geraldine listened to what Roselle had to say and was silent. Every time she looked at Wendy she felt the pain and the horror of what the girl had done. To keep that secret for so long and then to let it out must have been so hard.

Raped by her father then responsible for killing him. Watching her mother take the can. And all the time she was crying inside, unable to be normal, unable to be a girl again.

Geraldine knew how that felt.

Hadn't her own father been the same? Over friendly with his daughters. So friendly their mother wouldn't leave them in a room with him on their own. But still she wouldn't leave him and the good life he provided.

So she stayed and they had to learn to deal with him themselves as they grew older and wiser and stopped seeing it all as a big game their father played with them. It was the only time he'd shown them affection, during those awful games.

What he'd had left anyway.

Now one daughter was married to a man much like him and another was left with a hatred of men that was pathological at times. Geraldine knew she would never lose it.

'What do you want to do, Wendy?'

She sighed heavily, her lovely young face careworn.

'What do you think I should do?'

Geraldine took a deep draught of her brandy and coffee and shook her head.

'I really don't know. From a legal angle, your mother could come out tomorrow. But then, you know that. They'd take you and lock you up in her place. And you and I both know your mother didn't go to all the trouble she did just to see that happen. I think you should go with half the truth, tell them what he did to you. I think even your mother will compromise on that now, don't you? But are you ready to tell the world, that's the question?'

Wendy nodded sadly.

'All the time she's stuck in there, I feel it. Every day, every hour, every minute. I watched them decimate us as a family. I took everything Mrs Eappen and her lot could throw at me. I tried to look out for the others but inside I wanted to lie down and die. I can't take much more of this. Every kind act made me feel worse, every kind word made me feel a fraud, want to tell everyone to stop it. Stop being so nice because I was a terrible person. A terrible person who murdered her father with an empty bottle then let her mother take the blame. The mother of four kids who were left without her, needing her more than anything because she was all they had ever had.'

The words were spoken simply and without emotion. They were the truth.

'If you talk, you'll throw it all back in her face, Wendy. You know that's true. Do what Geraldine says. Tell them what led to the murder and leave the rest,' Roselle pleaded.

'Mum's sentence was because of the severity of the attack. She took Dad's head away because I'd bitten and scratched him, that was the only reason. Because of the forensics. No other reason. If she'd phoned Old Bill there and then, none of the other stuff would have happened. I know that and you both know it.'

Geraldine was getting annoyed and it showed.

'Listen, Wendy, your mother did it to stop you being put away and I'm inclined to agree with what she did. I think she was acting on instinct, looking out for you as she always had. You can't throw that back at her now, not after it's gone this far.'

Wendy looked at the floor. She moved her big toe in agitation and Geraldine and Roselle were reminded she was still a child, however much she'd had to grow up.

They were quiet, each collecting their thoughts.

Finally Roselle spoke.

'Come on, love. Just enough to get your mother out and leave it at that. For Susan's sake.'

Susan felt the steel sliding deeper into her skin. Swinging back one fist she knocked Matty from her with all the force she could muster. Which, in the confines of the cell, wasn't very far.

Matty hit the dresser heavily, making the doors open and everything inside fall to the floor. It acted as wardrobe, dressing table and shelving. As it collapsed, she disappeared under books, clothes and eating utensils.

Susan dragged herself off the bunk. She saw Matty get up at the same time, heard footsteps on the landing as the POs scrambled to get to the source of the noise.

A fight in a cell might be left if the women weren't likely to use blades. POs were reluctant to get involved in personal disputes.

But if an incident occurred where someone was seriously hurt then an inquiry would be called for. So hearing the crash from Enderby's cell made them move faster than usual.

Matty was up on her feet and swaying heavily. She was lashing out with a blade. Rushing towards Susan, she brought it up to Susan's face and attempted to hack at her with all the force she could muster.

'I'll kill you, Dalston. I'll rip your face off and watch you die. Like I watched Victor die.'

Susan was terrified. Matty looked demented in the half light – quite capable of doing what she'd threatened.

Susan grappled at Matty's throat and half dragged, half pushed her up against the bunks, kicking out as the blade moved dangerously close to her eyes and neck. She brought her head back and butted the screaming woman with all her might.

Even as Matty's nose collapsed under the blow, Susan felt her fingers scratching at her, and the blade in her right hand slicing by Susan's ear giving her even more strength and adrenalin. Susan realised that Matty was gone, completely gone.

Her eyes looked red now but it was the blood pouring into them that made her look like the devil. 'I'll kill you, Dalston, you watch me.'

Matty brought the blade up once more in line with Susan's face and neck. She was laughing now. 'You're dead, Dalston.'

Susan head-butted her again. And this time had the satisfaction of seeing Matilda Enderby drop to the floor.

As the cell door was opened Susan felt a great surge of relief. But Matty was getting up again. The blade had sliced into Matty's hand and still she felt nothing, no pain. As she threw herself at Susan she had her teeth bared like an animal. She was a mass of blood and energy.

The POs watched in amazement as Susan drew back a meaty fist and slammed it into Enderby's grinning face.

Finally, after what seemed an age, Matilda Enderby was out for the count. Yet she still managed to keep on her feet for a good ten seconds before she crumpled on to the floor. Nobody went near her. Fear was apparent in every face.

Susan looked at the POs and said heavily, 'You took your fucking time.'

June helped settle the children back into their beds. Little Barry put his arms up for a kiss and June hesitated, then smiling, she hugged him, feeling his sturdy little body against hers. It was a wonderful feeling.

'I love you, Nan.'

June's eyes filled with tears. She finally understood the appeal of children. Maybe she should have had sons. She'd always preferred males.

'I love you, little man.' The words came out instinctively.

'I love me mum best, though.'

June smiled. 'Of course you do, mate. Now go to sleep.'

As she walked from the room, Debbie was outside. 'Lovely, ain't they, Mum?'

June nodded but didn't answer. She was too choked to say anything.

'If Susan gets out all this will stop, you realise that, don't you?' Debbie sighed tiredly.

'I know that, Mum. But even if I don't have them long at least they'll know me. Know they have a second home here when they want it.'

June stared at her.

'You know something, Debbie?'

She shook her head.

'Tell me?'

'You're a nice person really.'

This was said in amazement. Debbie laughed but June was quick to notice she didn't return the compliment.

Susan sat on her bunk and shivered. It was freezing with the door wide open. The night PO, Lesley Gardiner, brought Susan in a hot cup of tea. She also placed a blanket across Susan's shoulders.

'You're shivering. The medics will be here in a minute, they still have Matty to deal with.'

Susan nodded.

'Did you hit her hard?'

She looked into the other woman's face and said tartly, 'Of course I hit her bloody hard! She had a knife to me Gregory, didn't she?'

The PO sighed and started again.

'How many times did you hit her?'

'Well, you know, it's funny but I wasn't counting. I was too busy trying to stop her from doing me permanent damage. Why?'

The PO raised her eyebrows.

'Remind me never to upset you, Susan Dalston.'

'Is she bad then?'

Gardiner smiled sadly.

'Put it this way, she was unconscious and none of us could find a pulse. I'd say she was in a bad way, wouldn't you?'

Susan swallowed down her fear.

'Listen, she was at my throat, ranting and raving a load of old cod's. She ain't all the ticket, you know that.'

Gardiner drank her own tea and they shared a cigarette.

'Well, you get my vote. But after they've given you the once over you're for the block. At least until they hold a proper investigation.'

Susan was terrified. This was all she needed.

Roselle went into the bedroom and hugged Wendy through the bedclothes.

'Are you all right now?'

She nodded. Her face seemed easier, she looked like a girl again.

'I feel much better just getting it off me chest. I've been lying awake nights for so long, just seeing him. Then I see meself hitting him with the bottle. The noise, Roselle, it was such an awful noise. Like a crunch. Every time I think of it, I feel sick. Then I think of Nanny Kate and her face when she realised what he'd done to me. Such disgust in every movement of her hands and in her eyes. I felt terrible. She gave me whisky to drink and she bathed me. Scrubbed me from head to foot. Then you came, much later, when I was falling asleep and took me home with you. I was glad to go. It was awful for her seeing me and being reminded what she had brought into the world.

'Then me mum doing what she did. When I heard I was so grateful at first, I really was. I wanted to hide away from it all. But you can't keep things inside for ever, Roselle, no matter how much you might want to. You can't keep things locked up.'

Roselle kissed her on the forehead.

'I think you know more about it all than I do, darlin'. I'll go along with you on that.'

'Me mum ain't capable of hurting anyone. Not even me dad. But she's the world's expert on hurting herself.'

Susan sat in her dark cell on the block. She knew she wouldn't sleep at all now. She was too hyper.

She'd had no intention of hurting Matty Enderby, none whatsoever, but hurt her she had.

Susan closed her eyes and sighed.

It was like Barry all over again, not knowing what to do or think. It would be ironic if now she finally had the chance to get out she was done for murder or manslaughter.

Life was certainly a bitch.

But she knew Gardiner believed her; all the screws realised Matty wasn't the full shilling and she'd already gone for Sarah.

Susan's mind raced.

But Sarah had taken the crunch for that. Put her little hand up. What was she going to do?

Susan paced the cell again, feeling as if the walls were closing in on her. If Matty died, any hope of walking out of this place was gone.

Susan sank to the floor and cried, long bitter tears. She was back to square one. Right back where she'd started. In a cell, on her own, wondering what the hell to do.

She had a feeling that somewhere Barry was laughing at her plight.

Matty opened her eyes to a glare of white light and a pain in her head that was excruciating.

A young male doctor leaned over her. She could smell his aftershave and cigarette smoke.

'At last you're back with us.'

He had a deep voice, surprising considering his age. He looked about twenty.

She stared at him.

'What happened?'

The doctor didn't answer her. Instead he took her OBs and checked her chart once more.

Matty closed her eyes and drifted back to sleep.

The young doctor on the psychiatric ward shook his head in despair. She had already taken out two male nurses and a care orderly, wrecked his treatment room and bitten and scratched him. It had to be the night he was in sole charge they got a really violent one. It had taken two separate injections of Librium to calm her enough to put on the restraining straps.

He wished she'd stayed unconscious, and that the woman who had knocked her out in the first place worked on this ward.

Christ knows they could have done with her.

The last thing he wanted was Matty Enderby up and about again. She'd already done enough damage.

Chapter Thirty-Two

The whole wing was quiet. Christmas decorations hung from the ceilings and gave the grim building a festive air. A radio was playing quietly in the background. The TV was on. Women milled about, drinking coffee and smoking, talking in low murmurs as if afraid to make any noise.

Rhianna, waiting for transfer after being sentenced, walked upstairs on to the fours and paused outside Susan's cell.

She could smell the deodorant she had used; looked at the hairbrush left carelessly on the bedclothes; smiled at the pictures of the kids on the wall.

It looked like a tip as usual.

She would miss Susan, really miss her. But she wouldn't mind that. She would just like to see her out. They all would. Each woman in here, from the prisoners to the POs. The only thing left of Matty was her posters. It seemed she didn't want them in Broadmoor. Apparently they had enough stuff there to keep her happy.

Rhianna still heard from her occasionally, rambling letters full of veiled threats and promises of undying friendship. Matty was really over the edge this time, had lost any ability to tell fantasy from reality. She lived on Depixol and dreams these days.

She was paranoid, apparently. That always made Rhianna laugh when she heard it. They were all paranoid, it was what prison did to you.

She closed the cell door and walked slowly back downstairs. She realised she had her fingers crossed and grinned, displaying her perfect teeth. A PO passing on the landing underneath looked up at her and shrugged.

There was no news yet.

But she could wait. After all, every woman here had time on her hands. All the time in the world. Most of them had been waiting all their lives.

June and Joey were in the pub. June had drunk more than she should have so early in the day, but she was in a good mood.

Joey looked old. She saw him clearly for the first time in years, really studied him, and realised he looked debauched. His life was written all over his features and his body, from his fat beer belly to the red cheeks threaded with spider veins after too much drinking and whoring.

She smiled to herself. He couldn't raise his pint these days, let alone anything else. He'd had a heart scare recently and that had taken its toll too. He hadn't drunk for a week and actually ate a salad.

Now, though, he was back to 'moderate' drinking. She watched him down a pint in two swallows and smiled again.

June thought for the first time in years about her Jimmy. Her eyes softened. She should have looked after him better, should have kept him. He had been her only chance at a good life. She felt a lump in her throat.

People still thought Joey had topped him. It had gone down in local folklore. Even the up and coming youngsters gave him his due for that, bought him a drink, talked to him as an equal.

If only they knew!

Joey placed a heavy hand on hers and grinned at her. His eyes, though, were on the new barmaid, a tiny blonde with big tits and a cast in her eye. Not that he had noticed the cast, of course. Joey never looked a woman in the face until he had bedded her.

It pleased June, though, that there was life in the old dog yet. As much as she hated him, she still cared about him. It was a habit she had acquired many years before and somehow she had never been able to kick it. Like smoking. You knew it would kill you in the end but, oh, God, that first fag of the day.

'I wish they'd hurry up, Joey. I feel all nervous and apprehensive.'

He shrugged.

'Stop getting your knickers in a twist. We'll know soon enough.'

June was suddenly annoyed.

'This is our daughter, our flesh and blood.'

Joey swallowed down his whisky chaser and stood up. He wanted to get another glimpse of that little bird's Bristols while he had the chance. She went off at two o'clock.

'So you keep telling me, Junie. So you keep telling me.'

He ambled towards the bar, a big man in a suit too small for his heavy frame, with hollows under his eyes and a sad downturned mouth.

June stared into her drink. What a wasted existence they'd led, the pair of them.

Rosie had dragged the Woolworth's silver tinsel tree across Debbie's lounge three times in the last hour. The other kids thought it was hilarious but Debbie was fast losing patience.

Now Rosie stood with her hands on her hips and cried, 'Bad, Rosie!' at the top of her voice.

This made the other two children laugh even more and even Debbie found a smile inside her.

One part of her wanted Susan home so badly she could taste it. Another part, the old selfish part, was terrified of what the consequences would be. These kids had wormed their way into her affections in a few short months, into her very body. She would kill for them now. They had shown her what life could be like, what Jamesie was enjoying. She understood now the hold Carol had over him. Every time she looked into their little faces she understood what life was all about.

But Susan would share them with her, she was big enough to do that. That was if she got out.

Little Barry picked up the tree and put it back in the corner of the room. Alana was collecting the balls and ornaments that were scattered across the floor. His eyes lingered on the presents, all gaily wrapped up awaiting little hands to tear off the paper and reveal the treasures hidden inside.

'This is the best Christmas ever, Auntie Debbie.'

Barry didn't know about the appeal. No one had wanted to get his hopes up, least of all his mother.

Alana looked at her aunt and smiled tightly, the strain of the knowledge heavy in her little heart-shaped face. People often thought Debbie and Alana were mother and daughter. The family resemblance was there for all to see.

She hugged the girl to her tightly.

'Everything will be all right, love.'

Alana looked at her gravely.

'I've heard that before, Auntie Debs. We all have.'

The little face was empty now, as if she had used up all her emotions and was waiting for a refill.

'Shall I make a cuppa?'

Debbie nodded.

The radio was on in the kitchen, and she knew the news was due. Alana wanted to listen in case something had happened. Debbie checked that the phone was in working order for the fiftieth time that day. Would it ever ring and put them out of their misery?

She picked up Rosie and hugged her, kissing the thick curly hair and enjoying the feel of her sturdy little body.

Rosie smiled and kissed her back.

All this unconditional love was heady stuff to Debbie. She wasn't sure she could survive without it.

Wendy sat on the steps of the Old Bailey. She watched the people walking backwards and forwards, all with lives to lead and places to go.

Roselle was standing down on the pavement, smoking furiously. It had to be her thirtieth cigarette of the day. Wendy watched her throw it to the ground and stub it out then immediately light another one.

She wished she could have a cigarette herself but had promised her mother she would give up and she had. Today the craving for nicotine was almost overwhelming.

Her bottom was numb from the concrete steps. She stood up, feeling the blood rush back into her legs and feet. They tingled, reminding her she was alive.

She stared over to where the TV cameras and the reporters were cordoned off and smiled. No one had sussed out who she was yet, Geraldine had made sure of that. For a little while longer she was just an attractive girl in a black designer suit, courtesy of Roselle. Everything was courtesy of Roselle. Shoes, bag, even her haircut. What a wonderful friend she had been to them all.

Soon Wendy would be the girl raped by her own father. The reason her mother had battered his head until he was unrecognisable as a person. Soon she would be all over the papers. Geraldine had warned her about this and they were all ready for it.

At least, she thought she was ready.

Either way it was done now.

Wendy only hoped it was enough to get her mother out and back home, in charge of her life and her children's lives once more. Back where she belonged and never should have left. She had sacrificed all her children for one. Wendy would remember that all her life. No matter what Mrs Eappen or any of them said.

Her mother was worth a hundred Mrs Eappens. A thousand even. Her mother was a heroine and always would be to Wendy, whatever the outcome today. She only hoped that the outcome was what they were all banking on. Otherwise Wendy Dalston wasn't sure she could live with herself. It had been hard enough up to now.

She wasn't sure what exactly would happen if they kept her mother locked up, and there was a good chance they would, even with the weight of public opinion and the women's groups who were all waiting outside with their placards and their Monsoon dresses.

Men in particular seemed to find her father's death more sinister than the usual murder. It was the obliterating of his whole head that did it. To hit someone with a claw hammer over a hundred times seemed the work of a maniac.

But Geraldine had argued that was because Susan Dalston had not been in her right mind at the time. Shocked by his rape of their daughter, she had wanted to expunge him from the earth.

The papers were going to have a field day with this. Gone was Barry Dalston the likeable rogue and in his place was the real man: diseased, violent, a pervert who'd wrecked his daughter's life.

Geraldine had seen to that.

She had scraped up everything she could about him and it made a very unpleasant tale. The tabloids thought they'd died and gone to heaven. All the papers wanted her mother out now.

Wendy hoped they got what they wanted. She needed her mother now more than she had ever needed her.

Susan was disappointed with her PO, an older woman with iron grey hair and buck teeth. She was one of the screws who felt they had to impose a sentence of their own on the prisoners. Susan had come across her kind many times. They stuck implicitly to the book and never deviated.

Susan smoked a cigarette and sipped at a lukewarm cup of tea. She had tried to make conversation with the woman twice and each time had been ignored. She could feel the animosity coming off her in waves.

The cell door was unlocked and Susan stood up expectantly. It was another PO. Ugly was going for her dinner break.

Susan relaxed.

This could go on all day and into the next. It had been known on appeal. She saw the other woman sit down on the hard chair and smile at her.

Susan smiled back.

This screw would dine out on her hour with Susan Dalston for years. She knew that, could see it in the woman's excited eyes and the way her hands fluttered.

Susan smiled at her once more, a big friendly smile.

'What's it like out there?'

The PO grinned.

'Everyone reckons you've got an out. I hope so, love, I really do.'

Susan was inordinately pleased at this friendly response.

'Well, fuck knows it's cost enough.'

Though it hadn't cost her or Roselle a penny. Geraldine had done it all for nothing, not even claiming legal aid. So far as she was concerned, this was for women everywhere. Women like Susan, with no one to speak up for them, no one to care what was happening to them in their own homes.

When she thought back to Barry now, it was as if it all had happened to a different person. A different Susan Dalston. Someone she once knew.

It didn't feel like it had all happened to her personally.

She had trouble at times remembering what he'd looked like. If she did see his face it was when they were both young. Before the kids and his discontent with life.

She had wasted all those years on a man who'd only wanted her because her father was a villain. A thug. Why had she never realised that at the time? Why had she thought so little of herself that she had gone along with it all?

She shook her head at the treachery of life. It jumped up and bit you on the arse and before you knew what had happened you had four kids, a black eye and a prison sentence hanging over your head.

Susan took a letter from her pocket and read it again: Peter wishing her all the best. Even his mother had written a postscript wishing her well.

There were nice people in the world, it had just taken her longer than most to meet some. It was strange but true that her best friend had been the love of her husband's life and another was a convicted prostitute and thief. Rhianna and she were closer than ever now. After the turn out with Matty, Susan wasn't sure what she would have done without her.

Now she was back to doing what she knew best, though.

Waiting.

Susan Dalston had been waiting for something all her life and until this moment she had not even known that fact.

She had always waited for something to happen.

Something to change her life for the better.

Well, it seemed that moment might have arrived if she could hold on just a little bit longer.

Doreen had regretted asking Ivy round while they waited for the verdict. The old woman was driving her mad.

'Even as a baby, Susan was me favourite.'

Doreen stared at Ivy as if she was fascinated by her every word. Inside she wondered if the older woman was finally going senile. Everyone knew what she had done to Susan as a child. Even if she had championed her granddaughter's innocence since the murder.

The news came on and both women listened in strained silence for anything about Susan's appeal.

Doreen looked around the room, at the Christmas tree and the presents, and wondered if her dear friend would be able to share it with them. She lit a Benson and Hedges and drew on it deeply.

Ivy's voice brought her back to reality.

'I mean, even though she killed him it wasn't like he was a real person was it. Not like he was a taxpayer. Mind you, from the moment I saw him I hated him. I warned her, you'll rue the day you took up with him, I said. But she wouldn't listen. In love she was.'

Doreen looked at the other woman and spoke softly.

'Ivy, love?'

'What?'

'Shut the fuck up!'

Ivy pursed her lips and sighed. Then pouring herself more Scotch, she started to talk again.

Kate Dalston sat up in bed in the nursing home. They had placed a TV set in her room and it was showing an inane afternoon soap opera. She turned the sound down with the remote and lay back against the pillows. The girls here were nice. Friendly, caring and kind.

Kate loved it.

She was a bit of a celebrity at the moment and she knew it. When Debbie had brought the kids in to see her there had been a near riot to have a nose at them. Cups of tea and biscuits were used as excuses to come into the room so they could all have a gander at the murderer's kids.

Kate was beyond caring about that.

Her health was finally broken on that terrible night when Wendy came to her, bloody and battered, and she had realised that her own son, whom she had raised and nurtured, loved and adored once, was responsible. The shock nearly killed her then. She still found it hard to believe at times.

But she had written a statement to be read out in court, explaining in graphic detail how he had treated his wife and children. She had made sure they knew what he was, and it had cleansed her. Made her feel she had paid for her part in all that grief.

After all, she had birthed him.

He had been her son.

If anyone knew what a piece of shite he really was, it was her. She prayed her statement would bring that girl home to her family where she belonged.

Kate felt the pain across her chest again and tried to regulate her breathing. She hadn't long left and only hoped it was enough to see Susan home once more. To touch her face and hand, tell her how much she loved and admired her for doing what she had.

Taking the law into her own workworn hands.

Kate's final wish was to shake the hand of the girl who had murdered her own son.

She picked up her rosary beads and started to say another decade of Hail Marys. Our Lady would understand, she had been a mother herself. She understood the difficulties of motherhood, the constant neediness of children.

For a split second Kate was back in Scotland with her husband and baby son. How handsome Barry had been, how people had remarked on his eyes and hair. She saw him on his first day at school, fat little legs encased in royal blue socks to match his jumper.

Where had that little boy gone?

Where had the man come from?

The vicious man. The bully. The wife beater. The rapist.

Her tears stung, their saltiness a reminder of the fact she was still alive. She was alive and that little boy was dead.

Kate clutched the rosary tighter, the beads cutting into her skin. She closed her eyes and her lips moved constantly in prayer.

Kate Dalston would leave nothing to chance.

* * *

It was nearly time for tea but the women were reluctant to leave the rec room. As they lined up to be fed they made as little noise as possible.

Rhianna sat by herself waiting for Sarah to bring her food as usual.

PO Blackstock sat opposite her.

'I have never in my life been so worried about a prisoner.'

Rhianna laughed.

'There's always a first time for everything, I hear.'

'I like old Susan. Everyone does.'

'What's not to like? She's a nice person. A lot of us are if you'd take the time to find it out.'

'I heard through the grapevine that Matty's been declared criminally insane at last. She's to be detained indefinitely.'

Rhianna shrugged.

'So what's new? Tell me something I didn't already know.'

The PO's eyes swept the room.

'Hang on, the news is on.'

She stood up and banged on the table with a tray. The room went quiet. The newscaster's voice was loud in the confines of the rec room.

'The appeal court today freed Susan Dalston . . .'

The whole place erupted. Women were shouting and hugging. POs and prisoners were hugging and shouting. The rest of the newscast was drowned out by the noise.

Their wing went first then the rest of the prison joined in. Plates were banged on tables, feet were stamped on floors. It was deafening.

Rhianna and Blackstock grinned at one another, Rhianna clenching her fists and jumping into the air, shouting, 'Yes!' over and over again.

In her office the governor allowed herself a smile before pressing her intercom and saying blandly, 'Leave them for a while. Let them get it out of their systems.'

Alana was screaming as was Barry. Rosie joined in because she didn't know what else to do. Debbie, half laughing and half crying, hugged them all to her.

Then, opening the larder, she took out a large frosted raspberry cake.

It was over, her sister was coming home.

Alana hugged her hard.

'Thanks for everything, Auntie Debbie. You're lovely, I love you.'

Debbie took her once more into her arms and said sadly, 'And I love you and all, darlin'. Remember that. You'll always have a home here. You know that, don't you?'

Alana nodded, eyes full of tears of happiness.

Barry, seeing his chance, stuck his finger into the frosting on the cake and ate it as fast as he could. It broke the tension. Then everyone stuffed their hands into the cake and grabbed at it. It turned into a fight and as Debbie saw her lovely fitted kitchen destroyed in front of her eyes she laughed like a woman who had never laughed before.

June saw the bottle of champagne and looked at Joey. He grinned at her.

'I arranged it earlier, I knew you'd want to celebrate. Old Jonescy said it's on the house like. What a touch, eh?'

June picked up her glass and held it in a toast.

'To my girl, home at last.'

Joey nodded and downed his drink in one mouthful. Belching loudly, he said, 'You can finish that crap, it gives me wind.'

But he grasped her hand as he said it and she smiled at him. After all the fights, all the trouble, all the heartache they had caused one another, they were finally, in their twilight years, a couple.

Susan was in a car being swept away from the Old Bailey to a destination unknown to anyone but Geraldine and Roselle. In fact they were going to a house in Essex that Roselle had found through Ivan. It was expensive to rent and in the middle of nowhere. Susan could get her head together there.

'I can't believe it! I can't believe I'm really out.'

Wendy held one of Susan's hands tightly and Roselle held the other. Geraldine sat in front with Danny, Roselle's trusted friend. He was going to mind them for a while until the deals with the newspapers had been done and the hysteria over the case had died down.

'Colin's waiting with champagne and fillet steak, Sue. We'll have a real party tonight. The kids will be there first thing in the morning and then your life will be complete.'

Susan looked into Geraldine's face.

'How can I ever thank you?'

She grinned.

'By having the time of your fucking life from now on!'

Geraldine's swearing made them all laugh, the nervous tension evaporating as they did so.

Roselle sat silently, her heart full.

But she was seeing Barry, the Barry she had loved. The man who had adored his Rosie so much he had not been able to part with her.

She saw him in her flat, changing the baby's nappy, his heart-wrenchingly handsome face smiling up at her.

She closed her eyes and felt the tears well. Susan grabbed her hand. Roselle looked at her and knew Susan was seeing what she was seeing. Had guessed what was going through her mind.

'I know, love, I know. But he's gone now and we're all still here.'

Wendy's voice came from the depths of her being.

'Amen to that.'

Kate Dalston passed away four days later, the day she took her daughter-in-law's hand and told her how much she loved and admired her.

She died peacefully, with nothing on her conscience.

Susan Dalston had made sure of that.

Epilogue

'Who'd have thought it, eh? The turn of the century. A new millennium.'

June's voice was hushed.

Debbie laughed.

'Me dad would have loved it, the piss up of the century!'

June laughed with her.

'Wait till I get up there, I'll slaughter him for leaving me to get drunk on my own tonight.'

Debbie put an arm across her mother's shoulders.

'You're not on your own, you've got us lot.'

'Another three months and he'd have seen the century out. But that was him all over. Never saw anything through to the end.'

Her voice was angry. For all that had happened over the years, she still missed him. She looked frail these days, old. The fighting and drinking woman was gone now. June had finally admitted she just didn't have the energy any more. Facing old age and loneliness, she embraced her children and her grandchildren, loving every moment she spent with them. Revelling in the forgiveness they had given her for their past lives.

Ivy sat in a chair, her eyes vacant as she tried to understand what was going on around her. June placed a hand on her leg.

'All right, girl?'

Ivy pushed her hand away shouting querulously, 'Who are you then? What are you doing in my house?'

Debbie bent over the chair and said gently, 'We're all at Susan's, Gran, remember?'

Ivy looked into a pair of kind eyes and smiled.

'Have they let her out then? About fucking time.'

'Senile old bat.' June's voice was upset.

Wendy came into the room with a large tray of food.

'Put that out, Debs, and I'll get the rest in.'

Debbie took the heavy platter from her and growled.

'Stop lifting in your condition.'

Wendy grinned.

'Don't be so silly. I'm having a baby, I'm not ill.'

Debbie snorted. She was a dumpy matron these days. They joked that she was the children's second mother by proxy.

She still lived in her house in Rainham, and still cleaned it constantly. But she was also a much happier woman. The closeness between Debbie and Susan had grown over the years and now they saw one another constantly, and spoke on the phone at least five times a day. They lived in each other's pockets.

Susan's voice bellowed from the kitchen.

'Leave her alone, Debs.'

Everyone laughed.

Wendy's husband came into the room then. David Hart was a tall, good-looking, quiet man who worshipped his fiery wife.

'Geraldine's here, I just saw her pull up. You want to see her new car, a Mercedes convertible.'

His tone said 'At her age' and they all laughed again.

Geraldine looked better at fifty-four than most women did at twenty-five. Still manless and happy with that state, she worked flat out for women's causes.

Susan bustled into the room, all heavy breasts, smiles and highlighted hair. She was a different woman to the one who had married Barry Dalston. She looked better now than she had ever looked and she knew it.

Susan was finally what she wanted to be, a confident woman with her family around her and no real problems. Still living for her children, she made her life around them, and they adored her as much as she adored them.

'Have you seen Geraldine?'

Geraldine followed her into the room and grinned at everyone, two magnums of champagne in her arms. In the background Robbie Williams was playing and it set the tone for everyone.

Alana came in then with Barry in tow.

'All right, Ger? You look marvellous.' It was a statement of fact.

'You don't look too bad yourself.'

Barry kissed her on the lips.

At twenty-four he was the living image of his dead father, but thankfully he was the opposite in personality and brains. He was working in computers and earning twenty-five grand a year, something Susan told anyone and everyone who would listen.

But sometimes it pained her to look at him.

Geraldine started to help with the food and when the front door opened again and Doreen walked in the house was once more in uproar.

'Jesus Christ, Sue, getting a cab is an impossibility. I had to pay triple fare.'

Her loud voice could be heard out in the back garden.

She was still thin, still bleached-blonde, and still had a fag hanging from the corner of her mouth. Other than a few more wrinkles she never seemed to change.

'My Michael's picking me up at ten to go to his house, as if I want to go there tonight of all nights with that bleeding wife of his.'

Wendy kissed her hello.

'She is a miserable mare, I'll give you that, Auntie Dor.'

'They're all going, apparently. I don't know how that came about. I was amazed I was invited let alone the others.'

She bent over Ivy's chair.

'All right, Ivy?' Her voice was even louder than usual.

Ivy nodded happily. 'Is my Joey here yet, dear?'

Doreen shook her head. 'I hope not love, we want to enjoy ourselves tonight.'

Even June laughed at that.

Susan put her arms around Wendy in the kitchen.

'You sure you're all right, love? You look pale.'

Wendy shrugged.

'I'm all right, Mum. David keeps his eye on me.'

'He's a good man, him. I hope the others do as well when their time comes.'

Her voice was full of hope and Wendy hugged her again.

'I hate the thought of history repeating itself.'

Wendy didn't answer her. Instead she changed the subject.

'He got his promotion. Head of English now if you don't mind. I was going to save it till later, but I wanted you to know first.'

Susan flapped her hand.

'It was a foregone conclusion. He's worked hard enough for it.'

'He's a good man, Mum, stop worrying about us all.'

'It's Rosie I worry about. Too attractive for her own good, that one.'

This was said with rough pride.

Geraldine came out to the kitchen and looked at Wendy.

'I hope this one doesn't decide to come tonight of all nights. The hospitals are empty by all accounts.'

Wendy patted her belly.

'Which is more than you can say for the pubs.'

The celebrations had been going on for days, the talk of power cuts and computer breakdowns forgotten in the excitement of being in on a little bit of history.

In the lounge June was shouting. 'Put the telly on – that Angus Deayton's doing his usual end of the year thing.'

'It's called *The End of the Year Show*, Gran.'

'I'd have gone after him a few years ago, he's lovely.'

'That would cheer him up no end if he knew.'

Rosie's voice was full of fun as she walked into the room.

Everyone looked at her. She was stunning.

Long blonde hair and deep blue eyes, she looked like a computer image of the perfect woman. She was training to be a nurse, and had set more than a few pulses racing. Alana, who was now a staff nurse, looked out for her. The two girls were very close.

But Rosie's secret was the fact she was really unaware of how lovely she was; this was the worry that Susan had for her youngest daughter. But Rosie had her head screwed on and managed her life just fine.

Alana grinned as June shouted out, 'This time it will be called *The End of the Millennium Show* anyway.'

Rosie and Alana groaned.

June always had to have the last word.

'Whatever you say, Gran.'

'The BBC are linking up with the rest of the world. We'll see this one in with the whole planet.'

June sounded pleased to be a part of something so big. Susan replaced her empty glass with a full one.

'She'll be asleep before it all starts and asleep when it's all over,' she predicted fondly. 'Her and old Ivy.'

Ivy nodded. 'Have you seen me teeth, Sue?'

'You've got them in your mouth, love!' Susan's voice was loud. 'Barry, help me unload the car, would you.'

He followed Geraldine from the house. Roselle was parking out on the road. She was with Danny, now her constant companion. They fitted together somehow, had a mutual respect and a deep love that transcended age and colour. They just were.

Roselle looked at the detached house, with its large in-and-out drive and sparkling windows. It was a far cry from Susan's beginnings, but she deserved it if anyone did. It had come from the money from the newspaper stories and the book about her life.

They strolled up the drive together, easy in each other's company.

The kitchen was baking hot and Susan opened the back door.

She felt a pair of hands push her out into the garden then grab her from behind. Cool lips touched the back of her neck.

'Happy, are you, Susan? Now you've got them all around you again?'

She turned and slid into Peter's arms.

'It's the second happiest night of me life.'

'You deserve it, mate.'

He looked at her lovingly. Peter could never quite believe she was his wife. It was a dream come true for him. Whenever he looked at her he saw the girl he had gone to school with, the girl who'd barely known he was alive back then.

When he loved her in the night it was with a ferocious passion that belied his quiet daytime appearance. And Susan loved him back. She had never known she could feel that way. That someone touching you could bring so much happiness, so much pleasure. With Barry it had all been taking, taking what he wanted, and her letting him. She pushed him from her mind. He wasn't going to ruin tonight.

He'd ruined enough of her life.

Peter had been a proper father to her children, and she would love him for that alone. She kissed him again, passionately.

'You never let a chance slip by, do you, Susan?'

The voice was deeper now, but held the same affection for her.

'Oh, Rhianna, you made it!'

She grinned.

'You didn't think I'd let the old crowd down tonight of all nights, did you?' Rhianna breezed in and out of Susan's life. It was how she was. But Susan had had a feeling she'd turn up tonight. It felt right somehow, that they were all together on this auspicious occasion.

'Colin and his kids have just pulled up. His wife ain't with him.'

Susan frowned. 'They've separated again! Still, Geraldine will cheer him up!'

She heard Colin's three daughters shouting with glee and June shouting back at them. They loved coming here though their mother thought Susan and her family were all common. The thought made Susan smile.

Silly cow that she was, all middle-class respectability and Blairism, Marks and Spencer's clothing and mystic medicine.

Feng Shui had been turned into cockney rhyming slang for fuck me and one of Colin's kids had picked up on it. Susan knew she had got the blame for that one as well. Yet without her Colin would still have been a no one, working for nothing. Her case had made him and he was grateful for that. They had all bonded after the appeal, kept together, stayed friends.

He smiled at her now.

'You'll be on the box tonight, Sue. They're going over all the big stories of the century.'

She raised her eyebrows in annoyance.

'I ain't watching that crap, I'm having a bleeding party.'

He kissed her gently. She smelled of Chloë as she always did.

'They're noisy gits, your lot.'

Colin grinned. 'Only when they're round here, Sue. It's the way you affect people.'

'I get the blame for everything, me!'

Later that night as they toasted the new millennium Susan looked around at her family and friends. She saw them all as they had been, younger but less hopeful somehow.

She saw Ivy, smiling and grinning and not understanding what was going on around her, and was amazed once more at what extreme age could do for a person. Everyone liked Ivy now, and she was adored in her old people's home. But they had not known her in her fighting days.

Susan saw her friends, all happy in their own ways, and glad to be here, glad to be with her.

She was Susan White now. A new person, a new woman in more ways than one. As she felt Peter grab her hand she was grateful that from the first time she had kissed him, she had been enveloped in the love and respect she had craved all her life. These feelings had grown stronger over the years. Nothing that had happened in the past could change what she had been given. Four happy children, a grandchild on the way and good friends. What more could she possibly want from this new century? She already had all she needed, all that she had craved as a little girl.

She felt Peter's hand safe in hers and smiled at him happily, knowing that when they finally went to bed she wouldn't be allowed to sleep for hours. Mind you, she couldn't think of a better way to be.

The thought made her smile wider and looking at Roselle they locked eyes. Roselle raised her glass in a private toast, just for the two of them and Susan did the same. They had both been the victims of Barry in their own ways and the bond had grown stronger over the years. Joseph was in New York with his wife, and Roselle knew that since burying Ivan, and her son finding out the truth of his beginnings, there had been a rift. Well, it was his loss, though she knew Roselle didn't quite see it that way. She felt the pain for her friend as though it was happening to her.

As Danny's arm went around Roselle she smiled happily and Susan could relax once more and enjoy herself.

Geraldine, worse for wear and flirting with Colin, was sitting on the arm of June's chair. Looking over at her mother, Susan screwed up her eyes with mirth. June had long ago been forgiven by her daughters.

'I told you, everyone! I said she'd sleep through it, and she has!'

'I think anyone who grew up on or near a council estate like I did understands my books, the background.'

Read on for more about Martina Cole . . .

> *'I've always been a book fanatic from when I was a little kid…'*

- Martina is the youngest of five children.

- Her nan taught her to read and write before she went to school.

- She secretly signed her mum and dad up to the library and borrowed books in their name.

- Her dad was a merchant seaman, away on the boats for long stretches. He'd come back for Christmas and bring the books that were big in America at the time.

- She used to bunk off school to go and read in the park.

- She was expelled from school – twice – and left school for good at 15: 'They said, don't come back.'

- She was expelled from a convent school for reading *The Carpetbaggers* by Harold Robbins ('They were nuns, how did they know what was in it?!')

- Her first boyfriend was a bank robber. He was really handsome, he had a Jag. 'We're still really really great friends.'

- The first book she remembers reading is Catherine Cookson's *The Round Tower* – she borrowed it from her nan.

- She reads on average two or three books a week.

- Martina wrote her first book when she was 14. It was about a girl who was at a convent but secretly worked for the CIA.

- Her first paid job as a writer was for her neighbour – a Mills & Boon fanatic who paid Martina in cigarettes to write her beautiful stories where they kissed on the swings at the end. Her neighbour's son used to steal the exercise books from school for her to write in!

- Her books are the most requested in prison – and the most stolen from bookshops.

- She sells hugely in Russia, and sometimes thinks it's because the Russians think it's a handbook to the London underworld.

- She has her own Film/TV production company with Lavinia Warner, the woman who produced *Tenko* – the first TV series with really great female characters.

- Alan Cumming did his own hair and make-up and singing for his part as Desrae in the TV adaptation of *The Runaway*.

- *The Faithless* made her the first British female adult-audience novelist to break the 50 million sales mark since Nielsen Bookscan records began.

- *The Take* won the British Book Award for Crime Thriller of the Year in 2006.

- Her fans include Rio Ferdinand – he was snapped with a copy of *Revenge*.

'I'm a great believer in anything that gets anyone reading...'

'They thought I'd be a one-hit wonder...'

MARTINA COLE was just 18 when she got pregnant with her son. Living in a council flat with no TV and no money to go out, she started writing to entertain herself.

It would be ten years before she did anything with what she wrote.

She chose her agent for his name – Darley Anderson – and sent him the manuscript, thinking he was a woman. That was on a Friday. Monday night, she was doing the vacuuming when she took the call: a man's voice said 'Martina Cole, you are going to be a big star'.

The rest is history: *Dangerous Lady* caused a sensation when it was published, and launched one of the best selling fiction writers of her generation. Martina has gone on to have more No. 1 original fiction bestsellers than any other author.

She won the British Book Award for Crime Thriller of the Year with *The Take*, which then went on to be a hit TV series for Sky 1. Four of her novels have made it to the screen, with more in production, and three have been adapted as stage plays.

She is proud to be an Ambassador for charities including Reading Ahead and Gingerbread, the council for one-parent families. In 2013, she was inducted to the Crime Writer's Association Hall of Fame, and in 2014 received a *Variety* Legends of Industry Award.

Her son is a grown man now, and she lives in Kent with her daughter – except when she chases the sun to Cyprus, where she has two bookshops.

Her unique, powerful storytelling is acclaimed for its hard-hitting, true-to-life style – there is no one else who writes like Martina Cole.

'I've always been an advocate of education in prisons'

For years Martina Cole has visited and worked within prisons across the UK. A passionate advocate of rehabilitation and education within the prison system, Martina has taught creative writing classes, given talks, and, in her role as ambassador for the Reading Agency's Six Book Challenge, she's seen how important increasing literacy is for educating inmates. In fact, it always surprises her how many young prisoners, especially male inmates, who can barely read and write when they get to prison, read their first book in this tough environment.

'My main function when I go in is to try and enthuse people to want to read or want to write. I show them it's possible to do it, that anyone can do it if they want'

Martina loves opening the door to the world of storytelling and language to people who have never picked up a book before. Her favourite moment in her creative writing classes within prisons is when she sees people who have never read a book in their life suddenly discovering storytelling and wanting to discuss books with her and their fellow prisoners.

'The one thing you need to read is time, and in prison you've got all the time in the world'

Martina's books are the most requested books within prison libraries and the most stolen from bookshops, a statistic she is very proud of – stealing aside! Because, for Martina, if her books are the first a person has ever picked up she's delighted to have encouraged them to start reading. She advises new readers to find their passion and read widely within it, be that crime, romance or science fiction. The book she recommends most to prisoners is *The Call of the Wild* by Jack London, a book she read and loved when she was young.

'When men go to prison they leave their kids with the person they trust most: their mum. But for women it's different – they often don't have anyone they trust enough to take care of their kids while they're inside'

Martina spends a lot of time working with women in prisons, trying to get families together, making sure these women get an education and can have the best chance of making something of their life once they've served their sentence and get out of the prison system. She's worked for organisations such as Women in Prison and she's a patron of Chelmsford Women's Aid.

'Prisons are tough, but the thing for us is we want to send them out better people than when they went in, right?'

As a supporter of initiatives to improve prison conditions with the aim of encouraging rehabilitation, Martina has been pleased at the positive changes she's seen over recent years in the prisons she visits regularly. The attitude towards rehabilitation has shifted in a positive direction in many institutions with better libraries and education programs in place. And Martina will continue to work tirelessly to support rehabilitation and education within prisons, as well as writing books that inmates and people everywhere will read and love.

> 'I'm not educated but I'm very well read...
> I read anything and everything. I can read
> a book a day. For me reading has been
> my biggest pleasure all my life.'

Martina's Top Books And Favourite Authors:

Hatter's Castle by A. J. Cronin – 'The book that stayed with me all my life'

Wedlock by Wendy Moore – 'A true story written like a novel'

The Godfather by Mario Puzo – 'The book was so much more powerful than the film'

Brighton Rock by Graham Greene – 'the book that changed my life'

Hollywood Wives and *Hollywood Husbands* – 'I was always a big Jackie Collins girl – these are two of my favourite books of all time'

The Hitchhiker's Guide to the Galaxy by Douglas Adams – 'Certain books are like old friends and this is one'

Room by Emma Donoghue – 'I thought it was so good – I read it on a flight to Cyprus and made sure we ordered copies for my bookshop as soon as I arrived'

Hermann Hesse – 'For pure beauty of writing. *Steppenwolf* had a big effect on me'

George R.R. Martin – 'He's given me back my love of fantasy'

Val McDermid – 'Love a good serial killer'

> *'She felt that all her Christmases and Birthdays had come at once...'*
> (Get Even)

Keep your eye on Facebook
f/OfficialMartinaCole to be the first to
hear when the next Martina Cole
is coming out.

And if you don't want to wait, treat
yourself to a nice bit of vintage Cole.
Here's a reminder of those blinding bestsellers
that have made Martina Cole the undisputed
matriarch of crime drama – and some quotes
from the lady herself to help you choose
which one you fancy reading...

'When I did Dangerous Lady, *they told me it was too violent and I said – she's hardly going to hit them with her handbag!'*

The book that first made Martina Cole's name – and its sequel
DANGEROUS LADY
MAURA'S GAME (Dangerous Lady 2)

The only time Martina's written from the Old Bill's perspective: her deadly DI Kate Burrows trilogy
THE LADYKILLER (DI Kate Burrows 1)
BROKEN (DI Kate Burrows 2)
HARD GIRLS (DI Kate Burrows 3)

You might have seen these on TV – but that doesn't mean you know what happens in the books!
THE TAKE
THE RUNAWAY

'I love the fact that my books are the most requested books in prison and the most stolen books in bookshops, I love the whole concept of that!'

Martina writes brilliantly about what it's like on The Inside. For gripping novels that tell the truth about prison, try
THE JUMP
FACELESS
TWO WOMEN
THE GOOD LIFE

'Your family is either the best thing that ever happened to you or it's the worst thing that ever happened to you.'

Family life is always at the heart of Martina's storytelling: loyalty, protection and how the ties that bind us can also sometimes choke the very thing we want to protect...

FACES
THE FAMILY
THE FAITHLESS
BETRAYAL

'I deal with the mums, the wives, the girlfriends, the sisters, the grandmothers whose children or family are caught up in this life.'

Anyone who's ever read Martina Cole knows her women are the best: strong, resilient, vengeful – nothing will get in the way of these ladies when they know what they want

GOODNIGHT LADY
THE KNOW
CLOSE
GET EVEN

'My books are very anti-violence. I say this is what happens to you if you get caught up in the violent life.'

With her unflinching talent, Martina's stories reveal a world that many would rather ignore

THE GRAFT
THE BUSINESS
THE LIFE
REVENGE

'I wrote what I'd like to read and as luck would have it other people liked to read them too – they either love them or they can't read them, they find them too shocking to read.'

'She's from the Essex darklands, and so are her books
– a brutal world of petty crime, and put-upon women,
and violent men. The voice on the page is her voice
in real life . . . She's a total one-off' *Guardian*

MARTINA COLE
THE KNOWLEDGE

For an indepth interview with Martina, and sample
chapters from all of her books, download the free
ebook – search The Knowledge.